Passion's Spel[illegible]

"Women like you have [illegible] ince the beginning of tim[illegible] ed, reluctantly realizing [illegible] ythical beauty in a [illegible] in the midst of a summ[illegible]

Beneath his [illegible] e person of Caitlin McGlory[illegible] neless, elegant Olympia immodest[illegible] ng her irresistible perfection. Quinn let [illegible] erce eyes caress all of Caitlin's finely wrought turnings and smooth swells before he flicked back his hair, sending a tiny shower of rain drops along her creamy, warm length. She shivered, and then, where the drops fell, Quinn's mouth followed, moving with excruciating slowness, barely touching her at first, brushing her lidded eyes and the smooth, white arch of her throat as her head fell back, then taking ravenous possession of her parted lips.

A subtle tremor passed through Caitlin, and she gathered him close. With wondrous delight, she felt her body responding, felt her own secret self parting and giving way to his strong hand's touch that sent flares of pleasure running all through her. She could no more stop him now than she could stop the rain from falling, the sun from setting. He had captured her, body and soul. . . .

BY
JOYCE
MYRUS

ZEBRA BOOKS
KENSINGTON PUBLISHING CORP.

ZEBRA BOOKS

are published by

Kensington Publishing Corp.
475 Park Avenue South
New York, NY 10016

First printing: March 1985

Printed in the United States of America

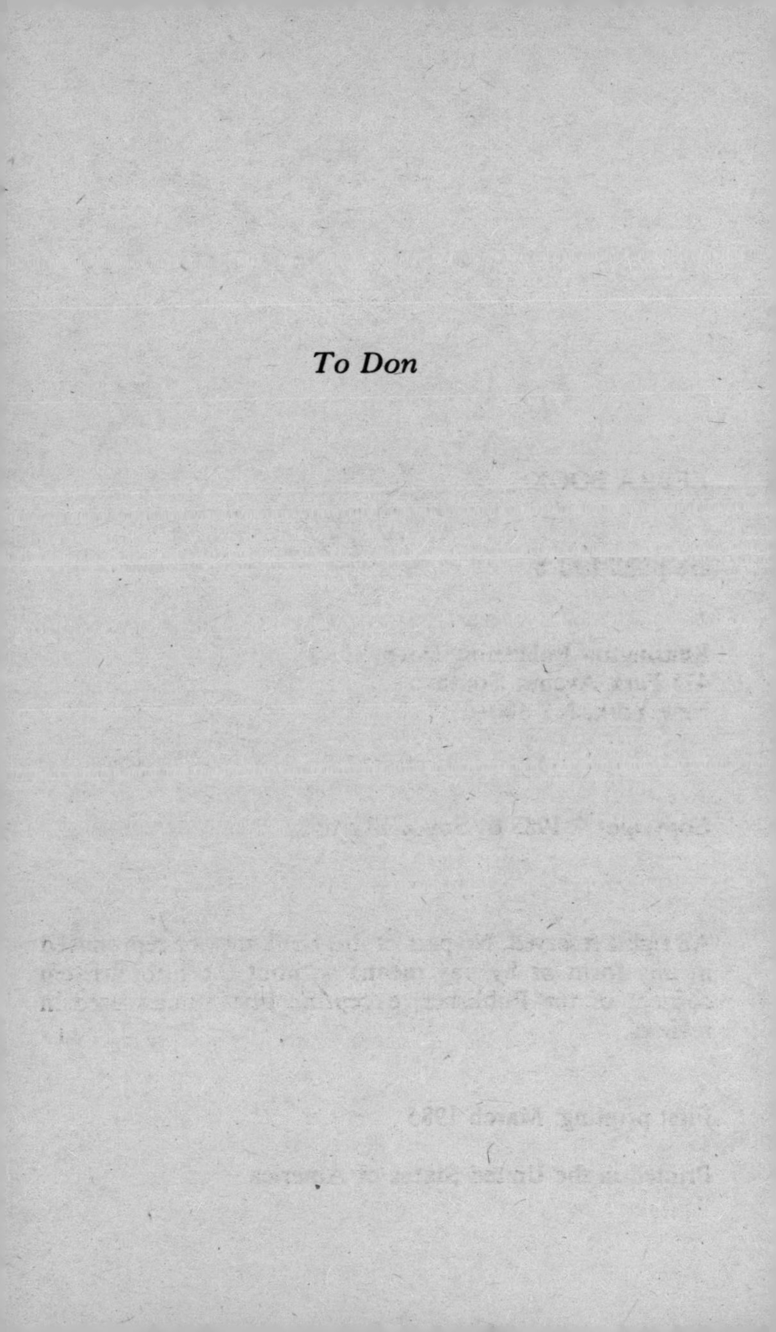

To Don

Chapter One

Caitlin McGlory, poised to descend from a hired livery, pointed a dainty, tasseled yellow slipper out of a froth of white petticoats. Glowing with excitement, she barely paused to glance down, expecting a waiting footman ready to hand her out. Instead, she found herself caught in the gaze of a pair of storm-gray eyes set deep in a lean, handsome, unsmiling face. The man who extended an upraised helping hand, Caitlin realized, was the rider who had preceded the livery up the long, curving drive to Silver Hill. His restive roan, dancing and high stepping under the shading oaks, had caught her eye. She had followed his progress until he had dismounted at the manor house portico and, with regal carelessness, tossed his reins to a stable boy. Then Caitlin's attention had been drawn to the party scene spread before her on wide lawns overlooking a bay.

It was the Fourth of July in the year 1871, a perfect pink and saffron summer afternoon. Caitlin, who was nearly eighteen and delighted with herself and the world at large, could hardly wait to make her entrance and get into the thick of the festivities. But then this man who was grasping her hand favored her with an absolutely incomparable smile and a cool tilt of his head, his glinting hair black satin in the summer sunlight. Caitlin felt a startling rush of delight all over, and everything else for the moment seemed dimmed and distanced. The golden day and the laughing voices, the scent of salt air and roses, were all dulled as she returned the smile, her own quite as dazzling as his, and made a hasty evaluation, starting at polished black Wellington boots. Whoever he was, he wore conspicuously well-made clothes and wore them well. He had long legs, fine, broad shoulders, and a handsome face with high, hard cheekbones. His strong jaw, faintly shadowed, lent him a lean, dangerous look Caitlin found perversely unsettlingly attractive.

Her inspection done, Caitlin alighted from the carriage and failed in her attempt to extricate her hand from his.

"You're a storybook princess come to life—or a brand new doll just unwrapped from tissue," he said softly. There was an intimate, conspiratorial tone in his smooth voice that caused Caitlin's glorious, natural high color to heighten slightly. An appealing look of confusion came into her blue eyes for just an instant before they began to spark with irritation.

His eyes, stormy again, went over her now very methodically, registering every detail. She was dressed and groomed exquisitely, the perfect image of a very expensive lady, despite the canny expression that he would have expected to see in some little street urchin or a practiced tease.

The girl wore a yellow, small-brimmed bonnet that revealed russet streaks in coiled auburn hair and framed a most extraordinary, unclassically beautiful face. With her widely spaced, large eyes and perfect nose, she reminded him of a rare wildcat he had seen once, long ago, in Sumatra. Uncatlike, though, was her lovely wide mouth, the bottom lip full and amazingly appealing. She wore a fragile white muslin dress with a tiny waist and full bishop sleeves. In one slim, white-gloved hand she carried a parasol, and from the other, the one he still held captive, there dangled a drawstring bag of crocheted lace decorated with yellow ribbons and yellow grosgrain roses.

Rising on tip toe and inclining toward him with the grace of a dancer, Caitlin smiled and, in a warm, husky, mischievous voice edged with a hint of anger, she said very sweetly, "You leave me go right now, Johnny, or you won't be looking so smug presently."

His fast smile that reached his dark eyes this time came and went again like lightning. "Quinn Jones is the name," he glowered, "and whoever dressed you up like a little doll, Princess, should have taught you to behave like one."

"If she's a princess, *I'm* her fairy godmother," an amused, slightly wearied voice interrupted. "And *you*, Mr. Jones, are still using that famous smile of yours to try and work your wiles. Has it ever failed you?"

"Never," Jones laughed. He turned, still not releasing Caitlin's hand but drawing her arm through his, to face a striking, slightly older woman being handed from the livery by a companion, a solidly packed, shaggy man with a battered but handsome brawler's face. The man's brown sack coat and checked trousers contrasted noticeably with his lady's understated elegance.

"Ann Overton." Jones nodded. "It's been a long time. You're looking as lovely as I remember. And I hear you're moving up in the world. I'm told you've gone away from Sag Harbor to become a great success at . . . stitchery, is it?"

"Stitchery?" the woman scoffed faintly. "Oh,

I suppose you could call it that. I've the most exclusive dress salon on the Ladies' Mile in New York now. When I said I was fairy godmother to the little princess, I was hardly exaggerating. Do you like her? I created her—her appearance at least. I've had less success with her manners. Miss Caitlin McGlory," Ann said with formal precision, turning to the girl, "allow me to present Quinn Jones, newly arrived . . . adventurer, shall we say, Quinn?"

"If you like." Jones shrugged. "It's as good a title as any."

"Quinn," Ann smiled a little, inclining her head, "the princess."

"Mr. Jones," Caitlin blurted, her pouting, velvety pink lips very naughty, "it's not right of Ann to be always teasing me so. What do *you* think?" she appealed with imploring innocence as she wrenched her hand free of Jones's grasp so violently she nearly lost her balance. Her dancing eyes, as she smiled into his, were reckless with her little triumph.

"I think you're probably a willful imp, too clever for your own good," he said, concentrating on her delicious mouth, trying to place the lovely faint accent that flavored her throaty little girl's voice—North Country British or Welsh, he couldn't be sure.

"Quinn," Ann Overton interrupted, "now meet Billy McGlory, guardian to the little princess, her uncle."

Jones noted with some interest that Ann's jaded eyes misted with apparent love when she looked at McGlory, who moved with a clumsy dignity to offer a thick-fingered hand.

"We've met," Jones said. "You run The White Elephant in New York."

"We did indeed meet," McGlory grinned. "I do remember you, my man. I see a whole lot of people in my trade, runnin' a dance hall like I do, but you are one I'd not forget easy. Our host today, my friend Hawkes, brought you to the Elephant when you just come home, wasn't it?"

"Yes. And I almost took your place apart, as I vaguely remember," Jones grinned back.

"I got your bank draft for the damages, and we're used to you young fellows creatin' a disturbance now and again. But you created the best disturbance we *ever* had. Well, a man's got a right to let off steam after bein' where you was an all. The Captain tells me you are settled down good now, Jones. He tells me you're goin' to be stayin' on out here in this quiet neighborhood for a while. So's my girl there, Caitlin, so maybe you could kind of see she doesn't get dull out here in the country—keep her entertained like."

Quinn cocked a dark brow at Caitlin, whose slight, slim form had been in motion all the while, like a fluttering leaf in a breeze.

"My pleasure, McGlory," Jones nodded. "If

there are no objections, I'll start now." He crooked an arm and Caitlin, about to slip hers into it again, held back for a moment.

"Only if you promise to let me go the very instant I say," she laughed.

"He'll promise you anything, Cate, so be on your guard," Ann said, shrugging thin, elegant shoulders in irritation as the two moved away toward the gathering of guests on the lawn. They certainly stood out, even in this fine crowd, Ann mused. They would anywhere—he, tall and slim, moving with the stealthy, controlled determination of a stalking wolf, and dainty, mercurial Caitlin, dancing along beside him like light on water, bubbling over with spontaneity and delighted with absolutely everything in a wonderful world unfolding, she seemed to assume, just for her alone.

"That girl!" Ann sighed, taking Billy's arm. "I've told her again and again life's a slippery proposition, and she'd best grab hold of something or she might take a nasty fall. But I suppose she'll always have some man wanting to care for her. This one, though, should not be encouraged. What do you really know about him?"

"Friend of the Captain's. Quite a cutthroat daredevil, it's rumored, just out of jail somewhere—Scotland, Wales—one or the other. I believe it. He still had a touch of the prison pallor on his face when I first saw him, even after his ocean crossing. It's also said he went to jail for someone else. Innocent, framed, or protecting a friend, I don't know which. And I believe that, too. From the look of him, he's no criminal. I'd swear to it. Now I've a question, Annie. What do *you* know about him? I saw your eyes glowin' when you looked at him, and I said to myself right then that there was something between you two one time. Am I right?"

"Fool," Ann sighed testily, at once on the offensive. "You've pulled that infant, Cate, out of the pan and thrown her into the fire, putting her in Quinn's charge. I *know*!"

"I'm sure you do, Annie, my love, but the Captain said Jones is a man of honor, and he's never wrong about such matters." Billy was adamant.

"Honor?" Ann repeated, assuming her usual detached manner. For one who was careful, as she was, not to lose her composure over anything, it was essential she regain her control quickly. "The man's a rogue and a drifter who's always got some girl infatuated with him. Love does burn in those dark eyes of his, until he gets what he wants, and then he's gone. Your little Cate is such an innocent, such an enthusiast. She responds to absolutely everything—the sky, the shore, sunsets and stars and sad songs and . . . and new hair ribbons, for heaven's sake—all with the same intensity. She must get herself in hand. I've told her that."

"Don't be too hard on my girl, Annie. She'll settle down in time. She's only seventeen, after all, and she's got a lovely, innocent sweetness I hope she never loses."

"She'll lose that precious innocence quick enough if you keep throwing her to the wolves this way."

"Is it my fault she grew up an orphan with no mother to tell her . . . things? Did I throw her to that Layton Weetch, the con man?" Billy demanded, shaking his large head angrily. "I did not!"

"But neither did you see to her education until she was nearly fifteen, or take her about to balls and theaters and operas as you should have. You let her dress like a tomboy and hang about with your fancy whores and barmaids. What did you expect?"

"She was everybody's baby, Annie. They all loved her so and I was busy makin' a livin' for us. I wasn't payin' attention to how she grew up so lovely. . . ." Billy's voice trailed off wistfully. He and Ann stood watching the fine carriages rolling up Silver Hill Drive, and he smiled to himself, remembering little Caitlin in the boy's knickers and suspenders and round-collared shirts she favored, propped on his long, gleaming, mahogany bar, swinging her legs, basking in the attention of the serving girls and tenders and his high-living customers who plied the beautiful child with sweets between their swallows of bourbon and turns about the dance floor. Caitlin was always happy about something—or nothing—and her happiness was infectious. She had thrived on all the attention, and she loved watching the night world through wide, delighted eyes, taking it all in, learning all sorts of things unknown to most little girls her age.

Then, when she was almost fifteen, something changed, not in her so much as in the men who frequented The White Elephant. They still teased her a little and still gave her sweets and affectionate pats on the head, but they began to linger about her longer, too, and smile at her differently, actually asking her to dance, though she still had long braids dangling to her waist. Despite it all, it wasn't until Billy saw Layton Weetch twine those braids about Caitlin's pretty throat and kiss her on the mouth that he realized he had a young woman on his hands, an especially beautiful one at that.

It was just as Billy's panic was taking hold that Caitlin began to notice the instants of exposed need in the eyes of men she'd known since she was little more than a baby. Their raw looks had unnerved her at first, but she soon became fascinated by these naked, imploring glances, began to search them out in the eyes of every man who met her own intent and beautiful violet stare.

Billy couldn't manage her any longer. On the advice of his friend, Slade Hawkes, he'd taken the girl to Ann Overton to be properly outfitted, and then he'd packed her off to school before she'd had time to think. But she was finished with that now, and it had been Ann's idea to leave Caitlin at Silver Hill for a while to keep her out of the dance hall and away from Layton Weetch, who had the stubborn tenacity of a terrier—at least where Caitlin McGlory was concerned.

"Billy," Ann pointed. "There's Slade Hawkes. You'd best tell him something about Caitlin so he'll have some idea what he's getting himself into. That's if she deigns to stay on here. Why on earth you gave her a choice in the matter I'll never understand."

"I can't say no to her when she looks at me the way she does. Never could," Billy grumbled.

Earlier, when the livery had turned off the high road in a cloud of summer dust and had begun the gentle ascent of Silver Hill Drive, Caitlin had taken Billy's hand.

"I don't want to stay here, Bill," she had said casually in a tone she always used when she was really serious about something. It had made Billy nervous.

"And why not, pray?" Ann had asked in her

most world-wearied manner.

"I don't—I can't bear being left, after my mother and all. Billy knows. I want to come home with you after this party, and that's—"

"I'm not desertin' you, Caty," Billy had explained quickly with an anxious glance at Ann. "Wait 'til you see the place at least, before you make up your mind against it. In only three weeks or four, I'll come for you like I said. Isn't it so, Ann?" He had looked to her for help.

"It is," she had nodded, gesturing with the faintest lift of her shoulder at Caitlin, whose eyes were following a mounted rider toward the manor house set at the crest of the hill.

"Is that where we're going, too?" Caitlin had asked with a smile and a toss of her pretty head.

Chapter Two

"Fairy godmother indeed! Wicked stepmother would be closer to the truth. Ann and Billy aren't even married, yet . . . and she's taken over everything. Ann Overton doesn't care for me at all," Caitlin announced, "and the feeling is completely mutual." Her arm was resting in Quinn's as they sauntered toward a windmill some distance from the house. They had mingled with the gathering of farm boys and girls, city ladies hiding beneath parasols, and their escorts in dark broadcloth wilting in the July heat. Caitlin and Quinn had been photographed together by an enthusiastic young man with a large camera, been greeted by their host and hostess, learned that dinner was an hour away, and decided to explore the estate on their own. As soon as they were off a little distance from the others, Caitlin loosed the anger she'd been holding back since early morning.

"I can't understand what Ann's doing with Billy anyway," she went on. "He's so direct with his unornamented speech and so wonderfully, appallingly vulgar and Ann's aloof and so—so elegant," Caitlin said, sucking in her cheeks and fluttering her long lashes in obvious imitation of Ann. "She just wants my uncle all to herself, so she's devised this diabolical way of getting rid of me."

"It is really vicious of her, exiling you to the finest country estate in Long Island," Jones agreed with feigned seriousness.

"It's all well and good for you to scoff. You probably like the countryside. I mean, it *is* lovely, nature and all, but I belong in the city. I'll miss the streets and the noise, the barrel organs at the corners, and The White Elephant filling in the evenings with my friends. I'll miss Billy most, though," she said simply.

"You're very fond of your uncle?" Quinn asked, lifting Caitlin over a wide puddle and catching the faintest fresh fragrance of orange and a hint of spice, aware of the soft, warm weight of her breast against his chest. Caitlin went on speaking, not missing a word.

"Fond of him?" she exclaimed. "I adore Billy. He's absolutely everything to me." She had tilted her parasol so that it shaded them both, and she rested her arm lightly along

Quinn's shoulders. "You really can set me down now, Mr. Jones," she smiled. "The danger is past, I think."

"You've no other family?" Jones asked, reluctantly releasing her and leading her to an old wooden bench at the mill door.

"None. But Billy's done his best to play father to me, even though the role didn't quite suit him. He's more like a big brother, all teasing and silly puns and clumsy tricks with coins. He saved my life with his circus antics and bear hugs. I'm convinced of it."

"How?" Jones asked, sitting and stretching long legs in front of him.

"By making me laugh when I was very, very sad," Caitlin answered. Shading her eyes, she peered into a mill window. "Very dusty," she commented.

"Sad . . . why?" Jones wanted to know, standing to follow her to the mill door that swung open when she tried the latch.

"Billy says I was missing my mother, but I don't—I can't remember." Caitlin was unusually still and quiet for a long moment then shrugged, and her smile lit her beautiful eyes again. "Billy always says," she told Quinn, stepping into the mill, "it's better to be born lucky than rich, so I shouldn't ever worry. Lucky as I am, I'm sure to get a rich husband." She leaned back so far to look toward the peak of the mill that she had to hold her yellow bonnet in place. "Look at the cobwebs!" she exclaimed. "Which were you born—lucky or rich?"

"Both," Quinn answered sarcastically, catching her hand and pulling her out into the sunlight again. "Do *you* want a rich husband, or is that your uncle's idea?"

"For all his kindness and generosity, Billy has never asked a thing of me," Caitlin said heatedly, "except to come when he calls, laugh at his jokes, and marry well. He's really concerned about position more than wealth. He's learned how to make money, he says, all we'll ever need, but I'm his only real means to social approval. I couldn't disappoint him. I just couldn't. And I do suppose," she burbled, looking up at Jones with mischievous eyes, "it will be just as easy to fall in love with an upstanding man as any other sort. Tell me, Mr. Jones, about *your* family now."

"There's only my father. I haven't seen him in years. We . . . don't get on," he answered coldly.

"Well, Billy and I got on perfectly until Ann Overton came along interfering where she's got no business at all. You and she were lovers once, weren't you?" Caitlin asked with disarming directness. "I could see it right off."

"What would a vestal innocent like you know about lovers?" He almost laughed.

"I saw a lot at The White Elephant," she

protested, "and the girls told me things. What about Ann?"

"I don't kiss and tell." He frowned. "And you shouldn't be so hard on her. She's had a rough time of it, a ne'er-do-well husband who passed young and left her with nothing. She's got no patience for anyone not as hard working and ambitious as she is." Jones undid his top collar stay and shook back his dark hair, ushering Caitlin ahead of him along a narrow, fern-lined path. Her waist was so exquisitely small, the subtle sway of her rounded hips and the toss of her bonneted head so appealing, that Quinn had to stop himself from catching her up and kissing her, the image of her perfect, pouting, very naughty mouth fresh in his thoughts. She stopped abruptly and he nearly ran into her, then moved against her, his arm circling her waist to steady them both. She moved away slightly, finding the momentary contact of their bodies even more unsettling than his amazing smile.

"Here," she glanced up at him over a pretty raised shoulder. "I'll leave this for our walk back. It's a bother, really." She furled her parasol, and he slipped its satin ribbon over a branch, leaving it dangling high above the path.

"Well," she said, "*I'm* here because of your friend Ann. Why are *you*?"

"I've some business in the neighborhood,"

he said laconically, leaving his jacket hanging beside her parasol. Taking her hand, he led her along the path that ended in a vast meadow dotted with dandelions and daisies. Caitlin caught her breath with pure delight, and suddenly she was on her knees gathering dandelions into the full white skirt of her dress that was billowing about her like a cloud. Quinn dropped to his knees beside her. Holding up a flower that had gone to seed, she pursed her lips and blew once, then studied the nearly denuded seed head intently.

"Count the ones left and you know what that tells you? It tells you how many children you will have. I'm having three," she bubbled happily. "It's always the same for me. You try. Oh, so you are having three, too!" she exclaimed after he'd breathed on a furry ball she held to his lips. Her rich, warm laughter rose, and then they were both very still suddenly, kneeling close, face to face. Quinn's hands were clenched at his sides, Caitlin's clasped behind her as she swayed a little, seeming to flow toward him and pull back all in one wavering, graceful gesture.

"The tramp with the golden crown," he said, a touch of a smile on his lean face. "The flower, the *dent-de-lion,*" he added, seeing the startled look in Caitlin's eyes. "The lion's tooth and the coquette's favorite. Did you know that about the dandelion?"

Caitlin shook her head and pushed off her bonnet, letting it dangle down her back as she rose. Quinn, resting on his heels, closed his eyes as she showered him with a rain of the little yellow flowers, then watched Caitlin smooth her dress and do a dainty dance step to shift her layers of petticoats back into place.

"I *didn't* know, but I still prefer dandelions to roses. Roses are so—so terribly beautiful," she said very seriously, "like jewels, but so fragile they're already beginning to wilt before they've unfurled a single petal. Roses make me . . . uneasy."

"I'll try to remember never to give you roses," he said, standing and catching up one of her white lace gloves. "How delicately made and little it is," he mused, placing it on his palm and spreading the fingers along his, his hand closing tightly when Caitlin reached out to reclaim it.

"You must return it," she announced with a little teasing sparkle in her eyes. "What will people think?"

"Do you care?" he asked, turning away.

"Well . . . yes. I'm supposed to care, aren't I? Your friend Ann gave me a little book to read so I'd know exactly how I was supposed to feel and think and behave at all times: nicely," she proclaimed with a devilish little laugh. "*The Young Ladies' Friend* the book is called, and it says . . . odd things—never sit close to a man, or let him read from the same book, or lift you on or off a horse, that sort of good advice."

"And do you follow it, all the good advice?" Quinn asked more seriously than he'd intended. They had returned to the path again that wound upland through pines and yews, away from the shoreside meadow. Quinn went ahead, and Caitlin found him wonderfully pleasing to watch. He moved with long, easy strides, his wide shoulders set, his narrow hips shifting a little. His dark hair fell over the collar of his well-tailored shirt that followed the muscled contours of his long back.

"Mr. Jones, you can't ask a lady such a question," she bantered. "I mean, what if I didn't follow the book's—?"

"Don't ever tell me I can't," he said in a menacing voice, turning on Caitlin, his mood suddenly changed. There was a dark threat in his eyes and an awesome furnace heat that panicked Caitlin for a long moment before it ignited the spark that had been glowing there in her own eyes from the first instant she had seen him. Before she had time to breath or even to think, she was locked in arms that were hard and strong, the curving, soft, warm line of her body bending to his, her lips parting to the thrust of his tongue. They stood, clinging, on the treelined path, golden in crossbeams of slanting sunlight, coils of Caitlin's auburn hair tumbling free, the summer breeze at her hem whipping lace petticoats about his leather-booted legs that pressed along the length of hers. She cared about nothing else then but the strength of his arms about her, the taste of the hot, hard mouth, the satin brush of his hair against her brow and beneath her caressing fingers.

"You are quick to take fire," Quinn was whispering along her brow, and then he set her a little away from him and stared down for a moment with bemused eyes now soft as gray velvet.

"Am I?" Caitlin breathed. "Is that . . . good?" Her violet eyes glistened as she stared back at this man, this stranger who had made her feel beautiful in a way she'd never even imagined she could. Everything seemed so perfect—Quinn and the place and the summer day—that Caitlin felt she could do anything and have everything she'd ever dreamed of.

"Let's go back now. I'm starved. Are you?" she smiled, extending a hand.

"You go. I've business elsewhere," he answered, adjusting white cuffs as he slipped on his jacket and raked back his hair. The flat coolness that had come into his eyes and the angle at which he held his handsome head as he stood at the edge of the wooded path reminded Caitlin of some sleek and dangerous animal come to test the air before slipping away again into the shadowy forest.

"My glove," she said huskily, wanting to hold him there, anticipating the quick stab of loss she would feel when he had gone.

"I'll return it to you . . . sometime," he winked. Then he was gone, and she could do nothing but stamp her foot and call his name, just once, in complete, furious indignation. She stood fuming, then paced a little before she sat and pulled off her slippers, the moss at the base of an old oak staining her dress. Her white silk stockings were next to be discarded, along with the one glove she'd managed to retain. Standing and stretching, she grasped the lowest branch of the oak and pulled herself up into the tree. She freed the parasol, let it drop, then paused to view the world from her elevated vantage. She could see the shoreline, the white sails on the bay, the manor house amidst its gardens, fields, and orchards, and, in the distance, the high road the livery had traveled carrying her to Silver Hill. With piqued interest, she noted a covered surrey pulled off into a sheltered clearing, its striped canopy matching the flounced hem of a blue gown—all Caitlin could see of the vehicle's occupant.

A tryst, she smiled to herself, about to descend when she saw Quinn Jones come striding across the road and brush his lips to an extended, gloved hand. He climbed in, took up the reins, and guided the surrey along the road in the direction of Sag Harbor.

Caitlin, caught in a swirl of amazement, was both furious and mortified at her own behavior. "Damn him!" she exploded aloud. "On his way to another woman and leading me on like—like some silly schoolgirl with no experience of men at all!" But that's exactly what she was, she had to admit to herself reluctantly with a little shrug. No matter how many love scenes she had watched played out at The White Elephant, and despite Layton Weetch's best efforts, she was an artless innocent, practically a simpleton, when it came to love games. Next time, if there were a next time, she'd be more careful with this Quinn Jones. Before she'd take him on again, she'd have to learn how to play at love as she'd seen others do. She'd need *practice*. Caitlin sighed aloud, leaning back in a crook of the tree to think. She closed her eyes, and a beam of light, falling through the leaves, found her face and blazed her sun-caught hair.

"It's only during snowstorms that angels are supposed to fly close to the ground. How did you get here on such a summer day as this?" At the foot of Caitlin's tree a young man with a drooping, gingery mustache and curious brown eyes stood smiling up at her. "I work here, miss, and if I can help . . . ?"

"It was my parasol, you see. It was . . . well, I had to get it out of the tree, and now I've mislaid a glove and torn a stocking, and I don't know what my uncle will say when he sees me."

Chapter Three

"I swear to you I really thought Caitlin *was* Billy's very young paramour when your husband first sent them to me. I've seen more unusual pairings," Ann Overton said with a quiet touch of humor. She sat with her hostess, Brigida Hawkes, beneath a magnificent silver-linden tree, watching a photographer at work wooing reluctant guests to stand for portraits in front of his large camera. "Where does he get the energy in this heat?" Ann asked.

"I don't know, but I'm glad he's up to it," Brigida said. "We'll be able to keep this lovely day forever because of him, and that's wonderful. Now . . . tell me more about my new charge."

"Your 'charge' is not much younger than you are—a year at most—but she's a child, a spoiled one, and she resents me, of course, coming between her and her uncle Billy. But she'll get over that. I'm going to let her model in the salon next season, now that you've turned me down. With her natural elegance and a seventeen-inch waist, she's perfect. Until the summer's over, do keep an eye on her, will you, Brigida? She's a born flirt. She thrives on masculine attention and she always gets it, but someday soon she may get more than she can handle."

"I see," Brigida nodded. "Tell me, who is the exceptional-looking man who's attention Caitlin has already captured?" she asked, beginning to maneuver Ann toward the manor house verandah.

"Quinn Jones. An old friend of your husband's. And mine," Ann said, slipping her arm through Brigida's, her voice taking on a rare, intimate fervor. "He's a rake and a drifter with a grand, cavalier style and shady dreams. I *know*. But I must tell you, Brigida, that in good conscience I couldn't tell any warm, free woman to pass by an opportunity to . . . enjoy his attentions. He's *extraordinary*, all passion and fire and shifting moods, but when he smiles . . . well, he appreciates a woman in the most extravagant ways. He finds perfection in the slant of a shoulder, in the turn of an ankle. He adores all one's secret softnesses." Ann was quiet for a moment, thoughtful. "It's all too intense to last, though," she added finally. "I couldn't have stood much more, and he's quickly sated and gone . . . and unforgettable."

"That's saying a great deal," Brigida said softly. As they neared the manor house, absorbed in talk, their pace slowed gradually until they came to a standstill some distance off.

"I could say much more," Ann sighed.

"And you speak with a voice of experience, I know."

"Of course. Lots of it. Before and after Quinn. But Caitlin is too young and impressionable to deal with him. Right now she thinks every flower in the world is blooming just for her. She's ready to give herself to the wind, to the sky . . . to the first man who sparks that lovely fire. That innocent girl has no inkling at all of the difference between love and seduction. For Quinn, there's *only* seduction, so please do watch out for her," Ann asked again with uncharacteristic concern.

"You *will* watch out for her, Captain? I'm afraid she'll be lonesome, away from home and all. She didn't have an easy time of it before she came to me, and I think it affected her. She can't stand me leaving her, and she was always asking about her mother when she was small. I never could find out anything much about the woman, not even a family name. Just Damaris is all I ever knew." Billy, with his hands thrust deep into his pockets, rocked back on his heels, his habit when agitated. "This Damaris," he went on, "run off with my brother Patrick, and the next I hear, Patrick's passed on, and *she's* up and left their child with Lady Something in Wales, who's been told to send Caitlin on to me. It was one of your father's ships brought her here, remember Slade? I came out to Sag Harbor to get her."

"What happened to the mother?" Hawkes asked.

"I've no idea. We've never heard from her once in all these years. I mean, can you imagine—walking away from your own child, and such a one as Caty?" Billy scowled, and deep furrows showed between his indignant blue eyes. "If only she'd been a boy. . . . It was all fine with us when she was a little thing, but imagine a bachelor like me raising such a headstrong young lady as she's grown into. It's not been easy, I'll tell you, and once the boys started payin' her attention . . . well, if you weren't so well married yourself, Slade, I'd not leave her here with you, if you know what I mean." Billy winked.

"Don't trouble about me, friend," Hawkes laughed, his intent eyes following his wife's graceful progress toward them with Ann in tow.

"Here come the ladies." Billy beamed. "Tell

me quick, before they get here. Who is this Jones anyway?"

"We were both with Sheridan during the war. Quinn needed a place to go for a while after it was over. I brought him here, and that's when Ann met him. Jones is from Illinois, a solid, old Galena banking family who made their money in the lead mining days out there. Quinn broke with them long ago, or he was disinherited. He's never said which, and I haven't asked. He was a wild boy—I heard that—always in trouble. Usually it was women."

"Sounds like someone else I know," Billy laughed. "No wonder you and him hit it off so good. Ah, here are the delightful ladies!"

"Slade," Ann began as soon as her foot touched the bottom porch step. "What is Quinn Jones doing here?"

"That's the question of the day, it seems." He frowned a little. "If you'll look over there, you'll be less concerned with Quinn, I think."

Out across the sun-splashed lawn, Caitlin, accompanied by a very attentive farm boy, was making her spectacular way toward them.

"Lord, what a lovely sight she is!" Billy laughed, and the Captain, with an arm about his wife and a warm look in his eye, readily agreed.

"Do you see the way Robin Edwards is staring at her?" Brigida asked. "If she gives him any encouragement at all, he'll be following her about like a lovesick hound."

"Encouragement?" Ann snapped. "I told you, she's a born flirt. But just looking at her, tousled and undone as she is, is all the encouragement any boy would need."

Caitlin's abundant, russet-streaked auburn hair was falling free, and her face was flushed. Her bonnet had slipped down her back, and she was barefooted, carrying her slippers. She no longer had gloves or a parasol or stockings either, Ann noted with annoyance. They all watched her smile and wave as her escort veered off toward the barn, and then she presented herself to the gathering on the manor house porch.

"Bill," she said in her special businesslike tone, looking charmingly serious, "I've decided. I *will* stay on at Silver Hill for a while, if that's all right with everyone."

Chapter Four

"Caitlin, close your eyes. Your heart's showing," Brigida Hawkes whispered, watching Quinn Jones come toward them through a rambling garden of captive, wild red roses.

"It's not like that, Brigida. I hardly know the man, and he has other interests," Caitlin protested. "I saw him with one of them. He's not even been here once since the party anyway."

"And that's nearly a whole week ago, isn't it?" Brigida smiled. "But a week can seem a lifetime, Caitlin, if you're in love. I know that better than anyone. I'm sorry to tease you, really, but you must be cautious. Quinn is a—a ladies' man and a rake, Ann tells me. He's always breaking someone's heart."

"Oh, Ann! She's always interfering," Caitlin pouted a little, concentrating on Quinn's slow approach, pleased with the set of his shoulders and the suggestion of movement in his low, narrow hips.

"But even my husband says Jones is just not ready for anything—respectable or . . . Here are Mary and Nan. We'd better talk about something else or they'll never stop teasing you."

Two well-favored farm girls, one carrying a basket of peaches, lighted like butterflies on the very green grass near Caitlin and Brigida, and they all turned their attention to a litter of retriever puppies tumbling about on a patchwork quilt.

"Who's that man coming?" Mary Edwards asked, looking up.

"Mr. Jones, a friend of the Captain's. He's here on business," Brigida explained with a glance at Caitlin, who was absorbed with the pups and seemed not to hear.

"Isn't he handsome? And dressed fine, but not like a dandy at all. I like a good dark suit on a man and a silk shirt," Mary's sister, Nan, announced, accidentally tipping her basket of peaches so that some flowed onto the lawn.

"I like cool gray eyes in a man," Mary twinkled. "Like his."

"Sometimes they aren't so . . . cool," Caitlin let slip, and the others sat still and looked at her for a moment with keen curiosity.

* * *

There was something, Quinn Jones decided, about girls cooing like doves over babies and little animals that was exactly the same everywhere, in any language, and completely captivating. It was the musical, unintelligible burble of young feminine voices that had attracted his attention as he was finishing up his business with Slade Hawkes, and he looked out of the study window to glimpse two pretty, shining heads—one fair, one darker—at the far edge of the rose garden below. By the time he was halfway there, Caitlin and Brigida had been joined by two other girls—one amply built as some mythic earth mother, the other a slender sylph. The captain's lady was the golden goddess of the charming cluster, and at its center, a fiery star shining, was Caitlin McGlory. They were all still for an instant, like players in a *tableau vivant* or the subjects of a painting, and Quinn was struck by the lush feminine display—graceful swan necks and willowy arms, bared, smooth, ruffle-touched shoulders, slim, sashed waists, rounded breasts beneath pastel summer dresses soft as rose petals, flirting hints of lace-edged petticoats and hair ribbons enough, pinks and blues and yellows, to deck the pole for a May Day dance. The tipped basket of ripe, fragrant peaches perfected the picture for Quinn, who had an educated, connoisseur's eye for art *and* women and collected both, though in different ways.

He never parted with a painting once he'd made up his mind to acquire it. Women he consumed intemperately, enjoyed enormously, and dismissed quickly.

Nearing this appealing group, Quinn had an almost irresistible desire to place a hand on the smooth cap of Caitlin's shiny hair that would, he knew, be sun warmed and silken to his touch.

"Quinn, help us," Brigida appealed. "The pups are all so perfect it's impossible to make a pick of the litter. You decide, but first meet Mary and Nan, my indispensable helpers. You already know Miss McGlory, I believe."

Quinn's smile pleased them all except Caitlin, who was more interested, it seemed, in the little dogs than in him, and he stood with his hands on his hips waiting for her to look up. When she did finally and her violet eyes met his, she felt a surge of her heart that took her breath away. Quinn was seeking her smile then, she could tell. She tried not to give it to him but failed.

"I've come for you," he announced bluntly, wondering why he'd done such a thing. Caitlin was a mere child, a guileless girl with all her feelings shining clear in her eyes for anyone to read. He preferred experienced women who knew how these games were played, who didn't expect him to wake up in love and never asked about tomorrow. Yet here he was, already seeing forever in Caitlin's eyes.

"I'm leaving soon," he said quickly. "I've done with my business in Sag Harbor, and I wanted to return this to you." Going down on one knee, he offered Caitlin her glove, then roughly fondled one of the pups, who bared sharp little milk teeth and yapped aggressively.

"Thank you, Mr. Jones, but I've no need of it now. I've lost the other," she said carelessly, trying and perhaps succeeding for the first time in her life in disguising her feelings.

He was leaving. It was over before it had even begun, and Brigida and Ann were both right. She'd best dismiss him from her thoughts now or she might indeed find herself very unhappy before long. She stood, smiling indifferently, and started toward the house. "Goodbye and good journey, Mr. Jones," she tossed over her shoulder in a manner that, she thought, would certainly dismiss him and send him on his way.

He overtook her beneath a trellised arbor, laden with full-blown roses, and tucked the glove into her waist sash. "About the other day," he began, and his low, intimate tone, the velvet softness of his gray eyes brought back every detail so clearly that Caitlin was pierced through with the sweetness of remembered pleasure.

"The other day?" she repeated. "Oh, yes, you *were* at the party, weren't you—briefly as I recall. Tell me, was your assignation with the lady in blue a success?"

"I wanted to tell you," he began in a voice taut with anger, "that if things were different with me. . . . Perhaps we'll meet again," he concluded hastily.

"And perhaps we won't. I can't see it matters much to either of us. Goodbye again, Mr. Jones." Caitlin dropped the glove and hurried toward the house. She tried to jerk her shoulder away in irritation as he swung her roughly about, but she couldn't stop herself from looking into his handsome face that was dangerous now and dark with anger.

"I'm going to give you something to remember me by," he gritted. He pulled her to him hard, and her hands fluttered to his muscled shoulders. Her body flowed to his as he kissed her, long and slow and deep, standing there in the middle of the rose garden, with the Captain, who'd come out, and Brigida and the girls, watching and the cook at the kitchen window. When he released her finally, he caught her raised hand before she could strike his face, then produced a blazing yellow cluster of dandelions from a jacket pocket and folded her slim fingers about it.

"And this must be something to forget you

by!" Caitlin snapped, knowing she'd begin to tremble in a moment if she didn't get away from him at once. She spun about on her heel and flounced off. "And *that*," she said to herself with a toss of her head, almost believing it, "is *that*!"

Chapter Five

"How I do dread washdays! I'd rather do anythin' else at all. What about you?" Nan Edwards asked, vigorously rubbing a sheet against a wooden washboard. She stopped to hear Caitlin's reply. Because of the heat, the work had been left to late afternoon and shifted outside to the kitchen dooryard.

"I've never done any washing." Caitlin smiled. "We always lived in lodgings or had a woman to do it. Would you like some help?" She placed her half-empty glass of lemonade on a stone bench to await an assignment and was set at once to stirring a boiling tub with a wooden wash stick.

"Now, you must move the things about a bit more, or there'll be yellow spots," Nan cautioned with motherly interest. It had been like that since she came to Silver Hill. Caitlin had been taken under wings, watched over, guided, instructed, and looked after by everyone. Mary had taught her to churn butter and make cheese; the old cook had given instruction in the art of baking; the lady of the house had demonstrated table setting and tea serving, and the captain, who had decided she should learn to ride, had put a gentle Welsh cob at her disposal for the duration of her visit and had instructed Robin Edwards to ride out with their guest every afternoon when his work was done and the day's heat subsiding.

Caitlin had learned quickly and pleased them all. She entranced the men, Robin particularly, with her innocent, flirtatious warmth and, as they all worked, she endlessly entertained the girls with what to them were wondrous tales of the wild goings on at The White Elephant.

A month after she had arrived at Silver Hill, Caitlin had to admit to herself that Ann Overton had been right. It *was* a wonderful place, and she'd been made one of the "family." It was all working perfectly, she told herself, so she should have been perfectly happy, but that wasn't quite true. All too often she was astir and skittish. Sunny, balmy summer days seemed to her restlessly calm, and there was something vague and elusive she fervidly sought in every breeze that touched her cheek.

Oddly unsettled, she tried to take refuge in the loveliness of the world about her. She went into ecstasies over fields filled with flowers, the clouds, birds flying. When that didn't work, when she still awoke suddenly from forgotten dreams suffused with inexplicable, tender, melancholy longings, she decided she must be homesick for the dance hall life and the city streets that were her true habitat after all. She wrote to Billy at once, relieved to have solved the problem, saying that it was time for her to leave Silver Hill. On the August afternoon that she came to help Nan Edwards with the washing, Caitlin was eagerly awaiting Billy's reply telling her when he would be coming to take her home.

As Nan scrubbed and Caitlin stirred, nearly lost in the rising steam, Robin Edwards entered the yard.

"Where's Caty?" he demanded. "It's time for her riding lesson. Ah, there she is. You, Nanny, are trying to hide her from me in that inferno of yours. Miss McGlory, get your lovely person away from that hot mess at once or you'll be looking like this." With a sly laugh, he held Nan's swollen, red hands up for display. The girl pulled them away and hid them behind her, her eyes filling with tears.

"You coward, Rob," Caitlin hissed, coming to Nan's defense. "Look how unhappy you've made her. Pick on someone who might be a match for you—not your own little sister."

"It's all right," Nan said, sniffling a little. "I'm used to him, after all. You go on for your ride now. Mary will be right along to help me finish up."

Caitlin came out from behind the washtub reluctantly and glowered at Rob, whom she had grown to dislike over the past weeks. She couldn't keep the contempt from her voice when she addressed him, something she tried to do now as infrequently as possible. She had been amused at first by his single-minded determination to lay claim to her affections, and she did, she admitted guiltily to herself, encourage him. That was a mistake, she realized, when he took to following her about, fawning over her like some pathetic hound, the look in his big, brown eyes imploring and pained when she made light of his protestations of love. Edwards was so dogged in his pursuit and so insensitive to Caitlin's gentle refusals that she was forced to become direct, then almost cruel in her rejection. It didn't seem to matter to him. He went on groveling like a beaten dog, and Caitlin completely lost sight of any redeeming qualities Edwards might have possessed. She saw only his faults, which were numerous. He had no dignity or self-respect. He was dishonest and sly and lazy, but worst of all he was a terrible bully. He dealt meanly with his sister and tormented the shy little stable boy endlessly, all the while paying court to those above him with apparently winning skill. Caitlin went to great lengths to avoid Robin Edwards completely, but still there were, at the Captain's direction, the afternoon rides, to which she determined to put an end after one last outing.

"Marry me, Cate. I'll change, I swear. I might even make something of myself," Robin said with the obsequious smile she'd come to detest. They'd ridden several miles east along the shore in total silence until they dismounted at Caitlin's favorite place, a part of the shore where a brackish pond nearly met the sea and the dunes were dark green with beach grass and ferns.

"Before you came," Robin went on, ignoring her obvious irritation, "I was hopelessly in love with the Captain's lady. Now I know you are my one true love."

"Tomorrow it will be someone else," she said archly, wishing he'd stop his talk and let her enjoy the quiet of the afternoon.

"No, it'll still be you tomorrow. You know, you've the sort of beauty a man would try to conquer the world to win."

"But you're not much of a man, so we needn't worry about you conquering anything, need we?" she said angrily and knew she'd gone too far when she saw him pale and his fists clench tightly at his sides. "I'm sorry Rob. I didn't mean it, really. It's just that I'm . . . homesick and restless and . . . well, my uncle will be coming for me soon . . . in a few days and. . . . Look, I need to be alone for a while. I'm going to walk along the pond a way before the rain starts," she said and strode off, wanting to get far away from him quickly, but he caught her before she'd gone very far and covered her mouth with his, his strong fingers closing about her throat.

"Robin, please stop before we're both sorry," she said calmly, smiling, trying to give him a way to withdraw with dignity.

"Don't say no to me, Cate, because I'm going to show you how much of a man I really am," he hissed, frantically kissing her brow and her ear, the curve of her throat, his hands moving over her until she hurled him off and began to run back toward the beach and the horses and the open sky that had become a roiling blue-gray mass of clouds that was torn suddenly by a twist of lightning as thunder exploded very loud and very close. Caitlin stumbled, her ankle caught and turning painfully in a tangle of vines, entrapping her under the wild storm as the rain began, cold and hard, and Robin was almost on her, the look in his eyes cruel and crazed.

"Don't!" she screamed, but her voice was lost

in the roar of the storm as he fell on her again and tore at her dress, opening it from neck to waist. She tried to fight him off, but she couldn't this time with her ankle caught and throbbing with pain. "Robin, Robin, I'll kill you, I swear. If you—"

She saw it then, coming at them like some satanic engine of doom, a surging horse bursting out of the mist and the blinding, leaden rain, its legs stretching in full gallop at every stride. The animal's ears were laid back flat, its nostrils flared large as saucers sucking wind and the great, draped, formless creature clinging to its back loosed an unearthly howl of rage. Caitlin, entangled, screamed and tried to pull away as she watched a massive arm rise and come crashing down across Robin's shoulders, then rise and fall again as a riding quirt cut across his face, which was still close enough to hers for her to see the ragged mark it made. Then Robin was gone, stumbling and crawling into the storm, and the rider was beside her, slashing at the vines that held her trapped, gathering her up, enveloping her in something soft and warm as strong arms closed about her.

Chapter Six

The crude shelter where Caitlin was deposited was dry and snug, though the door was only a deerskin flap and the window coverings greased parchment. There was a rough fire circle of stones beneath a small draft opening in the roof and a supply of wood stacked along one wall. Near this fireplace was a deep spread of pine boughs grown brown with age, that richly scented the air. And all at once, breathing deeply, she knew who it was that had saved her and what it was that had so filled her night dreams and her daydreams and set her yearning after every breeze. She finally knew what all her restlessness and bittersweet longings had really been about.

"Oh, Quinn! Oh, Quinn, I thought you'd gone," she barely whispered, shaking violently with delayed fear and cold as he moved about the shelter like some predatory animal in a lair, readying the place for habitation and securing it against the storm.

The fire flared; his long shadow leaped up the wall and, throwing off his cape, he turned to her then, his white stab of a grin flashing. The sight of him, of his smile and his fine gray eyes nearly made her heart stop, and Caitlin felt every part of her reach out to him. It was then her tears began.

"What are you crying about?" he asked. "You're safe now—more or less."

"Robin . . . he—he's some sort of monster," she managed to say between shuddering sobs.

"How do you know I'm not?" Quinn shrugged, and Caitlin followed his eyes down to her thrusting breasts that were naked to his wolfish stare. With his lips drawn into a thin grimace, he came toward her, shifting a silver knife from hand to hand.

"What are you *doing*?" Caitlin demanded, scrambling to her feet despite her paining ankle and turning away into the shadows. Deftly, he applied the blade to her wet, clinging clothes until they lay in a beribboned heap at her feet.

"Ann Overton does do nice work," he said, fingering, then pocketing a bit of delicate lingerie decorated with Caitlin's initials, CMM, embroidered in silken strands of her own soft, auburn hair. "What's the middle

M for?"

"I've no idea," she answered, facing him calmly then, moving naked into the firelight, her fawn-toned skin wet and glistening. She gazed up with beautiful, dark violet eyes that were innocent and trusting as a child's, yet held an unmistakable invitation that only a woman could offer. She looked for her reflection then, and a needy, wanting look in his eyes, but there was only cool, deliberate appraisal. She flushed and turned away, never seeing his eyes take fire or the look of greed that fleetingly touched his hard face.

Standing slender, poised, and still in the firelight, Caitlin appeared to Quinn as innocent and beautiful as Eve in the Garden must have been before the Fall. There was a glimmering brilliancy about her as long coils of russet-streaked hair tumbled, falling about her shoulders.

"Too cold for Eden," Quinn growled, purposely trying to shatter the spell that was beginning to envelop them both. "Get dry or you'll be ill," he ordered, dropping his leather cape about Caitlin's shoulders and slowly, methodically, pressing the inner, soft, sueded side against her sleek, wet body, touching her everywhere, his hands running over her shoulders and down the full length of her back before he reached around and pulled her against him. His deliberate, firm touch slid down over the swell of her breasts, lingering, and he and Caitlin both felt the peaks rise against the chafing suede. Pliant in his hands, she let his touch move along her hips and thighs and down her slim legs.

"Well, Caitlin McGlory, what've you got to say for yourself now?" he asked, turning her to him, his smooth, honeyed voice low, a new, concentrated luminescence in his eyes.

"Who the devil *are* you?" she asked, trembling again, but not with cold. "And what's this place?" She began to move about the fire, fluttering like a moth, drawn to it, yet fearful of singeing delicate wings.

"It's a traveler's shelter, built by some kind soul for stranded fools like us on nights like this." Quinn had stretched out, regally relaxed near the fire to watch her. He leaned on one elbow, and his straight hair, falling forward over his brow, was blue-black in the firelight. Caitlin's eyes traveled his long body's length and, when they came back to his face, she was wanting so desperately to be in his arms that she couldn't speak at all. Quinn stood with lupine quickness. "You didn't see the inscription carved on the doorpost," he said, taking her hand and leading her to it. "'Be not afraid to welcome strangers,'" he read, "'for thereby you may entertain angels unawares.' Are you hurt?" he demanded, seeing her favor her right ankle.

"It's all right. It's a little stiff, that's all," she lied as he lifted her and carried her back to the fire.

"Keep still," he ordered. "I'll be back. I've got to see to the roan, and if this storm turns into a full-blown hurricane, we'll need more wood before it's over." Wearing only a shirt and leather breeches, Quinn ducked through the low doorway.

"Take your cape," Caitlin called. "You'll drown out there."

"And leave you . . . disrobed? That would be a welcome for angels. And others. Keep these," he said, appearing in the doorway for a moment. He set down a silver flask, and, with a flick of his wrist, sent the silver dagger flying to lodge securely in a vertical post within Caitlin's easy reach.

Caitlin appeared to be asleep as she lay curled near the fire with Quinn's cape pulled up to her chin, her flushed cheek resting on a curved hand. Her eyes flickered open slowly, though he had hardly made a sound returning.

"Close them," he ordered, swallowing deeply from the now half-empty flask of brandy. "I'm taking these wet things off."

But Caitlin didn't close her eyes again. The fire had fallen apart, and she watched Quinn repair it to roaring height before he rose, his back to her, and begin to strip wet garments from his lanky, dark body. Flexed long muscles stood in his solid thighs and flanks. His hips were narrow, his shoulders wide, and when he shifted toward her, Caitlin saw that his sinewy chest was lightly furred. Quickly, a little afraid of him, she raised her eyes. In profile, his lean, regal face with prominent features and strong dark brows perfectly suited the moody prince he often seemed—suited, too, the boyish charmer he could be for fleeting moments when he flashed his amazing smile. He *is* a handsome animal, Caitlin thought, intrigued by the rippling contours of Quinn's hard-muscled body. Then, joltingly, their eyes met.

"I told you to close them," he glared, finding her curious, bold, violet stare astoundingly lovely.

"Aren't you cold?" she purred drowsily, made vague and soft by his brandy, luxuriating in the warm caress of his soft cape that was touching her bare skin everywhere.

With unpremeditated generosity—without thinking at all—she raised the cover, inviting him with a sleepy smile to share its warmth, her warmth. It's time for this now, she knew instinctively. It's time. She responded in her blood to the animal power she saw in Quinn, to his princely, sullen charm and rugged handsomeness. In some fallow, raw recess of her being, with every deep, regular pulsation of her heart, she wanted him.

When Quinn moved close to kneel over Caitlin, not smiling at all, she saw glistening raindrops caught in his black hair and inhaled the scent of pine on his cool skin. He lowered himself to her slowly, feeding on the sight of her efflorescent young body with its slim thighs and perfect contours. She reclined, pillowed by pine boughs, her extended arms uplifting beautiful, firm breasts. His connoiseur's eyes discovered in Caitlin then the ethereal loveliness of Titian's Venus and traces of Goya's gypsy seductress, Maja. But most clearly, Quinn saw in her that quintessential goddess of rampant femaleness, Manet's magnificent whore, Olympia, reclining nude like her centuries-older sisters, blatantly exhibiting a full, dazzling expanse of smooth, pale skin, her hint of a smile like Caitlin's, promising every pleasure a man could dream of.

"Women like you have bewitched men since the beginning of time," Quinn muttered, reluctantly realizing he'd found his own mythic beauty in a crude beach shelter in the midst of a tearing summer storm. Beneath his ready hand, in the person of Caitlin McGlory, was a shameless, elegant Olympia immodestly flaunting her irresistible perfection. Stalling, holding off, Quinn let his fierce eyes caress all of Caitlin's finely wrought turnings and smooth swells before he flicked back his hair, sending a tiny shower of rain drops along her creamy, warm length. She shivered, and then, where the drops fell, Quinn's mouth followed, moving with excruciating slowness, barely touching her at first, brushing her lidded eyes and the smooth, white arch of her throat as her head fell back, then taking ravenous possession of her parted lips. Her slender body shimmered into motion as she half rose, alarmed at what she was feeling, and Quinn traced the lovely, lilting curve of her silken breast with his hand, then his lips. She felt the boiling passion in him when his tongue and teeth found the prominent pink tips that were tight as new spring berries, and more tasty, Quinn thought, mouthing each in turn again and again.

A subtle tremor passed through Caitlin, and she extended a cautious hand to follow the line of his shoulder and the path of a flexed muscle down his arm. Drawing the cape about his shoulders too and smiling then, she gathered him close. His mouth was at hers again, and she welcomed the forcing thrust of his tongue. He moved his hand along the sleek planes of her hips and belly before he explored the joining line of her thighs, parting them and invading the tight, muscled passage between. With wondrous delight, Caitlin felt her body responding, felt her own secret self parting and giving way to his strong hand's probe that sent flares of pleasure running all through her.

When, carefully, staring into her eyes, he brushed a swollen, half-hidden swell of exquisite sensitivity, Caitlin cried out and would have bolted if he hadn't held her down.

"Be *still*, venturesome, wanton child, and tell me what you're feeling now. That'll make it even better." Quinn's voice flowed over Caitlin like rich, warmed honey, and it was then, when she was feeling more than she ever had, when she was on the brink of giving everything, that Caitlin, for the first time in her life, lost her nerve, panicked, changed her mind. What this man, this stranger, could do to her with the merest touch of his hand gave him a mastery she was unwilling and afraid to grant him.

All the terrible things she'd heard about him came rushing into her thoughts, feeding her fright. He was a ne'er-do-well drifter, with no ties and no position. He was a criminal and a rake and a rogue, and he'd be gone in the morning and leave her with that aching restlessness again, but this time it would be worse. This time she'd *know* what she was longing for.

Quinn was waiting for her to speak, inhaling the faint, crisp fragrance of orange and spice that clung to her silken skin. His sensitive hands molded the warm, curving swells of her body that was as perfect and controlled as a dancer's. "Go on, tell me," he prompted hoarsely, almost beyond waiting, but wanting to hear her lilting young voice gone throaty and warm with passion.

"Nothing *to* tell," she lied brightly. "I'm feeling nothing. It's just no good at all, Quinn. It won't work, I can tell, so let me go." She was parroting one of the bar girls she'd heard dismiss an importuning customer, and she didn't understand the implication of her words, the experience they implied she had had before, and their indifferent denial of his manly proficiency.

"I didn't ask you for a *damn* thing," he whispered roughly, genuinely surprised by her sophistication and angered by her jaded coolness. "It's you who made me a gracious invitation no gentleman would refuse. Why?"

"I owe you *something* for saving me, don't I?" she asked, appalled at her own crass vulgarity.

"I'm bedding a princess with all the sensibilities of a whore. You icy little bitch," he spat in a tight rage at her seeming indifference. "Even a whore would pretend to more feeling than you do."

"Let me go," Caitlin commanded, trying to resist his furious, searching probe as he knelt between her thighs, pressing her down, his hips thrusting against her.

"You've whetted my appetite, ice princess, so lie still and take what I'm giving you," he hissed.

"Oh, don't," she choked, tears of pain and anger misting her eyes as he prodded into her, pressing hard, harder than he thought he'd have to until one pistoning thrust broke the unexpected barrier. He drove in deep, realizing then what he'd done but not able to stop, and Caitlin's single, long, wounded cry tore through the summer night that had become soft and still without their even noticing. Then there was only a whisper of wind in the trees and the sound of surf pounding beneath a new August moon.

"You little fool, why didn't you tell me instead of putting on your act? You had reason to be fearful, but you're well unvirgined now," he said in a soft voice. Still deep inside her, he began to move again, and Caitlin began to weep softly and then, absolutely silently, folded her arms about him, moving against him hungrily in a free and wildly building response of pleasure, giving herself up to him completely now until she felt him tense with a rolling, long shudder. Then he was still.

"Foolish, seducing, virgin child, you should have *said*," he whispered, leaning to taste her tears. "There are kinder ways of doing these things. First I'd have breathed love songs all over your satin skin; there could have been . . . more. Don't cry. Now you're really ready for me to do all the things to you I haven't yet, all the things I've done to all the women I've had before."

"Haven't you done enough already?" Caitlin choked out in a confusion of soaring feeling that was more than she thought she could stand.

"Done enough?" Quinn thundered with a resurgent rage that frightened her breath away. "Virgin child, we've hardly even begun."

He reached for her again, and his ungentle taking of her petulant mouth, his easy, deliberate molding of her tautened breasts, then his hands gliding down over her belly to linger between her damp thighs sent long, rippling movements through her fawn-toned body. She felt set adrift, floating and weightless, lost in diffuse, unimpaired delight as long, sensual quiverings spread through her. By the time Quinn was poised over her again—lengths of glistening muscles flexed—and sliding his strong hands beneath her, lifting her body to his, he had made Caitlin so outrageously, wonderfully wild that she knew nothing, wanted nothing in all the world but to feel his fissuring, impaling surges of power again and again. He didn't disappoint her, and she gave way completely to all the lawless, unspeakable, beautiful sensations that, after an eternity, welled and broke in a turbulent upheaval that left her limpid and soft all over, urgently molding herself to the long, hard body that was subsiding beside her.

After a time, leaning to Quinn and over him, Caitlin found her reflection shimmering in his gray eyes. She smiled, and he almost smiled back before turning away. She rested her head on his shoulder after she'd pulled the cape up over them. Feeling weak and tired and oddly happy, she let her eyes drift upward with the fire smoke and felt as though she could touch the sky that was bejeweled now with low-sailing morning stars.

Chapter Seven

"You look as though you'd been naked since the day you were born," Quinn said slowly. "You look lightly buffed like pink cabochon coral." He watched Caitlin stretch awake and arch her back as her eyes fluttered against the dawn sunlight pouring through the shelter door behind him. To Caitlin, Quinn was a towering, dark shadow above her in the early morning brightness.

"I'm *starving*!" She smiled, rising up on one elbow, an outrageous abundance of glowing, soft hair falling across her shoulder. Shading her eyes, she saw that he was wearing only breeches, his upper body bare. "I must have thrown off the cover in the night," she said. "It's gotten warm again." She reached for Quinn's cape.

"Don't," he said, quickly going down on

one knee at her side, lifting handfuls of silken curls to expose her tremulous breasts, tracing their rounded, lilting curves with his hand then slowly tasting the tips that tightened and stood. Gently he laid her down again, looking into her exultant blue eyes that were asking for and offering everything.

Quinn's smooth, tanned face came close; his lips barely brushed hers. Then his eyes were like a velvet caress touching everywhere as he carefully kissed her fingertips, one by one. Braced on his arms, set to either side of Caitlin's hips, watching her eyes that were almost unbearably blue, Quinn stretched along her length and brought his mouth to hers again, a little more insistently this time and she traced the flexed muscles in his back and arms. She clung to his neck trying to draw him down to her, her full lips parting.

"Learn a little restraint, Caitlin; don't hurry it." There was a low, hot growl in Quinn's voice, a savage sensuality in his smile that gave Caitlin a stab of primitive fear as he suddenly reminded her again for an instant of a dangerous lupine animal, slipping out of the woods with the scent of pine and chilly springs clinging to his sleek, hard body.

"But I want to know everything . . . I'm aching to feel all there is," she sighed, her feathery body aquiver, irresistible.

"Oh, you will, I promise you," Quinn

answered very softly, searching Caitlin's face with a touch of skeptical delight, struck by her tantalizing innocence and the flamboyant passion he'd never before found, never expected to find, mingled in one beautiful woman. "I'll love every inch of your exquisite body starting with that naughty, pouting mouth of yours," he gritted, kissing her. "I'll rouse your senses until you're drunk with pleasure and you'll do the same for me."

Quinn tore himself away from Caitlin abruptly and rose to close in the shelter, dropping the door flap and the translucent window coverings, so that it became a cool and shadowy place, their bed—Quinn's cape over pine boughs—soft and sweet. Naked now, he knelt over her, his warm smile washing her with pure delight and pleasure as her hands moved down along his body, touching, carefully molding him. Wondrously awed at her own powers, she saw his expression change and his gray eyes darken. "You have . . . the softest hands," he whispered against her temple, his own hands moving over her, and she, too, breathed with inexpressible pleasure, lost in an innocent, unconditional ecstasy that seemed to Quinn, for some while, insatiable.

"I'm still starving." Caitlin smiled up at Quinn. "Aren't you ever going to feed me?"

"Not if you don't stop stretching like some exotic, wild cat. Here, put this on and get up." He tossed his silk shirt in her direction, slid on his leather jacket against bare skin, and tied a blue neckerchief about his throat. "I got us some eggs and wild blackberries from a dairy maid earlier, while you were still sound asleep."

"I think there's a problem." Caitlin shrugged, draping the shirt about her shoulders as she sat somewhat stiffly. I doubt I can stand. My ankle—"

"Blast! Why didn't you say something before!" Quinn exploded. "If it had been wrapped tight last night, it wouldn't have swelled this way to twice its size." With careful hands, he lifted her slim foot and gently moved it from side to side. He saw her face blanch with pain as she bit her lip to keep from crying out.

"Now what the devil am I to do with you? I've got to be in town in an hour and—" His quick anger had caught Caitlin off guard and she responded in kind without thinking. "The lady in blue, I presume? Don't let me keep you or cause you the slightest inconvenience," she snapped, struggling to her feet with a scream of pain as he caught her up in his arms, his expression changed from anger to indulgent exasperation which enraged Caitlin even more.

"Just leave me here—leave me and go about

your . . . your affairs." She choked, almost weeping. "I'll survive. I always have. I'll crawl along the beach without food or water like—like a castaway until someone . . . oh *don't,*" she sighed, futilely fighting him with all her strength as he brought his open mouth hard to hers and kept it there, probing and tasting until she softened against him. Her hands rested on his wide shoulders, and he shifted her so that her long legs twined his hips, and her breasts were pressed softly against his bare chest. He carred her out of the shelter, taking her lips again and again until he set her down on a blanket spread near a fire. Bacon was cooking, and coffee was boiling over.

"Temperamental, aren't we?" he laughed, buttoning the stays in Caitlin's shirt—his shirt—that would reach to her knees when she stood. The white silk followed the rise of her breasts and showed their prominent peaks as she leaned back on her elbows, carefully settling her swollen ankle.

"If you don't see to the coffee . . ." she pouted, looking away across the beach to the surf that was still wild after the past night's storm. "I hate being . . helpless," she complained, turning to watch Quinn break eggs into a heavy iron pan. Their odor as they bubbled mixed deliciously with the smell of bacon and coffee and toasting bread, and when Quinn passed her a full plate, Caitlin ate quickly, with intense pleasure and little ladylike reserve, then looked up to find Quinn watching her. "Well, I had no dinner," she explained with a lift of her head and a little smile, passing him her empty plate.

"You've interesting appetites, if not perfect manners. It's refreshing after some of the wilting flowers I've spent time with."

"What's wrong with my manners?" she demanded with a bemused laugh. "I don't turn my fork down any more. I hold it up the way Ann said, and I don't use my knife to—"

"A lady never ignores her dining companion, no matter what the circumstances or how hungry she is. In fact, a real lady never is hungry—not that she lets on, anyway."

Caitlin didn't answer, just pouted seriously in petulant silence for a while, watching Quinn sand-clean the pan and tin plates and return them to the cabin. He came out carrying two of her lace petticoats that were still intact and the suede cape. Helping her into them, he paused to taste her lips lightly.

"Caitlin," he began in a low, serious tone. "About last night—understand that promises not made can't be broken."

"Oh, I know *that*," she smiled up at him indulgently, as if she thought him a bit of a fool to be so serious. "I mean, I didn't ask you to love me forever, just for last night."

Her defiant yet gentle independence took

him by surprise, and then it was his turn to gaze off at the rolling ocean, his eyes steely, a deepening, troubled frown on his handsome face. "I've had a lot of ladies Caitlin, and I really loved them all, but I can hardly remember one. You'll be warm in my memory always. If I ever were . . . to settle down, it would be with . . . someone like you."

"But Mr. Jones," Caitlin smiled up with casual aplomb, her forget-me-not eyes clear as glass, "when I settle down it certainly won't be with someone like you. I've heard you're a rake and a rambler and a wanted man besides Is that true? And while you're about it, tell me what you're doing in this neighborhood still? You said weeks ago you were leaving."

"My—the yacht I'm sailing north was delayed. It's been a bad season for hurricanes, but I'll be away any time now," he answered, his incredible smile gone, the cold and dangerous arrogance returned to the noble profile he showed Caitlin. Raking back his dark hair, he again took on the demeanor of a wild, hunting wolf about to slip away into shielding shadows.

"Will you return me to Silver Hill now?" Caitlin fretted. "They'll be worrying."

"You need a doctor. There's a good one a few miles from here. Word will be sent as to your whereabouts."

Wrapped in the leather cape, Quinn's arms

about her as she sat sidesaddle before him, Caitlin glanced back just once at the rough cabin that had sheltered them. She'd remember it always—the slant of the roof, the shadows of the cross beams in sunlight and starlight, the fragrance of pine and wood smoke. "Be not afraid to welcome strangers . . ." she recalled the message on the doorpost. She glanced at the stranger holding her against him, the stranger she had welcomed to her arms, not caring then what he was, knowing now he'd bedevil her dreams forever.

Chapter Eight

"It may be broken, my dear, a fine fracture perhaps, though I'm not absolutely certain. Had a bit of an accident, had we?" Dr. Burleigh inquired of Caitlin who half-reclined in a deep leather wing chair in his office, her injured ankle propped on an embroidered foot stool.

"I was . . . running during the storm and gave it a twist." She nodded with big-eyed, almost childlike seriousness. "What's to be done?"

The doctor was a tall, bulky man, full at the belt, with a weathered face and a wild wilderness of steel gray hair and beard. His dark eyes were kind and sympathetic as he patted Caitlin's hand with one that was like a large, gentle paw. "We'll decide that later, after some of the swelling's gone down. It is fortunate Quinn came to the rescue. He seems to make a habit of doing that for distressed damsels and we—ah! Here's my wife back now from town. Cedre," he gestured to the woman who had appeared in the doorway. "Come look to Miss McGlory's ankle. She's turned it rather badly, I'm afraid."

"I heard all about her from Mr. Jones. I met him on the road and came quick as I could. That Quinn does seem to collect these fragile little things," Mrs. Burleigh clucked with maternal concern. Like her husband, she was of ample build, ruddy and strong featured.

"I may not be very tall, but I'm hardly fragile," Caitlin protested as the woman crossed the room in long, heavy strides, balancing a chunky baby on one hip. Unceremoniously, she deposited the child in Caitlin's lap and turned her attention to the injured ankle.

"My wife's a Rhode Island Sweet," the doctor explained to Caitlin. "The family have been famous bone setters for generations, trained from childhood, though they're not doctors. Farmers and fishermen with a rare skill. Sometimes it seems to me Cedre can see right through you. Well, my love, what do you think of our pretty patient?"

"Bad sprain," Cedre Burleigh pronounced authoritatively. "But," she went on, breaking into a big, dimpled smile, "even so, she will have to stay on with us for a few days anyway, so I can see she treats it properly. Now, you are not to worry yourself," she interrupted when Caitlin, who had been flirting with the baby, began to protest. "Mr. Jones will send word to Silver Hill of your whereabouts and ask them to have some of your things brought over. Until then, you'll have to make do with my little Honey's girlish pinafores packed away upstairs. Honey is our youngest daughter and the daintiest—about your size. She's gone off and married now, like all the others except for this little love." Cedre Burleigh laughed, reclaiming the baby who laughed too, and waved fat little arms as she nuzzled his neck.

"Cedre's always trying to snare prisoners like you, my dear," the doctor smiled at Caitlin. "My wife was happiest when this house was bursting at the seams with children, when all the coat hooks and nooks and crannies were full and there wasn't an instant's silence from morning to dark."

"Yes, just as a terrible quiet was settling over us and Wade was starting to suffer from middle-aged contentment"—Cedre rested an affectionate hand on her husband's shoulder—"along came this boy to keep us young. Am I right, Nealon?" she asked. The baby stared at her somberly then squealed with pleasure as two kittens chased through the room and out a garden door. "Not long now, he'll be running after them." Cedre beamed. "Now, Wade, if you'll help Miss McGlory upstairs, I'll be along when I've handed Nealon over to Jen in the kitchen."

"I never had a chance to thank Mr. Jones for coming to my rescue," Caitlin casually told Cedre Burleigh, who stood behind her brushing out her long, auburn hair. Caitlin had bathed with Cedre's help and now sat at a child's small pine dressing table in the Burleigh summer bedroom, wearing a plain cotton camisole and pantalettes.

Not used to the warm, motherly attentions she'd been receiving from Cedre, Caitlin's own reactions surprised her. She liked being taken care of, she realized, but Cedre's kindness was making her feel tender-hearted, even a bit shy—a unique sensation for Caitlin McGlory who had always faced the world head on with a fierce, self-sufficient independence.

"I don't think Mr. Jones expected any thanks." Cedre smiled, coiling a long curl about her finger. "Lovely hair. It does anything you ask it to." With the faintest pressure on Caitlin's shoulder, she turned her away from the dressing table and began to tightly wrap the injured ankle. "He did ask me to tell you, Caitlin"—Cedre went on, pausing to look up—"that he's not one for goodbyes."

"Nor am I," Caitlin responded quickly. Then, silent, she gazed about the room that was tucked under the steeply pitched roof of the doctor's old house in a remote wing, shaded by the wide-spread limbs of a towering yew. The small-paned windows, a whole wall of them, were open, and a breeze touched deeply fringed lace curtains. There were three small, neat brass beds in a row, with lace spreads, brass chamber sticks and snuffers on pine side tables, a wash stand with a pitcher and bowl, and a wood towel rack. To one side of the brass bed farthest from the window was a dome-lidded pine trunk, open. Lined with the same small-print paper that covered the walls, the trunk overflowed with dresses and sashes and bed gowns pulled out for Caitlin's inspection. "Honey has two sisters?" she asked.

"Two." Cedre nodded. "Charlotte and Rachel are older but only by a little. They were all three so alike, they were taken for triplets more than once. They were best friends, close as triplets, too," Cedre explained as she worked. "I do miss sitting in the garden now, of a summer evening like this will be, listening to their pretty voices drifting out on the warm air and hearing their silly, sleepy giggles over the boys who were always hanging on our garden gate. Someone was always in love, Caty, someone always off to a party or dance in the village . . . When I think of all the dark, springy curls I arranged, all the feathered embroidery I did and the dainty tucks taken in fitted bodices, all the yards of lace and linen that passed through this house, it astounds me! You mustn't mind if I mother you a bit while you're with us. It's a habit with me, you see. Now, tell me, have you any sisters, Caty?" Cedre asked, sitting back on her heels. She was touched by the distant expression on the girl's beautiful face.

"I have Uncle Billy," was the soft response. "I can't remember anyone else."

"That settles it! You'll have to be one of my girls, too. Now, let me help you." Cedre smiled, turning down the light summer quilt on the bed nearest the window. "You're to rest until dinner. I'll be back to help you dress."

Caitlin awoke as long shadows were beginning to fill the summer bedroom. She heard pleasant voices and laughter from below, and the festive clink of china and silver. Wanting to be part of things without delay, she decided not to wait for Cedre. Moving slowly, trying to keep her weight on her strong ankle, leaning first on one object, then another, Caitlin laboriously crossed the room to the open trunk. With difficulty, balancing precariously, she dressed, choosing a slim-fitted, natural, striped lawn dress that she slid over her head. It had a square-necked lace yoke and tiny, tatted lace buttons down the bodice. She found a pink sash, open-work stockings, and soft kid slippers, then made her difficult way back across the room to the dressing table near the door. She adjusted a string of tiny pearls about her throat then tried to see as much of herself as she could by bending and twisting before the too-small dressing table glass. Just at the door, Caitlin paused for a moment, looking about, thinking of the three little girls, the "best friends," who had grown up together in this charming room. She had just decided to ask their mother more about them, when she saw the pink satin sash coiled on the floor near the open trunk. "Blast!" she exploded, the effort of recrossing the suddenly immense room more than she could manage. She took herself by surprise by bursting into tears. It was such a silly thing, she reasoned, mystified at herself. She hardly ever cried, and never over silly things. "He went away and never said goodbye to me," she whispered aloud, finally admitting to herself what she had been steadfastly denying all afternoon. She needed to see Quinn more than she'd ever needed anything before; and for the first time in her life, she couldn't reach out and try to grasp what she wanted; Quinn had gone away.

As she stood clutching the back of the dressing table chair trying to get her rampant emotions in hand—something she wasn't at all good at—the door opened and she turned away, wiping a tear-damp cheek with the back of her hand.

"I told Mrs. Burleigh I'd just look in to see if you were awake. What the devil's the matter with you?" Quinn asked. Looks of irritation and concern alternately flitted across his severe, handsome face. Taking in Caitlin's agitated condition in one swift glance, he quickly stepped into the room and closed the door behind him.

Wildly happy to see him, not even trying to hide her feelings, she began to laugh and cry all at once. "My sash!" Caitlin cried, exploding into tears so impassioned it seemed as though her heart were breaking. "My sash. It's so far away." She pointed. "And besides that, you left without even saying *goodbye*!"

With the pink satin band coiled about the knuckles of his left hand, Quinn, arrow slim and sleek, came toward Caitlin with deliberate slowness and took her in his arms. He kissed her eyes gently and her lips not gently at all, then carried her to the pillowed window seat where he cradled her head against his shoulder until she had quieted. "Fool," he said softly, showing a quick, incredible smile that lit his gray eyes.

"You've called me that before." She smiled too, a bit weakly.

"It's true," he said and kissed her again, then began slowly to undo the little buttons on her rounded bodice as Caitlin wondered, fleetingly, what other deft hands had maneuvered those dainty fastening and what other girl's heart had raced, as hers did now, against the fragile lace. When Quinn's hand slid beneath it, cradling her breast, grazing the firming tip with a sure stroke, Caitlin was swept away by desire so intense she went weak. "I *want* you," she whispered, bringing her hands to his shoulder, her glistening lips to his.

"You can't always have what you want when you want it. Patience is a virtue," he said, his voice caressing as he moved away. "What you've had is a little hors d'oeuvre to whet your appetite. Dinner's to be served now. After . . . you'll get your just desserts," he teased. He twined the pink sash twice about her little waist, did up her buttons again, and looked her over with a critical eye. "I know you're starving," he scowled, lifting her, her arm resting across his shoulders.

"One question," she asked, gazing into his serious eyes. "What are you doing here?"

"The yacht needs work. I decided to come back and lay hands on you again as long as I had some more time to kill."

"You scoundrel! Set me down at once." She laughed, bringing her arm about his neck as if to strangle him just as Cedre Burleigh appeared at the door.

"She managed to dress herself," Quinn

explained, seeing the shocked expression on the woman's ruddy face. "She was ravenous, as usual—couldn't wait for dinner."

"Is that so?" Cedre nodded, taking note of Caitlin's joyful, almost giddy, manner and the subtle look of amusement in Quinn's eyes. "You'd best take her down then, hadn't you, Mr. Jones?" She smiled.

Though Cedre's table was set with white linen and silver candle sticks, the meal was an informal, lively affair. The food was served by the frazzled kitchen girl who scurried about mumbling to herself, forgetting a potato pie in the oven until dinner was nearly done. The exuberant baby, Nealon, presiding from his mother's lap, was fed a gruel of potato, bread crumbs, and arrowroot, that tended to fly about. He was virtually stuffed then set to gleefully rolling around the dining room clutching the horse-head handles of his riding chair, cooing with pleasure while Cedre popped up repeatedly to pull him out of the tight spots for which he seemed to have a penchant. The doctor, a man who exhibited a great capacity for enjoyment of everything, was comfortably ensconced at the head of the table, informally attired in shirtsleeves and suspenders. He ate heartily and consumed prodigious quantities of dark ale, sips of which he offered the baby whenever Nealon rolled close, explaining that the drink was full of good nourishment and would help the child sleep besides. Through it all, the doctor expounded in his rich, booming voice on the events of his day which, besides Caitlin's arrival, included pulling a tooth and doctoring a horse for which service he accepted in payment the three chickens and assorted vegetables that graced the dinner table that very night. Whenever he spoke, the doctor's entire body became involved. His grizzled head moved from side to side, his hands lifted and lowered, his shoulders shifted, and his bright eyes sparked with intelligent good humor.

He quite fascinated Caitlin who decided during the meal that she adored him. She asked questions about his work, laughed with delight at his little jibes and puns, watching him all the while with bemused pleasure as Quinn watched her in exactly the same way whenever he wasn't paying gracious court to his delighted hostess who couldn't have been happier with the whole noisy affair.

"'Among the remedies which it has pleased Almighty God to give to man to relieve his suffering,'" Dr. Burleigh announced with dessert, "'none is so universal and so efficacious as opium.' An English physician said that nearly two hundred years ago. Of course it's morphia we use today, one of the wonders of modern medicine, so if you're in any pain, my dear . . ." he told Caitlin, "you need only say."

"No one with an appetite like hers could be in pain," Quinn commented.

"I'm just keeping up my strength," she said with a little toss of her head, accepting a slice of warm peach pie from Jen.

"There'll be a taste of summer in Cedre's peach preserves next winter when we all need it most," remarked Burleigh. "The young lady is quite right, you know, Quinn. The best we doctors can do is assist the healing powers of nature when something's gone amiss, but to preserve your good health you must have good air, good food, and good sense."

"Wade became quite agitated with his medical colleagues years ago, Mr. Jones," Cedre explained. "That's how we happen to be way out here when the money in doctoring is to be made in the cities. Wade's mother was a Boston Bigelow, one of the old, well-connected medical families, and Wade could have been very well-to-do, couldn't you, dear?"

"All that Latin hocus pocus . . . it's just to take advantage of people and make them feel dumb," Burleigh grumbled. "There's no licensing, no controls, and educational standards vary so. The quackery in the profession is not to be believed."

"I've a friend, a Welshman, who'd have no difficulty believing anything you say about your less admirable colleagues, doctor. He's been misled and taken advantage of many times, though there have been entirely honest men—the more reputable practitioners usually—who've told him there's nothing they can do."

"What seems to be your friend's difficulty, sir?" Wade Burleigh wanted to know, a note of professional formality in his manner suddenly.

"He was shot some years ago, in the back."

"Fleeing the law?" Caitlin asked with a raised brow.

"Hunting accident," Quinn answered in a dangerous tone that silenced her. "The bones haven't knit properly. The pain is sometimes unendurable."

"Your friend needs Cedre's touch. I've never known anyone to work the magic she can with her wonderful hands. He's tried everything else available?"

"Yes, doctor, I saw to it he got the best medical attention England has to offer. Now he's gone over to faith healers, spiritualists, taken up vegetarianism. There was an American named Graham years ago who recommended regular baths and little crackers for whatever ailed you—that sort of thing."

"Oh, Sylvester Graham, of course." Wade smiled. "A Connecticut minister, friend of the family. Baths are well and good, my boy. Cleanliness *is* next to godliness, but giving up spirits and coffee as Sylvester insisted is quite another matter," he stated. "I suspect *you* agree with me on that, Quinn, so let us withdraw to the garden for a brandy while you tell me more about your injured Welshman. It is a lovely night. There won't be many more like it this summer!"

"I'll just assist the injured Miss McGlory to her room first, Doctor, to save you the trouble, then join you for that brandy," Quinn said, standing.

"I'll allow you that pleasure, young man." Wade winked. Then he and Cedre were both quiet, a little awed as they watched the ensuing scene. Caitlin raised her slender arms to Quinn, her upturned oval face beautiful as a clear cut gem, her violet eyes welcoming, dancing with warmth. Quinn's deep gray eyes, his angular handsome face, were touched by a fleeting flare of sensual heat as he lifted her in his arms, her russet-streaked hair tumbling like a curtain of subdued light over his shoulder, his own hair very black against it—like midnight and dawn, Cedre was thinking as her eyes met her husband's.

"I'll be up directly to see to Miss McGlory," she announced as Quinn started toward the steps.

They kissed on the first landing, again at the turning of the stairs, and when Quinn lowered Caitlin to the brass bed and lit a lamp, he rested his hands on her shoulders, then lightly ran them the length of her, molding her, pausing at the swell of her breasts and the turn of her tiny, satin-circled waist.

"Don't go anywhere. I'll be back," he whispered as steps approached the door. Leaning casually at the window, elegant as always in slim, dark clothes and fine linen, he bestowed his smile on Cedre as she entered, nodded to Caitlin, and left.

"That lovely fragrance in this room is the hops flowers mixed with the chaff in your mattress." Cedre smiled at Caitlin, helping her undress, then bringing a bed gown from the trunk. "This will keep you cozy. There's a touch of chill in the air. Summer is almost gone." Cedre sighed, smoothing Caitlin's quilt and fluffing a pillow. When the last candle was snuffed, yellow moonlight touched the shiny brass bedposts and made flickering leaf shadows on the slant of the low ceiling.

"The men will talk half the night," Cedre said happily, going to the window seat to look out over a long meadow that fell away toward the sea. "Wade enjoys nothing so much as good masculine company after a good company dinner. It's a favorite time for me, too. It's when my girls would tell me all their little secrets and their deepest ones also."

The sound of the men's voices—Wade's rumbling deeply, Quinn's low and smooth—drifted to the summer bedroom.

"The girls talked of love, of course?" Caitlin

asked, sitting up cross-legged, her hands folded in her lap.

"Yes, of course they did," Cedre answered, smiling to herself in the half dark.

"Well, I'm curious," Caitlin said in a light, chatty manner. "Did they think . . . do you think that there's only one true love for all your life?"

"They did. I always told them, though, that we've got inexhaustible supplies of it—love—that there are many kinds and probably many different men they each *could* love—but I did agree that only one would be a true love. When they found that one, I told my girls, they should hold on to him forever and a day."

"Well, what if . . ." Caitlin mused as if with careless unconcern, "what if one of your girls . . . Honey, for example—"

"Yes, go on," Cedre encouraged.

"What if she had told you she was in love—*really* in love—with a fugitive desperado drifter like . . . oh, like Quinn Jones, say?"

"Well," Cedre pretended to ponder the question—"if Honey had told me *she* loved Quinn, I would have thrown my arms about her and held her hard against my bosom until he had gone far, far away. He will go, you know," Cedre said softly. "I'd have told Honey that Quinn was a romantic daredevil, intemperate and wild, who'd lead her close to heaven through the turns of a tempestuous dance and then, probably, he'd break her heart. But I would also have told Honey"—Cedre said, holding Caitlin now, who was trembling faintly—"that Quinn was some sort of delinquent saint driven by a dark, sad secret and that if she thought she could save him with the holy fire of her love . . . she must go ahead and try."

"My wife, Quinn, is a remarkable woman," Wade Burleigh proclaimed and shifted his big, bear shoulders against the back of his chair. "She's warm and cheery as a good fire on a winter day and she has the truest maternal gifts of any woman I've ever known. She's already taken our delightful Caitlin to her ample bosom."

"Your wife *is* a charming lady," Quinn agreed, avoiding the subject of Caitlin.

"Cedre's not a great beauty like Caitlin, my boy. When Cedre's tired or a little down, it shows in her face at once, but I find her all the more lovable for her imperfections. 'Be to a woman's virtues kind/Be to her faults a little blind.' That's Matthew Prior I'm quoting, my favorite light verser. A brilliant fellow!" The doctor was enjoying himself so thoroughly, he showed no inclination to retire though the clocks had already counted twelve. Quinn, too, was relaxed by the brandy, and felt quite comfortable in the doctor's company.

As they talked, Quinn held his glass up in front of him from time to time, watching the moonlight turn the amber liquid to pale fire and gazing at Caitlin's darkened window, knowing his quarry would soon be in his hands.

"Tell me what you were up to in England, my boy," Wade asked. "It's been said you had difficulties of a legal nature. Your silence on the subject has set the rumor mill turning in this neighborhood, I can tell you that."

"I went to Wales to trace my family history, Doctor, possibly to claim heirship to a sizable fortune and an estate on the Gower Peninsula," Quinn offered. "My . . . research took me into some rough places. As to the rumors? I took up with a journalist, James Greenwood. We went into Merthyr Tydfil disguised as vagrants, then out to the countryside among the poachers. I did have a run-in with the authorities."

"I see," Wade nodded, almost as much in the dark as he was before Quinn made his unenlightening statement. "Well, Merthyr Tydfil's one of the most unsavory cities in the world right now. It's notorious for thievery and wife-selling and whoring. What sort of relatives do you have, Quinn, to be prowling about such a place looking for them?" the doctor jested.

"Through my mother, quite aristocratic ones, actually," Quinn laughed. "The Montressors trace direct descent on one side from William's 1066 incursion into England, and even further back to some wild, tribal princes. The family fortune was always ample and increased several centuries ago by speculation in the Dutch bulb market. All of it is claimed now only by me and a distant Montressor cousin, Melusina. But there's the problem of a missing heir more directly in line than either of us who'll inherit the lion's share and full title to the family seat in Wales if a claim is made on his . . . or her behalf within the year. If not, Melusina and I will share it all."

"Do you expect to find this lost cousin of yours among the princes or the poachers of Wales, my friend?"

"We—Melusina is involved in the search—don't expect to find our cousin at all. Every lead we've had has been a dead end, every clue false. But I will be absolutely sure before I abandon the hunt."

"You seem already a man of handsome means, Quinn. If your missing relative should surface, you won't be exactly destitute."

"It's the estate I want; it's my past, my history." Quinn abruptly tipped down the last of the brandy in his snifter. The doctor refilled it.

"Where is your home, man? You belong someplace, have some people," Wade insisted.

"My father's in Galena, in Illinois, but I'll

never go back there," Quinn answered, his voice flat. In the shadowy moonlight, his lean, angular face took on a marble coldness the doctor found very unsettling.

"I've got *homes*—several," Quinn continued with a harsh laugh. "In Canada, in Tennessee, another in California—the south of California. That's where I made my money, Doctor, in land speculation after the war when the droughts drove the large holders out. What I've already made there is a pittance to what the land I still hold will be worth when the railroads tie it all together."

"It seems to me," the doctor interjected with a twinkle in his eye, "an ambitious young man like yourself, Quinn, would be looking to a young country—California for instance—not back to the old world. Now if I were young and I had a fresh and vigorous little beauty like Caitlin McGlory at my side, I surely would go to California, though Caitlin, of course, would make a delightful chatelaine to the lord of any castle, I must say."

"I've a tentative alliance, Doctor, with Melusina. If we do decide to marry ours will be an unromantic, business-like marriage."

"Have you given your expedient plan careful thought, my boy? 'Marry in haste, repent at leisure' it's said, and you seem . . . quite taken with Caty."

"I've no place in my life for such a child as

Caitlin McGlory," Quinn answered laconically, "though I will say," he mused, stretching long legs in front of him and gazing off in the distance, "she is the most perfect beauty. She's a work of art come to life in my hands, a Leonardo sculpture, an Ingres nude incarnate. I've been thinking aloud, Doctor. I've been indiscreet," Quinn said, sitting up, flicking back dark hair. "I trust you'll keep our secret."

"What secret?" Wade Burleigh smiled. "One look at the lady's guileless eyes, a mere glance at the two of you together, tells all anyone would ever need to know about you and Caty McGlory."

Caitlin felt his shadow move over her. Her violet eyes, transparent in late moonlight, opened wide. Quinn stood with his back to the window, motionless and dark, his jacket draped over one shoulder, his white shirt half undone. Behind him, night trees moved against the face of the moon that was rolling low along the rim of the horizon.

"Prowler," Caitlin said, not moving, hardly breathing. "Sneak thief and prowler," she repeated, her voice low and sleepy, her beautiful face, framed by wild curls, a clear, cut, oval gem beveled by glacial moonlight.

"Poacher, maybe; ravisher surely. Never a thief," Quinn said in a precise, soft voice sounding to Caitlin as if secret communications in the dead of night were habit with him. "That yew is perfectly placed at your window." He'd dropped his jacket and pulled off his shirt. "Are you always such a restless sleeper? You're all ruffled, same as our night in the shelter when you kicked off the covers."

Caitlin's sheets and blanket were on the floor, her bed gown risen to her pretty thighs and, half unbuttoned, had fallen from one rounded shoulder. She smiled a little, waiting for him, glowing and warm as a soft star.

"Take off that flannel," Quinn directed, his forearms resting on the foot of the brass bed frame as he watched Caitlin intently with undisguised pleasure. She sat up, undid all her buttons, and then slipped free of Honey Burleigh's bed gown. She reclined again, gracefully, like a slow wave uncurling, then stretched, the lazy undulation arching her back, thrusting her breasts high, shimmering over her flat belly and down long, slender legs.

"You should be kept in some tropical paradise garden, perpetually naked and waiting for love. Nothing should ever touch your skin but shadow and light and lover's lips," Quinn whispered, a secret inner smile showing behind his blazing eyes. In the near-dawn silence and stillness that enveloped them, Quinn found again in Caitlin the mythic, timeless essence of woman more perfect than any idealized image he'd ever seen. "In India once," he said, moving to the side of the bed and gazing down, "I found a bronze Devi, a deified queen. She had close, high, round breasts . . . boldly tipped like these." One knee on the bed, he bent his mouth to Caitlin's upthrust nipples, a hand resting on the smooth plane of her belly dropping to the soft delta below. "The Devi," he said staring into Caitlin's softened vague eyes as he stood and pulled off the rest of his clothes. "The Devi had a diminutive waist, like this." He smiled and his hands encircled Caitlin's. "And long lovely thighs that made me ache to part them . . . like this." Quinn was kneeling over her, between her wide-spread legs, his mouth hot on hers, his hands slipping beneath her, bringing the open softness of her to him as she reached back to grasp a cool brass bedrail. He entered her quickly, possessively, surging deep, the first thrust and every one that followed wringing a suppressed low gasp of pleasure from Caitlin as she lost herself completely in Quinn's long, fierce, wild loving.

Chapter Nine

The old porch swing creaked louder and louder. Caitlin, deep in thought and pillows, reclined restlessly, furiously pushing herself at increasing speed with the gnarled and knotty walking stick provided by her Dr. Burleigh that morning when he'd delivered her to Silver Hill. Now, on a glorious, end-of-summer Saturday afternoon, the estate was nearly deserted. The Captain and his lady had left for Saratoga even before Caitlin's mishap. The girls were off to town with their young men, and none of the farm hands were in evidence. Only the old cook, Martha, seeing the doctor's gig rounding the last turn of Silver Hill Drive, was there to greet them at the door, wiping floury hands on her white apron and shaking her head in speechless amazement.

"She's nearly as good as new, Martha," the

doctor bellowed, handing Caitlin down. "She'll have to treat the ankle kindly for a bit but—Why what under heaven ails you, old woman?" he demanded, aware finally of Martha's stunned expression and agitated manner.

"We've been missing that girl for a week and more. We've been searching the woods and we've been combing the beaches. We've been weeping and waiting for the ocean to toss her poor drowned body up on the sands and when we just about give her up and decide, finally, she must have been carried away to sea by the storm as Robin thought she was, here she comes sound as a dollar prancing in here like—like nothing ever happened! We cabled your uncle, Caty. We couldn't wait any longer. He's due out on the afternoon train and I do hate to think of the poor man's worry all for nothing!"

"Oh, Martha, no!" Caitlin gasped. "But we sent you word. Quinn Jones sent a messenger the very day after the storm to tell you where I was and why. I wondered why no one ever delivered my things . . . I wondered why no one asked after me."

"Now, now ladies," Dr. Burleigh said, trying to calm them both. "There's been a—a misconnection somehow but it will be put to rights. 'There's always some accident in the best of things,' as Mr. Thoreau has written. The best of things for us all now would be a good cup of tea, a quiet moment on the veranda, and a little taste of sherry, Martha, please," he'd concluded with gentle authority, offering each of the ladies a crooked arm, leading Caitlin to the porch swing and sending Martha off to the kitchen for the refreshments.

"It's all Quinn's fault," Caitlin exploded as soon as she and the doctor were alone. "That—that rogue never *did* send word here as he promised to. Think of my poor, poor uncle."

"Your uncle will understand, I suspect, though I share your concern for him. To receive such news is . . . dreadful, dreadful—but think how pleased he'll be to have you back, so to speak. I'm sure there's an explanation, Caitlin, just as I'm sure Quinn is a man of his word. Don't judge him harshly until you know the truth of things," Wade Burleigh cautioned as he dropped into a wicker chair and patted Caitlin's hand with a large, affectionate paw.

"It hardly matters how I judge Mr. Jones. I'll never see him again anyway," Caitlin snapped. "And Doctor? . . ." she added softly.

"Yes, my dear?" he encouraged with fatherly patience.

"Doctor, my heart is breaking. I don't like the way that feels."

Burleigh nodded. "I know. It will heal, Caitlin."

"You . . . *know*?" Caitlin asked incredulously, sitting up very straight.

"No one seeing you and Quinn together, watching your expressive eyes and his, could not know. But I do have a question, my dear. You're a young lady of spirit and verve. Why are you . . . giving up on him so easily? Why don't you go after him?" the doctor demanded, slamming his hands down hard on the arms of his chair.

"You know as well as I what he is." Caitlin sighed, sinking back against the pillows in a corner of the swing. "He's a rogue, a thief, perhaps still a hunted man. I want something more than a drifter's life."

"My dear, I've met men like Quinn before, during the war. They came in off the frontier to fight, even from as far as California, some of them. They had one thing in common—a passion for danger. They were always testing themselves, these cool, self-reliant loners, and they were capable of anything, even killing, without a moment's hesitation. But there's more to Quinn than that. His background . . . You don't understand. He's—"

"Please don't try to defend him. Don't! Even if I were to throw care to the wind for such a man, it would break my uncle's heart. Billy expects more of me, and I couldn't hurt him after all he's done, especially after this dreadful mistake. Besides, Doctor, Mr. Jones bid me goodbye in no uncertain terms," Caitlin insisted.

The muted pleasure of sharing their secret with swift glances across the Burleigh's dinner table, their nights of unbridled passion and gentle, lingering, dawn partings were over, ended just hours ago, she thought sadly. There had been a soft dawn rain whispering against the windows. Tempered early light, filtering through lace curtains, lent the room a cool, shadowy feeling as Caitlin had wakened, awash in the sweet weariness of recent love. Already up, his back to her, Quinn pulled on Wellington boots and turned up the collar of his jacket.

"Good night," Caitlin had half sighed, half yawned, already drifting back toward sleep before he'd even gone. Quinn had faced her then, the blue shadow of beard darkening his lean cheeks. "Goodbye," he'd said in a clipped whisper, bringing her wide awake to find the old arrogance and ferocity back in his eyes and a remoteness in his manner that had said it all. "Cedre told me you aren't one for sentimental partings." She'd smiled, her beautiful, responsive eyes going quite cold. She was all ice and snow and frosty hauteur as she tossed back cascading curls and smiled fleetingly, catlike, seeming as arrogant and remote to Quinn as he to her. "So . . . goodbye," she said suddenly with an infuriating pertness, good-naturedly extending her hand as if to a mere acquaintance, a dull one at that. The whiplash anger in Quinn's stormy eyes told her she'd struck fire. Pressing her momentary advantage, she stretched deliciously, wrinkling her little nose and sinking into her pillows. "Godspeed and bon voyage, wherever you're going," she offered disinterestedly.

"I get more impassioned send offs than that from my lusty strumpets and paramours," he said, approaching the bed with a fierce grin.

"Tears do you mean, Quinn, and protestations of love?" Caitlin had asked with a taunting, sweet cheerfulness that prodded him to pull away her light cover and bury his hand deep in the lace of her gown, stopping her breath, making her feel she was balancing precariously on a high wire. She reached out to him as if to steady herself, and he lifted her, his arms hard about her, his mouth cruelly possessing hers, his hands intimately molding, delving, renewing his claim to what they both knew he'd already won. Her flower-smooth skin tautened under his hands, and with eloquent sensuality her lithe body pressed to his offering—almost irresistibly.

"That's more the sort of goodbye I had in mind," Quinn said abruptly in his hot, low growl, dropping Caitlin back in the middle of her bed. "Some fools are lucky at love," he went on. "They win on the first toss of the dice. I'm sorry, Caitlin, you aren't one of them."

"Are you suggesting, you arrogant rogue,

that I might be in love with you?" Caitlin hissed in controlled, whispered fury. "I told you the day we met I was born under a lucky star, on the sunny side of the hedge. I *will* find my true love one day *and* marry him *and* live on velvet, so you needn't be sorry for me, sir, and don't you call me a fool ever again!" She blurted it all out without taking a breath, kneeling on the bed, her fists clenched so tight at her sides her knuckles were white. Caitlin's small, slender frame was aquiver with indignation, her eyes ablaze with a blue flame of fury. Her color heightened, and there was a brilliancy about her that caught Quinn unaware.

"I would like to have seen those ambrosial curls of yours spread against fine lace," he said thoughtfully, fingering a coil of Caitlin's hair until she pulled away. "But I don't suppose I ever will now." He shrugged, bringing two fingers to his brow as if tipping an imaginary cap. "I'll remember you," he said, and then he was gone, leaving her only the memory of his perfect smile.

Now, an hour after her return to Silver Hill, Dr. Burleigh was gone, too, promising to come back after his rounds. Martha was off tending to one of the gardens, and Caitlin was left alone on the porch swing that—propelled by her angry thrusts with the walking stick—threatened to spill her to the floor with its every creaking rise and fall. The lazy summer afternoon at Silver Hill seemed intolerable to Caitlin after her stay at the doctor's thriving household. She'd hardly ever been alone there, night or day, she mused, through the whole week of enforced inactivity—"Of upright inactivity, at least," she said aloud, letting the swing slow, losing herself precipitously in a vivid daydream. She was caught by a swell of longing so intense it made her weak and dizzy, and with aching dismay she realized she was able to recall with crystal clarity every embrace and passionate joining she'd ever shared with Quinn.

"Damn and blast!" she swore, swiftly sitting up straight. Even though there was no one to see her, she blushed furiously then hid her face in her hands, appalled at herself for being so roused by mere memories, by clear, haunting, mind pictures that would, she knew, keep her longing for Quinn forever. "This will not do—it will *not,*" she gritted, trying to get herself in hand, wanting to roar with rage at her weakness, at Quinn, at absolutely everything, when she heard the rattle of carriage wheels on gravel that grew more distinct as the vehicle proceeded up Silver Hill Drive. By the time it had circled to a stop beneath the flagstoned portico, Caitlin was laughing almost wildly with joyful expectation, having glimpsed Billy peering out and raising a hand in greeting, she supposed.

The driver, slipping slowly down from his

bench, bemoaning his arthritic condition, reached the carriage door just as Billy burst from it and Caitlin hurled herself into his arms in a rush of tears and unintelligible words. She felt comforted instantly by his bulk and strength and warmth. "Oh, Billy!" she cried, inhaling the homey smell of his India water and cigars, the broadcloth of his suit rough against her cheek. "Oh, Billy, I was so *lonely* for you. I'm so *glad* you've come to fetch me home!"

When he hurled her away from him, Caitlin's head struck the carriage with enough force to stun her before she recognized the look in Billy's eyes as hot anger, the contemptuous grimace that twisted his mouth one she'd never seen before. Instinctively, like a trapped animal, she stood absolutely still, desperate, trying to make some sense of the threatening stranger before her.

"Wanton scarlet baggage!" he roared. "I got their wires. I know all about what you've been doin' over at that pandering doctor's every night—every night—with that rakehell criminal, Jones, letting us all suppose you dead, which you are to me now. And me havin' such false high hopes for you all those years, thinkin' the likes of *you* could bring *me* respectability. I should have known you'd turn out like your wanton mother, just like the both of 'em. Bad blood tells, Caitlin, it always does!" Billy was gesturing violently as Martha came around the corner of the house, her arms laden with roses, in time to see the girl go pale, clutching the spokes of the carriage wheel behind her, shrinking from words being spoken now too low for Martha to hear. She could see Billy McGlory's face contort with anger and Caitlin, slim and lithe, twist like a criminal under a lash before she began to run blindly, stumbling away, her hands covering her ears.

"I know everything, Caitlin! The second wire they sent told it *all*!" Martha heard McGlory shout. She dropped the roses and started after the girl, then hesitated as McGlory overtook her. "Leave her be," he commanded. "Just . . . leave her . . . Oh, lord what have I said?" he hissed, flinging his arms at the heavens then folding inward, seeming to grow smaller before Martha's eyes, deflating like a broken Montgolfier balloon she'd once seen at a fair, falling, trailing its beautiful silks in the dust. Glancing anxiously after Caitlin, Martha helped McGlory to the porch swing, abandoned his niece, and undid his collar stay before hurrying off to fetch the brandy he begged of her.

"I only sent one wire to you," Martha stated firmly some time later, seated opposite Mc-

Glory who leaned forward, head in hands, groaning aloud from time to time. The small woman, dark and stocky, had impassive eyes set in a large, plain face. There was in her manner toward Billy the polite deference of a servant, but after years of running Silver Hill there was also something of the tyrant about her. Clearly, she disapproved of the man's behavior. Billy looked up, misery and confusion in his eyes.

"The second telegraph come just as I was leavin' to ride out here, thinkin' her . . . gone, drowned, lost to me forever. It put me in such a stew of anger about that Jones, I boiled over the minute I seen her," Billy explained ruefully.

"Not to ask if it were true or let her tell her side—that was wrong of you," Martha said emphatically. "I sent Robin Edwards to the telegraph office with word Cate was missing. That's *all*, and if—" Martha looked away. "Robin Edwards was the one who told us she'd most likely drowned. He was in a bad way over Caty and I never . . ."

"I better go," Billy said suddenly. "She better stay on here with you folks a little, 'til she has time to calm some. Her temper . . . it's worse than mine. If she once gets her Irish up . . . well, you don't know what anger does to her. It makes her wild and blind and reckless. Tell her . . . will you tell her I'll be back? Tell her it'll be all right after a time, but she must stay on a bit now? Here," Billy said, pressing fifty dollars into Martha's hand before entering the waiting livery. "To get herself a little something to cheer her."

Rigid with fury, raking back wild, russet-tipped curls, Caitlin mounted her saddled cob from the paddock fence, then leaned to undo the gate latch. She missed on the first pass. "Damn and blast!" she exploded, pulling the gelding about to approach again.

"Let me. I insist," she heard as the gate swung inward and her horse, nearly unseating Caitlin, shied away from the figure of Robin Edwards planted in their path.

"Move or else I'll slash your face again, coward!" Caitlin spat, fighting to keep the dancing horse under control, her beautiful face set in a mask of cold contempt. The expression in Robin's eyes was pure hatred as he touched the mark of Quinn's blow still blazing across his cheek.

"How ever did you explain that, coward?" Caitlin taunted.

"A branch in the storm," he answered with a maddening, smug smile. "They believed me just like they believed me when I said you were probably drowned. I stopped Jones's message, see, the one telling where you were and all, and then, when they'd sent for your uncle I made sure he knew the truth about his virtuous little girl before he got here."

Caitlin drove her heels hard into the gelding's sides and the horse leaped forward, bearing down on Robin who rolled aside, then scrambled to his feet reaching up to pull her from her mount as she came at him again, blatant murder in her wild and beautiful ice-blue eyes.

She came down on top of him with an inarticulate scream of rage, and they rolled in the paddock dust, Caitlin grasping for Robin's throat, raking her long nails across his bruised cheek until he secured her wrists above her head, pressing her down beneath him, grimacing cruelly.

"We'll start where we left off, tart," Robin sneered with vicious softness before attacking Caitlin's mouth. "Now I'm going to take some of what you've been giving that bastard Jones every night."

"You'll take nothing. Get up off her." Martha stood with her hands on her hips in the open paddock gateway. "Get up and get away from Silver Hill and don't ever come back, or I'll tell Captain Hawkes all I heard and all you've done. Go on, you cur," she said in a commanding voice, to which Robin, shifty eyed, responded quickly. He released Caitlin and stood.

"One day I'll get what I want from you, and I'll pay back your lover, too, for what he did to me," he said quickly under his breath. Then he sidled away, glancing over his shoulder like a beaten dog.

"He's mean as a viper, that one, no matter about his big smile and always flashing those fine teeth. He fooled everyone else but he never fooled *me*," Martha said with righteous satisfaction, watching Caitlin try to brush some of the dust from her skirts. "You need a bath, my girl, and a change of clothes. Your hair . . . your face . . . , oh, you are a sight! Come up to the house like a good child and I'll help you—"

"No, I won't! I won't see Billy ever again." Caitlin stamped her foot and folded her arms across her chest looking as if she'd never move from the spot.

"He's gone away," Martha said, seeing Caitlin's adamant expression crumble. The girl's full lower lip began to quiver and a single tear made a muddy streak down her face.

"Don't be sad, child," Martha admonished, passing an arm about Caitlin's waist. "He's sorry for whatever it was he said to upset you so. He'll be back for you, he says, after you've both had a little time to calm. Your temper's worse than his. He said that. I could see he understands you, and he'll always love you no matter what—I could tell, and I'm never wrong about love." Martha patted at Caitlin's limpid blue eyes with an embroidered handkerchief. "Don't be too harsh with him. He had a shock, remember, and he means well. Here, he left this for you, to buy something pretty to cheer you." Martha offered Caitlin Billy's fifty dollars.

"That's just like him, to try to buy himself out of trouble"—Caitlin pouted—"but all the money in the world wouldn't be enough to make up for . . . for the things he said to me. I'll never take one penny from him again, *never*. I need to be alone, Martha. I'll be back before dark."

Caitlin walked into the water, letting the warm waves lap about her knees, her dress and petticoats floating like lily pads until, waist deep, she dove under a swell that washed the dust from her hair and face. Retreating to the dark, damp sand at the ocean's edge, she peeled off most of her wet things. Wearing only a clinging chemise and one petticoat, she twisted back her wet hair and walked deliberately up the beach toward the shelter where she and Quinn had spent their first night together. She spread her dress over a branch to dry, then sat leaning against the cabin, clasping her knees and lifting her face to the sun. It was time, she told herself, calm now and cool, time to decide what to do with the rest of her life. Like shifting sands in a summer storm, everything she'd known, all she'd planned and depended on was changed. She'd been cut loose, set completely free in the world with no ties or obligations. She was on her own for the first time ever. Despite the shock of it, she had to admit with a little secret smile that she was really happy to be mistress of her own fate, even happier to be relieved of the strictures and certainties of a predictable future.

"I can go *anywhere*, do *anything*, become whatever I *want*!" She laughed aloud, reaching at the sky, fluttering her eyelashes against strong afternoon sunlight. Taken by an euphoric restlessness, she stood and began pacing before the shelter then stopped and traced the words carved on the doorpost—"Be not afraid to welcome strangers, for thereby you may entertain angels unawares." She ducked into the cabin's shady depths and stopped still, stunned by the rich, remembered fragrance of pine and a sense of Quinn's presence so strong, she turned to run. "Damn him, damn him!" she hissed, tearing through the low doorway and colliding with a solid figure as she felt herself caught and gathered in arms like steel bands. "Damn you!" she repeated along with other angry words muffled by Quinn's laughing mouth as her arms enfolded his neck and the soft, warm curve of her body pressed to the hard line of his. She let her head fall back and his teeth found the tips of her breasts standing hard against her clinging, wet chemise. "What are you *doing* here? Why are you . . . ?"

"I came back to get my hands on these full, sloping flanks of yours one more time." He grinned, pressing her to him hard, moving against her with clear intent.

"But how did you know . . . I'd be here?" She sighed, breathless, reaching to his mouth with her perfect, moist, parted lips.

"I lied," he said, putting her aside. "I came back for this." He extracted his silver knife from the cabin wall where it had remained since their first shared night there. "It was a gift, a good luck piece. I couldn't go without it. I'm leaving on the late tide," Quinn said, polishing the knife against his sleeve.

"Take me with you?" Caitlin smiled, her eyes alive with pleasure, a touch of mischief in their blue depths.

"And what about your respectable future and your rich husband?" Quinn asked, leaning in the shelter door, studying Caitlin with canny eyes, no trace of his fine smile on his lips.

"All that's changed," she answered with a pretty lift of her shoulders, turning up her hands. "Billy has disowned me more or less. He was informed about you and me and he . . . he told me . . . well, now I know I belong with a daredevil cutthroat gypsy desperado like you,

Quinn Jones. We're two of a kind. Will you have me?"

"Perhaps for a while," he said very slowly, eyes gray as a storm, as intrigued by her unguarded, tantalizing innocence as he'd been the first time he'd seen her. He was taken again by her free, shimmering beauty, the glowing titian curls falling over smooth shoulders, the naughty, delicious mouth boldly smiling. Now she was playing the skilled flirt, calling up all her powers of sweet seduction to work her wiles and get her way.

"I'll repay you one day, I swear it, but for now I've been thrown on my own resources. They're rather limited at the moment," she said with whimsical charm.

"Not limited at all," Quinn couldn't resist commenting with a faint smile. "You can pay me as you did that night in this cabin for saving your life, remember?"

"Don't!" Caitlin flushed, turning away. "I just didn't know what to say to you, that's all, and . . ." She glanced up almost shyly and saw the lecherous leer of the satyr spread across Quinn's face, his dark brows wickedly upturned at the edges.

"If I *do* decide to take you with me, my avid little hedonist, I promise to carnalize you endlessly, understand, but that's the only promise I'll make. When it's over, it's over—no commitments, no ties, no matter when or where we may be. Understand that, too."

"I do, of course," Caitlin sparked, pleased with her own daring. "We'll sin sumptuously; we'll share wild, demonic passion and inexpressible pleasure," she laughed, "and when we're gorged and glutted and bored with each other, we'll go our own ways. I have plans of my own, you see."

"What plans?" Quinn demanded angrily, startled at the idea that she could even contemplate growing tired of him. No woman ever had.

"I'm going to make lots of money. In New York probably. Then I'll go to London where no one knows me and make them think I'm a rich American heiress or something. I'll catch the most noble, aristocratic, titled husband in all England, have a grand estate, and show Billy McGlory how wrong he was about me *and* about my mother. I might even invite him to high tea at my castle one day, if he tells me he's really, really sorry."

Caught up in daydreams of sweet revenge, Caitlin's thoughts turned inward and she stared off in the distance at the ocean, her pink and ivory mouth slightly open, a faint smile flickering like a candle. She seemed to Quinn the source of a lovely light between them, outshining the sun. He'd never seen her so still and remote, even in sleep, and he stared with something like a voyeur's pleasure, savoring all the swells and declivities of her rounded, silken body, the loveliness of her profile, the natural grace in the curve of her throat, in the tilt of her head. There was an elegant sensuality about her always, he decided, that was absolutely unique. He didn't move, not wanting to lose the moment, until she did, turning to him smiling, glittering, all light and movement and high spirits again.

"If you won't take me with you, will you love me here and now before you go?" she asked in the low, throaty voice Quinn found so captivating. "Just a little something to remember you by, like the dandelions?"

"There's not time," he said indifferently, watching confusion and disappointment fill her impossibly blue eyes, "so . . . I'll have to take you with me, won't I?" His wondrous, boyish smile broke over Caitlin like a warm wave as he grasped her hand and pulled her after him.

Chapter Ten

"Run off! Run off! What the bloody hell do you mean?" Billy McGlory exploded. Furious and uncomfortably warm in the early September New York heat, he stood in the middle of Ann Overton's small parlor where, as usual, no single horizontal surface except the floor remained uncluttered. In response to Ann's urgent message, Billy had left his bouncer in charge of The White Elephant and hurried to her rooms on Ninth Street.

Gathering up an armful of fabric swatches from a chintz-covered armchair, Ann wearily waved Billy to it. "Want a brandy?" she asked with her usual calm. Billy nodded, pulling off his jacket and tie.

"Caitlin's gone. What did you say to her? I know you didn't give your avuncular blessing to her passionate affair with Quinn Jones!"

Billy shrugged and gazed blankly about the room. Every time he arrived at Ann's, it took getting used to all over again. This place was very unlike her public presentation. The dress salon was richly but austerely decorated and her own appearance was always simply elegant. In contrast, this room, her private parlor, was feminine and soft with velvet festoons draping the windows, the piano, the mantle, and fluffy organdy ruffles shading the lamps. The wallpaper was a small floral print matching her chintz chairs. There was a spreading potted palm, cut lilies in vases, and an embroidered East Indian Flowering Tree of Life hung on a wall. A mahogany drum table that sank clawed feet into a rich, red Turkish carpet was covered with a lace cloth and doilies. On it, Ann now placed a tea set of translucent Irish Beleek china, a gift to her from Billy, and an Irish Waterford crystal decanter and glasses, her gift to him.

"How could the girl do this to me when I gave her such a good life all these years with all the advantages? I left word I'd be out to get her when we were both. . . ." Billy rested his elbows on his knees and hid his face in his big hands. When he spoke again, his voice was low and muffled. "I told somethin' evil to 'er, Ann." He took a big swallow of brandy. "But I was angry, thinkin' of her . . . so lovely, with that murderous Jones. You are the very one,

Ann, who told me he wasn't good for nothin' at all, a . . . a debaucher, a lecher, a—"

"Will you tell me what happened?" Ann asked patiently.

"I didn't really *mean* what I said to her. Caty should have *known* I didn't," Billy complained.

"Don't blame *her* for your mistakes, Billy McGlory. What *did* you say?" There was a note of real anxiety in Ann's voice now. She knew Billy's temper, knew the excesses to which it could goad him. When he calmed, he was always sorry and he'd do anything to make amends. This time she doubted he'd be given a chance to, and much as she'd criticized Caitlin, a permanent breach between the girl and Billy was not what Ann wanted at all.

"Billy, Caitlin's just a flighty girl, teary one minute, giggly the next, changeable as an April day. If you'd shown some delicacy and patience—"

"And what if you'd shown more softness to her?" he glowered.

"Billy, I hope you didn't . . . Billy, you'd better tell me what—"

"I said she had a defect of character like her mother."

"What else?"

"I said to her, to my own Caty . . . that her mum and dad was *both* wild and bad and had passed on their wickedness to her. Bad blood always shows, I told her that."

"Oh, Billy!" Ann exhaled in exasperation. "There's more, isn't there?"

"Damn!" Billy exploded, bringing a fist down on the table, shattering one of the fragile tea cups. "Never you mind about that. I'll get you another," he growled, knocking the shards to the floor. "I told Cate she was sunk to a sad depth of debasement with that Jones. Then, I said, her mother sent her to me to get rid of her because she didn't want her no more. And Annie?" Billy's voice broke. "I said it was her own mother put my poor foolish brother Patrick in his early grave."

Ann stood and turned back the deep gold-embroidered cuffs of her satin wrapper. She refilled both their brandy glasses nearly to the rims. Deftly, she rolled a cigarette, lit it with a taper from the small kettle fire, then resumed her place opposite Billy, who had been watching her with weary, worried eyes.

"What, exactly," Ann finally asked, exhaling a long plume of blue smoke, "did you mean by that?"

Later, when Billy had finished talking, Ann poured them each another brandy and led him to her bedroom, a place they'd both come to think of with something near to reverence during the half year they'd been together. It had taken Billy months of attentive, persistent pursuit to gain admittance there the first time, but the very morning after he did, Ann had begun to redecorate for him. Now there was a double brass-framed bed on a two-step dais and piles of down pillows on the chaise and on the rocking chair. A Turkish lantern, adapted for gas, could be raised and lowered from the ceiling by means of a brass chain, and Ann had purchased a richly patterned Afghan rug at considerable expense. On the walls she had hung calm, gentle oils—landscapes and seascapes done by a friend. The room had quickly become their private sanctum of sensuality and intimate comfort.

This evening, Ann turned down the bed as soon as they closed the door behind them. She knew how much Billy needed her comfort, how hungry he was for the feel of her in his arms. She knew, too, how quickly and completely she could soothe him with her long, eager body. It was like distracting a child with fantasy confections sweet beyond dreams, as Billy had told her more than once.

They were nearly of a height. She had to reach up only a little to brush her lips to his, tentatively, testing his mood. Billy shrugged and half smiled. "I don't know, Annie, if I'm up to . . . anything much now, after Caitlin . . .

and all."

"We'll see, shall we?" Ann smiled back, unfastening her heavy, dark hair that swung loose, tumbling about her shoulders and down her back. "Undress," she urged, removing Billy's starched white collar with tapered, long-nailed fingers. She placed the collar on the mantle then deftly extracted the other studs and slid off his shirt, baring his muscular shoulders and powerful, thick-furred chest. Her quick hands moved again like fluttering birds, loosing his belt and buttons, touching him, stroking and fondling with calculating, tactile intent and purpose until the subtle tremors she felt beneath her sensitive fingers built to flares of writhing energy, and Billy stood naked and hard, emanating a crude, raw power that made her moan with longing.

"You always do know what it is I want, before I know it myself," Billy whispered coarsely, catching Ann in his arms. He tore the white satin wrapper from her shoulders and brought his grasping mouth to her hard breast tips, each in turn. Her arms closed around his thick neck, and her head fell back as she arched her body to him. She slid free of the satin sheath that slithered down her hips to the floor and, twisting away, walked slowly to her side of the bed. Billy, leering, watched her firm, long muscles work beneath an amplitude of swelling flesh that took his breath from him every time. There was so much *more* of her, it seemed, unclothed. Not looking at him, knowing what she'd see—rampant, risen power, half-glazed, greedy eyes, and heaving chest—Ann gracefully mounted the two steps of the dais and fussily, using both hands, placed rimless spectacles with steel bows low on her nose. Still with her long back to Billy, she perched naked on the edge of the bed, knees primly together, pretending to look prudish and demure with a book in her hands. She smiled to hear a lusting, satanic laugh rumble from Billy's deep chest, then felt the bed shift under his weight as he lunged across it. His arms were about her waist, pulling her back and down and under him, both laughing wildly, until he kissed her and furiously drove deep into her welcoming depths. Then their rhythmically surging joined bodies were swept by the engulfing fury of their passion. With guttural moans and sighs, they shuddered and rolled in satiating pleasure, and Ann, lost to the world, felt all the universe throbbing in her wildly beating blood.

When she quietly arose some hours later, Ann stepped on her carelessly discarded spectacles, crushing them beyond repair. It didn't matter to her in the least. She stood looking down at Billy, exhilarated and a little incredulous still at finding this man in her bed, so full-fleshed and solidly muscled, so *substantial.* Ann had been married briefly and disastrously and was widowed young. Having escaped the ludicrous and pathetic title of "old maid," she had had, during her eight years alone, occasional lovers, but had dismissed all thoughts of love or marriage to concentrate her full energies on work. What she wanted was wealth and recognition, in that order. Men were just a bothersome necessity until Billy McGlory had invaded her life with his wonderful noise and untidy masculine messes. At first Ann had tried to frighten him off, had shown him only her acquisitive, ambitious side. She had lectured him at length—still did six months later—on a woman's proper sphere in the world, which was not, in Ann's view, the laundry or nursery or kitchen. She'd build her dream house without *those* rooms, thanks. A woman's exclusive place, according to Ann Overton, was the marketplace. The yardstick, she insisted, belonged in a woman's hand, *not* in a man's. She was absolutely convinced that men who stood about in retail establishments measuring ribbons and tapes degenerated quickly and should be put back behind plows with all speed to firm up their atrophied muscles.

That particular observation had earned her a deep, roaring laugh from Billy, soon followed by a proposal of marriage.

"What? And let you set a glass bell over me? Never!" She'd smiled, declining graciously. She was, nonetheless, touched by his offer and fell violently in love. Love, Ann found, was exhausting, invigorating, and though she was loathe to admit it, rather frightening. But she could handle it—now. The first time, sadly, she hadn't understood love at all.

"I'm jealous of Mr. Overton," Billy had told Ann the first morning he awoke in her narrow, virtually virginal bed.

"Oh? Why's that?" she'd asked, stretching against him with luxurious lewdness.

"Because he had you first, before me," Billy answered, gathering her into his big boxer's arms.

"You shouldn't be jealous at all. Mr. Overton was an ass, and it was never ever like this with him," Ann explained to Billy as he shifted her long body above his own sturdy form.

"You are one fine, matchless original, Annie," Billy grinned up, guiding her shifting moves with authoritative hands.

He had meant what he said. He found Ann's bizarre opinions charmingly outlandish; they didn't bother him at all. She was smart, elegant, cultured and quietly beautiful. She had a strong will and her own money. She was a ripe, grown woman. He liked all of it.

Billy McGlory would say, if asked, that he'd never had time to marry—he'd been too busy working all his life. During the worst year of the Irish famine, when his brother Patrick had turned vagrant and gone into Wales, Billy ran away to America. He was twelve years old and hired himself out as a boy of all work, cutting wood and hauling water for a farmer's widow outside Boston. Ten years later he was running a bar in Albany and making extra money boxing. Ten years later still, at the time he sent for Caitlin, he had enough money saved to buy The White Elephant, the best dance hall in New York City. It was the perfect situation for Billy McGlory. He was tough, shrewd, and affable; before long, he knew almost everyone in town. His business prospered and lately there had been talk among his friends of running him for city council.

Billy was entirely pleased with himself and his life, which had turned out a lot better than he'd ever expected. It had become better still when he met Ann Overton. Now, this summer, with Caitlin away, there had been no need to maintain even a veneer of respectability, and he and Ann had, as she put it, been playing house. In her jaded way she'd actually admitted to developing a certain tolerance for domesticity.

From Billy's point of view, this was a very promising development and, all in all, things couldn't have been better for him until that thoughtless Caitlin up and ran away and broke his heart right in two. Where on earth she was now, with that black sheep lover of hers he'd no idea at all.

Chapter Eleven

"I must be able to do something!" Caitlin shouted. "You haven't been still for an instant since we boarded." Her laughing words were carried off by the fresh wind that caught their sails as Quinn's boat cleared Cedar Point and flew silently out onto Gardner's Bay. Caitlin's arms were wound about his waist as he worked the wheel, her face pressed against his back whenever she wasn't peering around him to watch the feathery-white rows of waves rushing to meet them, breaking against their prow and filling the air with sparkling spray.

As they left Sag Harbor, the water had been littered with ships, some riding at anchor, some putting out with the tide, white sails swelled and gleaming. They'd soon swept by the larger vessels, Quinn's trim, thirty-six foot sloop, *Aglaia,* outdistancing the others.

"I'll teach you how it's done," Quinn said over the hiss of water and wind. He drew Caitlin in front of him, and with an arm about her waist, placed her hand on his that controlled the wheel. "Feel the sea play her like a lover?" he asked, bending his long body to Caitlin's. "Feel her respond?" The *Aglaia* was slamming the swells in the fresh wind. The air was warm, and the sky the royal blue of a late summer afternoon.

"Use two hands and hold her steady," Quinn ordered, watching Caitlin. When he'd unreefed the jib, the boat surged forward like a sensitive mare responding to the pressure of her rider's heels. "Quinn!" Caitlin called, caught off guard. Then she threw her head back and shook her hair free, letting it catch sun and wind. "Quinn, this is splendid!" She laughed, gripping the wheel, a surge of joy taking hold of her, feeling free and wild as she never had before.

"Hold her, Caitlin, as she goes. I'll pop the spinnaker," Quinn said, looking at the girl with pleasure, studying her as he liked to, finding her even more beautiful in this new setting. Her legs were braced wide, her slender body was gracefully swaying, her lips and eyes shining with delight. "Have you done this before?" he demanded.

"Never! And I hope it will *never* end!" she answered, looking perfectly at ease as though she belonged at the wheel of his yacht, as though she could pilot the craft through a hurricane laughing all the while like Triton's daughter, princess of the sea. All the while, her windblown, abundant brown curls, rich with rusty undertones, radiated a subdued brilliance that held Quinn's eye. "A titian-haired dream," he muttered aloud to himself. "The Venetian master painter would have done *her* full justice."

"I can't hear you!" Caitlin called. "Are you going to do that other thing you said or not? I want to go the fastest ever."

The spinnaker billowed and filled, and the sloop, almost planing the waves, shot ahead east toward the onrushing navy blue night, the slipping sun red behind them.

"We'll run close to the wind—like this—until we clear Orient Point," Quinn explained, passing his arms about Caitlin again to control the wheel, putting the *Aglaia* on a port tack. She heeled and gained still more speed.

"Then what? Will we stop at Orient?" Caitlin asked, resting her head back against Quinn's shoulder. "I see how you do that—hold her to the wind," she commented.

"Clever child. Tomorrow I'll teach you to rig the sails. Yes, we'll stop. But not at Orient. We'll reef and ride at anchor and have some time to play before full dark."

"And after dark?"

"If you're a good little girl, I might feed you. The sea air makes even dainty ladies a little hungry. *You'll* probably devour half the stores I've laid by for . . . where are you going?" Quinn called as Caitlin ducked beneath his arm and made toward the galley hatch forward of the small main cabin, moving, despite her flying skirt, with sure-footed ease along the pitched deck.

"I'm starving now, thanks. I want to see what you've got to eat."

"Only dried cod and water, a few onions and potatoes. I wasn't expecting company, remember? Wait there." Quinn lashed the wheel with a few turns of line, then followed Caitlin forward, and she watched him reef the jib and main, admiring the quick skill with which he worked, his severe, handsome face intense with concentration, his hair, dark as black lacquer, falling forward. He dropped the spinnaker, brought the sloop into the wind, and threw over the sea anchor. It was all done with a proficient quickness and masculine grace that Caitlin found inordinately attractive. Alone, miles to sea with no land in sight, Quinn was in absolute control, so sure of himself she would willingly sail with him around the world, even on this spare little craft that he treated with such fine respect.

"Who did you name her for?" Caitlin asked as Quinn was giving the lines a final check.

"The boat's called after one of the three Graces. *Aglaia,* who is brilliance, and her sisters, Charm and Grace, help love to bloom in splendor and joy. They often graced the affairs of the love gods, Eros and Aphrodite. Even the lusty Dionysus required their charms at his orgies. Do you know the myths?"

"I've only had a little schooling," Caitlin said. "You can tell the stories to me if we're becalmed. Or at night perhaps, if we need amusement," she teased with a pretty little laugh. "Oh! Look there!" She was reaching over the rail, enchanted by a school of small fish reflecting light just below the water's surface.

"I need a little amusement *now,*" Quinn whispered against her ear, his body following the forward curve of hers, pressing to her, her breasts filling his hands as he pulled her upright against him, then his touch slid down along her ribs as he tasted the nape of her arched neck. She was gripping the rail, her eyes half closed, feeling his hands at her waist, his quick fingers undoing her sash and freeing it to the insistent tug of the wind. Then he turned her to him, his expression as intense as when he worked the ropes and lines of the *Aglaia,* his fingers deft on the fastenings of her blouse which the wind took eagerly as it had the sash. "Aeolus is as ready as I to touch that peach-blossom skin of yours," Quinn said roughly.

"You're . . . hard on a girl's wardrobe," Caitlin breathed, undoing the catch at the waist of her skirt, stepping out of it, fumbling with the laces at her bosom until Quinn took his silver knife to them. "Aeolus?" she querried.

"God of the winds," he said moving quickly now, feeding Caitlin's flimsy underthings to the waiting wind one by one until she stood stripped on the faintly rocking deck in gilding sunlight, long legs slightly parted for balance. She watched breathless as Quinn's hard, slim body emerged from his own clothes, the warm air caressing and enwrapping them. They stepped toward each other, came into each other's arms with cautious reserve, wanting to heighten the pleasure of anticipation, both knowing that the first contact of skin to skin—her breast tips against his hard chest, hips and legs locking, mouths open and grasping—would loose the demonic passion they both craved and both willed, impossibly, to last forever.

"Wait," Quinn said hoarsely, looking into Caitlin's innocent, clear blue eyes, flashing a wolfish grin, his own eyes devouring her like a flame. "I want to look at you a while, just the way you are now . . . heated and warm and wanting. Turn and walk away from me."

"You're mad," she said in a throaty purr, smiling a little, her desire nearly enfeebling her as she acquiesced to his latest whim, the heat in his eyes warming her, the hunger in them endowing her with a power and beauty she adored.

Her body, he thought, was as perfectly controlled as a dancer's, firm and lithe, but softer than a dancer's and fuller, her fine muscles moving beneath taut silken skin.

He was behind her when she came to the rail, bending her forward so that her hair almost touched the surface of the clear water that, like the air about them, had gone quite still suddenly and smooth. Holding on at both sides, she let him part her thighs.

"Don't move," he gritted as his insistent touch between them made her gasp. Her half-lidded eyes opened wide to glimpse her indistinct reflection in the water below, overshadowed by his as he invaded the depths of her smooth, tight softness, all at once and totally. His strong hands were at her whittled waist, bringing her rounded body back to meet his with each battering thrust that released free, wild cries of pleasure from her throat, cries she'd been choking back, swallowing through all their previous clandestine nights of love. Wrapped now in golden isolation beneath the open sky, there was a pure, free, animal heat in their passion as their superb, perfectly matched bodies moved together. Everything else was still, hushed, as if the ancient gods of sea and sky all held their breaths to receive a timeless offering—the primitive, unrestrained fusion of two mortals joined in a consummate, consuming act of physical love.

When their ferocious passion sent the first tremors through her, Caitlin arched back and threw her head high, still grasping the rail as the thunder took her body and Quinn's together, rolling through them again and again until, wilting forward, they were mesmerized by their joined reflections undulating on the sea.

Caitlin didn't move when Quinn pulled away, until, seconds later, his body knifing the water shattered the image there and broke the silence. Surfacing, he flung the dark hair from his eyes and swam back toward the boat, moving fast and easy.

"Come on!" he called. "It'll be dark in a few minutes."

"I can't!" Caitlin answered, shaking her head. "I don't know how."

"I'll teach you," he said, reaching the side of the boat and extending a hand.

Without hesitation, she stepped over the rail and off the side, letting herself go down, feeling the water close over her, and then she was in Quinn's arms rising, breaking the watery surface, laughing and swallowing gulps of air, clinging to his neck.

"Fool. Don't just walk off the edge like that," he answered with a dubious half smile. His hands glided all over her and she kissed him quickly.

"I trust you," she said. "I knew you wouldn't lose me in the depths. Now, show me how to swim."

"You shouldn't trust anyone that much," he scowled, placing her hands on his shoulders. "Kick," he ordered, floating, drifting backward, not touching her until they circled the yacht once. Then he shook her hands from his shoulders and dove, leaving her alone to sink a little until he came up beneath her, lifting her to the deck.

"Why've you got only half a lifeboat?" Caitlin asked. She and Quinn were on deck after a supper of the halibut he'd caught and boiled potatoes, cooked on a two-burner lamp that also served as a stove in the small galley forward of the main cabin. Quinn had a case of wine aboard and some brandy which they enjoyed now in the still, warm evening, leaning back to back against the mast as the dusk turned to darkness and the stars began to shine.

"I cut the dory in half because there wasn't room for a whole one on deck," Quinn explained. "With the end sealed up, it makes a decent lifeboat and a more than decent bath tub."

"Clever." Caitlin nodded. "All very clever and shipshape, like your stove."

"Simple," Quinn said. "There's no extra object on board and everything serves a dual purpose." He stood and lit a large lantern which threw a good light about the yacht. "So no one will run us down in the dark," he explained, stretching out near Caitlin, an arm beneath his head. She came to lie beside him, her head resting in the hollow of his shoulder.

"Did you build her yourself?" she asked Quinn.

"Salvaged. Repaired, replanked, built the cabin, caulked her. She's as snug as anything afloat and sits in the water like a swan." He toyed with a curl of Caitlin's hair that had dried to a glistening rich brown after their day in the sun.

She smiled, rolling onto her stomach. Resting on her elbows, her chin on her clasped hands, she examined Quinn's strong profile. "Even a poor man with clever hands can have a yacht, you're saying?"

"No, that's what *you're* saying but I won't disagree," Quinn answered. "But all the money in the world couldn't buy a better craft than *Aglaia*. She was a working boat built in Nova Scotia of North Mountain spruce. That's the range that overlooks the Bay of Fundy and the Annapolis Valley where I've got a . . . place. That's where I'm going . . . where I'm taking you."

"So far!" Caitlin exclaimed, sitting upright.

"What if I don't want to stay . . . I told you I've plans. You could leave me in . . . in Boston or . . . Maine, couldn't you, Quinn, if I decide not to go all the distance with you?"

"I could *not,*" he stated flatly, sitting up also and bracing against the mast again, watching Caitlin. "I'm not putting in anywhere until Westport Harbor on Nova Scotia. That's Canada."

"Know what I think?" Caitlin demanded righteously. "I think you are a wanted man! I think you're trying to elude the police. That's it, isn't it?" she insisted, kneeling forward for emphasis.

"Would it disturb you to learn you're traveling with a renegade outlaw?" he smiled coolly, his eyes narrowing.

"Yes!" she exclaimed. "Oh, no!" she amended, flustered, jumping to her feet, eyes sparking. "How many times do I have to say it? I *belong* with renegade outlaw gypsies like you, Quinn Jones!"

"Why?" He shrugged, his hand closing about her ankle as she turned to stalk off. "Be still. There's no place for you to run, fool. We'll be sharing these close quarters for a time. We'll know each other . . . very well, so get yourself in charge. Now," he demanded sternly, "will you tell me what you're talking about—what it was your uncle said to disturb you so?"

"I won't." Caitlin pouted. "I won't *speak* of it. It's too awful, and I miss him. I do, even if he. . . . Leave me be, you. Oh, don't!" she protested as, with his hand behind her knee, Quinn brought her down into his lap, his arms enfolding her just as a storm of tears broke.

"You will tell me one day, when you're ready," he said, holding her, letting her hide her face against his shoulder, not moving or speaking again until she'd quieted. When he lifted her chin to look into her glistening blue eyes, she tried to smile at him and couldn't quite and cried again and stopped and kissed him hungrily. Kneeling in front of him, she pulled her shirt—his shirt really—over her head and, shaking back her hair, brought first one tremulous round breast, then the other, to his lips, her gentle aggression taking him so off guard his breath rasped in his throat. His hands, resting at the small of her back, dropped to the curves below, and he pulled Caitlin over him. She gripped his thigh as it slid between hers and her teeth nicked his shoulder through his shirt.

He rolled over her, pinning her hands above her head. "Of all the things I might teach you, Caitlin McGlory, of all the things you need to learn, a little slowness is the most important. Stay there now, savor what you're feeling. I'll be back."

"But where are you going?" she asked with

forlorn exaggeration.

"To dim the lantern. I want to see you in nothing but moonlight."

Through the warm, calm night, the boat rocked gently, water lapping the sides, the low galaxies rolling overhead. It was nearly dawn before Quinn carried Caitlin, who barely awoke, to the narrow bunk in the cabin below.

"The glass is falling. We're in for some weather," he explained when her uncomprehending eyes drowsily fluttered. She smiled. "Oh, good." She yawned to his amusement and was lost again, his name soft on her dreamer's lip and despite the approaching storm, he was transfixed by her loveliness and a heightened aura of trusting innocence about her as she slept so peacefully, flushed cheek on her hand, lips parted.

Quinn Jones had always slept well with his women. He'd liked most, loved none, and had never spent more than a few nights with any of them. That was all the time he'd ever needed to unravel little mysteries, plumb disappointingly shallow depths and grow bored. With cold calculation, he'd avoided long, tedious entanglements with members of the feminine species, preserving his freedom to pick and choose and play as desire and the moment dictated. So why, he asked himself, had he picked up this sensual waif, McGlory? He could be stuck with her for weeks, if the winds weren't fair. Quinn pulled a sweater over his head and found tall boots in a sea chest tucked under the cabin ladder. As he was about to ascend, Caitlin sighed, and he paused and looked at her again. Luckily, he admitted, she hadn't even begun to bore him—yet. She was so prodigiously, uncommonly beautiful he took a certain pleasure in merely gazing at her, just as he took pleasure in studying a work of art to try to fathom the mysteries of its perfection. If Caitlin never moved or spoke, he might never tire of her, Quinn mused. But like other beautiful women he'd had, she did both, of course. Unlike most of them though, she was neither vacuous nor vain and made no pretense of aloof detachment. Caitlin was incapable of concealment and proudly aware of the power of her beauty. Her completely natural immodesty was more seductive than any intended enticement could ever be. All pure spontaneity and instinctive response, Caitlin reminded Quinn of a warm, healthy animal who didn't even try to disguise her unabashed sensual pleasure whenever his eyes or his hands or his mouth touched her beautiful body. A little uneasy, Quinn moved the oil lamp closer to the bunk where Caitlin slept. Her covers were already askew and half fallen to the floor, revealing the lovely roundness of a bare hip, a smooth length of leg. Delilahs all! Quinn scowled. Even the plainest and dullest of them tried some subterfuge, some power play, to entrap a lover. Caitlin's game began with her kittenish purring response to his lightest stroking touch, the instantaneous quickening of her breath and glazing of her limpid blue eyes. She was, it seemed, always wanting him, always ready. Perpetually hot with a slow-burning fire, it took no more than his kiss to set an avalanche of sparks dancing.

"Thief. Prowler and thief," her sleepy voice broke into his thoughts as her blue stare, devilish and provoking, met his. She sat up, hair flowing, letting the quilt slip to her waist, gently brushing her breast with her hand, the unself-conscious gesture sending a fast rush of desire through Quinn.

"Why are you looking at me that way?" She smiled.

"Because you want me to look at you that way. Don't try to be coy. You can't pull it off." He frowned, resting his hand over hers, feeling her quickened heartbeat beneath. He pulled her to her feet. "Wait," he said curtly, going to the trunk again. "Try these." He watched Caitlin slip into his white cable sweater that fell halfway to her knees. She turned in front of him with an inquiring smile as his eyes brushed the undulating curves, front and back, her body made in the soft wool.

"It suits you," he said, head to one side, hands on his hips, black hair sleek in lantern light. As he gazed down at her, his gray eyes concealed his admiration for her extraordinary sensuality that would hold his interest until he'd completely plumbed its depths and explored all its tempting possibilities. He would have to force her to the outer boundaries of her inventiveness, test all the expressive limits of her superb and undissembling erotic genius before he'd be ready to walk away, indifferent and sated as he always had. That was the real reason he'd agreed to take her with him, he told himself, relieved. A smile touched his lips and she stepped toward him. She wanted him now, he thought, wanted him again . . . always. She adored being taken . . . possessed by him . . . but then . . . maybe any man could turn those beautiful violet eyes vague with longing, touch the secret softnesses, and make her needy, imploring.

"Quinn . . . what is it?" Caitlin asked almost cautiously.

He turned away, not wanting her to see his face as a blow of possessive desire stunned him with its brutal strength. Jealousy, he knew, was a cursed and savage emotion that he'd never felt before.

They rode out the storm anchored in the lee

of Great Gull Island, hearing the wind rattle among the low trees ashore. They rarely left the cabin, only reluctantly deserted the narrow bunk and each other's arms until the storms within and without began to abate. In the languid, intimate afterglow, they talked as they hadn't before. Rather Caitlin talked, encouraged by Quinn's occasional question or easy laugh, telling him, she swore, all she remembered of her childhood in England before she'd been sent to Billy. There *had* been good times, rolling hills and dogs and horses and a warm, safe nursery high in a great house. Then there had been flight through dark night woods and a terrible, depthless sadness that kept coming back to her again and again. In her dreams, Caitlin called out forever to someone who never answered and never came.

When her silent tears began to fall, Quinn held Caitlin in his arms for a long while, as if sheltering a lost little girl from all the world's sadness, wanting to keep her safe forever. Like a trusting child, she'd fallen asleep in his embrace and only awoke as the sky lightened into a cool, gray dawn.

"I've never told anyone all that before." She smiled with a puzzled look. "I didn't think I could remember so much or ever talk of it. Especially the saddest part—standing at the stone arch, watching her turn away."

"But you didn't tell me that before," Quinn

said, standing suddenly and tossing Caitlin her sweater. "Who turned away?"

"My mother, I suppose. She *did* desert me," Caitlin said thoughtfully, "just as Billy said. I can't really remember her at all—only the forest and the smell of the sea and feeling . . . lost."

"We *will* be lost if we don't look lively," Quinn said, holding her safe in his arms once more before climbing the cabin ladder to the deck.

They set an easterly course, in a fog as thick as a pall, toward Nantucket. Caitlin, who was quickly becoming a competent hand, took soundings as Quinn maneuvered the double-reefed *Aglaia* through a sea of low swells, sometimes in dangerously shallow water. In freshening winds, they rounded Cape Cod. In festive sunshine and after many dull days, with the autumn smell of bonfires drifting from land, they passed Gloucester and sailed through the crowd of boats on the westerly fishing banks, heading northeast. A week later, they approached Nova Scotia and tore into Westport Harbor, hurled up the Bay of Fundy by a fierce riptide that demanded all Quinn's navigational skills. Though Caitlin was as wild as the waves with excitement, she skillfully downed the jib at Quinn's sharp command and the *Aglaia*, which had seemed on a crash course, rested her flank daintily against the wharf like a perfect lady.

"Throw us a line there, kid. I'll secure her for you! Well, look smart, lad, or are you slow-witted?" a laughing voice demanded. Caitlin gave the gesturing fellow on the dock her best approximation of a disdainful glare.

"Kid indeed!" she frowned. He was young enough himself—no older than she, Caitlin decided. He had a narrow, boyish face with a small nose, a wide, sensitive mouth, and very large, very green eyes beneath yellow hair brushed to one side. He was of medium height, wiry and slim.

"If that whelp was in my employ," the fellow went on, addressing Quinn, "I'd give him a good going over as you should yourself, sir, him gawking about with work to be done."

"The loafer is green, never been to sea before, never done a day's work either." Quinn laughed. "I'm trying to be patient, though."

Caitlin's look of indignation turned to confusion, then to dawning understanding as she glanced at her attire—big sweater and rolled men's pants. About to snatch off the peaked cap that hid her auburn curls, she thought better of it, nodded, and smiled at the indignant figure on shore and hurled him a line that fell a few feet short and had to be tossed again.

"If I may be so bold, sir, I think . . ." the man said, looking at Caitlin with narrowed eyes, "I think this chap isn't made out to be a sailor. Now I've just come across from England, sir, officer in Her Majesty's Navy and I'm seeking honest employment in the New World, so called, as I heard was to be had for young men wanting to make their fortunes, and it seems to me, sir, seeing the fix you are in with this lazy lout, you could make use of my services. I know how to handle a craft under full sail, sir."

"I can do that myself, single-handed." Quinn winked. "What else can you offer?"

"I know how a gentleman likes to be looked after. I could keep your clothes in order and your linen in repair. I'd see to your mistress and your mount and your wine cellar. I cook and I know about—"

"You're hired," Quinn said.

"The last thing *you* need is a valet," Caitlin quipped. "On your way to jail and all," she added, lowering her voice.

"I'm hired, did you say, sir? Did I hear you right?" the boy asked a little skeptically, climbing aboard, scowling at Caitlin. "What's to be done with him? Fresh as he is, I wouldn't want to put anyone on the street with nothing to his name and nowhere to go. I'd teach him proper ways, sir, if you let him stay."

"Oh, don't worry so!" Caitlin said, touched by the boy's concern. "I'm not . . . I mean . . . well, see!" she exclaimed, pulling off the cap and letting her hair flow down.

"No wonder he kept you on even though you handle a line like a . . . a cream puff!" The boy laughed, his green eyes full of admiration as they flitted over Caitlin's trim form, returning again and again to her beautiful face. "I'd not have been so forward, sir, if I'd known the lad was your . . . wife and all."

"He's not Quinn's wife." Caitlin laughed. "I mean, *I'm* not," she amended, tilting her head prettily, her natural flirtatiousness beginning to light her eyes.

"He . . . he's not," the boy said more than asked. "Well, I can be useful to you *both* and I won't disturb your . . . your voyage d'amour. I'll sleep on deck," he added, his eyes on Caitlin.

"You know all about proper English gentlemen, it would seem," she said quite seriously. "I mean, you know what they expect and how they do things and where—"

"The lady has a particular interest in the British aristocracy," Quinn remarked sarcastically. "She plans to marry into it, so any information you can offer would be appreciated. Now, if you're working for *me*, you'll stop staring at *her* and go see if the inn's got two rooms to let. Two," Quinn emphasized, in the face of Caitlin's questioning look. "One for you, boy, one for us, and see, too, what's being provided for supper there, and if you can buy the lady a reasonable respectable ready-made frock of some sort. From the way you've been studying her, I'd suppose you had all her dimensions well in mind." There was an edge in Quinn's voice that chilled the atmosphere for a moment until the boy pulled off his cap and bowed low with exaggerated courtesy. There was a flash of undisguised mischief in his green eyes.

"Beg your pardon, sir, but no manly fellow *could* forget the delineations of such a lady as you have. Her dimensions are close, though not exactly the same as those of my sister waiting at the inn to see what employment I find in this remote place. Dancy will have some outfit for . . . ?" The boy paused. "I don't know your name, sir, or the lady's, but if you will only say—"

"Jones." Caitlin nodded. "He's Quinn Jones. My name is Caitlin McGlory." She smiled her prettiest.

"David Pallett at your service." The boy smiled back, turning up the collar of his faded jacket as a cool gust crossed the deck.

"We are going to Mr. Jones's place along the bay somewhere . . . am I right, Quinn?" she asked, her head to one side with a gentle deference. He only nodded, watching her begin to glimmer like a firefly in the early dusk, charming their visitor as she did him with her flirtatious warmth.

"Well . . . perhaps your sister could come

along unless she has other commitments, and *if* Mr. Jones doesn't object. Do you, Quinn?"

"I'd never turn away a lady with such a pretty name as Dancy." He flashed a grin. "And if her person is even half as charming as her name . . . She must be ready to leave on the early tide if the morning's fair."

"We learned a bit about this place the little time we've been here. The tide does govern life on the bay. Your craft sitting in the mud one minute is then lifted twenty, thirty feet by the tide, even more than that, I've heard, down the bay. What sort of place have you got and where is it, Mr. Jones?"

"In the North Mountains off Minas Channel. Now, you'll start earning your pay by finding a respectable costume for this waif—and David, ask at the tailor's shop if there's a letter for me, will you? I'm expecting one."

"I thought I should never ever see him again this side of the grave, but I never gave up hope and one day he just came into the draper's shop where I was . . . working in Cardiff." Dancy Pallett and Caitlin stood in the bow of the *Aglaia* the next afternoon as the yacht worked down Fundy Bay, Quinn at the wheel, catching a windblown, lilting laugh and fragments of their conversation as he observed them with pleasure. He'd always liked watching women in their unself-conscious moments, when they were unaware of his attention. Anticipation of seeing some pretty thing—with whom he was otherwise finished—at her morning toilette had kept him in more than one bed overnight and drew him, too, to bordellos in lax, early afternoon hours when their inhabitants were just arising. These two now, Caitlin and Dancy, were chattering away like old friends or long lost cousins though they'd only met the day before. They were almost of a height, Quinn noted as they stood shoulder to shoulder, their backs to him in identical, plain, dark dresses, both Dancy's. Caitlin's figure was the softer and fuller. There was an almost boyish flatness about Dancy Pallett, front and back. She, though, would have been considered a beauty in Elizabethan times, Quinn decided, with a lace ruff and her long neck, bodice flat and tight over her little breasts.

"We're twins. Did David tell you?" Quinn heard the girl ask before a new slant of wind stole his attention.

"No, but I can see it," Caitlin answered. "Everything about you two is the same, except your hair."

Dancy was fair skinned and green eyed like her brother but with carrot red curling hair so heavy, the brisk wind barely lifted it.

"*And* my freckles." The girl laughed self-consciously, glancing over her shoulder at

David who was setting a mainsail winch. "I can't help but stare at him whenever he's about me. It was ten years we'd been parted. Grandfather lost our farm and died of heartbreak, Ma said. Our father took David and left Mother and me all on our own, deserted." Dancy shook her head sadly and glanced over her shoulder again. "I was only ten when it happened, but I was stronger than Mother, poor thing. She could do nothing but cry. I was sent into . . . service in a fine house, and the lady there took a fancy to me and made me governess to her children."

"But why were you working for a draper?" Caitlin asked. "Here, have another apple." There was a barrel of them—fine Nova Scotia apples—taken aboard at Parker's Cove.

"I left Lady Outerbridge because I wanted to look for David," she said quickly. "Mm, just the fragrance of these apples makes me miss our . . . farm." Dancy smiled, polishing one against her sleeve. "When the boughs of the trees were heavy with them and the fields were fallow, it was really autumn and soon it would be winter and there'd be apples in the Christmas tree. David!" she called. "Have one!"

He caught the shiny fruit she tossed. "Reminds me of . . . home," he called in a muffled voice, his mouth full.

"See, we *are* just alike." Dancy laughed, turning back to Caitlin. "I don't suppose we'll ever call any place home again," she sighed. "Certainly we can't go back to England ever again."

"Why not?" Caitlin asked, startled. "Come below and help with the meal while you tell me. Is it to do with David jumping ship?"

"Jumping ship?" Dancy asked, apparently puzzled for an instant. "Oh, he promised me he wouldn't tell tales. David . . . he . . . I've learned in the few months we've been together again that he just . . . lies. About everything. For no reason most times. It's a habit with him. It's harmless. I suppose he can't help it. He told you he was in the royal navy, didn't he? Well, he never was. He was a stowaway on a liner. We only had enough money for one fare. We had to get out of Cardiff fast and . . . we got put ashore at Halifax after I gave the captain every cent we had left. And my trunk. That's why I had only two dresses, the one I'm wearing and yours." Dancy's green eyes were filled with tears. Caitlin lit the large lantern and set a pot of water boiling for potatoes. Before she could speak, the girl lifted her chin bravely. "If you and Mr. Jones don't want to be traveling with such as David and me, put us ashore next harbor and we'll fend on our own." She sniffed, her very fair skin going a little blotchy.

"We will have to abandon you at the very next port," Caitlin announced. "No doubt of it. I, after all, am the deserted daughter of a pair of wild, irresponsible runaways; and I've just been cast out penniless by my saloon-keeper uncle because bad blood always tells, as my *uncle* tells it. Quinn's some sort of wanted desperado cutthroat, and though he's far from penniless, I'm afraid to ask how his ill-gotten wealth was gained. So you see, Dancy, we couldn't possibly spend another instant with a low pair like you and David. Here, peel these," Caitlin said, setting a bowl of potatoes before Dancy who stared at her wide eyed before breaking into peals of laughter.

"Oh dear, birds of a feather, it is. I'll tell you now, Caty, we ran from Cardiff because . . . because I attacked a constable with drapers' shears when he tried to arrest David as a vagrant. They have the Poor Laws in England . . . they can just pick up anyone. But you must never repeat what I've told you," she added with an anxious look.

"We'll keep each other's secrets." Caitlin nodded very seriously. "Shall we?"

"We will, I *swear,*" Dancy agreed just as seriously. "Now that we're friends, tell me one thing more. How long have you been in love with Quinn Jones?"

"I never was!" Caitlin whispered, nearly dropping the large basket of mussels she'd gathered at low tide on the shoals before they'd left Newport. Her warm coloring didn't hide the flush that suffused her face.

"I see those mysterious looks of love pass between you two, but if you won't admit to it . . ." Dancy shrugged.

"If you ever breathe one word to any living soul—even to your David—I swear I'll . . . I won't speak to you ever again," Caitlin whispered fiercely. "You are right, of course," she went on when Dancy had nodded agreement, taking the basket from her and starting up the cabin ladder. "But he'll never know, nor will anyone but you and I, because I'm going to leave him as soon as . . . We made a . . . He's promised to teach me things I need to know before I can do what I plan to. I *am* going to marry into the British nobility. I'll have a duke or a baron—nothing less."

"Whatever for?" Dancy asked, bemused. "And why would you willingly leave a man you love?"

"For respectability and position and wealth, that's all. And to show my dear uncle how wrong he is about me and about my mother, that's why," Caitlin added angrily. "Now!" She smiled, brightening as abruptly as she'd dimmed. "We'd best clean these little monsters, or we'll have two ravenous men on our hands before long."

"How do you plan to cook these funny fishes?" Dancy asked as she emerged on deck.

"I've no idea. I've never laid a finger on such

things before." Caitlin poured sea water from a bucket into the half life boat, and, taking up a brush, she began scrubbing at a mussel. "How's that?" she asked, holding up her work for Quinn's inspection as he passed.

"Sparkling." He stopped and knelt beside her and cleaned a few, quickly. "But it's not diamonds you're polishing. If you don't go at it faster, we won't eat until full dark. Miss Pallett knows how, I see."

"Oh, really?" Caitlin said with feigned coolness, refusing to acknowledge the tinge of irritation and jealousy she felt. "I'll just leave the whole business to you and Miss Pallett then, Quinn. I've no talent for cooking and such. David and I will have a nice talk. Won't we, David?" she called.

The boy, drowsing on the cabin hatch, lifted his head, sleepy green eyes puzzled. "What say, Miss McGlory?" He smiled as she climbed up beside him.

"Mr. Jones and your sister are doing the evening meal so you can just tell me all about you now. Dancy and I are great friends already." She smiled, tossing back her rich curls with a flirtatious lift of her head.

"Take the wheel, mate," Quinn ordered David, dipping up another bucket of sea water. "Mussels *mariniere*, Dancy?" Caitlin heard him ask, his voice on the edge of those warm, low tones she claimed as her own, exclusively.

Unsettled, she looked off in the distance, startled to see the moon in full daylight sitting on the *Aglaia*'s prow, the old man in it laughing at her for all she was worth. She shook her fist at him once then turned to David Pallett who was watching her attentively.

"Dancy tells me you and she hadn't seen each other for years when you met again quite by accident. How did such a thing ever happen?" Caitlin asked almost absently as she watched Quinn from the corner of her eye disappearing below decks with Dancy.

"Father died of the cholera a young man," David said, his green eyes narrowing.

"Oh?" Caitlin said. "I thought he took you and—"

"Mother was nearly destroyed by his death. She lost interest in . . . the farm. Sheep it was we raised. And feed. The Gower Peninsula is wild and beautiful like Nova Scotia, which is why we came here, though Dancy still wants to go to New York City. I never would have left home but Mother married again—to a bleak sort of man from the Devil's Bridge hill country. Maybe that's why he saw the devil everywhere, even in Dancy. I couldn't abide him tellin' her all the time that the devil had given her wild red hair. He was lusting after her. I knew that and so did he. He'd have killed me or me him if I hadn't run away to sea."

"Dancy says she misses home even so,"

Caitlin offered, stunned by David's story.

"Of course. You've never been to Wales, or it would not seem so remarkable to you that she does. Our wild mountains are deep gladed and rocky—like those." He pointed at the coastline where the trees, in the fall evening, were already holding night and a hint of winter in their branches. "There are deep glades in our mountains with moss and bracken on the rocks. There's fern along the banks of cascading streams, and vapor rises from them on summer nights, making the branches above silvery and wild."

David stood and rested his forehead against the mast. "We can't ever go back again, so I will build us a home in the uplands here, a long and low and whitewashed house like the farm at home. There'll be sheep and black Welsh cattle and rocks and streams."

"But your sister said . . ." Caitlin began.

"Don't mind what Dancy says and don't ever say I told this, but she's got a way of . . . making up things. It helps her . . . not to think bad thoughts." David's boyish face seemed very old and sad for an instant. "Do you suppose those two are ready to eat?" he asked. Because he had seemed to have forgotten the *Aglaia* in his perturbation, Caitlin took the wheel as the sails began to luff, bringing the boat back into the wind.

"Go below, David, and hurry them along,"

she said. He shrugged lightly and vaulted the ladder rail in a sudden burst of energy and reviving high spirits.

"The lady and I are starving," she heard him announce as he disappeared into the cabin. "What are you two doing with those mussels?"

Alone on deck in the quiet wilds of Fundy, pleased at finding herself in control of a fine craft, Caitlin let a faint unease begin to blossom in her mind. Though she already felt a warm affection for David and Dancy, a kind of kinship of impoverished, homeless drifters, she had been taken off guard by their contradictory tales. That they were very close and that they cared for each other very much was clear, but nothing else about them was. Thinking over their stories and their requests for strictest secrecy, Caitlin decided that one of the twins was either quite clever . . . or perhaps just a little mad. Though which of them it was, she had no clue.

Well, Caitlin mused silently, two days in the intimate confines of this boat and then weeks perhaps at Quinn's isolated cabin or house—whatever it actually was—would reveal a lot about all of them, even that desperado Jones. "I've walked right into a lair of thieves or into a lair with thieves," Caitlin said aloud happily, wondering again why on earth she had done such a thing.

Just then Quinn's dark head, followed by his

broad shoulders emerged from the cabin, and he turned his fine smile in her direction.

That's why, she told herself.

Quinn recognized the positive lift of her chin, knowing it accompanied serious thought. "Cate, you're doing well with the *Aglaia*, but the wind's freshening. We'll lay over in that cove. Then in the morning, we'll sail for Minas Channel. We should be there by noon."

Chapter Twelve

"Is that it, Quinn?" Caitlin asked with barely contained excitement, leaning forward in her saddle. "I wasn't expecting . . . well, it's very grand, isn't it?" The rough, winding road they were traveling ascended into the mountains, following the bank of a cascading brook that was blue where afternoon sunlight touched it and foaming white as it fell over jutting rocks. Through overhanging branches already aflame with the first fire colors of autumn, Caitlin glimpsed a large structure clinging to a craggy mountainside.

"Reminds me of home!" David Pallett called. He and Dancy rode in a small, sturdy cart built to maneuver the narrow, twisting road. They followed the mounted riders who had paused to wait for them at a wooden bridge.

"You'll have to take the cart up the long way. We'll meet you there." Quinn gestured when they'd all clattered across the stream. The road forked, one prong widening and rising gradually, the other disappearing in a sharp, almost vertical turn.

"Lean well forward," he instructed Caitlin as, taking the bridle to lead her balky horse, he began the ascent through shadowy pines. Caitlin tucked closer about her a wool tapestry-weave shawl of soft pastels Quinn had purchased for her in the village below and did as she was told, holding fast until they came to a clearing where Quinn reined in and dismounted. When he lifted her down, he never released her from his arms as his mouth found hers. Her shawl fell as her arms went about his strong back and they sank together on a bed of springy, soft moss at the base of a towering pine, their bodies fired and ready the instant they touched. Her fastenings were undone, her round, lovely breasts exposed to sunlight and air and the caress of his lips as he rolled her above him and thrust up hard. Looking into his half-lidded gray eyes, seeing in his severe face the cruel animal grimace that was fearsome and arousing at once, Caitlin lost herself in the sweep of wild love, fast as a knife flash this time, and especially sweet for its urgent brevity.

"They'll be waiting," she whispered, wilting

on Quinn's chest, her face against the cool channel of his throat as his hands played over her with the precision of a sculptor molding, or a blind man memorizing.

"Gordon will tend to them. He stays on the place."

"Alone?" Caitlin asked softly. Lost deep in the insular closeness of the moment, she didn't really care about anything beyond the fine, strong curve of Quinn's jaw that filled her eyes when she opened them.

"Gordon Finley's a hermit at heart," Quinn explained.

"I think I may be, too!" Caitlin laughed, sitting up to begin on her buttons. "After these past days in the *Aglaia* with the twins—delightful company as they are—it was rather too restricting . . ."

"But not for a clever, uninhibited little temptress like you," Quinn said, resting back, hands behind his head. "*You* found a way. I think having David and Dancy asleep below decks added to your . . . pleasure. Secretiveness does that to some women."

"But it wasn't . . . just that one time on the boat and . . ." Caitlin's amorous violet eyes met his, and a soft smile played at her parted lips until he laughed. She blushed at her own thoughts and, furious at Quinn, rose quickly. Her slight, slim form aflutter with anger, was silhouetted above him for a moment in a blaze of afternoon sunlight, before she pranced off with an inarticulate exclamation.

"Stay away from that horse," he commanded right behind her, his hands at her waist, turning her to him as she tried to mount.

"You mustn't laugh at me about such things," she pouted, struggling against him, not meeting his eyes. "Now see! You've made me tear Dancy's dress and she hasn't another I can borrow. Let me go!"

"Before I'm done with you, Caitlin McGlory," Quinn said evenly, "you'll ride like an Arab. No matter how good you look on horseback, you can't handle that animal now in this mountain country, so don't behave like a fool. And I wasn't laughing at you," he added. She looked up quickly.

"But you *were*," she insisted with a stamp of her foot like a stubborn child, Quinn thought, tempted to laugh again.

"I was paying you a compliment. Inventive and clever as you are about loving, you'll certainly please your British lord, in bed anyway."

"And when you've taught me to ride like an Arab and to pour tea like a princess, I'll please him in the field and in the drawing room as well," Caitlin said, her low, trilling laugh and mercurial change of mood catching Quinn off guard.

"There's a little more to it than that." He

glared at her, inexplicably angry all at once. "And if I'm to turn a scruffy waif like you into a *real* lady, the sooner we begin the better. Let's go."

Rough-hewn, steep, wide, stone steps rose up a terraced hillside, narrowing to pass through a high, vaulted stone arch overgrown with climbing vines, standing deep in the remnants of summer wild flowers. Caitlin got a fuller view of the house gazing up through the arch as she and Quinn reined in and dismounted.

"It's a *mansion* Quinn!" She laughed as he took her hand to lead her to it. He turned when she hung back at the arch, finding her lost in one of her dreamy trances, eyes distant, that lovely, flickering smile playing over her full lips. She had pulled her shawl closer as if an icy wind had touched her and just stared at the house. Its Palladian façade with tall, mullioned windows and uniform pilasters was severe and calm and very elegant.

"What's wrong?" Quinn demanded when she resisted the pressure of his hand.

"It reminds me of something, though I can't tell . . . my dream. I feel I've stood in this arch before, looking at this grand house," she answered, still not moving. "Silly of me, isn't it?" She laughed, suddenly skipping ahead of

Quinn and pulling him after her.

"You've seen pictures probably of Greek temples or English country estates. The long, horizontal lines are much alike in all of them."

"No, it feels as though I've seen this very house, not pictures. But anyway, it suits you," Caitlin said, thinking that the calm severity of the structure, its stylish, understated elegance *was* just like Quinn Jones. Even now, after weeks at sea and these last hours overland on horseback, everything about him was right, quite perfect . . . the well-cut riding breeches and Wellington boots, his felted jacket worn over a dark sweater, emphasizing broad shoulders and slim hips. The only thing out of place—the small detail *he'd* taught her to recognize—was a shock of black hair that he raked back from his brow.

"This place suits you, also," he said thoughtfully, not really having meant to but feeling about Caitlin now, as he had aboard the *Aglaia*, that she was in her element. This setting, too, was right for her. She belonged here, completing an unfinished picture as she stood beneath the soaring arch with the wind in her hair, the long, fringed shawl flung about her. And she belonged somewhere else as well, Quinn felt with a haunting sense of *déjà vu*, as if he'd seen her, in some shadowy, elusive past, on the wild and dappled ancient Cambrian Mountains of Wales. Blazing in all her exuberant, vivid beauty, Caitlin became for him a Celtic princess of antiquity surveying her craggy realm, or the proud daughter of a conquering warrior who'd crossed the sea with William centuries before to take hold of England. Those Norman lords had been granted earldoms, and the Welsh Marches they created—the half-timbered black and white manors they'd built—formed a protective buffer for William between subdued England and wild Wales that still, even into the nineteenth century, clung defiantly to its proud past.

Interested in everything, as usual, Caitlin only hesitated a moment before dancing up the rough steps, not stopping again until she'd reached the top. There, she glanced down the long evergreen valley below, already in half darkness. Above, ribbons of smoke rose from the mansion's chimneys that were hidden behind the pilasters and the raised cornice of the roof.

"But Quinn, it isn't finished!" she exclaimed.

The perfect symmetry of the classic, vine-covered structure was thrown into chaos by wooden scaffolding outlining the shape of a missing wing that would have completed a balanced H. The open foundation was filled with wild greenery that had had a season or two to take hold.

"There's something . . . so sad about half-built houses," Caitlin said. "Why did you stop?"

"I lost interest," Quinn answered brusquely, striding ahead across the court, boot heels striking stone emphatically.

"But *why* did you?" she demanded, hurrying to catch up and take his arm. He didn't slow when she did. "You know," Caitlin went on, "I tell you absolutely *everything*. I've hardly any secrets from you but you never tell me what I want to know. It's not fair!"

He only laughed, amused by her directness and knowing she was right, of course. During their weeks alone together at sea, she'd charmed and amused him with her ingenuous, spontaneous responses to everything—sea and sky and wind and stars, the boats they'd hailed, the shapes of clouds, storms and calms and colors. Under the darkening sky then, or curled in the cabin later when the air went cold, she had, like Scheherazade, kept him entertained night after night with her clever, funny stories of the New York waiter girls and their blades and dandies, the Tammany politicians and confidence men, the sports, "the fancy" and the uptown society boys whose antics she'd grown up astutely observing. She had told him, too, in the soft nights, in the close calms between storms of love, as precisely as words would allow, how incredibly beautiful he had made her feel . . .

how she wanted to feel again, what she'd do to him and he to her in the delight of loving. She wanted . . . intended, she had said, to experience everything there was in every setting under the sun, and she pressed him to describe to her all he'd ever done before, with whom and where. But he was more inclined, at such times, to demonstrate, and she was easily distracted.

In her rare, subdued moments, when she talked to him of the mother she couldn't remember, spinning lovely fantasies of a childhood that might have been, Caitlin had stirred dorment, nearly forgotten protective feelings in Quinn. It was at such times he had told her a little about his past . . . his boyhood in Galena, roaming the red cliffs high above the Mississippi, and told her, too, of the magnificence he'd seen in India and the Orient. A direct question, though, about home, immediately elicited stony stares and angry silences.

"What did you mean by 'hardly any secrets'? I want to know *all* your secrets," he pronounced with a sudden provocative grin.

"We'll make it a trade—secret for secret—in the future, or nothing doing," Caitlin countered. "It'll be much easier for you. You've got all your little ones to start with. I've only big, important secrets left. Now . . . I demand to know why you didn't complete this magnificent mansion."

"A copy won't do, now that I've seen the original," he said cryptically.

"Oh, isn't that informative of you," she scolded with mild sarcasm. "Copy of what?"

"A manor on a Welsh hillside so perfect it seemed part of the sky. Before I ever saw it, it was described to me in . . . longing detail by someone I cared very much for. Ah! There's Gordon," Quinn announced, his thoughtful tone changing abruptly as the doors of the mansion swung wide. A tall, thin, slightly stooped man of indeterminate age, wearing neither jacket nor shoes, stepped out into the court and wearily raised a lank hand in greeting. He had unkempt, nut-brown hair and keen, observant, dark eyes. A frayed cigarette burned at the corner of his thin lips.

"The whole blasted place is cold as a cave, Quinn," the man said testily. "I just made fires when I spotted that wagon coming up the long hill. I sent for the house staff. You've got quite a crowd on the way up here, I see. This one," the man said, looking with interest at Caitlin, "appears impossibly young." A long ash dropped from his cigarette, making a gray smudge down his trouser leg as it fell unnoticed.

"I brought you tailor-mades, *No-name 24s*, and *Latakias* from Bedrossian, the tobacconist to the New York carriage trade. They're in the wagon," Quinn said, clasping the man's hand.

"Caitlin McGlory, meet Gordon," he added then, taking her hand, too, and waiting almost expectantly, she felt, for the man's reaction.

"Delighted," she said with a pert little curtsy.

"Likewise," Gordon answered dourly.

"Liar," she smiled, "but you'll just have to put up with our invading your hermitage. We won't stay forever. I promise."

"I can stand it. I've stood worse. Just look at me, carved by age as I am, cosmically cheated by fate and low women of intrigue, rescued from drowning in a sea of poverty by this most noble man here, Jones." Gordon nodded. "Do you know," he asked in a gravelly, rasping voice, offering Caitlin his arm, "that guests are like fish?"

"How?" she responded suspiciously, glancing up at Quinn who shrugged and winked and followed them inside.

"I'll tell you how," Gordon pontificated. "Guests *and* fish are best the first day, dull the second, stinking the third!" he bellowed ferociously before a fit of coughing shook him.

"That *is* an awful thing to say," Caitlin replied flirtatiously when he'd quieted, staring into his eyes with mock horror before her suppressed light laughter broke free.

"Gordon, one only speaks badly when one really has nothing to say," she scolded, trying, without success, to sound stern.

"And only a librarian or a schoolmarm—not my favorite sorts of ladies—would quote Voltaire at me," Gordon complained to Quinn. "Where did you find *her*?"

"Washed up on a Long Island beach, bedraggled as sea weed and just as clinging," Quinn answered, displaying his best boyish smile. "I haven't been able to shake her off since."

"Say such a thing to me again, you low life gallows bird, I'll be out your blasted door and gone quick as that," Caitlin flared with a snap of her fingers, the accent of the street urchin clear in her angry voice.

"Ho! No school teacher this! She *has* got a nasty temper, hasn't she now?" Gordon laughed. "But the world would be such a dull place without a bit of nastiness. A lady of spirit is Miss Caitlin McGlory. Good. She'll keep you in your place and me entertained while she's doing it. But why does she call you a . . . what was it? A gallows bird?" Gordon asked. "I can't fathom that one at all." At a sharp glance from Quinn though, he dropped the subject and turned back to Caitlin. "There's nothing more I'd ask of a house guest, my girl, then a bit of lively fun and good repartee." He beamed at her. "Friends?" Gordon offered.

"Friends!" Caitlin agreed. Placated, she began looking about, Gordon's compliment and her natural curiosity overcoming her quick anger.

The vast entrance hall of the mansion soared two stories to a glass conservatory roof. Empty symmetrical arched niches, each flanked by pillars, ran the length of the room to a staircase that curved upward with the grace of a long wave, its slim marble balustrade and posts continuing along the hall above.

"The *care* it took!" Caitlin marveled, fingering one of the pillars.

"This vestibule—" Gordon began, "vestibulum where the Romans divested themselves of their vestes, you know—is all Connamara marble, including the floor."

"Gordon's full of bits of intriguing information, you'll find," Quinn interjected. "He's a big talker, a wild drinker, and a roisterer who'll keep you up and fascinated all night if you let him. Give us another obscure fact now, Gordon," Quinn prompted.

"Um . . . let me . . . Oh, yes!" Gordon's eyes snapped with pleasure. "Alexander the Great was buried in a coffin full of honey. Didn't know *that,* did you, Caitlin McGlory?"

"Of course I didn't," she purred with suppressed laughter. "Why honey?"

"Preservative." Gordon smiled smugly. He rolled, then lit a fresh cigarette from one that was burning too close to his lips. "What else do you want to know?"

"That'll do, thanks," Quinn said. "Why

don't you go meet the wagon and get your factory smokes while I show Caitlin about?"

"I know when I'm not wanted," Gordon grumbled, ambling toward the door, "which is most of the time. *Cigarette*," he pronounced, pausing on the threshold as if beginning a formal lecture. "The word comes to us from the French via a clever Egyptian cannoneer. At the siege of Acre, he broke his only clay pipe and was forced to roll tobacco in gun powder papers. See you folks anon."

"Odd hermit who never stops talking," Caitlin remarked with a laugh.

"Odd in more ways than one," Quinn agreed, grasping her hand and leading her to a pair of beautifully carved mahogany doors embellished with brass fittings. They opened into a large, paneled room with deep, ornate moldings and festoons of glittering gold leaf. The room was completely empty but for an immense rug spreading like a spring garden over the white marble floor.

"It's a Turkish carpet from Izmir," Quinn said, seeing Caitlin hesitate at the center medallion, then move toward the fire. "It's nearly three centuries old," he added. "The Ottomans virtually live on such magnificence—talk, eat, love on their carpets, get to know their most subtle, intimate details."

"It *is* a magical thing," Caitlin whispered, her violet eyes dreamy with delight. The firelight raked her glowing hair which was caught up in a soft sweep with a golden comb. As she stood poised in one of her rare moments of complete composure, her every line a study in physical perfection, Quinn realized he had memorized her in full and luscious detail. Undraping her with his eyes, he caressed in his mind her silken shoulders with the thrusting, rounded swell of her floating breasts, then the fine narrowing of her flexible waist. She turned, unknowingly offering his imagination her long, tapering back and the tempting full flare of flank and hip.

"Caitlin?" he said in a low voice, willing her to smile.

When she looked up at him, warm and inquisitive, he found himself sheathing her in white satin, surrounding her with clouds of palest pink chiffon. When he encircled her throat with ropes of pearls, he knew without doubt he'd have to see her that way, just as he had to see her naked and eager, shimmering in the deep, soft nest of his down-filled bed, spread on his silken sheets, her russet-touched hair beautiful against antique ivory lace. That was, after all, one of the reasons he'd brought her here, he insisted to himself.

"I'll show you . . . other things," he said in a tone she'd rarely heard him use before—soft but sinister and vaguely threatening.

Grasping her hand, he pulled her after him

through room after echoing room, paneled, papered in gold, dripping with swags of fruits and flowers, their footfalls ringing on marble. They stopped only briefly while Caitlin admired the one perfect object each contained: in the library a Chippendale secretary bookcase of inlaid mahogany with swan-necked pediments; in a small drawing room a Queen Ann molded walnut lowboy with a beaded border and cabriole legs; a Flemish tapestry was hung in a hallway; a classically shaped Empire side chair stood at a stair landing; in a glass-roofed sun room on the second floor was one star-caned wicker rocker, curlicued and arabesqued, with rolled back arms and lattice work. Caitlin sat rocking until Quinn tipped her from it impatiently, hurrying her on, hurling open all the doors along the second floor corridor, revealing empty, paneled bed chambers filling with gray evening light that fell through long leaded windows.

"Why are you rushing so?" she asked, coming to a stubborn stop. "I won't budge until you tell me."

"You'll see," was all Quinn answered, unceremoniously lifting her off her feet and striding purposefully to the end of the hallway. The closed doors in their path gave way to one thrust of his booted foot and he stepped into a room that seemed to be floating magically in midair. The mountainside fell away beneath a curving wall of long windows filled with cloud-streaked sky. Amidst the pines below that were mere points in the distance, cottage roof tops were barely visible. Far off, there was a glint of water.

"It makes me almost dizzy, this glorious height. It's . . . like soaring!" Caitlin gasped when Quinn set her down in the window bay.

"Turn round," he ordered, "and don't move. I want you there with the light behind you."

"Oh, Quinn, don't be so dramatic. I am *not* one of your paintings or a possession of yours to be studied as if I weren't really here at all. You make me feel like . . . like some trophy you've won, and I don't like it."

"Can't you ever keep still?" he demanded.

When she faced him, he was glaring at her, sinister and handsome, his eyes like soft summer smoke. "If you insist," Caitlin said, "I'll humor you this once, but don't think . . ." She lapsed into silence and simply waited for his next unpredictable move. Behind him at the far side of the room a fire burned, and paired candles flickered on a carved walnut mantle. The floor was intricately parqueted, and at its center hexagon there was a wide, high canopy bed, its graceful spindle posts free of drapery. There was a chaise longue upholstered in tailored blue wool moreen beside a low walnut table inlaid with ebony and fruitwoods. A single painting hung on each blue-gray paneled wall, with several drawings above the mantel.

"If I'm to stand bored and dull waiting for you to do something, tell me about your paintings."

"The nude after the bath there, coiling her hair with one hand, drying with the other," Quinn said, discarding his jacket, "was done by an old friend, a Parisian banker's son, De Gas, or Degas as he now calls himself."

"You? Old friends with a banker's son?" Caitlin gently scoffed, slipping into the chaise and curling up comfortably.

"Well, go on. Who's the lady with the large . . . blue eyes?"

"An acquaintance of Edouard Monet. She's got the most perfectly beautiful breasts I'd ever seen—until yours," he said, cupping Caitlin's in his hands when he came behind her. She let her head rest back against the chaise, and slowly he brought his lips down to hers.

"Get out of this dress," he said against her brow. "I'm tired of seeing you try to look like some prim little governess. You can't."

"But I haven't another and this one's already torn. What am I to wear?"

Quinn half-smiled and the hot growl was in his voice when he spoke. "I told you before: Nothing should ever touch your skin but shadow and light and lover's lips. I told you I'd keep you naked and ready in some sequestered seraglio and carnalize you . . . endlessly."

"It hasn't been *exactly* endlessly," Caitlin teased. "But close. There's not much I can do about it, is there, now you've lured me to your thief's hideaway."

"You begged to come with me, remember?" Quinn grinned.

"Begged isn't exactly the right word," Caitlin protested with a toss of her head. "And we do have . . . an arrangement. You will teach me certain things about playing the lady and in appreciation I'll, um . . . favor you with a little caress now and then, with a chaste stolen kiss when no one's there to see and—oh! Do stop," she giggled as he unceremoniously tumbled her onto the bed, the small tear in the bodice of the dress continuing its full length.

"I'll steal more than kisses, you hypocritical little tease," Quinn threatened, leaning above her, his lips at hers, his precise hands lost in her silken underthings.

"You always do," Caitlin said, working at his buttons, stopping to rake back his dark hair from his brow. "Well, all this thievery, my gypsy desperado, will cost you your fortune and your heart one day, and don't forget it."

"Don't you think you can threaten me, urchin," he half-laughed. "Do your worst. It'll do you no good. I'm a heartless heartbreaker, and I've never paid for my crimes yet."

"There's always a first time," Caitlin said softly.

Quinn rolled away and got to his feet to look at her as she lay in the downy softness of the big bed, her perfectly beautiful body aglow in soft lamp light, titian curls flowing over lace-covered pillows. Against this backdrop, she was all he could have imagined and more. But as he went to her now, the memory of their first time together in the rough beach shelter with the storm raging, the scent of pine and wood smoke swirling, came sweeping back. He saw her, felt her, as she'd been then, the wild, willing child-woman who'd loved him as no one had ever before.

When Caitlin awoke it was dark, and the long windows were black, reflecting the room. It was bathed in a rosy pink glow cast by what seemed dozens of oil lamps, their white porcelain bases intricately carved and cut away to expose the fine ruby glass beneath. The doors of a spacious armoire, mirrored on the inside, were thrown open, exposing a row of gowns in rainbow hues and, Caitlin found when she arose and crossed the floor to examine them, of superb material and manufacture. Extracting one, a blue silk with long sleeves and a square, low decolletage, Caitlin stood at the mirror, deciding it would fit almost perfectly. Draping it across the chaise, she moved toward a sliver of light at the edge of a door and opened it to find a small room—small for this mansion at any rate, she mused, barely twelve feet square, although the ceiling was high as in the other rooms. Angled across one corner was a small fireplace of white tile and mottled pink marble. There was a very large tub, full and steaming, also of pink marble. Above a matching dressing table an extraordinary painting was hung, a close view of a lavish nude woman sprawling back, legs apart, seeming almost to writhe with passion.

"How remarkable," Caitlin said as Quinn appeared in the doorway.

"Gustave Courbet did that on commission a few years ago for Khalil Bey, who was the Turkish ambassador to St. Petersburg for a time. It's called 'Origin of the World,' appropriately, I think. I took it off the Bey's hands when he was short of funds. Her flesh is as beautiful as a Renaissance nude."

"You keep dropping these . . . these ranks and titles—Turkish Beys and ambassadors, bankers' sons. Who is this Courbet now? A titled aristocrat, I suppose, who does this sort of brazen work as a hobby."

"Hardly. He's in jail at the moment."

"He sounds more your type—one of the criminal element."

"Gustave Courbet is a political prisoner

sentenced to death for helping run the Paris commune that's just fallen. He is a superb painter, a realistic one, and that's not in fashion. You can see all the voluptuous, naked women you want in European galleries, playing with cloven-hoofed satyrs or being seduced by swans in pastoral settings. But if an artist forgets to name his naked lady Leda or Aphrodite, his work is attacked as prurient. Speaking of brazen . . ." He lounged in the doorway, running his warm eyes over Caitlin. "You go about like some elemental mountain nymph, hiding nothing."

"But you said that's the way it should be," she flirted, stepping into the deliciously warm tub that Quinn had ordered to be filled. "And you like to look, so why complain?"

"Oh, I *do* like to look. And touch. And taste," Quinn answered with a wolfish glare that said even more than his words as Caitlin's satiny form disappeared beneath foamy bubbles.

"But we've serious business to get on with," he added reluctantly. "Turning a little urchin like you into a fine lady may take . . . a while. We'll start tonight by dressing for dinner. There are scents and combs in the table there, lingerie in the semanier, and gowns in the armoire. Dancy will be in to help you."

"But I want *you* to help me, not Dancy," Caitlin complained with a provocative laugh, sending a splash of water at Quinn's disappearing back. He pivoted about and was at the side of the tub in two long strides, pulling off his shirt.

"I'm not interested in hooks and lacing, so if you want help from me, you'll have to take it now. I'll start with your back. Lean forward," he ordered, going down on one knee at the side of the tub.

His fine hands, soap-smoothed, slid along Caitlin's back as she rolled her shoulders and purred like a petted kitten. When she rested back again luxuriously, arms crossed behind her head, her full breasts were lifted out of the water and Quinn brushed wisps of rainbow bubbles from the pink tip of each before his smooth hands began to mold, then his fingers to agitate them, bringing the nipples to standing firmness. He lightly kissed Caitlin's sweet, dreamy smile before he turned his caress to her slender legs, moving very slowly, tantalizingly, up along their firm, shapely length to linger between them. She sighed, her body beginning to undulate irresistibly as she arched forward to taste his lips, and then he was discarding the rest of his clothes, looming tall and dark over her for a brief moment until he stepped into the tub and knelt across her hips, his strong arms about her as he kissed her hungrily.

"Now," he growled, pulling her to her

knees, "you tend to me."

Facing him, their wet bodies glistening, Caitlin quickly ran a soft sliver of soap over one of Quinn's shoulders, then the other, and across his hard chest. Brushing against him purposefully, she reached around to do his back and his narrow hips and flanks before her touch slid down his belly to the full swell of him pressing against her. Laughing, the agitated water surging over the tub rim, they rinsed the last traces of soap from each other's bodies and backs and stood. Quinn lifted Caitlin with him as he stepped from the tub to stand dripping on the rug before the fire, and, when she brought her arms about his neck, her legs about his waist, he let her sleek, wet body slide down along his as he slowly invaded her soft depths.

"This whole wardrobe closet full of *beautiful* clothes—everything is new, never worn. Why?" Caitlin was inspecting herself in the armoire mirrors, back, front and sides, as Quinn emerged from his dressing room opposite the bath chamber.

"They were made for a lady who had a change of heart," he observed coldly. "The fit is almost perfect for you."

"I nipped in the waist and would've dropped the hem a half-inch if there'd been time, but otherwise the fit *is* perfect," Dancy commented. "But she needs some adornment at the throat with that low decolletage."

"Her natural attributes are adornment enough for the time." Quinn grinned, adjusting the cuffs of his dinner jacket over a silk shirt. "You, Dancy, are looking lovely, too."

She wore a dark green silk dress draped at the bosom and bustled, rounding her angular figure.

"Caitlin chose it for me from her . . . *your* collection." Dancy smiled.

"I haven't so looked forward to an evening since the last masked ball at The White Elephant!" Caitlin bubbled with her usual glittering exuberance. "*Do* let's go down. I'm starving and I want to see David Pallett and that Gordon, too, in dinner dress and . . . well, come *on*!" she insisted, taking Quinn's arm. He offered the other to Dancy and they swept from the room in a flourish of silk and Caitlin's pretty laughter.

"Miss Pallett, may I relieve Quinn of half of his delightful burden?" Gordon asked, crooking an elbow at Dancy. He was pacing and pivoting at the bottom of the stairs, a burning cigarette at the corner of his lips. His dinner jacket was loose and his shirt collar too large, but he'd shaved and brushed his dark hair and seemed genuinely pleased with the evening's prospects.

A bit flustered, embarrassment blotching her fair skin, Dancy slipped her arm through his as they entered the large drawing room where David was waiting. He, too, was dressed for dinner in the formal dark pants and double-breasted blazer of the Royal Navy, brass buttons polished, two stripes on his arm. His yellow hair was slicked to one side, and he seemed to Caitlin, in uniform, older and somewhat more serious than before.

"The cook's helper pressed these for me," he explained to his sister's startled exclamation. "They've been in the bottom of my duffel—"

"Should you be wearing *those* clothes, David?" she interrupted. "I mean, is it allowed . . . on shore and all?" Dancy questioned.

"Certainly no one here will ever give David away," Caitlin interjected, looking from one twin to the other, unable to decide which of them was fabricating. Both seemed ill at ease for a tense moment, until they smiled their matching smiles and the conversation, directed by Gordon, took another turn. Settling himself into one of the arm chairs brought to the drawing room from elsewhere in the house, waving the ladies to a settee, he took a swallow of the drink Quinn had handed him, smacked his lips, and raised his glass.

"Welcome home, Major. It's been a long time," Gordon rumbled.

"Major? Major of what?" Caitlin asked with

a prankish look over the rim of her sherry glass. "I didn't know that rough-scruff rabble fingersmiths conferred rank on their leaders."

"Young woman," Gordon exclaimed with a perplexed frown, blinking as smoke from his too-short cigarette bleared his eye. "Why do you keep making these slanderous remarks about Jones? He served his cause with great distinction at—"

"Don't try to protect me, Gordon," Quinn interrupted, catching the man's watery eye. "It's all right. Miss McGlory knows *something* about my alarming past and the *real* reason I've come here now, which is to lie low, what with the authorities and all. Understand, Gordon?"

Nodding, exploding into laughter that was quickly covered by a racking cough, Gordon lit a fresh smoke, emptied his glass, and resettled himself in his chair, wiping his eyes with a pocket handkerchief. "Blast it, Quinn, should you be saying such things in front of . . . well, can you trust her, or them?" He waved a hand in the direction of the twins.

"They won't give us away. They're fugitives, taken to the tall timber, like me," Quinn said very seriously, leaning on the mantle, elegantly relaxed. When Gordon nodded back at him just as seriously, he turned away from the company to face the fire.

"Is *she* wanted for something, too?" Gordon

gave Caitlin a piercing stare.

"No, not wanted, not *yet,* but she's one of us," Quinn said, glancing at Caitlin. "Her mother and father were wild and wicked. She's got their bad blood, of course. Her uncle told her so and worse that she won't even repeat."

"I'd never give any of you away, I *swear*!" Caitlin said, her very blue eyes wide and solemn. She sat up straight, her hands tightly clasped in her lap.

"Of course you wouldn't." Gordon nodded vehemently, leaning to pat her shoulder.

"But, Caitlin," Dancy protested, "you've no reason . . . you've never done a wicked thing in your life, I'd swear!"

"That is definitely not what my uncle thinks," Caitlin said angrily. "He says I'm a . . . fallen woman, ruined, with no future. But I'll show him if it takes the rest of my days!"

"Miss McGlory has a plan for her future," Quinn announced in an almost malevolent tone that made Caitlin uneasy. With the fire behind him, his face was in shadow. His hands were on his hips, his long legs planted wide. "And we're all going to help Caitlin accomplish her ends," he concluded.

"Of course we are," Gordon nodded sagely with a blink of his eyes for emphasis and a shake of his dark head. "But how?" he asked, "and, bye the bye, what *is* this plan?"

"Miss McGlory, my friends"—Quinn laughed coldly striding to the center of the vast, candle lit room—"Miss McGlory, sitting so sweet and innocent among us even now, is planning to become . . . an adventuress!"

"A *what*?" Gordon bellowed. "This angelic child wants to be . . . ?"

"Exactly right, sir." Quinn laughed, flicking back an errant lock of dark hair.

Gordon's eyes narrowed and he held silent, waiting for Quinn to go on.

"This angelic child, as Gordon describes her, is intent upon becoming a *lady*—superficially, at least—so that she can take herself off to England and snare a rich, titled lord under false pretenses, then invite her saloon keeper uncle to tea at the castle . . . by way of revenge, you understand."

"How cruel of her," Gordon offered, with mock seriousness.

"Don't jest," Caitlin commanded with brittle determination. "I mean to do what I plan."

"How may we help?" Gordon asked eagerly.

"We've got to polish the lady's beautiful, though slightly rough edges, gentle her speech, teach her the finer points of manners and manner—to move with mincing, tiny steps instead of striding aggressively across a room, to hold her hands limply at her waist and keep her head at a coquettish tilt, or, in other words, turn her into the kind of fragile, frigid creature that certain Englishmen expect their wives to be, though not their mistresses, of course," Quinn pronounced, his tone heavy with sarcasm. "You, Gordon, must converse with Miss McGlory, teach her the art of repartee, help her develop the wit and quickness of mind needed by an intriguer who would charm her victim into a trap."

"Fortunately, the raw material we've got to work with is superb. She is already witty and charming and beautiful enough to captivate a king, but I'll do what I can," Gordon promised with a laugh.

"Dancy, as a former member—governess, wasn't it?—of a great English house, you know how to run a schoolroom, which you will do here, every morning," Quinn continued, pacing, his voice ringing in the nearly empty room, his footfalls lost in the depth of the grand carpet.

"I've *been* to school," Caitlin protested.

"She quotes Voltaire to me," Gordon rumbled.

"She picked *that* up from my friend, Dr. Burleigh. She's got a good memory, but an education . . . She attended, briefly, some silly dame school for the daughters of ambitious American tradesmen. If she's to entangle a Duke of . . . oh, Gloucester, of Westminster, or Buccleuch, she must have a taste of French, of drawing, of music of course, but more important she must understand how her prey thinks and lull him into a false contentment and security by behaving exactly as a grandly brought up daughter of an English Duke would behave."

"They *are* unique," Dancy said, laughing. The Outerbridge girls that I grew up with tended to care for their ponies and dogs more than anything else in the world. They were always surrounded by beautiful things that they seemed to have absolutely no interest in at all. I mean, the family statues had all their noses broken by cricket balls and no one even seemed to notice. That sort of thing."

"Really?" Caitlin giggled. "How odd, but must I know *that* sort of thing?"

"Can't hurt," Gordon said, "and these eccentricities are amusing when related so charmingly by Miss Pallett."

Dancy's face blotched a little when she acknowledged the compliment with a smile, then she hurriedly looked away. "And what use will David be in all this, Mr. Jones?" she asked.

"David signed on the *Aglaia* as a man's man, a jack of all trades, including valet, so he must know how to take orders. The stripes on his sleeve lead me to think he can give them, too. He'll be able to teach Caitlin to run a staff, to keep her liveried servants moving, quiet, and efficient, through the long corridors of a great house. Will you do it, David?"

David nodded once with a calculating stare at Quinn as though gauging him anew, reevaluating him somehow.

"But you could teach the lady the manner of command as well as I could, *Major*," he said quietly, "*if* she needs teaching at all."

"Thank *you*, David," Caitlin said. Then, looking archly at Quinn with a touch of irritation, she asked, "What will be *your* contribution to my transformation?"

"Me? Why, you *know*," he scoffed, his suggestive smile bringing a quick flush to Caitlin's cheek. He winked before she could loose a verbal attack and added, "To ride and shoot, of course, like a Cossack."

"Like an Arab, I thought." She smiled, her eyes ablaze with anticipation.

"Whichever you prefer. Now, may I escort you to dinner?" he asked as a uniformed servant appeared at the drawing room door.

"What do I do for a . . . *crust*?" Gordon repeated, looking aghast at David Pallett until understanding changed his expression to one of delight. "You mean, how do I earn my living! Quaintly phrased, boy. Right now, I don't do anything. I rely on the generosity of a friend and for considerably more than a crust as the remains of this meal testify. I did do work once. I was an investigator for Dunn & Co."

"A detective, Gordon? You?" Caitlin asked as the serving girl began to clear away.

"Of a sort. I did credit reports about Western businessmen for Dunn. He sold the information to New York wholesalers. That's how I first met Quinn, in Galena, at his father's bank, just before the war."

"His father's . . . ?" Caitlin questioned again.

"Yes, father kept what little he had at the First National Bank of Galena," Quinn explained, shaking his head sadly. "He was trying to order yard goods on credit from an eastern merchant when Gordon came poking about. I never blamed you, Gordon, for telling the truth about Dad."

"Generous of you, Quinn. I've said so before." Gordon nodded. "Yes, Jones Senior had a fiery temper; got him in trouble; got him threatened with criminal prosecution once. I had to report that—I had no choice—but that was the last of those reports I ever did for Dunn. The war broke out and I went home to Georgia to fight, dreaming all the while of boughs laden with peaches and peaceful, slow summer days. After it ended, I fled civilization which I found corrupt and cruel. I went into the mountains, the Appalachians, to gather wild ginseng that I traded for tea mostly, in China."

"I should have liked to see China, but I never did get a ship destined for Far Eastern ports," David said wistfully as Dancy coughed into her napkin.

"Macao is an unequaled city of sin. The flower boats offer everything a man could dream of and some things he couldn't even imagine."

"Flower boats?" David asked.

"Floating brothels. Pardon me, ladies," Gordon huffed. "Well, when my host throws me out"—he coughed—"come with me to the Amazon, boy, for rubber. Actually for seeds of the rubber plant. The first man to smuggle them out will make a small fortune, or, a large one."

"Gold, diamonds, now it's rubber fever." David nodded. "But where will you grow the seeds if you do get them out of Brazil? The climate—"

"Ceylon, boy, or Java. Climate's perfect politically and geographically. The British know how to make the most of a valuable resource. It'll be banana fever next, mark me. If you want to know another way to make a fortune, now's the time to build a plantation in the tropics and get a head start on bananas."

"David doesn't need to build a fortune," Dancy insisted. "We need a home, but surely not in the tropics with all those insects and crawly things. You Americans would do *anything* for money. Lord Outerbridge says money's the only thing that tells you who you are."

"But Dancy, dear, one must have money. You don't want to spend your days amidst cheese parings and candle ends," Caitlin protested.

"There's nothing so respectable in America, Dancy, as turning a profit," Gordon said quickly, dominating the conversation again. "And really, young woman, thrown on one's own resources as each of us in this room has been one way or another, what's one to do but become master of one's own fate? As much as one ever can, of course. Especially in tempestuous rags-to-riches times like these, it takes an act of the imagination to succeed. Besides, 'Those who have done nothing in life are not qualified to judge those who have done little.' Like me. Dr. Johnson said it and I—"

"Gordon, really! We're ganging up on her and that's not fair," Caitlin complained. "You've no idea what Dancy may have done before. Besides, Democratus said, 'To do all the talking and not be willing to listen is a form of greed.'" Caitlin laughed. "You are *very* greedy, Gordon."

There was a moment of stunned silence during which Gordon lit a new cigarette and, to Quinn's amusement, actually blushed.

Dancy's stricken expression changed to one of vindication. David, long fingers restlessly tracing first his spoon, then his cup, and finally his glass, let a smile touch one corner of his lips and light his green eyes.

"If there's one thing I absolutely detest in a woman, Quinn," Gordon said finally with a mournful look and gloomy smile, "it's reticence and ambiguity, qualities totally lacking in *this* woman. Caitlin, I think we shall be fast friends." He grinned. "And Miss Pallett?" He turned to Dancy. "My apologies. Actually, I admire your emphatic respectability. I'd be quite willing to drown with decorum with just such a lady as you, enjoying the safe comforts of the fireside, but, alas, those pleasures will never be mine, I'm afraid. The only women who've ever been willing to put up with me have been Cyprians and sluts, and calculating, tasteless little tarts who've drained me of my strength and wealth and left me as you see me now, my friends—an empty husk, a shadow of my former, too-trusting, robust self." Gordon sighed dramatically, exhaling a long plume of smoke.

"You've been unlucky at love, poor Gordon!" Caitlin commiserated, and Dancy leaned toward him across the table, her eyes brimming with sympathy.

"Isn't everyone?" Gordon sighed more deeply, rolling his eyes at the ceiling.

"Not Caitlin McGlory. She was born under a lucky star," Quinn announced with a touch of irony. He stood, pushed back his chair, and held hers while Gordon helped Dancy. "Dancy." Quinn winked, catching her eye. "Be careful. This reprobate, Gordon, is trying to play on your sympathies and weaken your defenses. There's coffee in the music room."

A bent-side mahogany spinet and a harp stood near tall windows at one end of the music room that was papered with scenic landscapes surrounded by scrolls and flourishes. A tray waited on a low table between matched Chippendale love seats and upholstered chairs.

"Caitlin will do the honors. She needs the experience," Quinn said, delivering her to a love seat and settling beside her.

"You pour very prettily," David said with a smile, accepting a filled cup. "For all your good intentions, Major, I don't think any of us has much to teach *her*."

"She does do everything with a certain natural grace and style. Where did you learn to do *this*?" Quinn asked in the velvety low voice Caitlin warmed to so quickly.

"I don't know, really." She smiled, handing him a gold-rimmed cup in a fine china saucer. "It's as if I'd watched someone pour formal tea . . . coffee, in this case, but I can't think where. Surely not at Billy's. I've so many untraced memories I can't call up. I had the same feeling as we came through the stone arch this afternoon. I told you so. What are you doing?"

Quinn poured rum from his silver flask into the steaming cups of coffee they were drinking and Dancy sipped hers cautiously before pronouncing it pleasantly palatable.

"Uncle Billy served an Irish coffee made with whiskey and sugar syrup and whipped cream that was always a favorite on fall and winter evenings," Caitlin recalled. Suddenly restless and warmed by the rum, she became all at once mercurial and agitated. Unable to sit still, she rose to explore the room, the smallest and most completely furnished of any in Quinn's magnificent, half-built mansion.

"I almost peroxided my hair once, did I tell you?" she asked, catching her own reflection in a darkened window as she released her sweep of auburn curls to tumble in flamboyant abundance about her shoulders.

"Now, Caitlin, really," Gordon huffed. "To describe *your* hair as merely 'light brown' doesn't begin to do you justice, but you and Stephen Foster's *Jeannie* hold center stage in this day and time. Fashions do change, of course, but right now blondes are considered . . . a little insipid, brunettes, spirited and warm. Redheads"—he winked at Dancy—"are said to be positively afire with passion. So why on earth, Caitlin, would you even consider making such an alteration in your extraordinary appearance?"

"It was the British blondes. They came to The White Elephant, you see, and they were so adored that all the girls wanted to be like them," Caitlin explained patiently.

"The *what* came to *where*?" David laughed, crossing the room to stand beside Caitlin at the window. As the evening had progressed, his manner had changed very subtly from boyish deference to subdued confidence. In his well-cut uniform, puffing one of Gordon's tailor-made cigarettes and sipping his coffee, David projected an urbane sophistication that perplexed Caitlin a little and further piqued her interest in the twins.

"The White Elephant is my uncle's dance hall, and the British blondes are a burlesque troupe from England, of course, who all peroxided. They are very popular in New York. Their stage door johnnies would bring them to our place to dance after they'd finished their show. They sang really bawdy songs at the music hall but only taught me sweet ones." Caitlin giggled. "Is the spinet to be used or is it for show?" she asked Quinn, lifting the lid.

"To be used, of course," he said quizzically, bemused by Caitlin once again as, adjusting the bench, her full skirts billowing about her, she touched the keys with tapered fingers and launched into a coquettish burlesque ballad that she performed with all the charm of a skilled comedienne. The words, milder than those of most concert saloon songs, made Dancy's face very blotchy none-the-less.

"Miss Pallett, there's no need for embarrassment over *this* stuff. Now, there are certain Elizabethan ballads that bring a blush even to my sallow, sunken cheeks, in gentle company at any rate. The popular song, once a Paean to gods of fertility, has always had a certain risqué quality." Coming to lean at the piano, round shouldered and gaunt, Gordon applauded enthusiastically.

"Bravo! Bravo, Caitlin. I saw the Blondes in Boston two years ago when they began their tour. There's not one of them does that number better, is there, Quinn?"

"Probably not," Quinn mused, loosening his tie and stretching his legs toward the fire, "though Eliza Buck did a creditable performance costumed in fleshings and high boots that always brought down the house."

"She was dressed in what?" Dancy asked, wide-eyed.

"Fleshings . . . skin-toned tight things that hug the body *very* closely. Some of the burlesque troupes reproduce nude scenes from the classics dressed that way. They might just as well have really been naked, *I* heard," Caitlin explained. "The police were always raiding them and the ones who do the high kicks, but they're never closed down for long."

"You *are* well informed about New York lowlifers, aren't you?" Gordon remarked. "Give us another song while I serve up some brandy."

"Oh, I've a funny one! It's done usually by a girl wearing lots of petticoats," Caitlin explained. "I'll just . . . sing it."

"I've a little pink petty from Peter
And a little blue petty from John
One green and one yellow from some other fellow
And one that I haven't got on.
I've a lovely one made of red satin
That came from an old Dublin store,
But the point that I'm at is that underneath that
I haven't got on any more!"

"Encore! Encore!" Gordon cheered again over a rush of notes. "Do it over—this time with all the right moves."

"Oh, she *wouldn't*," Dancy squealed. "David, aren't you sorry now we didn't go to New York? See what you've missed!" She laughed.

"Caitlin, your titled British lord may be startled by your repertoire"—Quinn gifted her with one of those incomparable smiles—"but your musical talents are apparent. Now, if you can draw at all, there'll be only riding and shooting for you to be taught, and a few subtleties of behavior."

"Taught by you, of course," she flirted, full mouth pursed.

"You just want to keep her all to herself, Major," David complained half-jokingly.

"He's always been possessive of his new toys," Gordon offered. "I've known him since—"

"Toys?" Caitlin exclaimed. "Stow it, gents. I'm no one's toy and I never will be!" She stood, brought down the spinet lid with an emphatic thud, and stalked toward the door, her bouncing curls adding emphasis to her curt good night.

"Caitlin, don't go! You'll give us all the glooms if you do," Dancy pleaded, starting after her. "And we're having such a nice time, nicer than I can remember in so long."

"I always say the wrong thing, damn it," Gordon moaned. "That's why no self-respecting woman's ever had anything to do with me . . . for long. You're so sweet natured and kind, Caitlin. Don't go and make me suffer pangs of guilt and regret all night long because I've chased you away. If you stay, we'll have a game of table croquet or bezique or tiddly winks."

"I once got a double bezique—two Queens of spades, two knaves of diamonds—five hundred points right off," Caitlin said, turning to face the company just at the door, her dazzling cheerfulness restored with the childlike quickness that always made Quinn smile.

"I'll forgive you this time, Gordon," Caitlin offered with a lift of her shoulders. "Let's try croquet and gin. I used to enjoy a nip at The White Elephant before bedtime."

"You *have* had an . . . interesting upbringing. Don't take offense, Caitlin, but in England the better classes consider gin's only for sailors and whores," David said.

"I shall have to give it up then, won't I? But not until I'm there. What else should I know?" She helped set out the little wire wickets on a green felt-covered table as Dancy distributed miniature mallets.

"Well, for one thing, if you want to maintain your vivacity, the etiquette books say you must refuse to play at games late into the evening. Avoid reading novels, of course, especially by candlelight if you want clear eyes and a fresh complexion."

"I've often stayed up 'til dawn watching the goings on at Billy's place, and that doesn't seem to have done much to my vivacity. Quinn, will you play?" Caitlin wanted to know.

"No. I'm going to look over the paintings once more. They'll be catalogued and crated with everything else, starting tomorrow." He slipped out of his jacket and turned back the cuffs of his shirt as he left the room.

"What's he mean 'crated'?" Gordon demanded as he eyed the croquet table eagerly, brandishing his little mallet.

"Didn't he tell you? He's closing the place down," Caitlin explained.

"I suppose it's the Amazon for me, then, sooner than anticipated," Gordon answered disinterestedly, but he had gone a little pale, Caitlin thought, as a large ash dropped from the cigarette he held in a shaking hand.

Chapter Thirteen

Caitlin was standing partly undressed, at the long windows of the bedroom, soaked in autumn moonlight.

"What will Gordon do when you turn him out?" she asked when Quinn entered.

"Don't worry about Gordon. Come here," he answered with a little snap of his fingers.

"I'll never come to any man's whistle, or the equivalent," she said with a silvery laugh, starting toward him, "unless I choose to. He cheats at croquet."

"If you're as lucky at love as you claim to be, you'll fling yourself into someone's arms before the last whistle note fades," Quinn said as she came into his arms eagerly, her pert breasts brushing his chest as she let her shawl, which had been draped over her bare shoulders, fall away. He gathered up handfuls of her auburn hair that was glossy in the moonlight.

"Yes, Gordon does cheat at games, but you can trust him with important things—like your life and your honor—unless he's under the influence of too much joy water. He gets in his cups on rare occasions. You're cold. Come to the fire. I've something for you to wear."

He brought an ivory satin gown from the armoire, lace ruching to the waist, on the bodice, and along the straps. The matching robe was full and flowing, with puffed shoulders and deep, banded sleeves.

"Even when Ann made all those *lovely* things for me, she never did such a sumptuous thing as this!" Caitlin sighed. "It's like pictures of Juliet in a book I had at school. Come onto the balcony with me!" she laughed, twirling before the mirror, then flinging open the doors and gliding to the parapet, her natural elegance heightened by the billowing gown and wrap as she waited smiling in the moonlight for Quinn to follow. When he didn't come quickly enough to suit her, she climbed onto the marble railing and sat dangling her legs over the side, the forest swirling in a rising wind like a dark ocean far below.

"Get down," Quinn commanded furiously, "and come in here!"

She stood, laughing, her curls lifted by the wind, the soft gown sheathing her slender body like a glove and flaring out behind her, then tiptoed the parapet with the unconcern of a tightrope walker, her balancing arms extended out to either side until Quinn, taking her by surprise, folded his arms about her and tipped her over his shoulder. He delivered a serious slap to her conveniently positioned bottom before he let her slide along his length to the terrace stones that were dampened now by a sprinkling of icy rain. The moon was cut by ragged, fast-moving clouds that almost obscured its light.

"What did you do that for?" Caitlin pouted, pulling away angrily.

"You were behaving like a naughtly little girl and not too clever a one at that. One false step. . . ."

"I was looking for Romeo," she teased, fluttering long lashes at him. "You're behaving like some fusty old dolt."

"No Romeo ever climbed to a balcony hundreds of feet above a forest, not with a storm howling in his ears that's roared a thousand miles up the Atlantic to this wreck-haunted coast. If he'd had to do that, there'd have been no story. Now get inside before I do turn you over my knee," he concluded ominously.

"How sensible we are," she taunted, laughing, edging toward the door. "You never take chances, I suppose? Well, I'll go in because I'm cold, not because—oh, don't you dare!" Caitlin giggled as Quinn started toward her, scampering away to wait shivering near the fire while he secured the balcony doors.

The storm had rapidly become a gale roaring round the mountain, isolating them in its blanket of sound. The fire flared and jumped in the strong chimney draft and the candles flickered.

"Not stupid chances, I don't. There's always a reason when I put myself at risk," Quinn answered with a scowl. He pulled a satin quilt from the bed, draped it over his bare shoulders like a cape, then gathered Caitlin inside it too, his hard mouth finding hers moist and soft and deliciously warm.

"Now, the part of *Romeo and Juliet* I like best isn't the balcony scene. It's where he helps her out of her clothes, with all their Renaissance charm and detail, like the pretty fastening at the throat of your gown, and those along the bodice."

Quinn had let the comforter fall. He gently slid Caitlin's robe from her shoulders, letting it drop away before carrying her to the soft, big bed and placing her at its center, her hair flowing over satin sheets and lace pillows, one strap of the bed gown slipping from a rounded shoulder. Everything about Caitlin—her innocent and inviting half-smile, her soft eyes, violet as a dawn sky, the easy placement of graceful limbs—seemed a near perfect picture to Quinn as he studied her with the detached, evaluating look she was coming to find infuriating.

"You're doing it again, studying me like I was some sort of statue or picture, as if I weren't here, really." Caitlin shivered and his expression was at once warmed by his smile.

"You should have been painted by Ingrés," he whispered, leaning to her lips, then extending his hard body along hers, his fine hands sculpting, moving, working her supple body, starting in motion those galactic swirls of pleasure that made her weak limbed and warm and wanting.

"Who's Ingrés?" Caitlin had been awake since the first light, covertly watching Quinn. Through the open bath chamber door she'd seen him rise from the tub and towel himself dry before a blazing fire. With a towel about his hips, he'd shaved at the glass above the wash stand. He'd crossed to his dressing room and emerged soon after in well-fitted, worn suede and tweed before he went to the bedroom door for his Wellingtons, polished and left by a servant before dawn.

Caitlin spoke, thinking he was about to leave, wanting to keep him in her sight. He seemed to her Adonis and Hercules in one, sleekly handsome but rugged, too, and strong. The ruthless, lupine look in his severe face and in his fine gray eyes was stunning.

"Billy used to let me watch *him* shaving," she said, sitting up naked and stretching, her ineffable vibrancy lighting her eyes. "He did it at the fire, too, in his room, wearing a red silk dressing gown. He kept his old boxing gloves hanging on the mantle . . . always five or six bottles of Krug's Extra Dry on the sideboard."

"He has good taste. But you're not supposed to be spying on me—that's my prerogative." A warming expression displaced the animal coldness in Quinn's face. "You're missing Billy," he said, watching Caitlin pull a lace-edged sheet up over her breasts as a knock sounded at their door. Quinn took a large tray laden with covered silver dishes from a maid and crossed the room to set it on the table placed near the long windows.

"Join me for breakfast?" he asked, draping a linen napkin over a chair arm.

"Of course I miss Billy. I used to love him, remember? It doesn't just stop . . . love. Who was Ingrés?" she asked again abruptly, her violet eyes that had betrayed a moment's sadness almost belligerently bright again.

"A Parisian painter obsessed with the nude form—of women, of course."

"Of course." Caitlin laughed. She draped a quilt about her in a Grecian fall and came to the table, uncovering one dish after another to appraise their contents with pleasure.

"It's a very English breakfast—part of your education," Quinn offered in the tone that was a little cruel and edged with anger.

"How very helpful of you," she responded with a wicked laugh. "My English lord will owe you a debt he'll never even be aware of. What's this?"

"Oatcake soaked in buttermilk—that's Welsh—but Nova Scotia's been heavily settled by Scots, so there's Aberdeen sausage and quince marmalade from Dundee, fried eggs, kippers, ham, tongue, green and brown teas, chocolate—very British—coffee, of course—American. You'll serve."

She did, with her usual grace that Quinn found so pleasing, as if she presided over a grand table, even though her hair was still lovely in sleep-tossed disorder and her quilt needed constant readjustment to preserve any semblence of modesty. She ate enthusiastically in silence except for occasional comments about the food as she tried one dish after another, until she looked up with a little start and met Quinn's amused eyes.

"Oh, sorry! I forgot to make proper table talk." She laughed, settling back in her chair to sip gunpowder-green tea, thick with sugar and cream.

"What a beautiful cup," she commented, holding it to the light, "and this silver and the stemware . . . it's all lovely. Some people would keep such fine things under glass, just for looking at."

"They *are* old and valuable," Quinn said, "and beautiful. But if they were kept in a vitrine like museum pieces, I'd forget to look at them and they'd give me no pleasure. Using them, I enjoy them and—*now* what are you doing?"

She'd risen to inspect the room in daylight, moving about like a kitten after dust motes, drawn at random from one object to another, very pleased with it all.

"The forest is *blazing*!" she announced when she reached the windows and gazed out into morning light that was like fire in the wet trees. "Let's ride now! Is that all right?" she appealed.

"It's all right," Quinn answered, "*if* you'll sit down and try to converse just until I finish my coffee. You can do your studies with the others later, when I tend to some business."

"What shall we talk about?" she asked, perching tentatively at the edge of her chair. "I know—the twins! Which one of them do *you* think is protecting the other?"

"What makes you think either is?" Quinn asked, testing her, though he'd decided the same himself.

"It's the only explanation that makes any sense at all," she answered. "I mean, they tell these stories that are somewhat alike, but not really the same, about what's happened to them and why they are here. None of it seems quite right somehow. I don't think they ever were servants or drapers' helpers or whatever. He's so soft spoken and self-assured and she's so, so . . . polished and ladylike."

"And she seems spun out and nervous whenever he mentions certain things . . . the Navy, for example." Quinn passed his cup for refilling.

"Well, which one do you think is lying?" Caitlin asked, refilling his cup.

"Both," Quinn answered with a fast smile. "I'll make inquiries. My contacts in Wales will know."

"*Your* contacts," Caitlin scoffed, "won't know about *those* two. David and Dancy aren't of the criminal classes, that's clear."

"Why don't *you* try to learn the truth?" Quinn shrugged. "If you blink your innocent eyes at him, or tell him one of your own little secrets, that might work."

"Confidences can't be shared, though," she said with her childlike seriousness. "I wouldn't be able to tell *you* anything."

"I'll go about it in my own fashion and let you know what I discover. That way, you won't be put in an awkward position, will you? Now, get dressed. I want to see you in the wine wool riding costume, the one with the plaited leather buttons. It should fit you nicely."

"Of course it will. All of these clothes were made for the same woman, or did you have several lined up, in case one didn't suit you?"

The wardrobe closet, overflowing with magnificent things, inflamed Caitlin's curiosity and jealousy, too, she had to admit. Someone, some time, not so long ago, had moved Quinn to extraordinary expense and generosity, had so captured his attention that he'd obviously given great care and thought to every item of clothing she'd wear, every fragment of lace and satin that would touch her skin. Each brooch and pin and ring in the jewel chest was perfectly beautiful. Hair bands and gloves were finely made, boots and wraps were suede and leather and the finest wools, some even lined with fur. The ball gowns alone, with magnificent skirts and yards of fabric, required a separate closet.

"Will you ever tell me who these were made for?" Caitlin asked again when she'd dressed and was standing before Quinn, who eyed her from the hem up slowly, then stood and loosened her hair that had been primly coiled and undid the plaited buttons from the throat to the top swell of her breasts.

"Maybe they were made for you. Anyway, they're yours."

"Don't you trifle with me," she admonished, an edge of irritation in her voice.

"I'm not trifling. You should have them, but remember one thing—don't ever go about done up so tight. Women who do seem to be binding in their warmth and desires as if they were afraid of their own passion."

He encircled Caitlin's tiny waist, then slid his hands up along her ribs to her soft breasts. "That's not at all what you're about, is it, holding back your passions?" He kissed her lightly.

"No. It won't ever be," she agreed with a sparkling glance. "But if you don't tell who these clothes were made for . . . you didn't even know me, so how could—"

"I always knew you," he interrupted laconically, guiding her to the door with a firm hand at the small of her back.

"Now, get going and don't chatter at me. I've more to do than dally with you all morning, and the others will be waiting to begin their instructions as soon as you return from your riding and shooting lessons with me."

Caitlin and Quinn breakfasted then rode every morning of that long, slow Nova Scotia autumn, a memorably golden one in a country notable for sweeping fall fogs and damp. They were only gradually able, after the night's intimacies, to relinquish each other to the day's demands. Their growing reluctance to be apart at all led them to lengthening excursions through the apple-laden orchards of the Annapolis Valley and even farther, to the shores of Fundy Bay. They raced over the glistening mud flats, past fishermen harvesting the day's catch in horse-drawn wagons, the stranded creatures struggling in vertical nets left silhouetted against the sky by the outrush of the wild Fundy tides. It was there that Caitlin really learned to ride. Supple and confident as a circus performer, she could, before long, keep her seat perfectly at full gallop, holding a pistol in each hand and never missing her target.

Exhilarated by her own skill and daring, responding to everything about her with her usual breathless intensity, Caitlin was ready to hurl herself into Quinn's arms as soon as they reached their special place in the pines—a rough shelter he'd built on their first ride out. Her jubilant abandon would make him laugh aloud as he tackled her to bring her down on top of him. The two, rolling about like a pair of rough and tumble young animals, playfully scuffled beneath the tall trees until the fragrance of the pines had its usual aphrodisiac effect on them both and changed the nature of the amorous game they played.

The constancy and generosity of his attentions, his total if temporary absorption with her, delighted Caitlin. She responded with a gentleness taught by deepening, though hidden love and a heightening sensitivity to everything about her, particularly to Quinn. She began to anticipate his dark, sweeping changes of mood and found she was often able to distract him by enticing him into a ride or walk or by gathering the others for cards or charades, a parlor game at which her particular comedic talents shone.

Her favorite times with Quinn were after their morning rides. He seemed to take the greatest pleasure in watching her dress and comb and fuss at her dressing table. She glowed in the warmth of this pointed attention. He picked her dress for the day from the pastel rainbow in the closet and told her it pleased him to see her with a cameo at the throat and with a ribbon in her hair, always worn, as he'd demanded, soft and flowing. Before he would let her leave the room, he would insist on some small change in her costume—a different sash or brooch, a pearl ring instead of a ruby, or more rings, so that often she wore one on every slender finger. It was as if he were putting his imprint on her somehow or asserting possession, and Caitlin, who found her image in his gray eyes growing more vivid with each passing day, made no protest or complaint.

Finally, he'd deliver her to Dancy, who was waiting patiently in the sun room where more rattan and wicker furnishings had materialized. He'd slide into a chair or lean in the doorway listening to the sound of the girls' pretty voices before he'd finally be ready to deprive himself of Caitlin's company—for a while, at least.

"Caitlin, the man's in love with you. I *know* it," Dancy pronounced one day as soon as Quinn had gone. It was during the second week of their stay at the mansion in the hills.

"Idiot," Caitlin giggled happily, "he's no such thing! I was told all about him by one who knew quite well whereof she spoke—Miss Overton, a family friend." Caitlin rolled her eyes dramatically heavenward and clasped her hands over her heart before going on. "Quinn Jones loves *all* women, every one of us, and his intimate, appreciate manner and devastating boyish smile are just the tools of his philanderer's trade. So says Ann. Women are collectables for Quinn, like his paintings and antiques, though he really does seem to enjoy feminine company immensely. Anyway, I've had fair warning and I intend to try to heed it. Now, shall we get on with the day's lessons or is there something else on your mind?"

"It's your company he enjoys," Dancy insisted as they started with French, which was always a pleasure for them both. Caitlin's drawings, on the other hand, totally lacked perspective and became a great joke between them, though her calligraphy was perfect, her letters beautifully formed, gracefully thickened, and curled.

David took Caitlin in charge when Dancy had done with her for the day. On their first afternoon together he briefly explained that the housekeeper and butler of a noble establishment ran everything, as the couple brought up from Halifax did here at the mansion. If her plan to snare a rich aristocrat did succeed, as David had no doubt it would, she'd never have to trouble herself about domestic matters at all.

This pleased Caitlin very much, and from then on she and David, wearing sheepskin boots and wool capes, took to the grass paths that circled the mansion and walked briskly in the chilling fall afternoons, round and round it, David speaking without pause about his home in the accented lilt she loved. She listened intently, even when he unconsciously lapsed from English into Welsh—his native tongue, he said. The first time he'd done it, she's just let the lovely musical flow of sound surround her until she found herself, to her surprise, actually understanding some of what he said. This so delighted David that he decided their hours together could best be spent in his teaching her the old Celtic language of his ancestors that was still spoken in Wales. It was to be their secret, an intended surprise for the others, especially Dancy, who, David was sure, would be delighted to hear the language of home from someone besides himself.

Caitlin's sessions with Gordon were riotous, contentious, and loud. They took place in the music room because he liked her to perform her rowdy dancehall songs while he sat slumped in a deep chair, wreathed in cigarette smoke, brandy bottle in easy reach, laughing and applauding when the spirit moved him. Caitlin would begin by indulging him with one abbreviated song; then, sitting like a child at his feet, she would employ her best flirtatious wiles, hoping to pry information about Quinn's past from Gordon's lips, which were—on that subject alone—sealed.

"I grew up in a large white farmhouse, my girl, with shade trees all around and five brothers and sisters, and three orphan cousins we were raising, too. Father was a doctor, an educated doctor, a gentleman, who never made nearly enough to feed us all, so we worked the farm." Gordon made this informative statement in response to a question from Caitlin about Quinn's relations. "Now, my little sister, Marigold," he continued, "whom I haven't seen in five years, married a Hoyt, I think, and moved to—"

"Gordon, my love," Caitlin smiled, patting his hand, "I'm sure Marigold is a charming girl, but I asked you to tell me about Quinn's family, didn't I?"

"Quinn's got no sisters or brothers, either,"

Gordon said quickly. "Now, when I first left home, when I came away from that Georgia farm, I wasn't as much of a country lout as some, Father being a doctor and people always in the parlor waiting, ready to talk to a boy."

An ash dropped on his sleeve. Caitlin brushed it away. "Did you go to Galena straight off and meet Quinn there or—"

"To New Orleans, the queen of cities, Caitlin, a paradise softened by the sea and the French and those beautiful octoroons with mocha skin and lilting voices. I took my hard-earned pittance to the turf and gaming tables and to the cock fights, and I won and won and won! And that, Miss McGlory, I'll have you know, was my downfall. Prosperity was more than my virtue could bear. Well, money's bad for some people, does something to them, and of course, youngster that I was, with a respectable upbringing, I had no savvy. I was prey to every come-hither smile and suggestive glance from every fornicatrix and Delilah in The Quarter. Sadly, my girl, we no more choose our passions than the color of our eyes." He sighed dramatically.

"I heard that Quinn was wild as a boy, too—always getting into scrapes with the ladies."

"There's not a woman in the world Quinn couldn't keep under his thumb if he wanted, which he doesn't, and of course, wealth never upset *his* equilibrium. He was born to the silver spoon . . ."

"Silver spoon? I thought his father was a failed merchant," Caitlin said, getting to her feet in a flurry.

"On his mother's side . . . it was the mother came from wealth, but of course she didn't have it long, once the old man got his hands on it," Gordon answered, taking a long swallow of brandy and staring into the fire when Caitlin tried to read his eyes.

"Did I ever tell you how I did meet Quinn?" he asked, knowing the subject would distract her quickly. "After New Orleans—I left there stone broke and broken hearted, down and out, and fleeced by one tart or another—I made my way to New York, put on the one suit of good clothes I still had, and became a professional guest in the best parlors, gifting one and all with my wit and charm. Life was just one long party . . . for a time."

"Professional guest? I never heard of such a thing." Caitlin laughed. "You, of all people!"

"In England, hostesses do actually pay a witty, charming man such as myself to attend their evenings and weekends if an invited guest should fall ill and unbalance the table. Fill my glass once more, there's a nice girl," Gordon said, barely stopping for breath. "In New York, payment is less direct, but only a little—an inside tip on a horse, on railroad stock, lots for sale—that sort of thing helps a boy get ahead and I did. Ah, Caitlin!" Gordon sighed heavily. "'What a fine comedy this world would be if one didn't have to play a part in it.' Know who said that?"

She shook her head vehemently, near exasperation at his verbal meandering when what she was most interested in, he avoided with clever cunning.

"Diderot," Gordon said. "The French philosopher—eighteenth century, very influential."

"Oh," she answered, turning from him, clenching her fists and pacing, her silk skirt swirling. "How very, very interesting, you . . . you remarkable rogue!" she exclaimed, his bemused, innocent look reducing her to affectionate laughter. "You've outsmarted me again, haven't you, Gordon? It's tea time and the others are waiting, but I give you warning: one of these days you *are* going to tell me what I want to know."

Gordon, silent for once, grinned, shrugged, and stood, dropped his cigarette end in the fire, and gallantly offered Caitlin his arm.

"Will you be sad to leave here, Dancy?" Caitlin asked. They were in the drawing room at tea time, working on floral needlepoint inserts for velvet pillows they'd begun weeks before when they'd all arrived at the nearly empty North Mountain mansion. Gradually, all the sparsely scattered fine furnishings of the house had been gathered in the most frequented places, and there was a lovely comfort and warmth about the drawing room on a late fall afternoon. The woods and forests below the house, already in autumn fire when they'd come, were now, by mid November, stripped nearly bare except for the evergreens.

"I shall be heartbroken to quit this place, of course," Dancy answered warmly. "And so will you, Cate. I can see that; anyone could. Why do you even mention it?"

"Because I've been here . . . too long already," Caitlin snapped. "I've other—"

"Yes, we know very well you've got other plans," Dancy said a bit shortly. "Caitlin, really, it is so beautiful and . . . and safe here, and we've all become so close. Do you really want to disturb everything? You and Quinn . . . well, to turn your back on happiness . . . it's mad!"

"Damn it, *you* stay here then, Dancy," Caitlin exploded, hurling her needlepoint across the room. Going to stand at the window, she saw Quinn a long way off. He was guiding a glossy black mare up along the wagon road, and she felt her heart surge at the sight of him, her first in nearly a week since he and Gordon had sailed to Halifax, on the far side of Nova Scotia. She sighed deeply, admitting to herself that everything Dancy said was true.

The mountain mansion *was* idyllic and they all *did* get on well together, too well, Caitlin had decided. That was the problem. She and Quinn were almost always together, touching and talking. They always sat close, often shared the same cup, offered each other tastes of foods and sweets and disappeared together for hours at a time at the indulgence of the others to the privacy of their cloud-touched room at the top of the mansion.

"They're almost here," Caitlin said, her voice a little throaty at the sharp remembrance of those stolen hours. Dancy came to stand at the window at her side.

"You're so short tempered because you've been missing him. Isn't that so, Caty?" Dancy smiled.

"Yes, I guess." Caitlin shrugged resignedly. "And if I don't tear myself away from him once and for all very soon, I won't be able to, and then he'll leave me one day and there I'll be—empty and aching and furious at myself for being . . . for being so bloody *weak*!"

"He'll never leave *you*, Cate, believe me!" Dancy pronounced. "I come from a long line of seers and Welsh witches. I've the second sight, you know, so don't doubt what I tell you. My," she said happily, "how sprightly Gordon seems, talking full speed as usual, but there's no cigarette dangling, is there?"

"You've done wonders for him." Caitlin

laughed. "There's even a touch of color in those sallow, sunken cheeks of his."

"And you want to get us all thrown out into the cold," Dancy admonished. "Now that Quinn's art work is all dispatched to wherever he is going, the only thing holding him here is you."

"Dancy, much as I'd like to, I can't stay, so you'd best get used to the idea of leaving," Caitlin said adamantly. "What are you really doing here anyway, you and David, hiding in these woods as you are? Yes, *hiding*," she added before Dancy could speak. "Good friends as we're supposed to be, you haven't even told me the important things about you. I mean, you want me to throw my life away on that cutthroat gypsy, Jones, all for your sake, *and* for Gordon's because he doesn't want to face the real world, and even for David who could, it seems, go on forever wandering these hills and pretending he's in Wales. Oh! Don't look at me that way. I'm sorry!" she implored as Dancy's bright green eyes swam with tears.

"But you're right about me, Caitlin," she sobbed. "I'm not as strong as you are, and I *am* hiding, and I'm keeping David from living his life. Oh, I don't know what to do!"

"Friends help each other, Dancy, but if you won't tell us what's wrong, how can we?" Caitlin asked kindly.

"I could never tell anyone but you, Cate,

what it was that happened," she whispered, clutching Caitlin's hands. "So you must swear never—oh," Dancy gasped as the doors flew open and David strode into the room. Instantly aware of his sister's distraught condition, his green eyes narrowed to points of rage.

"Don't say anything more, Dancy, you fool. You let her be," he almost snarled at Caitlin. "It isn't your affair. It's ours. We'll take care of each other, thanks."

"David," Dancy said tearfully, "Caitlin was trying to help."

"She can't. Talking about it just makes you half mad," he said desperately before pivoting and fleeing the room as abruptly as he'd entered, leaving Caitlin astounded and his sister silent, as though she'd been struck dumb.

When he entered the room with Gordon after their days away, Quinn was jolted anew by Caitlin's vivid beauty, her high coloring and radiant warmth more captivating than ever, if that were possible. She was gazing fixedly at the drawing room rug. Dancy was staring out into the dusk as they sat in the window seat forming one of those delicate set pieces of nubile femininity that so pleased him. Caitlin was in pale blue silk and Dancy in green, the red hair and auburn curls contrasting and setting each other off.

About to speak, Quinn was stopped by something in Caitlin's attitude, an unnatural stillness. Silently, he crossed the room, dusty Wellingtons sinking quietly into the thick carpet. Caitlin didn't move until he stopped in front of her, so close his knee brushed hers. When she did raise her eyes, the expression in them was distraught and appealing.

"Dancy won't move," she said in a hushed whisper. "She won't speak to me, either. She was about to tell me something terrible, I think, but David stopped her and now I don't know what—"

With a little sob, Caitlin hurled herself into Quinn's arms that folded about her protectively, their lips meeting, bodies bending together urgently. He lifted and carried her across the room to the fireside to sink, holding her on his lap, into the soft, deep settee. She curled against him, clinging, her mouth desperate and demanding on his lips that parted and tasted, then devoured what was so intemperately offered, his hand beneath a breast, thumb chafing the tip that he felt swell firmly to his touch beneath the silk.

"Have you been practicing while I've been gone?" he asked softly, brushing aside a titian curl that partially hid her beautiful profile.

"Riding and shooting." She nodded with the childlike seriousness that made Quinn smile as he toyed with her small, soft hand, bringing it to his lips.

"I can hit the second ring or better every time, at full gallop, side saddle or astride. Now I want you to take me upstairs," she said, catching his ear in sharp little teeth then letting her head sink into his shoulder, "But Dancy—"

"I think I've learned what's wrong with her, with them both. We'll try to help."

"But what?" asked Caitlin, sitting up straight. "Is it really something so terrible?" Her eyes were apprehensive.

"She should tell you herself. Even that will help her, but Caitlin . . . *I* want to tell you something," he said, his voice going into the low, intimate undertones she always melted to. "I've been thinking, during this time apart, that I could stay with you . . . for a while." He shrugged. "Maybe longer. We'll talk about it when I *do* take you upstairs. You help Dancy to bed first, will you?"

With relief Caitlin realized he'd taken charge again and became acutely aware of how much she'd come to depend on his authority during the short time they'd been together. Studying him with a new, tentative admiration, she found him even more manly and handsome than she'd remembered. Silken black hair fell about his brow, and long-lashed, gray velvet eyes somewhat softened the ruthless severity of his face. Meeting her eyes, he flashed his intriguing, volatile grin that transformed him totally and made Caitlin think she might not really care at all what he'd done or been before. The present was all that mattered, now that he'd mentioned there might be a future.

"I don't think Dancy will come with me. She won't even *look* at Gordon," Caitlin said, glancing at the couple over Quinn's shoulder. Gordon, shifting from foot to foot, bent his frail, bony frame to Dancy and directed a steady stream of words at her rigid back.

Extricating himself from Caitlin's embrace, Quinn went to the girl who was sitting erect and stiff as a statue. He whispered something in her ear and, over Gordon's protestations, extended his hand. Dancy turned, took it, and accompanied Quinn from the room, leaving Caitlin and Gordon alone.

"Pour me a brandy like a good little girl," he whined, his hands shaking as he lit a cigarette, one of the last of the tailor-mades Quinn had brought from New York. "He *always* does it. He has the magic touch with the ladies . . . gets them right under his thumb. She wouldn't speak to *me*, wouldn't even look at me. He whispers in her ear and—damn him!"

"Gordon, don't. Quinn's been such a good friend to you. How can you? Dancy wouldn't speak to *me* either. Something's wrong now, but I know Dancy . . . she cares a great deal for you. I think she might even be in love with you."

"Too bad. Love and regret go hand in hand where I'm concerned. Quinn sees to *that*," Gordon sneered before great paroxysms of coughing wracked him. He dropped into a chair to drink down great gulps of brandy straight from the bottle.

"What do you mean 'Quinn sees to that'?" Caitlin asked when Gordon gave her a sly glance, and she knew instinctively that she didn't want to hear what he was about to say; knew, too, she couldn't stop his saying it or stop herself from listening.

"Sit down. I'm going to tell you about my wife."

"Your *wife*?" Caitlin repeated. "You were—"

"Hard as it may be for you to imagine, I—even I—actually had a wife once. She wasn't much, I'll admit. Oh, she was very pretty, but she lacked certain qualities one wants in a wife—devotion and fidelity, for instance. Little things, but they do make a difference, wouldn't you agree?"

"I'd agree, yes." Caitlin nodded with a sense of foreboding as Gordon's expression become morose and his speech slurred with drink.

"Everything I ever hoped for was destined not to be," he muttered. "My little Flora was a woman of easy virtue, a strumpet, a floozy. She'd bedded half the men in town before I wed her, the other half after."

"I'm sorry, Gordon," Caitlin said, starting toward him.

"Quinn was one of them," he added with a perverse pleasure and a nasty smile as Caitlin stopped at the center medallion of the massive carpet, first stunned, then doubting.

"Quinn? Your friend who practically saved your life, gave you this place to live, put food on your table and . . . I don't believe you," she said adamantly. "I've seen how honorable and generous he's been with all of us."

"You saw him walk off with Dancy, just as he did with Flora those years ago. He's trying to make up to me for that—that's all his generosity is about. And as for honor . . . when he leaves you to go off and marry his English heiress, as planned, then talk to me about honor. And here you are, looking at him as if he'd hung the stars in the sky for you alone. Fill my glass?" Gordon asked, suddenly sheepish and slumped in his chair. In silence, Caitlin did as he asked, and, as she was about to turn away from him, he grasped her wrist in strong, bony fingers.

"Don't look that way," he pleaded, beginning to cough. There was a lethal calm about her, an ethereal coolness that frightened him. "Strike me dead, Caitlin, if every word I just said wasn't inspired by the devil. It was all lies. Because I'm jealous of Quinn."

"If you say so." She smiled icily.

"Don't tell Quinn."

"Of course not," she agreed in a patronizing tone.

"Don't tell Quinn what?" They both turned, Gordon with an oath, Caitlin with her frozen smile melting almost to tears, to find the subject of their conversation standing in the doorway. He came toward them, the hunting stealth of the wolf in his long strides.

"I haven't seen him this way in years," Quinn said, helping Gordon to his feet. "Usually he handles it well but alcohol can play havoc with him when he's disturbed about something," he told Caitlin. "I'll just put him to bed now . . ."

"It's the drinking made me tell her about Flora, Quinn. Not *all* about Flora, just . . . some of it. I told her it was lies." Gordon winked with obvious exaggeration.

"What else did you two talk about while I was gone?" Quinn asked affably, guiding Gordon toward the hall.

"That's all, all—I swear to you." Gordon raised his right hand, tottered, and leaned on Quinn's shoulder.

"Why don't you just throw him out? You're so generous, Quinn, and he's so disloyal and loathsome," Caitlin said coldly. Barely breathing, she watched them both, desperate for some sign that what she'd been told really was all lies. Though the possibility hadn't even existed hours ago, she now wanted her future with Quinn, wanted it terribly. If Gordon was right, they had no future at all.

Quinn and Gordon stared back at her for a moment, chilled by her icy tone as much as by words that were so unlike her.

"My debt to Gordon, Caitlin, will never be paid," Quinn said slowly. "I'll never throw him out, no matter what the fool does."

"I see." Caitlin nodded, accepting his words as all the confirmation she needed that Gordon had told the truth about Flora and about . . . everything else. Quinn was amusing himself, playing with her until some rich English lady became his wife. Now, his closing this fine mansion began to make some sense.

"'A man might just as well go to bed with a razor as be intimate with a foolish friend,'" Gordon said sadly. "I can't remember who said that. I'm sorry, Quinn, to be such a foolish friend to you." He shrugged and lurched from the room.

"I'll just put *him* to bed now and be right down. We'll have dinner alone. I'll tell you about Flora." Quinn placed his hands on Caitlin's shoulders and gave her a small shake. "Don't take Gordon so seriously. *He* doesn't."

"Why dinner alone?" was Caitlin's only response.

"Dancy's asleep, David's taken to the woods again after one look at her, and you've seen

Gordon for yourself."

"Things do seem to be coming apart, don't they?" she said with a frigid, disarming smile. "You'll be dining completely alone. I'm leaving."

Quinn's expression was instantly as cold as hers, his wolfish stare flat and cruel. He raked back his hair. "How and when do you think you're going to do that?" he demanded. "There's no way out of here tonight without my help."

"In an hour or two is when. One of the serving girls is going home to Halifax. I'll get a ship from there for Boston or New York. You'd better see to Gordon. He seems to be stumbling about in the hall," she said, hearing a small crash.

"I'll see to him. And then to you." Quinn scowled, abandoning Caitlin in the drawing room as rain began to splatter against the windows.

"I'm wearing Dancy's dress so I won't be needing anything of yours except this shawl, but I'll pay you for it as soon as I earn my first dollar." Caitlin smiled, calm and totally aloof as Quinn came through the bedroom doors, then leaned back against them, ominously still.

"If you want the shawl, pay for it *now*," he said viciously.

"I can't. I haven't any money. How do you expect—" Caitlin's innocent eyes widened with understanding.

"Yes, in your usual way," he laughed, his intentions becoming obvious as he undid his collar and dropped his jacket.

"No," she said flatly, trying to control her temper as he strode across the room and tore open the wardrobe doors.

"You'd best select a few more things, because I intend to take ample payment in advance. Here, have these sheepskin boots," he gritted, flinging them toward her. "*And* the wool traveling suit—it can be cold at sea this time of year. Ah, lined gloves . . . fur muff, matching hat, tea gown, morning dress . . ." As he went on reciting the long list in a clipped, barely controlled voice, he hurled gowns and wraps and gloves across the room in a building rage until the floor was littered and the closet bare. He moved then, purposefully, toward Caitlin who stood frozen amidst the opulent devastation, her beautiful face beveled by anger, hard as a clear, cut gem and her large eyes burning with a blue flame.

"I hate you!" she choked, her face hot, head pounding. Nearly blind with rage, she flew at him and he caught her in his arms.

"You don't hate me," he growled, "but it wouldn't matter if you did. You know I can have your undisciplined little body warmed and wantoned in no time, any time I choose, even if you aren't willing . . . at first." Securing her arms behind her, his hips and thighs pressing to her, he bent her back, his tongue forcing and prying between her resistant lips. She tried to twist away from him, and, freeing one hand, she beat at his hard shoulder furiously until, weeping with rage, she began to soften to his demanding body thrusting against hers. Hesitantly, reluctantly, she traced the corded muscles of his back as her silken tongue darted, meeting his, her hips surging to him. Her dress—Dancy's dress—ripped to the waist at Quinn's tug and slid from Caitlin's shoulders. His silver dagger flashed once, twice, and her lustrous, undulating body was laid completely bare. Quinn let her go and moved away a little to stare down at her with Dionysian menace as a smile touched his hard lips. She returned the smile, the devil dancing in her violet eyes as she made a quick, sudden dart toward the door, feinting to one side and laughing wildly as he reached for her, evading his arms and retreating toward the balcony. Then she was out and tiptoeing across wet stones, a warm downpour of Indian summer rain polishing her lustrous skin, sleeking her hair.

"I want to *dance*!" she called to him, taunting, her eyes reckless and provoking as Quinn came after her. Before he could catch her, though, she was up on the parapet, reaching at the heavens, offering herself to the wind. Mercurial and slight, she moved at the very edge as if wooing the spectral forest far below. "Don't!" she howled, fists raised, when Quinn pulled her down. "I'm dancing, you spoilsport! I've always wanted to dance naked in the rain!" He turned her back to him with a bone-rattling shake and delivered two fast, strong slaps. Disregarding her outraged protest, he propelled her inside and across the room to the bed and sent her sprawling over it with another sharp slap before she twisted to face him, her eyes ablaze with angry tears.

"Don't," she whispered, velvety lips atremble. "I'll do what you want."

"I *know* you will," he answered, towering over her. The dangerous hot purr was in his voice that always set her tingling, this time with a slowly thickening fear. Grasping her ankle, he roughly pulled her to the foot of the bed. He secured one leg to a post with a silk stocking before she could even realize what he was doing and begin to struggle again. Catching up a chiffon scarf from the littered floor, he knelt over her twisting body, pressing her down, securing her other ankle as she pounded furiously, ineffectually, at his back. When he faced her, his severe face was dark with anger, his eyes like steel. She raged inarticulately while he twined a torn strip of petticoat about her wrists, then secured them above her head, leaving enough slack for her to move as his hands, with leisurely precision began to mold her writhing body. She went rigid as he lightly brushed the rounded outer curve of her breasts, traced along the slim, narrow line of her ribs to the perfect niche of her tiny waist and the flare below of round hips and sleek thighs.

"Get done with me. I want to leave here," she said through clenched teeth, defiant, blazing blue eyes meeting his with a challenge before she assumed an expression of contemptuous boredom that made him laugh angrily.

"I said I'd teach you slowness, Caitlin McGlory, and I will. You're going to live centuries before *this* night is done." His strong jaw was set in stubborn determination.

Straining against her bonds, Caitlin arched up to watch him cross to the bath chamber and return with a sheet of toweling that he applied to her wet skin with precise care, as though polishing some extraordinarily valuable object left out by mistake in the rain. He peeled off his own clothes and dried his hard body, shaking droplets of water from the nocturnal swirl of his hair before slipping on a silk robe and starting for the door. Casually, almost as an afterthought, he returned to pull a quilt over Caitlin's straining form.

"Don't leave me this way!" she implored,

but he merely shrugged and promised, not too convincingly, he wouldn't be long.

The scallop bisque Quinn brought from the kitchen was pungently laced with sherry. "Sustenance. You'll need it," he said laconically, placing a pillow beneath Caitlin's head, letting her russet-tipped curls flow over it. When he held the bowl that he shared with her to her pursed mouth, she sipped gratefully, staring at him in silence over the rim with large, insolent eyes that fluttered closed each time he licked small drops from her sherried lips. When she'd finished, he set the bowl aside and very slowly turned back the quilt that had warmed her, exposing her splendid body—warm, pale corral against ivory satin—as though unwrapping a rare jewel. His narrowed eyes were gray as smoke, touching her everywhere, and then his lips went to her breast tips and his hand brushed the smooth concavity of her belly as it slid between her bound, parted legs, caressing only gently and superficially, not moving in the way that Caitlin expected.

"Don't tease me, Quinn. Let me loose and do what . . . I need you to," she barely whispered, a delicious languor beginning to seep through her entrapped limbs, darts of pleasure, icy and hot, shooting through her.

"Slowly, Caitlin, slowly," he growled, leering down. "Did I ever tell you about the

Tantrikas of India, my impatient little waif? I think not. Now's as good a time as any," he said, his voice all smoke and gravel, never pausing in his languid, teasing manipulations.

"As good a time as any?" she repeated, her tongue tracing her lips as his had just done, the faintest hint of humor in her look. "You can't do such a thing to me. I won't stand for it!"

"The Tantrikas perform—" He stopped to taste her mouth, "—they perform rituals of love . . . a man and a woman together . . . or several," he persisted, the intervals of silence as he kissed her growing longer, "—in their pursuit of heavenly bliss." Quinn stretched to his full length, warm against Caitlin, his chin resting on the palm of his hand, his hair falling forward as he looked down at her. He brushed his lips beneath the shell curve of her ear, then lost himself in her depthless, imploring blue eyes. "In the sacred pursuit of heavenly bliss, they would stop often, fully joined, to sip cups of tea—even," he whispered, "to shoot at tigers, it's said, to prolong the intensity of their . . . pleasure." He brushed Caitlin's fluttering lids with his lips.

"And not . . . interrupt their . . . play?" she asked in a throaty sigh, twisting toward him. "Loose me, please."

"The act of love is divine to them." He laughed low, ignoring her words. "The full power of it . . . of love, if the yogas are mastered, is said to sear the soul with ecstasy. We haven't time for such mastery, more's the pity, but we'll find our own ecstasy," he promised, sliding over her, his upper body raised on rigid, strong arms.

"Are they . . . still there, in India?" Caitlin half-smiled, no longer struggling, weak with longing. Quinn's teeth touched the raised pink tips of her breasts before he sat back on his heels above her and stripped off the silk robe.

"Oh yes, they are certainly there," he answered. "The proper English have forced the cult to pursue its rituals in secret, but they *are* there, after centuries, still serving the gods of love."

"And we're *here*," she implored, "and I want you so I can hardly bear it!"

"Savor it, Caitlin, feel it all. This is the last time; don't waste it. It might not be as good again, ever . . ." He tested the smooth, elastic depths of her, his other hand spanning her breasts, working the points to rigid, responsive knots of pure sensitivity. With precise, slow gestures and strokes and sleights of hand, he quickened her turbulence unbearably, his lips tuning her body, whetting and sharpening her craving until, after a time, it seemed she almost ceased to breathe as he knelt over her, aggravating her need, still concentrating it first in one place, then another until finally, he was ready to relent to her sighing entreaties. He lifted her hips toward his body that was hard as warm ivory and began his invasion, piercing slowly. Caitlin twisted wildly against her restraints, surging up to his controlled, deliberately shallow probes.

"I want you *now,*" she breathed. "*All* . . . I want *all* of you."

Grudgingly it seemed, he did give a little more and a little more still, until, to Caitlin's astonishment and confusion, he paused. Unmoving he looked down at her, his stormy eyes gray as smoke and ash.

"Don't . . . stop," she implored in her husky, little girl's voice. "Quinn, free me . . . I need to touch you." Her eyes caressed the muscled contours of his broad shoulders then met his stare again. "Is this when your Indians would sip their tea and shoot their tigers?" she asked, moving against his flexed, hard body. "We've neither tea nor tigers so . . . Quinn, don't make me wait."

He didn't, could have, but didn't want to any longer, knowing he'd already taken her farther than he ever had, needing now to press to the very limits of her glorious sensuality. With a wild and savage tenderness, his every instinct responded to the plea in her credulous eyes that were shining with a promise of forever.

The silver knife flashed and she was free, holding to him, laughing and sobbing in his arms until the first tempestuous upheaval, when it came, tore them both free of time and place and season, and in the sweet violence of love, in the searing heat of their joining, anything . . . everything Caitlin had been before was desolated, laid waste, and she was recreated by Quinn, transformed into his own superb and beautiful possession.

She encircled his neck, pressing close and clinging, only gradually becoming aware, as the surges subsided, that her arms ached and one hand, bruised against his shoulder, throbbed painfully. Quinn took it to his lips, holding her, furious that he'd let anything hurt her.

"You do damage easily," he said, gathering her even closer.

"I don't feel anything now but you." She smiled, nuzzling his throat as she slipped toward sleep in his encircling arms.

"The first time and the last are always best," Quinn whispered, brushing his lips to her brow. But Caitlin was beyond hearing, already lost in dreams of his love-soft, fine gray eyes that would haunt her sleep forever.

Chapter Fourteen

It was the sound of hammering that ended Caitlin's sleep finally, after a night of many soft stirrings. Quinn had kissed her awake, again and again, as the ebb and flow of his passions moved him. She had responded each time with all her hungry sensual innocence, first in fading firelight, then in dawn glow, her body lush as mother-of-pearl and pink gold, ruby tipped and warm. Her arms had been as difficult to break free of as a siren's, but Quinn had done it. He was dressed and booted, a lambskin great coat over one shoulder, when he felt her eyes caress him. Forget-me-not blue and smiling, the undisguised invitation he read there drew him to her.

"What is the noise?" she asked, lying back luxuriously against the pillows, enticingly flushed and disordered. "And where were you so early without me?"

"Tending to business. They're beginning to board up the windows." Quinn's tone was cool, his expression calculating as he gambled on what he thought, after last night, were pretty fair odds in his favor. He'd watched Caitlin a long while in the spreading light of dawn. Vulnerable as she'd seemed in sleep—a childlike, angelic innocent—he'd had to remind himself of her wilful determination about almost everything from what she'd eat for breakfast to what she'd do with the rest of her life. She was going to live it with *him*—he'd already determined that, confident he could distract her from her precious plans—and he wasn't about to let her think she could ever win at the kind of game she'd tried to play with him yesterday. Her uncle may have indulged all her little whims and backed down in the face of her threats and tantrums, but Quinn would have none of it, and he wanted her to understand that now.

Caitlin sat bolt upright in bed, recalling her threat of the night before to leave. She'd already retracted it so totally in her mind, she'd forgotten she hadn't told Quinn so. As she was about to, he spoke again in a remote, indifferent tone that made her rigid with anger.

"We're leaving for England on the next steamer out of Halifax. The others are coming with me. It's all been decided. You too, if—"

"Been decided? Who are you to decide anything for me? The answer is no, thank you!" she shook her head emphatically. "I'm sure you've got plans, once you arrive, that won't include me, and I've plans of my own. I'm going to New York. I told you so yesterday, only now I've missed my ride because of you and I. . . ." Near tears, she appeared to become, all at once, cold as an icy stream, glittering with anger.

"I can arrange for a boat to get you to Portland in Maine. There are trains from there, but Caitlin . . ." he hesitated, his manner gentling.

She looked up, her breaking heart showing in her eyes, she knew, unable to hide it, not wanting to at all. But he had turned away, showing her his set shoulders and long back as he gazed down the valley beyond the sky-filled windows, deciding on a change of strategy.

"Take . . . anything you want from here. After last night—" He pivoted about to face her again, the beguiling, boyish grin lighting his handsome face. "—after last night, there's a credit balance in your favor."

"I wouldn't have anything of yours if . . . if I had to go naked from here to New York," she exploded, flouncing out of bed and, as he'd done the night before, furiously flinging clothes about until she unearthed Dancy's torn, faded dress. "Now I'll have to repair it for the second time, again thanks to you," she snapped, flushing as she realized that his eyes were going over her trembling body. "Stop looking liquorishly at me and get out," she ordered, draping a sheet about her.

"Caitlin . . . listen to me," Quinn began intently. "You turned your back on your uncle and left everything you had behind you. Now you're about to do the same again. I told you yesterday I want you with me. I'm asking you now to come with us . . . with *me*, to England. We get on, you and I, and that's not so . . . ordinary. You can't just keep walking out like . . . like a reckless gypsy." He shrugged, teasing a little, his winning smile lighting his handsome face, his black lacquer hair falling over his brow.

"Oh, can't I? Watch me." Caitlin smiled, serenely smug to see his eyes go flat and cold. "Quinn!" She laughed with exaggerated gaiety. "We had good times, didn't we? We laughed a lot. Remember that when you think of me. I mean, if you ever do think of me." She turned away and stood at the windows, biting her lower lip to keep from crying.

"Don't you feel anything," he growled, starting toward her. "I can't believe—"

"For a criminal like you? No, nothing," she lied. "Besides, feelings are treacherous. They change," she added in a choked voice, about to flee when he caught her up and kissed her brutally, his hard body working against hers as he forced her down onto the bed and loomed over her.

"That's so you won't forget me," he snarled with arrogant ferocity.

"You're already a fading memory," she answered defiantly.

"Listen, my capricious, brazen little adventuress, you and I *are* going to meet again. Someday . . . somewhere, I'm going to find you waiting in the dark for me, ready to offer everything."

"Liar! Leave me alone," Caitlin hissed, covering her ears, not wanting to hear any more. He forced her hands down.

"Some women, Caitlin, are attracted to brigands, to dangerous liaisons with low characters." There was a biting, cruel edge to his voice. "And if they're cheating, there's even more excitement in it for sham princesses who would be whores. Gordon's wife, Flora, was one. You're another, and you'll come looking for me again no matter what else you do. Goodbye for now, *Princess* McGlory." He bowed with mock servility, his face dark with anger, turned up the collar of his coat, and strode from the room, leaving the doors flung wide behind him. As the ring of boots on marble faded away and she heard the door slam below, desolate sadness seized Caitlin with nearly overwhelming force.

An hour later, though, when she quit the room herself, no one seeing the beautiful young woman with dancing blue eyes could have guessed at the devastation of the heart masked by her warm and ready smile.

Chapter Fifteen

"Ah . . . living testimony to the brevity of love," Ann Overton said in a disinterested, jaded tone. Wearing a gold satin dressing gown, her heavy dark hair down about her shoulders, she had opened her door at two in the morning expecting Billy McGlory and finding Caitlin instead. The girl was looking beautiful as always and not in the least uncomfortable despite her unaccountable absence of two months or more.

"What a warm greeting, Ann." Caitlin laughed. "It does make one feel welcome. What do you mean by it?"

"Saucy as ever, aren't we?" Ann almost smiled, admiring Caitlin's verve but not wanting to say so. "What I mean is, he's left you or you wouldn't be here. Come in. The night air is cold. No luggage?"

"I always travel light," Caitlin said airily, following Ann through a darkened hallway and up a flight of stairs to a parlor where a cheery fire burned.

"It's just like your other place, all this clutter and fringe. Even the chintz pattern and wallpaper are the same," Caitlin commented, dropping into a chair after sweeping a pile of fabric scraps onto the floor. "The bouncer at The White Elephant told me where to find you."

In the parlor light, Ann was surprised to see that Caitlin was shabbily turned out beneath a very expensive woven shawl wrap. She wore a plain, almost threadbare dress of too light a fabric for the autumn weather, and the hem of her skirt was soiled and tattered.

"You're looking like a down-at-the-heels governess, or something—not Quinn Jones's style at all. He likes his women picture perfect as I recall, dressed or undressed."

"Don't tease about him, Ann, please," Caitlin said, staring into the fire. "How did you know I was with him?"

"The others thought you ran off with Robin Edwards, but I couldn't buy that and neither could Martha," Ann answered, offering Caitlin a cup of tea and resting a hand on her shoulder in passing.

"Robin Edwards!" Caitlin spat with a grimace. "You know, there's a phrase the French have: *âme-de-boue*—soul of mud—*that's* Robin Edwards."

The suggestion of a smile curled Ann's downturned lips.

"Perfect, perfect. I quite agree with the description, but tell me, who taught you French? I'm impressed." Ann rolled and lit a cigarette, poured herself an absinthe, and settled opposite Caitlin near the fire to study her unexpected guest. There was something changed about the girl that piqued Ann's interest though she couldn't quite put her finger on exactly what it was. Superficially, the child certainly looked the same. The face was exquisite with its fine bones and wide-spaced, gloriously blue eyes. The pouty mouth, a little fuller perhaps than fashion sanctioned, had to be as tempting as forbidden fruit to every man who saw it and the envy of every woman. It was Caitlin's manner that was different, Ann decided. She seemed softened and subdued.

"I was taught French by an English girl we . . . I met, a governess whose dress this is," Caitlin explained. "Her brother taught me some Welsh, too. Why did you move your salon?" she asked, accepting a dish of sweet biscuits and devouring them quickly.

"I borrowed the money from Slade Hawkes to buy this townhouse. Broadway is the ideal location with all the best modistes and department stores here and horse cars bringing the ladies in droves. It was an opportunity not to be missed, the acquisition of this structure. It's intimate and elegant, and there's space for my work rooms on the garden level a bit below the street and for the salon a bit above the sidewalk. We find the living areas ideal."

"Oh, 'we,' is it?" Caitlin asked with a raised brow.

"Your uncle has given up his rooms. He's got his own den here, replete with boxing gloves. He packed away all your things with loving care, Caitlin, so when you want them, you need only ask."

"I want father's pocket watch and mother's lace book with the poems copied out—nothing else from Billy or . . . any man." There was a stubborn, angry determination in Caitlin's manner that took Ann by surprise.

"Caitlin . . ." she began, "do you want to tell me about it before Billy gets here?"

"If Billy's due, I'm leaving," she said, standing.

"Don't be a fool. It's three in the morning and you have to face him sooner or later. You broke his heart, you know. I'm sorry, Caitlin, I didn't mean to say that," Ann added, irritated by the self-righteous tone of her own voice.

"He broke mine, too," Caitlin answered. "I'm going. I only came to talk with you about the job you offered me once, but if you don't want me, I'll understand."

"But I do. Stay tonight at least. There's an unused room at the back of the house with a day bed, but that's all it's got, I'm afraid. It may be rough but it is a place to lay your head. Have a bath in my room and scamper right up. You can decide about Billy in the morning after I've had a chance to prepare him. No rational decision was ever made at this time of night. Or morning. It's too late for dreams, too early for birds, and too lonely to be walking the streets alone. Well?"

"Ann," Caitlin said, more serious for a fleeting instant than the older woman had ever seen her, "thank you for having me. And don't talk about rough living." She laughed. "Have you ever seen Portland, Maine? It's a lumber camp and . . . well, a sophisticate like you wouldn't believe the way other people live. I will stay tonight. Tomorrow's another day, isn't it?"

The special quiet of Sunday morning enveloped the house as Caitlin awoke. Her nearly bare room was tucked up beneath a sharply pitched roof and, with the heavy door closed, no sound reached her from below, though the tantalizing smells of bacon and coffee had drifted there and teased her awake. Her dress, she saw, washed and pressed and neatly repaired, was worn by an old mannequin that also sported a blue felt bonnet askew on a handle where a head might have been. There was nothing else in the room but the narrow, tarnished brass day bed from which Caitlin emerged cautiously, not knowing what to expect amidst the dust on the floor. The leaded windows were too dirt streaked to see through, but, thrown open, they offered a view between rooftops and chimneys north toward the park and the new rail station uptown. Watching a lone cat saunter in leisurely fashion across the cobbles of the deserted street below, Caitlin was assaulted by a lost and lonely Sunday sadness that stunned her, and she had to close her eyes tight and take several deep breaths before she felt in control again.

"Five hundred hours," she whispered to herself. "Three weeks, three whole weeks, and the thought of that brigand can still make me weak and soft and desperate, damn him!"

Sunday is not a day to be homeless and alone with nothing but memories, she decided with an unconscious, bold lift of her chin. It's a time to belong somewhere, to be with someone. Tomorrow, when the world went on about its business again, she'd be better, Caitlin knew. The city would welcome her home, would captivate and distract and delight her as it always had. With a remnant of a childlike belief in magic, she still felt that the city belonged to her, that everything in it was hers for the taking. The furs and jewels and carriages of wealthy society ladies had been promised somehow to a laughing little girl, her nose pressed to a boarding house window, her aspirations soaring as she watched the passing parade. It was the flaunting factory girls and saloon waitresses, though, taking to the city streets in bright colors, streaming feathers and flowers, who had once seemed to her the most glamorous creatures on earth. The exuberant, impressionable child Caitlin had been not long ago had felt—known with an unshakable certainty—that everything she saw and admired would be hers one day. It was all waiting just beyond her reach for her to grow up and stretch out her hand, and that's exactly what she'd come back to do. She was going to have it all! That desperado, Jones, wasn't going to bring *her* down. She wouldn't ever let his memory stand in her way. He was out of her life and out of her heart, too, she tried to insist, except for those terrible lucid moments, always so unexpected and stunning, when it all came rushing back.

"Enough!" she exploded, facing the mannequin. "So dreadfully sorry to leave you alone, my dear," she addressed the old wireworks dummy, "but if I spend a solitary Sunday in this forsaken garret, I'll really come unstrung. Dear, dear, your skinny ribs are showing." She laughed, pulling the dress over its shoulders and slipping into it. "But then," she sighed, doing up the buttons, "nothing should ever touch your . . . your fine wires but light and shadow and lovers' lips." She laughed sadly. "Damn Quinn Jones!" she flared, hurling open the door with a bang and fleeing the room as though she were pursued by demons that declined to be left behind.

Shawl wrapped, auburn curls bouncing to her waist, Caitlin skipped down the last flight of steps and had the front door handle in her grasp when a gruff voice spun her around as emphatically as a hand on her shoulder.

"And just where do you think you're off to?" she heard as, heart pounding, she peered into the shady hall, willing Quinn to step out of the gloom. "Here was I, countin' on a game of checkers like we always had of a Sunday morning and here's you slippin' off without one word of greeting for your poor old uncle whose heart you left broken all in little pieces!"

"Hello, Billy," Caitlin said with remote courtesy, watching him rock back on his heels, a sign, she knew, of the agitation he was feeling.

"That's it? Hello Billy?" he bellowed, his big leathery hands reaching out to her.

She offered him a restrained smile, torn between rushing away and hurling herself into his protective arms. The last time she'd done that, she recalled, had been one of the worst moments of her life. She held back.

"You are lookin' more beautiful than ever and . . . more genteel, sort of, like a real princess, my little Caty, even if you are kind of ragged. I got all those fine things saved for you." Billy hesitated, made cautious by her silence. "You've changed some way. I never seen you so standoffish. My little girl was always ready with smiles and kisses for her old uncle, wasn't she?"

"I am changed, Billy. No, no don't deny it," she said as he shook his head starting toward her. "And I'm not your little girl any more, I'm afraid. I've grown up . . . some."

"We'll just see about all that." He winked. "You're just feelin' low now, ain't you?"

Too proud to lie, Caitlin nodded and turned away, her reserve beginning to falter, weakened by the essential kindness of Billy's manner and the warm, familiar twinkle in his blue eyes.

"I was just the one could always cheer you, couldn't I? And I still can, even if you are all grown up like you say, which I don't buy as easy as all that." Looking fierce as some wild, North Sea pirate until a sheepish grin spread over his battered face, Billy took a step toward Caitlin. She edged away.

"Oh, don't run from *me*, Caty," he implored in a strangled voice. "You are everythin' to me, you know that, and I never meant to say . . . about your mother and that, but worry over you got my temper hot and loosened my tongue. All I ever wanted to do was to give you everything in the world I could and now—" His voice broke and he stood looking clumsy and helpless, hands thrust deep in his pockets, rocking back on his heels. "Here," he said suddenly, "I think there's a quarter in your ear, Miss." He brushed at Caitlin's cheek with a fist as he thrust a coin up between his clenched fingers. "Look! Another back of your neck," he crowed, pulling her against him.

He was solid and sturdy and as strong as a wall as he folded her in a bone-crushing bear hug that nearly took her breath away and seemed to force the hard-held tears from her eyes.

"Oh, *Billy*!" she cried helplessly, hiding her face against his red satin dressing gown. "Billy, I missed you so much and . . . and I'm so sad I can hardly bear it."

"Caty, my pretty little love, life's full of cruel surprises, and I tried so hard to shelter you from them. I was nothin' but a dismal failure, wasn't I?" he questioned, desperately holding her close to him.

"Oh, don't say such a thing!" she protested angrily, tears coursing as he patted his pockets for a handkerchief. "I don't let anyone else talk you down that way."

"You don't? That means you are still my little princess and we're friends again!" Billy roared like a jubilant bear, swinging her about as they both laughed and cried until she protested and he set her down, not letting go of her hand.

"Billy," she said in her most businesslike manner, "we'll be friends again, but . . . you must realize, I'm changed. I'm not your little girl and you can't take care of me any more and I won't take anything from you and if you don't agree to that—"

"You stubborn, headstrong, brat!" he roared with laughter. "You'll soon be beggin' me for frills and laces and bonnets just as before, see if you ain't. I know how you like fine, fancy things. You women are all alike!"

"Care to hazard a stake on that, McGlory?" she demanded with a challenging smile.

"Why not?" He nodded, serious all at once. Gambling was no light matter to Billy. "What stakes?"

"Two hundred dollars and a brace of the best pistols money can buy. That's in three months from now if I haven't asked you for anything more than the time of day between now and then."

"That's *all*?" He laughed.

"Oh, I don't mean miniature ladies' guns. I want full-size, long-barreled, pearl-handled Colts, perfectly balanced and sized to my grip. Nothing less." Her precision and intensity took Billy off guard.

"What the devil do you know about guns?"

"Everything." She smiled smugly, folding her arms across her chest. "Now, what is it you want from me if you win, which you won't?"

"I want you to marry a man *I* pick and have half a dozen little blue-eyed brats tugging at your skirts in as many years, so I'll have someone to leave my wealth to."

"That's all you *ever* asked of me. You'll get that in spades. If you win. Anything else?"

"Yes, something else. When they run me for the city council a year from now like they've planned, I want you at my side, smiling your winning smile and flashing those big blue eyes."

"It's a deal." Caitlin nodded seriously, extending her hand that disappeared into Billy's enthusiastic shake.

"Ann!" he roared at the top of his large lungs. "Ann! Come see who I got here smiling up at me like she never left!"

The parlor door opened more quickly than either Billy or Caitlin would have expected, and Ann emerged, almost smiling.

"Well, I'm glad you've got all that settled," she said, nodding. "You certainly made enough noise doing it. Now, Caitlin and I have more important things to do than stand about gloating. We've serious business to discuss."

"Not today, Annie. My little girl and me . . . oh, beg pardon, Cate . . . not my little girl, my *niece* and me, we are going to do what we always do on a Sunday, and you, my love, are welcome to join us or not, as you please."

"Join you for what, pray tell?" Ann asked wearily, lifting fine shoulders beneath a soft, slim, black jersey morning dress.

"Our game of checkers, then a carriage turn in the park and our usual stop at The Dairy for a chat with the cows and some fresh milk, this being Sunday, and—"

"—and after a big roast beef dinner, Billy will dapper up and meet his Tammany cronies, and I'll curl up to read a French novel and eat fudge. Right, Billy?" Caitlin laughed, dancing about him elfish and agile, glimmering, Ann thought, like a polished diamond. She watched the girl stretch up to plant a kiss on Billy's cheek, aware again of a difference about Caitlin, a reserve, a new refinement that enhanced the child's natural elegance of style.

"Well, all right," Ann nodded. "I'll play with you two today, but first thing tomorrow we'll descend to particulars, Cate and I, no two ways about it."

"Three dollars a week is what all the new girls get. That's what you'll get, too. If I find your value to me increases, I'll pay you more." With her usual jaded expression on her calm, classical face, Ann rested an elegant elbow on a satinwood *bonheur du jour* in her small office. Like everything else in the room, the desk was pristinely neat and obviously very expensive. Ann gave the same impression, organized, crisp and businesslike early Monday morning, unobtrusively, beautifully dressed, hair smooth and upswept. She sat on one of the two Queen Ann needlepoint chairs in the room, facing Caitlin who occupied the other, a French porcelain tea service with gilded rims and spouts on a low table between them. The *chinoiserie* embellishments on the cups and pots—pagoda parasols held by servants above the bowed heads of fan-fluttering ladies with downcast eyes—had amused Caitlin while she'd waited for Ann, who came gliding into the room finally in a rustle of nubbed pale gray silk. Her exquisite narrow-skirted dress was form-following in front and bustled, its understated bodice the perfect backdrop for a beautiful and unusual necklace of glass and gold beads.

"Yes, an antique," Ann acknowledged Caitlin's questioning look. "The larger beads are Roman millefiori glass, actually, very rare, but if I kept it under lock and key, I'd rarely bother to look at it. I'd get little pleasure from it that way. Wearing it, I enjoy it whenever I please. Now, I'll use it as a device to explain my—Why, what's the matter? You've gone a touch ghostly on me."

"Quinn Jones said exactly the same thing to

me once, about a tea service, actually," Caitlin half smiled, clutching the arms of her chair to stop herself from bolting.

"A memorable man, Quinn. One learns much from him if one is receptive. He makes an impression one doesn't forget, does one? Do you want to tell me about it?" Ann asked.

"No!" Caitlin exclaimed emphatically. "I can't. Not yet, Ann," she added, softening her tone. "What did you want to explain?"

"My basic view of fashion, which is that dramatic simplicity and quality are worth wagon loads of frills and feathers. These beads caught your eye because nothing else was calling for your attention."

"But I like a little flash and color." Caitlin smiled, sipping tea thick with sugar and cream. "Working girls, who aren't inhibited by the proprieties and restrictions that hamper upper class ladies, have a flair I've always admired."

"You and I know, Caitlin, that fashion does come from the street as well as from Murray Hill mansions and the dancers and actresses. And . . . others who come here with their wealthy lovers know that, too, but most of my ladies don't. They are exactly those wealthy, snobbish women you mentioned, who consider themselves the elite arbiters of style in this city. The only real business of life for them is beauty, as *Godey's* told them it should be.

That's not the worst view of life, in my opinion. Beauty is power, Caitlin, and you in particular should never forget that. But most of my ladies not so graciously gifted as you've been by nature, equate beauty with fashion. They live in terror of being seen in any but the latest styles, and they are virtually enslaved to fashion, consequently to *me*. I look to the French for inspiration. No customer of *mine* will ever meet herself on the street. The things I design are rare and beautiful and right, because I say they are, and they are very, very costly. Do you understand?" Ann opened a desk drawer to extract a package of cigarettes and struck a light. "*Now* what's reminded you of Jones?" she demanded as Caitlin stood and began pacing.

"Your ready-made cigarettes, *No Name 24s*," Caitlin answered with a single self-deprecating laugh. "*Damn* the man!"

"Caitlin, if you talk about it—"

"Don't mind me Ann. Just go on," Caitlin said, resting her brow against the cool window pane. "Your girls are arriving."

"Good! Four minutes early," Ann noted with a sharp glance at the clock above her desk. "They stay here through the week, in the other rooms near yours, so they're never late, but after work on Saturday, they go off. Monday mornings are often hard for them."

"Do they go home?" Caitlin asked, watching

the three seamstresses climb the stone steps to the entrance. "How pretty they look—two of them, anyway."

"May and Judy are my tinseled butterflies." Ann smiled a little. "They have an absolutely insatiable desire for fancy new clothes, but that happens to a lot of girls in this business. They can make up their own things, of course, and I let them have fabric remnants at . . . a fair price."

"You actually sell them your scraps, Ann?" Caitlin asked with a quizzical laugh. "Would you use the stuff if they didn't?"

"That's beside the point entirely. You don't expect me to *give* them the goods, do you?" Ann responded, her look mildly shocked and quite self-righteous. "You do, I see. Well, sit down, miss, and I'll tell you how I run my business. I give nothing away. I never have and I never will. I worked sixteen hours a day, year after year, ruining my eyes in poor light, burning lard-soaked rags instead of candles to save money. I pricked my fingers until they bled, and later I sat hunched over my machine, my back aching, making finery for rich, privileged women. I never discarded a scrap or a button; I never was late with an order; I never charged too high a price, but I always demanded, and got, exactly what I thought I was worth. That is how I built this business, and now that I'm secure—secure as I'll ever be, because I've still got very hungry memories—I am not about to hand out charitable contributions to strong, healthy girls who are capable of doing the same as I did if they want to, and that includes you, Caitlin McGlory, understand?"

Ann paused for breath and Caitlin nodded, awed by the lengthy tirade and impressed to see calm, cool Ann Overton more animated than she ever had.

"I don't expect special favors," Caitlin said.

"Good, because you won't get any. I'll start you at three dollars a week, same as all my new girls, and consider yourself lucky; some dressmakers pay only twenty-five or thirty cents a day. You'll model when needed. We'll keep you busy with other things when not. We work eight to six, except Saturday when we stop at two unless there's a special order. Then we don't stop at all until it's done. Prove your worth and I'll pay you more. Room and board will be deducted from your wages and so will the cost of anything you use from the remnant room to do up your little attic. You'll be my guest for Sunday dinner but only because of Billy, you understand. Any questions?"

"Yes. What's the top wage you pay?"

"Twelve dollars a week to an experienced forewoman, but you won't—"

"I will"—Caitlin smiled—"quicker than you might suppose."

"All the better for us both, but don't be overconfident. It's a tougher business than you can imagine. Now . . . I've one complaint right off—that namby-pamby governess dress. Burn it," Ann said with cool disgust. "You'll chase off customers otherwise, even pretty as you are."

"I've nothing else. After I earn—"

"After you earn enough to outfit yourself? Not by a long chalk, my little friend. I've had your wardrobe unpacked and pressed, and it's ready for you now if—"

"Not by a long chalk yourself, Miss Overton." Caitlin grinned. "I don't want special favors, and I can't pay."

"I've already been paid . . . by your uncle, remember?" Ann snapped back, secretly pleased by Caitlin's independent spirit.

"So much the worse," Caitlin insisted, arms folded stubbornly across her chest, chin uptilted. "I told you, I'll never take anything from him . . . or any man, again."

Ann nodded once. "I see," she said, going to the door. "One word of caution. Someday, you may want to let . . . someone take care of you again . . . a little. Don't be so inflexibly independent that you won't remember how to be cherished should you want to be."

"But look at you, Ann. You're the most brittle, determinedly independent woman I've ever met."

"Don't do as I *do*, miss. Do as I say." Ann shrugged irritably. Opening the door, she beckoned with a long hand that brought a pretty young woman with a narrow face and jet-black hair hurrying into the office. "Measure her up, May." Ann shifted a shoulder at Caitlin. "I know it's Monday, but try not to look so *dull*. She's Caitlin McGlory, the new girl. She needs outfitting. What she's wearing is all she's got. It won't do, obviously. Measure her up and take her over to Mr. Macy for ready-mades—dowlas shifts and plain stuff gowns, two of each, one black, one brown. Her boots and shawl will have to do her until she can afford better for herself."

"Nothing wrong with 'er shawl," the girl said behind Ann's back with a wink at Caitlin, who responded with a raised brow and a little questioning shrug.

"Did I ask you for an opinion?" Ann demanded, winking at Caitlin herself, out of May's sight.

"Thank you, Ann," Caitlin managed to say without laughing at them both.

"Don't thank 'er. She's charging you for every stitch, and for my time to go an' shop with you," May said in a thick brogue. "Let's be off. I got to finish Miss Carpenter's trousseau this week. All the shifts and bed gowns need embroidering, and it's the practice here to use the bride's own hair, only this one's locks are that fine, it'll keep me occupied longer than Miss Overton might think necessary," May said sassily, glancing at Ann.

"There's no one to equal you, May, for fine work; we all know that," Ann flattered, as if placating a child, maneuvering the girl toward the door. Puffed up like a proud hen, May almost clucked with pleasure. "I'll meet you at the door, Cate," she said. "I'll just get the others started, the lazy things!"

"Twelve dollars a week?" Caitlin inquired when May had gone.

"Ten fifty," Ann answered with a pinched look. "They're good, she and her cousin, Judy, but just off the boat and still learning. They're a wild pair on their own time, I've heard. They've come over alone, just the two of them. There's no family to hold them to the old ways. Poor innocent Kathleen was horrified by them at first."

"Your third stitcher?"

"Yes, a plain, colorless little creature, a bit thick, it seems. I've never met anyone so unimaginatively upright, but she does beautiful hand work. Every Saturday, when the two butterflies flutter out of here in red boots and short skirts, Kathleen's father collects her, relieves her of her wages, and keeps her slaving over the family's washing and ironing until he brings her back on Monday. There are five brothers who harried the poor mother into her grave years ago. But this girl is either going to rebel or break. I can see it in the way she stares at the fancy men always waiting for May and for Judy." There was a silent moment before Ann clapped her hands and stood. "I'm not paying you to sit about and chatter. And May's waiting."

Picking up her shawl, Caitlin left the office and crossed the salon, glancing at the coffered ceiling and hanging *portières* done in pale shades of blue and turquoise. There was a triple love seat at one end of the room, a deep Turkish sofa at the other, and arm chairs and tea tables scattered between in pleasant groupings. Sculpted rugs in shades of blue, corner chairs, and filigreed screens faced a long wall of mirrors. Chevals stood about at random. The overall effect, achieved at considerable expense, was something between an intimate boudoir and a formal, elegant drawing room.

"Caitlin," Ann called after her. "Remember, you may take what you wish from the storeroom to do up your bedchamber—fabric ends and such."

"You'll deduct, of course, from my wages for what I use," she teased, twirling in front of one of the long mirrors.

"Of course, but out of the goodness of my heart and to protect my investment, I will have a small coal stove installed at my own expense. You'll be no use to me at all as a model with red eyes and sniffles if you take cold."

"Come *on*! Caitlin, *do* come on. I can't wait an instant longer, I'm that excited." May Browne pounded at Caitlin's door as her cousin, Judy, paced the narrow attic hall, her red boots clicking on the hardwood floor. The two were ready for an outing. Both were dressed in red, with bright yellow wraps and bonnets streaming tri-colored ribbons. Judy, in contrast to her taller, sultry cousin, was tiny, blond, and plump as a partridge, as Ann described her, with carmined lips and large hazel eyes that seemed perpetually wide with surprise.

They both waited impatiently for Caitlin to join them until, in exasperation, she threw open the door of her room and invited them inside.

"You made it so pretty in here, it's no wonder you are in no hurry to leave." Judy smiled, hands on her hips, looking about. "It's always like spring, isn't it, with your dried dandelions there?" The tiny room had been whitewashed and the moldings painted yellow. The bed skirt and curtains were of a yellow ruffled dotted swiss fabric. An embroidered canvas rug was placed before a small stove. Framed, chain-stitched nosegays hung on the walls, and heart-shaped lace pillows were piled on the bed that served during the day as a settee.

"Delightful as it is in here, if you don't get a wiggle on you, you'll never know what Mr. Mummler's spirits have to tell. You do want to find out about your mother and dad, don't you?" May plucked at Caitlin's sleeves. "Come on or we'll be too late."

"It's all so . . . shady," Caitlin complained, wrapping her beautiful shawl about her shoulders and glancing into an old, oak-framed mirror. She'd rescued it from Ann's dust man who was about to cart it away. "I want to go dancing. I told you that!" she added, twirling in front of the glass. Like the other girls, she was dressed for an outing, too, in a blue, narrow-sleeved, unruffled wool dress that followed her figure closely, the skirt short enough to show fine ankles in high-laced, high-heeled boots of bright bottle green.

"We'll dance *after*," Judy almost whined. "We know you've got new boots."

"I've spent almost everything I've made on them in the two weeks I've been here . . . everything Ann didn't withhold for expenses, that is, and you want me to sit in the dark and hide them under some medium's rigged table."

Judy and May each took one of Caitlin's arms and propelled her toward the door. "Do you think we'd give up a night of dancing at Harry Hill's or at your uncle Billy's place?"

May asked.

"Do you think we left home and came on our own on that coffin ship, risking our lives with half the people around us fallin' like flies with the typhoid, to do anything *but* dance?" Judy questioned.

"But you'd pay good money for imaginary spirits—" Caitlin began.

"We know herself has already given you one raise in just the short time you've been here," May sniffed. "You can afford it."

"And if'd you'd accept it, Billy McGlory'd give you the world," Judy added.

Caitlin stopped still in her tracks. "I won't take anything from him again and you both know it," she said. "And if you ever mention such a thing—"

"Never, never, I swear, I won't say that again about Billy, nor will May. Will you, May?" Judy prompted as they tripped down the steps and gained the street at last. Arms linked, stepping boldly, laughing and talking in a burst of high spirits, the three girls captured the unabashed attention of every man they passed as well as the furtive glances of the more sedate women strolling along the sidewalk from shop to shop in the bright Saturday afternoon sunshine. When Caitlin glanced back over her shoulder to wave at Billy smiling from the salon window, she saw Kathleen, the third sewing girl, waiting forlornly on the street below, skinny wrists protruding from the sleeves of a faded, coat, long outgrown.

"We *will* have to take her with us one day," Caitlin told the others. "I feel badly, leaving her looking so downhearted."

"If you'd a father like *that*"—May indicated a heavyset figure coming toward them—"you'd look a bit downhearted yourself. Afternoon, Mr. Toole," she sang out, nearly colliding with the man whose brutish, scowling stare preceded a low oath.

"Out of my way, you baggage," he muttered as Judy curtseyed in front of him.

"Don't!" May whispered, pulling her cousin along. "He'll only take it out on poor Kathleen. Cate's right; we *must* take her with us as soon as we can and show *him*!"

"She'll never!" Judy said.

"We finally got *this* one to come along, didn't we?" May retorted, nodding toward her new friend.

It was Caitlin's first real outing since she'd arrived at Ann's door two weeks before. She had tried a solitary walk one evening soon after she had come, confidently expecting the city sights and sounds to engage her as always and to distract her from almost constant thoughts of Quinn. She joined the promenade on Broadway where, it seemed, all the world came together. Pale armies of sewing girls who had crouched over whirring machines for long hours and the red-eyed factory children who had spent their days laboring in unnatural silence came to life after five to mingle with the street walkers from adjacent Five Points, the city's most notorious slum. Flower sellers and apple vendors were everywhere. Curbstone singers gathered tossed pennies from the cobbles at their feet, and organ grinders at almost every corner kept jacketed monkeys jangling tin cups of coins, soliciting more. Young men, drab clerks in the city's banks and mercantile houses by day, became the dandies of the evening. Sleekly barbered, displaying gold neck chains and tasseled walking sticks, they lolled at the entrances of hotels and athletic clubs, flirting with the working girls who met their stares with coquettish confidence. Sounds of music and laughter drifted from saloons and dance halls, and crowded horse cars clattered past, carrying workers home to the boarding-houses uptown. Lacquered carriages conveyed the more reclusive rich to Murray Hill mansions as dusk turned to dark and street lamps were lit.

Moving through the carnival night world she had always loved—that she had always thought of as *home*—Caitlin felt oddly detached and lonely, not part of it all as she always had been before. She slowed her pace and looked about quizzically, trying to decide what was wrong, when her eyes fixed on a tall, dark man moving along the street ahead of her, the easy strides and set of wide shoulders oddly familiar. "It *can't* be," she whispered, her heart pounding wildly as she started after him. "A trick of the imagination," she insisted to herself when she'd almost overtaken her quarry who disappeared into a men's grill before she could be absolutely certain it wasn't Quinn.

"Damn and blast!" she said aloud. "Damn and blast that gypsy, Jones! He's ruined *everything*." Face flushed, she pivoted about and started back toward the salon, walking briskly. Stopped by traffic at a busy intersection, she glimpsed the same tall figure again, she thought, behind her this time, with a hat pulled low and shadowing the face. Determined to prove herself wrong, she started after him, but he eluded her again. Caitlin returned home furious at herself, deciding to keep her mind on business and nothing but, until she was mistress of her own emotions again. After nearly two weeks of nothing but work, she was, she thought, ready to take on the world and had agreed to this Saturday outing with Judy and May.

"I'm glad to see the girl off for some fun," Billy said, turning away from the salon window, "but those three look more like General Hooker's camp followers than good little working girls enjoying their Saturday out. How can you allow it?" he demanded of Ann accusingly. She was half reclining in a deep chair, going over the week's figures.

"I'm not a nursemaid," she said disinterestedly. "Caitlin's done a good job with the books. I'll turn them over to her altogether, starting next week."

"And pay her more?" Billy frowned.

"A little," Ann snapped. "Oh, now you've made me lose count. I'll have to start this column over."

"Never mind that. Put it by and listen to me, Annie. I don't want the girl earnin' any more money."

"What do you mean like Hooker's camp followers?" Ann asked, still preoccupied with her figures. "Caitlin's magnificent, a dashing creature with her strong features, cheeks glowing with health and pleasure. She's bold now going out with the Browne girls, but here, working, she's simply elegant, just spirited and showy enough to sell but not enough to intimidate my less well-endowed customers. It's the best thing ever . . . what was that you said?" Ann looked up, a doubting expression on her face.

"I said I don't want her earnin' any more money." With his hands in his pockets, Billy rocked back on his heels, jaws clenched emphatically.

"What an underhanded way to try and win your bet," Ann admonished. "You know I never overpay anyone, but I am fair, and Caitlin will deserve another increase—a little one to be sure—if she keeps on as she has been. Her flare for style is rare and so is her head for business, particularly in a woman."

"I don't care," Billy grumbled. "All this money . . . makes her too independent. It's not good for a young girl. And her going about with those two, that's not good either. They are easily tipped, the pair of them, and Caitlin . . . she could still marry well, even after this dalliance with that Jones. Who'd ever be the wiser?"

"I don't think I believe what I'm hearing," Ann said with deceptive calm. "You thick-skinned peasant lout," she went on in the overly sweet tone that always hid her anger, "that was something more than a dalliance, and the girl's not over him yet. Can't you tell her heart is breaking? All that relentless energy of hers, that passionate intensity about everything, is meant to hide it from us, from herself, too, probably, and I'm reaping the benefits of her attempted subterfuge. That's what's made her throw herself so completely into this business of mine. You know she's at work before anyone in the morning, and she's still in the office when it's striking midnight working at the figures or the bills, and that's after a full day with my very demanding customers."

"I want her married and—" Billy began to fume.

"She is so clever at this business," Ann interrupted. "The things she's thought of—the plate glass window she'll model in, our own fragrance we'll sell to only our best customers, invitational showings at mid-season besides the usual spring and fall displays—all sorts of other things. Come, Billy, don't begrudge her a Saturday night's dancing. She deserves it, and perhaps she'll meet someone who'll help her forget that rake, Jones."

"I want her settled and having babies, damn it!" Billy roared.

"You want her under your thumb is what you really want. But don't expect me to conspire with you to keep her poor and dependent. Let her go, Billy. It's time." Ann stood, gathering up her papers.

"It's not good for her to be so independent," Billy insisted stubbornly.

"I suppose you don't think it's good for me, either?" Ann asked coolly.

"I never said that, did I? You are puttin' words in my mouth as usual, shrew, but . . . well, if the truth were known"—Billy grinned—"you'd have married me long ago if you wasn't a wealthy woman with this blasted business of yours, and don't deny it."

"Oh, I see." Ann nodded archly. "Tell me,

McGlory, didn't you think I was 'easily tipped' as you so delicately phrased it? I'm surprised you'd want to marry a loose lady like me, a man with your oppressive view of women."

"You put up *some* resistance, but I always knew it was just for show." Billy laughed as her papers went flying everywhere and Ann, very much out of character, rushed at him only to come up against his blunt, solid strength and find herself caught in his heavy arms. "Harridan! Marry me," he whispered against her ear. "Haven't you woke up singin' every mornin' since the first mornin'?"

"Well, yes, I have, as a matter of fact," she said disinterestedly, as if involved in the most casual conversation, though she was struggling ineffectually against him. "But that's only because I know I can throw you the devil out of here whenever I choose."

"Annie, don't say such a thing. We're bound to each other forever." Billy's eyes showed a touching vulnerability as he released Ann. Despite his bulky strength and noisy bravado, he seemed almost helpless then, at a complete loss as to what to do next. Moved, she smiled, her long, cool hand caressing his craggy face.

"We are bound," she said softly, " no matter what happens. I'm just . . . not ready for family ties. I thought you were happy the way we are."

"You haven't really committed to me, Annie.

You're keeping at a safe distance from me still, and that's the easy way, the safe way. You just said it yourself. In the back of your mind you always know you can get out any time, and, even if you never do leave me in a hundred years, there's that thought like a wall a mile high between us." Billy shook his large head sadly.

"Don't look at me that way." Ann sighed. "I've given you more than I ever have any man. If you're willing to go on slowly, one day perhaps . . ." She shrugged and looked away. "How did we get into this again? We started talking about Caitlin and—"

"You never want to talk about it, about me and you, Ann. You want everything polite and arranged perfect. I want more," Billy roared. "I'm not young as I once was, and you ain't no trembling girl at nearly thirty either. I need to settle my life. I've kicked about this world alone long enough, and now you say I must turn loose my Caty. Ann," he said, his gruff voice soft and imploring. "I want to see the generations unfolding for us, for you and me together. Don't you want that?"

"I . . . don't know," she said, coming into his arms. "I think I'm afraid."

"But I'll take care of you," he said simply. And, for a long moment, wrapped in Billy's masculine strength, Ann let herself feel protected and cared for. Beginning to enjoy the sensation, she abruptly pulled away.

"Wait a little longer, can't you, Billy?" she asked so gently he had to relent.

"You think you can just twist me 'round your little finger whenever you like. You're right." He laughed. "But you got to give me something now like a compensation prize, sort of."

"What might you have in mind?" She laughed back, loosening her hair. When she'd undone pearl buttons to her waist, exposing the soft, pale curves of her breasts, Billy approached her and slid her dark silk dress from her shoulders that were very white in contrast. Then, with long fingers, Ann undid Billy's collar stay and, with increasing urgency they dealt with each other's fastenings, items of clothing falling away until his muscled, furred body enfolded her willowy length, their eyes on a level as their lips met and their joined reflection in the salon's angled mirrors swirled about them in infinite, depthless duplication.

Chapter Sixteen

"Say 'potatoes,' say 'prunes' to get your pretty mouth into a perfect pout," the photographer suggested to Caitlin, who sat at the center of his studio in an extraordinarily elaborate, twisted wicker posing chair.

"Mr. Mummler," she asked, "do . . . living persons show up as extras in your spirit pictures, or is it only—"

"Only those who have passed over, Miss McGlory. Who is it you wish to see?" Mummler asked, angling his camera.

"I'm not telling," Caitlin giggled, setting May and Judy off, too, as they observed the proceedings from the side of the room.

Mummler, a soft, balding man, with small, sharp features, flushed scarlet. "If you would peek into the windows of heaven, you must be serious. If you disbelieve, if you are in a hurry to meet your young man, or if anything distracts you, this simply will not work. Now, you two had best be silent or you'll frighten away the very spirits your friend hopes to see."

"She wants to see her mum and she's got no young man. The only one she wants is gone away," May sniffed, a bit affronted by Mr. Mummler's scolding.

"Miss McGlory, think about your mother now; call her image into your heart," Mummler instructed.

"But . . . I can't remember her at all," Caitlin said with a small shrug.

"Do you have anything that belonged to her—a ring, a scarf, anything? Yes? Good! Concentrate on that with all your might," Mummler added when Caitlin gave him a short nod. When he decided, four minutes later, that she'd concentrated long enough, he pressed the bulb of his camera, then passed the glass plate to an assistant who only extended a hand from the dark room.

To conserve funds, May and Judy sat together before the camera, deciding to call up the spirit of their mutual grandmother.

"She was going real strong when we left, but it's been four years. Not a one of us at home could write, so we decided to check on granny this way. If she's still among the living, we won't see her, will we, Mr. Mummler?"

"No, but my associates, who are extraordinary clairvoyants, may be able to contact her for you," he said. "Why don't you wait in the next room, Miss McGlory? Your friends will be along directly."

Caitlin found two elderly women already seated at a polished mahogany table when she entered the séance chamber. She took a chair herself and looked about. The room was heavily draped and lit only by a pair of candles in sconces to either side of the door she had just passed through. There was nothing else except a carafe of water and a glass on a mantle above a cold hearth.

"First time?" one of the old ladies inquired pleasantly of Caitlin.

"Yes, and you?" she responded. The two frail creatures tittered as if she'd said something hilariously funny.

"We've been doing this for more than twenty years. We've been to the best," one of the ladies answered.

"And to the worst," her companion added.

"These two, the DeLisles, where do they fall in the scale?"

"They are very good, indeed, with the living and those passed away. So good, in fact, it's said by some that *he's* part spirit himself. DeLisle comes and goes with never a sound and never speaks except with the voice of . . . the *others*. It is through him that Madame makes contact, you see. The DeLisles are the only ones who could ever locate our Alanzo. He's at the bottom of a pit in the Yucatan. He's been there a long while."

"Yes?" Caitlin asked politely, trying not to laugh. "How did he get in the pit? Do you know?"

"We put him there. He did us both wrong," one of the ladies answered with a smile. "Engaged first to Aggie Wily there." She nodded at the other who took up the story.

". . . then to Charlotte Wily," Aggie said, nodding at her sister in turn. "Ran off with our fortune. We only had one fortune between us and he was a fortune hunter. You must watch out for them if you've got one. Do you?" They stared like a pair of little birds, sharp eyes magnified behind thick lenses.

"Poor as a church mouse, I'm afraid," Caitlin answered, delighted with the little murderesses.

"That's probably fortunate," Charlotte tittered.

"That's a pun," Aggie giggled. "Perhaps you'll marry one."

"One what?" Caitlin asked, finding her companions amusing, if a bit macabre.

"A fortune, a fortune! What else would you marry with your looks. A great beauty like you can pick and choose. *We* settled for Alanzo," Aggie said.

"But we settled *his* hash," Charlotte pronounced with a smug little smile. "You must never settle for anything less than your heart's desire. Ah, who have we here?"

"My friends," Caitlin explained as May and Judy tripped in, blinking in the semi-darkness, and tried several chairs each before alighting.

Aggie pushed her glasses up higher on her nose.

"First time?" she asked.

"Yes. You, too?" May answered politely. "Cute as a bug's ear, aren't they?" she whispered to Caitlin.

"We've been doing this for twenty years. We've been to the best," Charlotte nodded.

"*And* the worst," Caitlin added, about to break into what she knew would be uncontrollable laughter as the door opened again and a dark-eyed, olive-skinned woman, black hair streaming to her waist from beneath a white turban, stepped soundlessly into the room on slippered feet. Trailing diaphanous layers of cloth, she took a chair. Almost at once the candles went out, their odor thick in the air of the close room. A faint glow, as of a shrouded oil lamp, slowly brightened so that Caitlin could see just the medium and another figure, a man who had appeared to stand silently behind her, his face in shadow. The woman's eyes fluttered closed, her lips parted, and she sighed deeply before she spoke in a sweet, almost childlike voice.

"If our new guests will tell us who it is they wish to contact— No, no, Alanzo! Not *yet*," Madame DeLisle admonished gently. "You must give someone else a chance, you naughty boy."

"Don't send him away, please!" one of the Wily sisters implored.

"He'll be back, Aggie. His is a very persistent spirit. He's been monopolizing the show for days. There are three newcomers among us, and it isn't polite of him." The medium took another deep breath and placed her hands at her temples, opening her eyes very wide. The light behind her dimmed even more, and her gossamer draperies began to flutter, then to billow eerily. The heavy table on which the participants rested their hands shifted slightly, and May gasped. "Oh, Lord, maybe it's Granny!" she whispered.

"The spirits are coming to us now . . . in a great, sweeping wind . . . crossing the seas . . ." Madame DeLisle blinked her eyes repeatedly and threw back her head. The room was plunged into inky darkness for a moment as faint music began, softly at first, swelling louder as a fiddle blended with the sounds of a flute.

"Oh, you hear what's playin'? Do you *hear* it?" Judy asked. "Somethin' has brushed my face," she whispered, half standing and clutching her cousin's hand.

"Yes, yes," May responded. "It's . . . it's like spider webs and smoke and fingers touching all over."

The medium's head snapped forward, her eyes opened wide, and she began to sing in a cracking, quavering, old woman's voice, "Would I were Erin's apple blossoms o'er you . . ."

"It *is* Granny! She was always singin' that song," Judy said in an awed voice.

"And she still is, it seems," May tittered nervously. "The old biddy must be goin' strong yet, bless her."

"May! How can you?" Caitlin whispered. "Now hush. I want to see if—"

The room began to brighten in one corner and the draperies to swell in a wave that circled the room as Madame DeLisle turned toward Caitlin, the whites of her eyes and her coiled white turban seeming to glow out of the dimness. "What is it *you* want of us?" she asked, resting her hands palms up on the surface of the table, indicating that the others must do the same.

"I want to know my future." Caitlin smiled, taking the whole event rather lightly. She had quickly decided it was a harmless enough entertainment, nothing more, and intended to enjoy herself.

"We are not fortune tellers, miss. We don't use leaves or the tarots. I can only say of your future that you will be unusually successful in business."

"What can you say of my past?" Caitlin questioned, leaning forward a little.

"The past is hidden in yourself. Search inwardly," Madame said, her eyes fluttering closed.

"But can't you help me in my search? You *have* found Alanzo and Granny Browne for the others," Caitlin pressed a little, annoyed to find herself actually hoping for some small hint, a tiny clue that would become a key to her elusive memory.

Madame DeLisle's lips began to tremble, then to soundlessly form words. When she finally spoke, it was with a man's low, muffled voice coming from what seemed a long way off.

"Be afraid to welcome strangers," the voice began, "for thereby you may entertain devils unawares."

"No!" Caitlin cried out, getting to her feet so quickly she upset her chair. "You *can't* know about that, you—"

"Be still, be *still,*" Aggie cautioned as the medium began to thrash about wildly. "You could cause her damage if you anger the spirits now."

Appalled, Caitlin watched Madame's hand tremble and her arms flail wildly. "The names . . . the names . . . are coming." Madame gasped before she screamed once and fell back into a deep swoon.

"Look at her *arms,*" Charlotte whispered. "Look!"

Her heart pounding, Caitlin cautiously drew closer to the unconscious woman and saw, in a moment of real fear, that the medium's forearms were covered with raw, blood red markings.

"It's spirit writing," Aggie breathed. "She's known for it. The left arm is evil, the right, good."

"Alanzo never wrote to *us,*" Charlotte complained. "Well, what does it say, for pity sake?"

"Water, please." Madame DeLisle barely spoke. Hurriedly filling a glass from a decanter on the mantle, Caitlin held it to the woman's lips then almost reluctantly dropped her eyes to the fragile outstretched arms. On each, a single word, a name, had appeared—on the right, Edwards; on the left, Jones.

With her emotions rolling between wild laughter and hysterical tears, Caitlin froze, unable to move as the medium's head lolled back and from her barely parted lips a luminous vapor oozed slowly, spreading about the hushed room. Caitlin stared a moment longer then fled, tearing right through the middle of a photo session taking place in the next room.

"Young woman, young woman!" Mummler called after her. "You've frightened off this man's spirits, and you haven't even paid for your picture. It's crowded with extras!"

"Let her go. I'll cover the cost." A man had followed Caitlin out of the dimly lit séance chamber and now leaned in the doorway stroking his drooping mustache, a satisfied smile on his face.

"What are you doing? Get out of here," Mummler snapped with a meaningful glance at the miffed gentleman waiting before the camera. He stood and snatched his stove-pipe hat from the rack.

"Mr. Mummler, my concentration's broke, what with all the fuss. How can I summon Mr. Lincoln with all *this* going on? I'll return later. My wife really did enjoy seeing me seated with Messrs. Adams and Franklin."

"Do return later, Mr. Podmore. I'm sure Mr. Lincoln's spirit was quite close indeed. I feel he was about to stand beside you for his last and perhaps best photograph." Mummler smiled, seeing his customer to the door, then turned on the man now lounging in the chair before the camera.

"Are you trying to ruin us?" Mummler demanded, his voice squeaking with anger. "You chased off that girl somehow and now this poor dupe and . . . what do you mean, *you'll* pay. You never paid for anything in your life you didn't have to, you skinflint, even though you are getting rich with Madame and me."

"Relax, Mummler," Robin Edwards sneered. "You and your so-called Madame didn't do half so well before I showed you a few tricks of the spirit trade. That baryta water and a touch of dioxide, for example, does make a lovely cloud seeping from a medium's mouth. Gets the customers every time. Here," he added, separating a ten dollar bill from a thick wad in his pocket. "Whatever it costs me, it'll be well worth it, every cent, to get back at that smug little bitch, McGlory." He ducked into the dark room just in time to avoid May and Judy as they emerged from the dim séance chamber, blinking slightly then hurrying after Caitlin when they discovered she had gone.

Chapter Seventeen

"You must pay the most careful attention to how a ruffle is cut . . . how a seam is set, of course, but the heart of fashion is really in the whorls of silk, in the drape of a fine wool. The quality of fabric is everything," Ann lectured a silent Caitlin as they arranged scarves on a low display table and awaited their first Monday morning customer. "Rich velvet subterfuges can hide many imperfections in a woman. Medici collars disguise others. Leg of mutton sleeves are simply delicious with potatoes, and you are not paying one whit of attention to a single word I'm saying, are you?" Inflection changed, Ann inserted the quip and question and got no response. "Caitlin!" she exploded. "I'm talking to you!"

"Sorry?" Caitlin asked, looking up with a little scowl, her beautiful blue eyes startled and a touch guilty.

"You'll spoil your looks with such frowns," Ann admonished, wishing the girl would just say what was on her mind. But she knew from past experience that the headstrong child would speak only when—or if—she was good and ready. Shrugging her shoulders resignedly, Ann continued her instructive lecture.

"The suffragettes have been trying to demolish fashion for twenty years now, since Cady Stanton and Amelia Bloomer appeared in public in their calf-length skirts and baggy trousers. What an outcry that raised."

"I don't recall," Caitlin said as she cleverly draped a scarf, a long rope of pearls, and an ermine wrap about the shoulders of the wire-works mannequin that she had taken from her garret room and gilded as a cage for a pair of doves, much to Ann's delight.

"Of course you don't recall." Ann smiled. "You weren't even born then. The ladies were rebelling against the tyranny of fashion to which, they said and still say, we are all enslaved. I do have a certain sympathy for the suffragette position, believe it or not."

"You?" Caitlin asked with a sharp look. "You shouldn't bite the hand that feeds you."

"Well, have you ever known *me* to put anyone into a Grecian bend?" Ann asked languidly, rolling a cigarette and consulting the appointment book. "I need a bit of tobacco before Miss . . . Mrs. Faithful arrives. She's a rich widow, English, a professional beauty not so long ago. She'll no doubt arrive with her younger paramour in tow."

"Grecian bend?" Caitlin queried with only mild interest as she cast a final, critical glance about the salon to be sure all was in order.

"Those wretched corsets that make the bosom bulge above and the *derrière* protrude below," explained Ann. "Worn with very high-heeled slippers, the thrusts are even further exaggerated. The effect seems to me an open invitation. One might as well wear a sign saying, 'Grab these,' mightn't one?"

"I suppose." Caitlin smiled vaguely.

"That style does incapacitate a woman totally and—have you fed the doves?" Ann asked sharply, aware that Caitlin's attention had wandered again.

"Pardon? I didn't hear—"

"If you don't tell me what's wrong with you, Caitlin McGlory, there'll be hell to pay," Ann said matter-of-factly. "I don't talk for my own enlightenment. If you want to learn this business, there are things you must know, and you are not—"

"Damn and blast, I was almost over him, I was, until Saturday!" Caitlin exploded, a blue flame of fury alight in her eyes, her color heightening, her dreamy manner vanished and replaced by the high-strung, mercurial energy more typical of her.

"Well, *that's* a relief," Ann sighed wearily.

"A relief? How?"

"To see your verve and spirit restored, my girl. Are you ready, finally, to tell me about Saturday? And before?"

"We haven't time now," Caitlin snapped. "Your Mrs. Faithful's due in quarter of an hour."

"A long story, is it?" Ann teased mildly. "They're always late, these rich widows. Come into the office for a sherry and get right to the point. You'll feel better, I promise."

"I don't feel better, I *don't*, and you *promised*!" Caitlin proclaimed, laughing at herself, really, and trying to agitate the unflappable Ann who had sat silent, nodding now and then, through a twenty minute avalanche of words, not always rational ones, describing Caitlin's weeks with Quinn in unsparing detail and concluding with the disturbing visit to the spiritualist two days before. "She . . . someone actually spoke words almost the same as those carved on the shelter door where . . . where we were first together. It all came rushing back to me even though our angels had turned to devils and . . . well, aren't you going to say anything?" Caitlin implored, throwing up her hands.

"Yes, I am." Ann smiled her jaded smile, her downturned mouth curving just a little. "Four or five things actually." To Caitlin's annoyance, she sipped her sherry and lit a new cigarette before she was ready to begin. "Firstly," Ann said, "there is some explanation for your medium's clever tricks. Second, you were warned by me *and* by Brigida Hawkes. I'll refrain from saying I told you so, but you should have known all about Quinn Jones, about his keen appetites and extraordinary appreciation that makes a woman—any woman he graces with that glorious smile—feel like the most beautiful creature on earth. You *were* told all that. I know he himself told you from the first that he was going to leave you, but you didn't believe him, did you, until he was gone?"

"But I *did* believe him. That's one reason I wouldn't go to England. But Ann, I didn't realize you still—"

"Third," Ann interrupted brusquely, "you *will* get over Quinn Jones. I did. Almost everyone recovers from this sort of affair, except for the rare jilted spinster who goes to her virgin—or perhaps not so virgin—grave, after pathetically longing her life away. There's no excuse for that. Better to shoot the bastard and pay the consequences, *if* you can find him."

"Yes, I agree." Caitlin laughed, thinking of

Aggie and Charlotte.

"Fourth, Miss McGlory, why are you spending your rather hard-earned money on such humbugs as spiritualists? They thrive on the wishful thinking of poor, lonely unfortunates."

"It was just meant for a lark, Ann. Haven't you ever tried it?" Caitlin asked, glancing into a mirror as they heard a carriage stop in the street below. She smoothed her lustrous hair, coiled it up softly, and patted the embroidered pocket of her lace-trimmed pinafore apron, hoping to find a clasp that wasn't there.

"That thumping about and ghostly music is not for me." Ann sniffed. "Monstrous rubbish, all of it, but just on the off chance that there might be a little something there, I stay far away. I'd rather not shake up any of *my* ghosts, thanks. Caitlin?" she asked quietly, glancing through the half-open office door into the salon, "are you familiar with the phrase 'speak of the devil'?"

"Of course. Why do you ask?" Caitlin laughed.

"Well, yours has just walked in."

At the entrance to the salon, a gentleman was helping a lady off with her wrap. The woman was tall and striking, with broad shoulders and generously proportioned hips and bosom. The man was Quinn Jones.

"Will you be able to handle it? A professional could." Ann addressed Caitlin who was leaning back against the desk, her hands loosely clasped in front of her, changes of expression flitting over her face so rapidly—disbelief and delight and mute despair—that Ann hadn't time to respond to any of them. "I'll understand if you'd rather I dealt with him myself," she offered, finishing her sherry.

She waited patiently for Caitlin's response, which was slow in coming.

"But . . . she's old! And she's fat!" Caitlin said at last in a furious, appalled whisper that actually made Ann laugh aloud.

"Darling child, don't take that as a personal affront. Did you expect him to be true to your type, if not to you? Quinn's always had broad tastes. He adores women, all of them. Besides, Mrs. Faithful is hardly old, my age is all," Ann said archly. "And though she's a touch . . . overripe, her type is called voluptuous these days, my little pet. The look is very much in fashion, though I've always thought, and still do"—she went on slowly, stalling for time, trying to gauge Caitlin's true state of mind—"that the real aristocrat is always slender. Knights and ladies on medieval tomb rubbings are all elegant and thin. Go upstairs, Caitlin, I'll call you when they've gone."

"No, I'll call *you*. Allow *me*, Miss Overton, to handle this my own way," Caitlin said, striding forward boldly.

"Not if you're going to carry on like some jealous princess. Don't be viperish. I won't have it," Ann cautioned, but Caitlin had already gained the salon, her shining eyes dancing as she crossed toward the couple engaged in a whispered *tête-à-tête* at the far end of the room. "Mr. Jones! What an unexpected pleasure," she interrupted, pausing in the middle of the room, glowing in all her matchless, exuberant beauty that was reflected and duplicated in the surrounding mirrors.

Quinn stood and started toward her, holding her frozen in his dangerous gray stare. Her lustrous cloud of auburn hair perfectly framed her exotic, beautiful face, lit now as always by unbearably blue eyes, wide spaced and catlike. All her undisguised feelings shone from their transparent depths, entreating, imploring, promising Quinn everything, and she seemed to him for an instant the guileless waif she'd been on the day he'd found her. Then, she smiled a smile that changed everything, a smile he remembered perfectly. It brushed her tantalizing innocence with a veneer of ineffable femininity. She was ingenuous child and seductive woman flawlessly combined. When she spoke his name, her low, smoky voice called up in Quinn vivid remembrances of her rare, unreigned sensuality, and he took a step toward her. Caitlin held her ground, wanting him near her, her eyes savoring his dark, sleek grace.

"Quinn?" she repeated with a slight quaver as he took her hand to his lips. The dark exultation she read in his eyes when they met hers again, the undisguised rapaciousness roused an almost irresistible, tactile urgency in her to trace his long, violent muscles working beneath smooth skin, to taste his mouth, to feel his hands. She pulled away then very quickly, careful, now that it was too late, to avoid even the slightest touch, knowing how she'd be devastated by it.

"Welcome to our little *atelier*, Mrs. Faithful," she said to the woman who'd been serenely observing the scene from the soft depths of the Turkish sofa. "A tea tray will be brought up in a few moments," she added, touching an embroidered bell pull.

"A boutique perhaps, but hardly an *atelier*, my dear," Mrs. Faithful burbled, extending a soft hand. "You are Miss McGlory. Quinn described you in quite perfect detail." The woman smiled, gracious and warm, forcing Caitlin to admit that she was indeed a beauty with her abundantly endowed figure and classical face.

"How may we be of service to you today?" Caitlin asked, watching Quinn's reflection in one of the small table mirrors in front of her. Her composure recovered somewhat, she was all business.

Ann, who had held back, emerged from her office and, offering Quinn a nod, began to unfurl rolls of gloriously patterned silks and satins all around Caitlin and her customer.

"I want an entire new wardrobe," Mrs. Faithful announced emphatically. "What I've brought with me from England won't do here. It's all far too dull for America. Quinn . . . Mr. Jones agrees, don't you, darling?"

He nodded, fingering a piece of amber silk, his eyes on Caitlin, his look now politely sinister.

"Come sit by me and advise," the woman invited him, patting the thick cushion at her side.

"Before Mrs. Faithful purchases a stitch, I want everything you have, Ann, modeled by Caitlin," Quinn commanded. "Your walking suits, ball dresses, at-homes . . . I particularly want to see a wedding gown, if you've a design for one."

Ann saw Caitlin pale before she flushed as she stood with her head high at the center of the salon.

"She *is* a beauty"—Mrs. Faithful smiled in Caitlin's direction—"but such a delicate, aristocratic little thing, perfect as a fashion doll. How am I to know if what looks well on her will suit my more generous proportions?"

"Everyone knows English women are far . . . healthier, we'll say, than any others." Quinn laughed as he ducked Mrs. Faithful's playful fist.

"Darling, if you'd starved as I did before I married Mr. Faithful, the poor, dear departed, you'd take plumpness in a woman as a sign of prosperity as I do."

"An eighteen-inch waistline doesn't come cheaply, Mrs. Faithful," Ann commented with a subtle and surprising hint of sharpness.

"Oh, I quite agree. A diet of potatoes and bread and other such pasty stuff couldn't produce a perfect figure like hers," Mrs. Faithful responded with an agreeable, warm laugh. "But here in America, I've been informed, a fat bank account will give a *man* a fat belly, though not Quinn, of course, who is our own Apollo Belvedere, a near-perfect example of manly beauty, don't you agree?"

"Women can be beautiful with grace. Beautiful men become diffcult," Ann said, dogmatically positive.

While the two women politely squabbled for a moment longer, Caitlin's amused eyes met Quinn's, and they exchanged fast, conspiratorial smiles as they'd often done across the Burleighs' dinner table before she hastily turned away .

"Ah, tea and biscuits and sandwiches, too," Mrs. Faithful beamed. "*Just* what I need. We barely had breakfast in our hurry to get here. Isn't that so, darling?" she asked, turning to Quinn.

"I always seem to find myself with women of prodigious appetite," he answered, his superb smile lighting his handsome face. "Will you pour, Caitlin?" he asked, placing a chair for her at the lace-covered tea table.

His last remark earned him a withering look as she took her seat, wondering if she'd been overconfident, taking on Quinn and his expansive new mistress, alone. Ann had abandoned her, going off to arrange the gowns for showing.

"Will you and Mr. Jones be married very soon, Mrs. Faithful?" she couldn't resist asking with a little smile as she passed the English woman a tea with milk and two sugars.

"Married? Oh, my dear!" Mrs. Faithful exclaimed. "We've only just met a few weeks ago and on the high seas at that." She turned to Quinn who had declined tea and had settled back languidly into the depths of the sofa to observe the two women with apparent pleasure, though Caitlin's superb composure was beginning to annoy him.

"Imagine, darling, you and I married!" Mrs. Faithful said with a suggestive, loose laugh, familiarly touching Quinn's knee for emphasis.

"Mr. Jones did ask to look at wedding gowns," Caitlin responded, quickly getting to her feet to rearrange the fans displayed on a side table.

"Mr. Jones, I've learned in just the short time we've been acquainted, has a unique appreciation of the feminine form. He is gratified by viewing it in all possible drapings *and* undrapings. His interest in wedding gowns, at least as far as I'm concerned, is purely aesthetic. Besides, I'm enjoying my widowhood too much to even consider marriage, and . . . he hasn't asked me." Mrs. Faithful smiled and bounced a little on her cushion, accepting another watercress sandwich from Caitlin who had resumed her place.

"So!" Caitlin began clapping her hands, her good nature somewhat restored. "You two met a few weeks ago on the high seas? Tell me *all* about it," she asked, reminding Quinn of a young girl gossiping with her best friend. Mrs. Faithful responded in kind.

"Oh, it was wonderfully dramatic," she offered warmly, sitting up straighter at the edge of her seat. "We thought it was pirates or icebergs, stopping like that, four days east of Halifax, and then *he* came aboard in a great animal-skin coat and high, furred boots, looking like some wild North American mountain man. Until he removed his wraps, that is. A more elegant, cultured gentleman isn't to be found anywhere." Mrs. Faithful smiled. "But then, Quinn is an art collector who surrounds himself with beauty, a connoisseur who seeks perfection in all things, a—"

"I don't understand," Caitlin interrupted with artless charm, cutting off Mrs. Faithful's rush of praise for Quinn in mid-sentence. "How on earth did you both get here if you were part way to England only a short time ago?"

"Dear, you don't *seem* slow on first impression," Mrs. Faithful bantered. "Our ships were passing in the night . . . almost the night. It was dawn actually when Quinn was brought by dory from his steamer, bound for England, to ours, bound for Halifax, Boston, then New York. He suddenly remembered some unfinished business. Isn't that right, Quinn?"

"Now I see." Caitlin nodded. "And what of your traveling companions, Mr. Jones? Did they continue on?" She rose and pulled the tapestry bell cord that quickly brought a servant to remove the tea tray.

"Yes. The twins and Gordon will be comfortably entertained by a trusted friend until I join them. What have you there?" he asked as Caitlin began placing various objects on the table before Mrs. Faithful: a burl glove box trimmed with brass, ivory glove stretchers, lace collars and cuffs and jewelry box covers, jeweled smelling salts bottles, and a collection of folded fans.

"The lady will perhaps find something

among these trinkets she'd like to have"—Caitlin smiled at Mrs. Faithful—"and the gentleman will perhaps buy it for her." She nodded at Quinn. "It was my idea to bring these small things into the salon to keep people amused during my changes of costume. They sell very well, too."

"This *is* lovely!" Mrs. Faithful exclaimed, taking up a small cut glass bottle decorated with diamonds. "Though the last thing *I* need is smelling salts, vulgarly robust as I am."

"It will do for scent as well," Caitlin suggested. "Here's something very lovely. You know that lace is coming back into fashion again now. The best of it is being made on Burano Island near Venice. The copies from there are so perfect, the new can't be distinguished from the old. But see *this* magnificent creation." Caitlin adjusted a deep-yellow silk lace collar that reached nearly to her waist. "The original was made about two hundred years ago, and for a man. One of our own sewing girls, Kathleen, copied it from an old pattern book just republished."

As Caitlin turned slowly, Mrs. Faithful's eyes, fixed on the collar, began to glow with avid desire. Quinn's eyes, fixed on Caitlin's serene, lovely face, showed a similar look.

"I *must* have it," Mrs. Faithful announced. "But I want the scent bottle, too, and it would be scandalous indulgence to take them both. Which would you choose, Quinn, if you were I?"

"Both, definitely." He smiled. "Or neither. Perhaps there's something else Miss McGlory would display?"

"The fans are my favorites," she responded at once with her dazzling smile. "When I make my fortune, I'll have hundreds of them, all displayed in crystal cases. I'll use a different one for every ballet and opera and concert of the season." She removed the lace collar and placed it within Mrs. Faithful's reach, and the woman's eager fingers, irresistibly drawn, traced the fine pattern of knotted silk stitches and loops as Caitlin began spreading fans on the tea table.

"These of painted parchment with the little silhouettes are Italian; this of engraved painted paper with ivory sticks is French, the scenes are of *The Barber of Seville*. We've other operas, a few battles, an exploding Mt. Vesuvius, and my favorite, though it's too dear for me to buy yet on my meager wage."

The miniature painting, in pale pinks and blues and greens, showed the Roman goddess, Flora, in her blooming garden that was made to glisten by tiny, light-capturing chips of mica set over the flowers.

"It isn't very old, but aren't the colors beautiful?" Caitlin asked, coquettishly fluttering the fan before her face, her taunting blue eyes meeting Quinn's penetrating stare above it.

"I'll buy it," he said casually.

"But . . . you *can't*!" Caitlin stamped her foot, her long-simmering temper finally breaking free. "I said I wanted it, and you—" Mrs. Faithful's astounded look silenced her, and Caitlin's expression changed instantly from spirited anger to austere and ethereal cold-eyed scorn.

"Here, take it as a gift," she said. "No charge."

"Caitlin, how unlike the clever businesswoman you usually are," Ann scoffed in a mildly critical tone. Reentering the salon, she adjusted the drapery to soften hard edges of light that were striping the room.

"Deduct the cost from my wages," Caitlin snapped. "Are we finally ready to begin?"

"But she must be exhausted, Quinn. You've kept her at this for hours," Mrs. Faithful admonished, her hand resting casually on his knee. Caitlin hesitated, glancing from one to the other, as much amused as irritated by Quinn's persistence.

"I'm not at all tired," she told Mrs. Faithful, who had ordered one, and sometimes two, of every item shown her, the duplicate for her daughter in England. "If Mr. Jones insists upon seeing our lingerie modeled . . . well, it *is* my job to . . . satisfy his demands," she smiled.

Despite her exuberant manner, Caitlin was beginning to tire, and at the moment she was growing very warm, swathed to her lovely eyes in a criminally expensive cashmere wrap. Her performance, carried off so far with perfectly disciplined grace, had already lasted more than two hours. She'd paraded the salon's entire collection before Quinn, who lingered over every detail of every gown, directing her turns and swirls with an infuriating arrogance. She'd changed her hair style several times with Judy's help, worn at least ten different pairs of slippers and boots, as many pairs of gloves, several sets of worked stockings, pearls, rings, feathers, and even Ann's antique glass bead necklace that Quinn knew at first glance was priceless but tried, none-the-less, to buy.

When, rarely, Caitlin met Quinn's appraising stare, she found it threatening with a seductive heat that she pretended to ignore, though she could feel his eyes touching her as his hands had once, caressing every swell and curve and exquisitely sensitive secret place.

The others, it seemed, remained unaware of the stubborn contest taking place in their midst, of the test of strength Caitlin and Quinn each expected to win. He'd thrown down a a gauntlet just by walking into the salon. She'd accepted his challenge and had no intention of backing down now . . . or ever.

To Quinn, Caitlin's perfectly aloof, icy beauty was a taunting reminder of the audacious, warm innocent he'd expected to find and thought he had found in the first moments of their meeting again. Now, all she would offer him was a false, enigmatic smile, and that only briefly before she turned her vague, beautiful stare to the window, to the ceiling, in any direction but his. Determined to strike a nerve beneath her brittle, beautiful exterior, he'd kept her working and at his beck and call much longer than he'd intended. He was both irritated and intrigued that she showed no signs of strain, dancing through her command performance with such charming, extravagant elegance he began to wonder who was manipulating whom in their private battle of wills. To step up the pace of the game, Quinn changed his tactics, laying hands on Caitlin in a way that propriety forbade, making no excuses.

"Now, that is a perfectly designed costume on an *almost* perfect body," Quinn commented when Caitlin discarded the cashmere wrap to reveal a dotted muslin spencer worn with a narrow, bustled silk skirt.

"What do you mean 'almost' perfect?" Caitlin flirted with a little pout. Quinn ignored the question, handling her as he might the wireworks mannequin beside her.

"This body nicely exemplifies Hogarth's thesis that the curved line . . . as here"—he ran a hand lightly over Caitlin's breast, expecting some reaction, but she only blinked—"and here, as well." He shaped her little waist in his two hands, drawing her toward him, his head lowered as though to try her lips. It was then that Ann caught Caitlin's fleeting look of exquisite helplessness and came to her rescue. Stepping between the two, she turned Caitlin toward the mirror.

"She is a good example as well of Professor Lavater's Physionomic Law. If one can determine character from facial structure as the professor wrote and many believe, Caitlin is a sterling young woman. The nose must be equal in length to the depth of the forehead . . . so"—Ann touched Caitlin's brow—"and should almost join the arch of the orbit of the eye, as here. Lavater also thought that a nose neither hard, nor muscular, nor pointed, nor broad, always indicted an excellent character. Hmm, yours is a touch broad at the bridge, Caty, so you're not quite perfect after all. What do you think, Mr. Jones?"

"Close enough." He glared at Ann, casually resuming his place on the deep sofa next to Mrs. Faithful, who seemed quite oblivious to the subtleties of the conversation, overcome with pleasure about her purchase of the lace collar and Quinn's generous gift of the diamond-encrusted scent bottle.

"The wedding gown, if you please. We'll forego the lingerie . . . for the present." Quinn tried his smile on Caitlin, who gave him one of her own. "For the present? But I believe Mrs. Faithful has ordered all she could possibly need. You're not planning to favor us with another visit on your own, are you, Mr. Jones?"

Caitlin had started toward the dressing room door, loosening her titian hair and, completely unself-consciously, beginning on her bodice buttons.

"No, not on my own!" He laughed and she spun about to face him, speechless for a moment, blue eyes flaming.

"I understand. Well, visit as often as you choose," she said in a mockingly pleasant tone. "If *all* your lady friends are as pleased with our work as Mrs. Faithful, we'll be more than pleased to see them and you."

He made no answer, just touched two fingers to his brow as though tipping an imaginary cap, acknowledging she'd scored a point in their private contest.

"The wedding dress, Miss McGlory?" he reminded her in a patronizing tone that sent her hurrying from the room in a pique.

* * *

"Some girls, Caitlin, are simply born to be brides. You, my dear"—Mrs. Faithful sighed—"are one of them."

Caitlin stood poised at the center of the salon wearing an antique ivory satin wedding gown completely lavished with lace in an intricately filagreed bird and floral pattern. The slender, form-following sheath, banded beneath the bosom, had long, sheer sleeves and what seemed acres of train that Ann arranged in a swirl about Caitlin's feet. Lace cap streamers fell to her waist with a flamboyant cascade of titian curls and a feather-light veil touched her perfect profile. In lace-gloved hands, Caitlin held a bouquet of dandelions dried to a bright bisque yellow, the only flowers, she explained, available on such short notice.

"You should be deluged with them, looking as you do—lily-of-the-valley and forget-me-not, white wild orchids and pinks." Mrs. Faithful smiled. "When you *are* a bride, you will hide a pink somewhere about you beneath all that satin and lace. The groom will search for it and find it . . . eventually. It's an old English custom. You will make some lucky fellow very happy, Caitlin. Won't she, Quinn?" the woman asked. Standing, she set her hat on her head and began pulling on her gloves.

"I'm sure she will," Quinn amiably agreed.

"That design particularly suits her. I've seen her in—and out—of something very like it, playing Juliet as I recall. Good day, Miss McGlory."

Caitlin's coloring heightened and her eyes flashed.

"Scoundrel!" she mouthed behind Mrs. Faithful's back as Quinn helped the woman on with her wraps. He winked, putting on his own black top coat that was velvet collared in gray and slim at the waist.

"Isn't he the most manly fellow?" Mrs. Faithful beamed, slipping her arm through his possessively.

"And so elegant, too," Caitlin agreed with exaggerated enthusiasm.

"Most American men aren't. They dress so . . . so dully. Too busy making money to care how they look; that's what the English say," Mrs. Faithful reported. "Well, thank you, Caitlin, for a lovely morning," she said, turning to Quinn. "Shall we go, darling? We're to lunch with my solicitor . . . my lawyer, as you call them, or my silk, as dear, departed Mr. Faithful invariably referred to his legal advisor. Whatever, he's to be at—"

"Shall we really expect you again, Mr. Jones?" Caitlin asked with more feeling than she'd meant to, struck by the hollow, sinking sensation she'd always felt before when Quinn was about to leave her.

Mrs. Faithful, at the threshold of the salon, turned back, her sympathetic eyes enlightened and knowing now as she approached Caitlin again.

"My dear, you mustn't bother about *this* charming rogue. You're much too young and innocent for his sort. It will take an experienced woman to keep him in line. I would like to send a delightful gentleman to call on you if I may, a young Britisher, Richard Montanari. He was aboard our steamer, recovering from a broken heart. A sea voyage is so purifying, good for whatever ails one, and it seems to have done wonders for the boy. He's ready now to go back to work. He's let a small studio not far from here."

"Is he an artist?" Caitlin asked with interest.

"Richard Montanari is a doll maker, one of the best in Europe, and always looking for new models. He will simply adore you, and perhaps you would do him the kindness of sitting for a few sketches."

"I'm sure Miss McGlory has better things to do with her time than waste it on Richard," Quinn said coldly, his look severe and a little cruel all at once.

"But you're wrong, Quinn," Caitlin disagreed. "I'd love to pose for a doll maker, of all things. Mrs. Faithful, do ask him to call. I've plenty of time. Saturdays are my own, though I've promised part of this one to the girls. We're going dancing in the evening, but I could give Mr. Montanari the afternoon."

"Where do you do this dancing?" Quinn asked disinterestedly, slapping his palm with a pair of gray doeskin gloves.

"At Harry Hill's hall," Caitlin said, turning back her veil, seeming to take no notice of his changed mood.

"Dance halls! Oh, now I understand why the returning British are always so taken aback by you young American girls. You're all so independent, going about unescorted and unchaperoned, flirting with strangers on the streets, actually dancing with men you know nothing about. It isn't done at home. Think what might happen!" Mrs. Faithful, staring into the mirror, set her hat pin emphatically.

"Yes, just *think*," Caitlin said with a humorous inflection. "Some inexperienced girl just off the farm or the boat, all alone in the city, could be taken advantage of by . . . well, by a crafty fellow like Mr. Jones, for example. New York's full of these marginal drifters, with no place and no ties."

"Like . . . Quinn?" Mrs. Faithful asked, genuinely puzzled. "But he's not—"

"We must go, Leila. The carriage is waiting," Quinn interrupted, ushering her out of the salon before him. Then he turned back to Caitlin with a quick, conspiratorial wink, all at once the mischievous boy taking her into his confidence.

"Don't give me away now, Caitlin. This is a very rich widow. She needs someone to help her invest her fortune, and she's found just the right man."

"Invest? What do you know about investing? Thievery is more in your line and—oh!" Caitlin exploded indignantly, hands on her hips, disapproving eyes wide. "I understand your mean little game. You are going to dupe her out of her inheritance. And she's such a nice woman and— Don't! Don't you come near me, Quinn Jones," she ordered, panicked as he started toward her with a dangerous smile.

When she tried to flee, Caitlin found herself ensnared by the long train of the wedding gown that had been so picturesquely arranged about her feet.

"Damn and blast!" she exploded, tripping directly into Quinn's arms, the remembered feel of them that she'd so longed for, his hot, gray eyes staring into hers, instantly turning her soft and almost helpless against him. He was forcing her mouth as she tried to twist away, and then her inarticulate protestations died on her lips as she began to respond, pressing to him as though she couldn't get close enough, her fingers raking his dark, satin hair, his hands possessively molding the slim lines of her body through lace and satin, reclaiming her so totally she hadn't the strength or desire to resist him at all.

"If you tear that wedding dress, Quinn Jones, you'll have to buy it. It's very dear and you are the last person I'd ever expect to have need of it," Ann said calmly. She'd entered the salon unnoticed, cigarette in one hand, feather duster in the other, and paused. "Call me when you've done, will you?" she added, turning to leave again as Caitlin, still clinging to Quinn, hid her face against his shoulder, her trembling voice muffled when she finally managed to speak.

"Oh dear! How embarrassing," she said.

Quinn lifted her chin and smiled into her eyes. "You always were quick to take fire," he said in the low voice that had, from the first time she'd heard it, set Caitlin's heart pounding.

"You'd better go now," she said, disengaging herself from his arms, her own melodic voice husky and warm. She gathered up the train of the gown and held it over one extended arm, prepared for flight if he approached her again.

"I've a suite at the Fifth Avenue Hotel. Come to me later, when you're free. We'll finish what we started here."

"No, I can't," Caitlin answered vehemently,

shaking her head.

"Come tomorrow, then." Quinn turned up his collar.

"Never." Caitlin smiled.

"Liar." He smiled back and then he was gone.

Chapter Eighteen

"Who is it to be today?" Caitlin asked a bit testily, not looking up from the ledger book before her.

"Alyce Brice," Ann answered. "Quite a well-known bareback rider. She often dresses like a streetwalker, but then these days so many do that it's hard to tell the amateurs from the professionals. Caitlin . . . if you've had enough of this game with Quinn, I will understand. He's been here every day this week, putting you through hoops for his various ladies. There's no point tying yourself into knots over him."

"I won't give him the satisfaction of quitting now. It's Saturday. He can't come tomorrow and that will give me a chance to untie the knots. What's this girl look like?"

"More like you, actually, than any of the others. Mrs. Faithful was overripe, the actress was elfin and boyish, the two bar maids on Wednesday Amazonian. I can't remember Thursday . . ." Ann puzzled.

"He came alone and chose special sorts of things to take to England, he said, including my fan and the wedding gown," Caitlin snapped.

"Oh, of course. How could I forget?" Ann asked wearily. "It was the same day he brought us that extraordinary gem-encrusted fabric from the Parisian embroiderer, Michonet. It must have cost Quinn a small fortune, and I'm charging him another to make up the ball gown he described."

"And Friday it was that stuck-up Miss Gouvenour." Caitlin glowered. "With her short upper lip and upturned nose, she looked like . . . like a pug dog."

"She's very old New York, Society Register rich and she can't do anything about her nose. Miss Brice *is* more attractive, though rather less respectable. She's your height and of similar figure, though not as well proportioned. I'd say you've got her by an inch at the waist. Hers is eighteen or—horrors—perhaps even *nineteen*," Ann mildly jibed. "Her bosom's smallish, not bad, but it can't compare to—"

"Don't tease me about him," Caitlin said so plaintively that Ann actually took her hand.

"Caitlin, do you know what it is Quinn wants of you?"

"Nothing he hasn't already had and, Ann

. . . if he doesn't let up soon . . . I can't hold out much longer." Caitlin closed the ledger with a snap.

"What if you did spend a night with him? Just to get rid of him, of course," Ann suggested, watching Caitlin intently.

"Buy him off, do you mean? That's contemptible. Besides," she said with a flickering smile, "I've already thought of that. It won't work. I might not want to leave him again."

"Perhaps you wouldn't have to," Ann said, smiling herself now as Caitlin looked up in amazement.

"Whatever do you mean by that?" she asked.

"I've seen him look at you, I've watched you two together all this week, and I think it just might be possible that the man's in love with you."

Caitlin tilted her head to one side quizzically. "Really, Ann? And what if he is?" she asked with an attempt at a blank stare. "I've no intention of spending my life, or any part of it, with that . . . that benighted gypster, no matter how he makes me feel."

"The landscape of the heart is full of hidden pitfalls, Caitlin. Love's not to be treated so lightly," Ann answered, unsettled by the girl's adamance.

"Love's got nothing to do with this," Caitlin insisted.

"But he did ask you to go to England with

him. For Quinn Jones, that's . . . remarkable."

"And, you're the one who told me to be independent. In fact, you're the one showing me how to do it, or have you agreed to marry Billy?"

"I've told you before not to do as I do, but to do as I say." Ann shrugged. "I never meant you to be so unbending, so independent that you could never let a man think he's taking care of you just a little. It's fine to be a free spirit, Caitlin, but too free is *lonely*. That silly wager with your uncle! Poor Billy fussed over you so long, he doesn't know what to do with himself now that you won't let him do anything for you. There are times when graciously accepting what one is offered is true generosity. You haven't let Billy spend even his time on you, to say nothing of money, since that Sunday you came home."

"It's difficult, Ann, him working all night and me all day. I can't see when—"

"You haven't really forgiven Billy, have you, for what he said that day at Silver Hill?" Ann asked, shaking her head disapprovingly. "You, miss, are even more stubborn than he is."

"I trusted him and he turned on me," Caitlin persisted. "He told me such . . . awful things."

"But you know his temper. Half of what he said probably isn't even true."

"Well, I am going to England one day soon to find out for myself," Caitlin announced with a pout.

"And Quinn?"

"*He* . . . left me, just walked away." Caitlin's lower lip quivered a little.

"I know you think that's absolutely unforgivable but I think . . ." Ann's thoughtful expression piqued Caitlin's curiosity.

"What do you think?"

"You helped him on his way alone, Miss McGlory."

"I had cause," Caitlin objected, turning back to the figures in her book. "He's . . . about to marry an English girl, the one he's buying all these beautiful things for, including the wedding gown and *my* fan!" Caitlin stood and stamped her foot.

"Quinn? Marry anyone but you? I don't believe it for a moment." Ann responded with sceptical surprise, slowly coming to her feet.

"I had it from a very good source. And I refuse to have any more to do with Quinn Jones. I've done all I can to make myself unavailable and unattractive to him," Caitlin said seriously.

"Oh, I see *that.*" Ann nodded, equally serious. "You've pulled your hair into a tight knot and brought your little governess dress back into service. None of it works, darling girl. Yours is the sort of beauty that will never disappoint. You're trying to play it safe and that's not your style."

"And what would you suggest?" Caitlin demanded, flinging open a window and taking several deep breaths.

"Be bold and daring, Cate. Try to beat him at his own game." Ann smiled with quiet relish. "You've given him a good match so far, but go farther. Flaunt your admirers at *him*. Go out on the town every night with a different adoring escort. Dress superbly, be gay, charming, laugh a lot and flirt outrageously with everyone, including our Mr. Jones. That's the way to show him he's just one more Tom to you, no different than any other man."

"When you put it that way . . . well, I'd better go up and change before he arrives." Caitlin laughed, her eyes dancing with mischievous pleasure. "I can hardly wait to get on with the game now that you've shown me how to win it! Ann Overton, *you* are brilliant!" she called, hurrying off to her room.

"You've no idea yet, my sensible little girl, how really brilliant I am," Ann thought with a congratulatory nod at her reflection in the mirror, "or how maneuverable you are," she added before turning her attention to the ledger book abandoned by Caitlin for more pressing pursuits.

It was the third night out of Halifax that Quinn Jones knew he had made a mistake.

Pacing the deck of the steamer alone at four in the morning, hands sunk deep in his pockets, collar turned up against the wind, he had decided he wasn't through with Caitlin McGlory, not yet, had even begun to suspect he might never be, would know that for a certainty the first instant he saw her again in all her mercurial, restless beauty.

But striding the deck in a restless rage that night beneath indifferent stars, he was sure of one thing: he had to see her again, had to compare her reality with the vision growing more perfect in memory with each passing day and mile. Caitlin's innocent, unquenchable passion had been a fantasy come true. Her gentle aggressions, untainted by coyness or restraint, were committed with a bountiful liberality that had made him want to give her, in turn, more than he had before ever—infinite, endless delight. When she'd moved against him . . . above . . . below . . . or when she was coiled quivering in his arms, her responsive eyes wondrous with anticipation, and after, vague and beautiful with drowsy satiety, he'd felt he'd possessed her completely. She had been flawless, perfect and she belonged to him then as no woman ever had, but as his paintings did, or the other beautiful things with which he'd surrounded himself.

When he'd turned and walked away from her, thinking he'd had enough, thinking it would be as easy to leave Caitlin as it had the others before, it had been a serious mistake, one of the few he'd ever made, and Quinn intended to put it right without delay.

He was striding toward the captain's cabin to have the ship turned back to port when he spotted the distant lights of a westbound steamer approaching off the starboard bow.

Now, for the sixth day straight, Quinn feasted his hungry eyes on Caitlin, devouring every detail of her extraordinary appearance with a voyeur's pleasure as she came toward him across the salon with her willowy walk. Today there was something different about her, he noticed instantly. Her eyes were shining in a new way, and there was a small, secret smile lurking about her delicious, velvety lips that unsettled him a little and made him doubt what he saw.

Quinn had become more certain with each passing day that Caitlin's resistance was weakening, that she'd be in his arms and in his bed before another night passed. Yet here she was, refreshed and lovely as springtime coming in at the door, and so preoccupied with some private thought, she didn't notice him at all. Scowling, Quinn stood, nearly upsetting her display of silk scarves draped over a standing lace window screen.

"You're like a bull in a rose garden," she complained with a laugh, thinking he was anything but, admiring his lean, rangy build and easy grace. "Don't fuss; I'll see to the scarves," she added offhandedly.

"I've no intention of fussing." He glared. "What makes you so chipper?"

"I'm looking forward to my afternoon off," she answered, rising on tiptoe to coil one of the scarves about his neck. "That suits you. It would do for a man as well as for a woman, don't you agree, Miss Brice?" Caitlin asked pertly, pulling the bell cord for tea.

"We'll pass on the refreshments today, thanks," Quinn said before his companion could answer. "The lady will look at lingerie only. I've no time to waste, so if you'd proceed . . ."

"Don't mind Mr. Jones. He's often irritable this way when he's bored," Alyce Brice explained helpfully to Caitlin.

"Is he often bored in your company, Miss Brice?" Caitlin asked so sweetly that the woman, not sure if she'd been insulted or not, hesitated to answer.

"She'll be far from boring in some flattering bed attire," Quinn said in a low, menacing voice, leaning against the mantel. "Do you think you could stop chattering and get on with it?"

Miffed at being dismissed like a servant,

Caitlin swept from the room with a withering glare at Quinn, her good humor giving way to irritability. "He can just wait and whistle," she said to herself, deciding to take her own good time returning. When she did, nearly half an hour later, Quinn and Alyce, smiling and relaxed, were standing very close, deeply engrossed in conversation. They moved apart guiltily, Caitlin decided, when she cleared her throat and took the floor to stand rigidly still at the center of the salon wearing a discreet, innocent ensemble she'd purposely chosen, a high-necked cotton bed gown worn beneath a matching wrapper with a pink drawstring tie at the waist. Slants of sunlight fired her russet-tipped hair where a pink bow was set amidst the curls.

"Turn," Quinn said gesturing, knowing exactly how her smooth body would look stripped of the robe and the brushed cotton gown, remembering its sculpted ivory perfection as the firm, lithe muscles tightened. Caitlin's full lips parted just a little as he studied her, her half-lidded eyes warmed, and he knew exactly what she was wanting. He could almost feel her in his arms, softening and flowing to him, her compelling fragility heightened by infinite tenderness.

"Take off the wrap, Caitlin," Quinn said in a softened, caressing voice, and she looked directly at him then with searching eyes. He saw the yearning not quite hidden in the glorious blue depths, and he read forever there as he had from the very start. But pride ran in her as strong as passion, he knew, and he had committed the worst crime in her catalog of transgressions. He had turned his back and walked away; he had deserted her, and now she was trying to shut him out forever, to hide her true feelings from him and from herself, too. She had little skill at subtlety and subterfuge, though. She was still, and would always be for Quinn, a guileless girl with all her emotions shining. He had seen enough to know the game was still worth the candle, and he was willing to give it some time. In fact, he was willing to give it forever.

"Take off the robe," he repeated gently.

"Quinn, really!" Alyce protested. "She can't do any such thing. She'll be as good as naked."

"I've seen it before," he said, grinning, his arms folded over his chest, never taking his darkening gray eyes from Caitlin.

"You scoundrel," she said pleasantly, a disarming trick she'd learned from Ann, who could make the most devastating remark more cutting by delivering it in the mildest manner.

Very slowly, Caitlin undid the satin-covered hooks running to her waist and loosened the pink ribbon tie. Then she turned her back to Quinn, lifting a shoulder a little to suggest he help her out of the wrap, forcing him to touch her, enveloping him in waves of fragrance. He slid the robe from her shoulders, letting it fall, and he saw in the mirror through the light cotton gown the curving lines of her perfect body with its darker shadows and peaks and soft, smooth plains.

"Do you like our new scent?" she asked in a burnished whisper, feeling ravaged by his raw stare. She turned about once, well aware of the effect on Quinn, then reclaimed the robe, slipping into it quickly. "We call our fragrance Cream of Lily. Miss Brice should have a sample," Caitlin said as she unstoppered a ruffled, opalescent glass bottle, fluted in the form of an opening lily.

"I prefer your orange and spice," Quinn said gruffly.

"Do you?" she responded lightly. "I can't see *that* matters . . . now."

"Can't you?" he asked with a slight, incomprehensible smile. "We'll be going," he added abruptly, turning away.

"But you've only just got here," Caitlin protested, "and Miss Brice hasn't seen—"

"Send one of everything for her to my hotel," he said, his bearing all at once that of an aristocratically impractical prince, grandly profligate.

"Don't be so impulsive, Quinn. I don't need *everything*," Alyce said mildly.

"It's the simplest thing to do. I'm in a

hurry," Quinn answered, holding his companion's cloak at the ready. "And it is Saturday. The salon closes early today as I recall."

"Will you be back next week?" Caitlin blurted, as usual not wanting him to go and wishing to heaven she'd never met him.

"I don't expect so," he said, his now-veiled eyes unreadable, disguising a nearly uncontrollable urge to catch her up in his arms and carry her off. There was a vulnerability about Caitlin at that moment, a plea in her eyes, that made it hard for him to leave. He took a step toward her then turned away.

"We're going, Alyce," he called, already through the salon door.

"Sorry," the woman said with a superior smile. "I've never seen Quinn this way exactly, so quickly bored and restless. Thank you for your time, miss," she added, rushing out after him.

Forehead pressed to the cool window pane, Caitlin watched their carriage as it pulled away from the curb into the flow of traffic and was gone from sight.

"I've got to get out of here for a while," she announced furiously, turning from the window as Ann entered the room.

"I suggest you change first," Ann said, taking in Caitlin's flimsy attire with a mildly amused glance. "How did it go?"

"Wonderfully! I don't think he's ever going

to bother me again," Caitlin reported with a catch in her voice. "He has no plans to return here and never had, so I needn't have worried at all."

"I don't think I really believe you, but if it's true, you can just stop mooning about and get on with your work. You still owe me half an hour," Ann said, rearranging the scarves.

"I'll need more money," Caitlin announced.

"Call off your silly bet with Billy. You know he'll give you whatever you want," Ann said, occupied now with the draperies.

"You don't understand. I want more money from *you,*" Caitlin snapped, expecting an explosion of protest as Ann turned toward her languidly and stared.

"I'm already paying you five dollars a week. You've just had a two dollar raise," she said with mild indignation. "I'm running a business here, not a charity for wayward girls, which is the way it often seems."

"I've been approached by Rowland Macy and his second-in-command, Margaret Gretchell. They asked me to model and to start a making-up department for them, like Altman did."

"Macy has already got furniture and crockery in that store of his and now a making-up department?" Ann sniffed critically. "None of the better sort of women will frequent his establishment. That cousin of his, Margaret, does everything for him—writes the ads, supervises the staff, even locks up at night. Did she tell you she spent weeks training a pair of cats to sleep in the furniture department? Margaret's absolutely loyal to Rowland, not like some overly ambitious little upstarts I could mention." Ann was actually becoming quite agitated at the very prospect of increasing Caitlin's pay for the second time in less than a month.

Amused but staunch, Caitlin persisted. "I told Miss Gretchell that with her talents, she should go out on her own," she gently goaded Ann, who took the bait without hesitation.

"And I suppose you've thought about doing the same?" Ann sniffed, "after your vast experience of a few weeks here? Well, keep this in mind. That Nantucket Quaker, Macy, was a dismal failure at everything he'd ever tried before—whaling, stockbroking, real estate and more—and Margaret is very much responsible for his success now, but I am not Macy, Miss McGlory, and you are not Gretchell, and if you suppose—"

"Really, Mrs. Overton!" Caitlin interjected with a laugh as Ann paced the room, puffing blue plumes of smoke from her cigarette. "I don't want to go out on my own. All I'm asking is that you pay me properly. If you sell just one fan, you've made my week's wages three times over, and it was my idea, after all."

"Well . . . how much did they offer you," Ann asked sheepishly, coming to light in a window seat.

"Ten a week," Caitlin answered quickly, tacking on a dollar.

"Ten dollars to play about with pots of face creams and boxes of powder? Ridiculous!"

"It's turning a really good profit, enameling and making-up," Caitlin answered patiently.

"Really? Well, I suppose there could be something to it," Ann reluctantly acknowledged. "I did have a very fashionable young beauty in here not long ago, carrying a Portable Complexion. She redid her paint before she left. We'd have to have the very best enameler, though. If the arsenic paste isn't applied just right, the pale shell over the face tends to crack. We couldn't have our ladies—"

"The best of course!" Caitlin bubbled over with excitement. "We could have other cosmetics, too, and a hairdresser. There's lots of space if we divide the salon."

"My better customers see their doctors *and* their hairdressers in the privacy of their own boudoirs. You know that on a night before a ball the man of the moment works into the small hours putting up curls, then rushes from house to house next day combing out. But I suppose"—Ann's jaded eyes began to light up a little—"I *do* suppose that a very sought-after hair stylist and a skilled enameler could bring a great many new customers to our doors. We'll do it. Caitlin, you are so clever, you actually remind me of me at your age."

"So you will increase my pay then?" Caitlin gently pressed.

"Damn it, yes! Ten a week; not a penny more!"

"Ann, I can hardly believe you're agreeing to all this so quickly," Caitlin said a little suspiciously. "Why?"

"You're blackmailing me, that's why. If Macy doesn't hire you away, someone else will one of these days. We both know that, don't we? Besides," Ann added, staring out the window, her back to Caitlin, "there's a special bond between us, you know. We've loved the same men, you and I."

Touched by this rare personal revelation from Ann, who so diligently kept her feelings to herself, Caitlin was quiet for a moment. "Billy and Quinn," she said finally in a very soft voice. "Oh, Ann!"

"Don't feel sorry for *me*, my pet. I got over Mr. Jones fast. I had to. He got over me faster," Ann snapped, her veneer of indifference back in place. "It's past two. You're off duty. What are you doing here still?"

"Ann?" Caitlin began again. "There is one other thing."

"And what can that be, pray tell?" Ann asked with affectionate sarcasm.

"I want a percentage of the profit on the making-up business and on my little trinkets—the fans and scarves and such," Caitlin blurted.

"You little ingrate!" Ann exclaimed, now shocked and barely masking a grudging admiration at this latest demand. "After all I've done, all I've given you, how can you . . . ?"

"You taught me everything I know, and I know ten dollars a week just won't get me where I want to go, that's all," Caitlin explained calmly.

There was nearly a full minute's silence before Ann spoke. "I'll consider it and let you know in a few weeks time, once I've had a chance to see how it all will work. Fair enough?" she asked with a gloating smile.

"Fair enough!" Caitlin nodded, giving Ann a fast hug as she hurried past her. "Now I'm off for a ride in the park. I'm taking Billy's stallion!"

Chapter Nineteen

"Let's you and me kick up our heels a bit, Mack," Caitlin said, patting the velvet nose of a handsome stallion with a bright, coppery coat. She led the animal to a mounting block and gained the saddle with an acrobat's lithe ease, then had a stable hand shorten the stirrups so that, sitting astride, she rode almost as far forward and as high as a jockey. In a short, cropped jacket, jodhpurs, and knee high boots visible beneath an open cape that draped the horse's flanks, she was an arresting sight on the bridle path in Central Park. Her flowing, long, wild curls bounced free as, with some effort, she held the stallion to a quick trot, waiting for the traffic to clear before giving him a free rein. She enjoyed the perceivable stir she caused riding against the prevailing flow as most other riders turned south toward the entrance gates. The day had gone cold and a fine mist hung in the air.

"Just a little farther, Mack, and we'll let go," she promised her now-prancing mount with an exuberant laugh just as a group of young men passed. One wheeled his horse about to trot in silence at her side. Bemused, Caitlin glanced at him expectantly, waiting for him to speak.

"Well . . . aren't you going to say *something*?" she asked with a hint of annoyance.

"I can't," the boy said somberly. "You've taken my breath away. And my heart. Let's run off to . . . to Araby . . . to Persia . . . to the moon," he implored. "You are like one of the *lionne*'s of Paris, those most magnificent of women who ride and shoot and fence with the best *and* smoke cigars—when they aren't making wild, free love under the stars. Is that you? Am I right?"

"Well, I don't smoke cigars," Caitlin flirted wickedly.

"Warren Abingdon, at your service." The boy laughed, lifting his hat. "Respectable old New York on both sides. The Warrens and the Abingdons are solid, rich, and well connected. Marry me!"

"I can't, more's the pity," Caitlin said with a deep, mock sigh. "I'm after an earl or a duke, a viscount at the very least. But perhaps we could take tea one day. It's been a pleasure, Mr.

Abingdon," she said, touching her heels to the stallion's ribs to send him flying forward.

"Don't go! How will I find you? I don't even know your name, and you're taking my heart!" the boy called as he was rejoined by his curious friends who had been following a short distance behind.

"Well, who *is* she?" one demanded. "Did you find out?"

"No," Warren shrugged with a laugh. "But I will. A beauty like that can't escape notice long in this city full of gossips. My mystery princess will turn up somewhere—skating, dining, at the theatre. I want you all to give this your single-minded attention," he ordered, glancing back over his shoulder in time to see another rider come up even with Caitlin and fall into stride before they rounded a bend at a canter and disappeared from sight.

"I said good day politely to Mr. Abingdon," Caitlin began, "but . . . *you* . . . !"

"Polite may work with some, Caitlin; not with me." Quinn Jones laughed, changing horses with the daredevil ease of a circus rider, his arms coming about her waist, his legs following the line of hers as he forced the stallion off the path and into a sheltering glade of trees. Dismounting, he pulled Caitlin from the saddle and into his arms all in one flowing, easy movement, his mouth taking hers, his hands at her waist bending her to him then following the swells below, outlined by the close-fitting jodhpurs. Her dark cape billowed like a flag in the wind, exposing its red satin lining, her flying hair's russet streaks a visual echo. Her gloved hands rested on Quinn's wide shoulders as she pressed hard against his thigh forced between hers, her soft angularities melting to the urgent hardness of his long body. She didn't resist the feathery flowers of heat uncurling inside her, making her weak and wild and more than willing until his low voice rasped in her ear.

"Let's go home," he said, lifting her and striding toward the stallion.

"No, Quinn!" she protested, struggling in his arms. "I won't. I don't want to."

"Liar. I could take you here and now if I chose to," he laughed demoniacally, forcing her lips and not loosening his grasp until he cursed low, then set her down with bone-rattling force. He brought a finger to his bleeding lower lip as she pulled a scented handkerchief from her jacket pocket and dabbed at the little wound she had inflicted.

"I'm sorry," she offered, meaning it, her eyes soft with sympathy.

"Liar," he said again, this time smiling, responding to her gentle concern.

"But you must . . . stop this, Quinn. I don't

want you bedeviling me day after day. It's unkind and pointless and . . . dangerous. We've both got other plans that don't include . . ." Her beautiful eyes blazed with tears then that wouldn't fall.

"I'm your destiny, Caitlin. The sooner you admit it the better for us both." Quinn held her handkerchief at his lips, inhaling the intoxicating fragrance of orange and spice. "I don't mean . . . forever," he amended, "but for the moment, for now, we belong together. Fate, it seems, keeps arranging it."

"My fate is in my own hands," she gritted. "I must go. I've an engagement and . . . oh, damn and blast! Why did you come back?"

"To see you in a ball gown," Quinn answered matter-of-factly, entranced by her volatile, almost feverish intensity. "Do you know, you're like sea coal, Caitlin McGlory? That's what the Welsh call the stuff they get from watery mines. It's all flash and sparkle burning, and like a whirlwind when it's disturbed. It doesn't glow steadliy and predictably, like the other sort." He stood with his hands in his pants pockets, coat thrown open, tall and lean and dark, his hair falling forward until he flung it back. "Caitlin," he began in a rough-edged voice. "What do you really want?"

"Everything," she answered without an instant's hesitation, in his arms again before she really knew what she was doing, lips wide and pressed to his.

"Come to me tonight," he breathed against her ear. "I'll be waiting for you." He broke away then, caught in the vague blue haze of her beautiful eyes before he strode off.

Caitlin stood bereft watching him go, turning up the collar of his riding coat before remounting his own horse. Leaning weakly against her pawing stallion, she relaxed a tightly clenched fist to find the key Quinn had pressed upon her. She had clutched it so desperately it had etched an outline on the palm of her soft leather glove.

"Damn and blast!" she swore, about to hurl the object away with all her strength before changing her mind and tucking it into her boot. Extricating a folded tweed cap from her jacket pocket and pulling it low over her angry eyes, she jammed her hair up into it before mounting again and taking off in full, furious gallop.

Still in riding clothes, the black cape pulled close, hair tucked into the tweed cap, Caitlin ran along Fourteenth Street, passing by the usual Saturday evening crowds outside Barnum's Museum. Late for her appointment with Richard Montanari, the doll maker, she hadn't bothered to change after returning Billy's horse to the stable. Cold and wet nearly through, she sighed with relief when she sighted the building to which she had been directed. There was a shabby restaurant on the ground level. His studio, Montanari had said in his note, was two floors above. Near the entrance, bonnetless, gaudily dressed women milled about, occasionally entering into subdued negotiations with passersby. A man leaving the building stopped to hold an upturned bottle to his lips, leaning precariously against a side wall plastered with posters and handbills exhorting temperance.

"Care for a swallow?" he slurred, falling into the doorway, blocking Caitlin's progress.

In the ensuing scuffle as she tried to pass, her cap was put askew and her hair tumbled. "You're a real improvement over the usual quality here, girlie. I'll just come back on up for another helping," the man leered. "You must be going to that English artist up top. He does do well for himself by the look of you and the other one that's up there sky-clad, bare as the back of my hand. I peeked," the drunk confessed with a laugh. He shattered his empty bottle against the postered wall, falling toward Caitlin again. She side-stepped him nimbly and danced up the first flight of steps where, at the landing, a door stood partly ajar. She glimpsed a scantily clad woman reclining on a sofa, smiling up at a man who leaned over her, grasping her full, pale breasts.

"Join our party, pretty?" he invited, sending Caitlin up to the floor above.

"I can't talk to you just at present," she was told disinterestedly by a man who never even looked up from the sketch pad on his knee as Caitlin entered the studio. The room was lit to almost daytime brightness by oil lamps placed on every surface. A very hot fire blazed and near it a nude model leaned forward on a raised platform, showing the artist the cleft between her breasts that were partially hidden by her long, blond hair her only covering.

"I've a cramp, Mr. Montanari," she complained, flexing a dirty foot and wincing.

"Take a break then, Heather," he sighed, looking up at Caitlin at last. "You're even more beautiful than Leila Faithful described you," he said thoughtfully, taking Caitlin's hand and leading her to the bright center of the room. "Heather, brush out her splendid hair!" Montanari laughed with delight as Caitlin perched on the edge of the model's platform, the red lining of her open cape spreading about her.

Heather, who had wrapped herself in a sheet and had padded across the room, was lavishing butter on two thick slices of bread.

"Heather, Miss McGlory, full bodied as she is, is attempting to become even fuller," Montanari explained, circling Caitlin as he sharpened a pencil with a small pocket knife.

"I wouldn't make my twenty-five dollars a day, would I, if I didn't keep my weight up?" Heather mumbled through a mouthful of bread, spewing crumbs half across the room.

"Twenty-five?" Caitlin repeated. "I don't make half that a week modeling."

"But you do keep your clothes on, I'd bet," Heather said.

"It's not worth it." Caitlin laughed.

"It is a bit more respectable, though uppity society thinks any kind of model is a fallen woman." Heather moved behind a screen to dress, emerging after a time the image of a modest young matron. "Shall I come on Monday, Richard?" she asked and had to ask again to break into his total absorption with Caitlin, whose profile he had already committed to paper.

"No, no Heather. Today will be all for a while," he said putting down his sketch pad only long enough to pay and dismiss her with a kiss on the cheek before turning back to Caitlin. He said nothing for a time, except to request that Caitlin change her position, lift her chin or coil up her hair so that the graceful line of her neck could be duplicated on paper. He worked with intensity, filling page after page, his fine, well-cared for hands moving quickly. Montanari was a small man with a full head of brown curls and small, regular features. His long-lashed, dark eyes were very serious as he worked.

"There!" he proclaimed finally, looking up with a satisfied smile. "I've got you on paper, at least. If you should disappear this instant, I'll not have lost you completely!"

"But why should I disappear?" Caitlin laughed, letting her hair fall and standing to stretch before beginning to explore the studio with her typical curiosity.

"Anything as perfectly lovely as you are, Miss McGlory, can't be quite real. You are a figment of my imagination, surely."

"Oh, I'm real, thank you," she protested, "but if I were a figment of your imagination as you put it, what would you do with me?" There was a flirtatious, teasing edge in her voice.

"Like Pygmalion, I would fall hopelessly in love with my own creation, of course, but as it is I shall have to be content with turning you into the most beautiful doll ever made. Would you like to see some of our work?" he asked, beginning to open a series of cases that stood lined up beneath the bare window of the studio. When he had finished and stepped back, a row of magnificent dolls stood on display with their complete wardrobes, elegant down to tiny boots, gloves, even miniature folded fans, and Caitlin was on her knees, ohing and ahing with the unself-conscious delight of a child. She especially marveled over a dark-haired beauty in a cashmere coat and a brown hat with Nile green plumes.

"But she had *twelve* dresses! That's more than I own," Caitlin complained. "Three cloaks, nine hats, a muff, and—oh, dear! Long lace mitts in a red kid glove box. It can't be even three inches long."

"Open her vanity case," Montanari suggested, beaming.

"Nail brush, tooth brush, a tiny knife . . . what little girl wouldn't go wild over such minuscule treasures? Is this her card case, this ivory dot? It isn't an inch square, and the calling cards are smaller still!" As she lifted each doll, Caitlin's professional expertise informed her inspection of the gowns and lace petticoats and tassled kid boots.

"The clothes we design and sell to our customers are not better made than these, Mr. Montanari," she said with admiration. "And the dolls' features are so . . . lifelike, so perfect!"

"There is an entire industry in France that works in miniature for dolls—modistes, shoemakers, wig makers; even diminutive artificial flowers are to be had," Montanari explained.

"But how did you ever come to do such delightful work?" Caitlin asked, holding in her hand a pair of tiny red silk garters removed from a doll in a striped pink taffeta dress.

"A family business. My mother began making rag dolls. Father was a modeler in wax—statues and effigies. The natural result of their marriage was me and these little ladies. There is a long tradition of the fashion doll, you know. It's said that Henry IV first sent Marie DeMedici small dolls in French outfits, and that, for centuries after, these little ambassadresses visited all the royal courts of Europe."

"Could they be larger and still so lifelike and lovely?" Caitlin asked.

"My, how intense you are all at once, Miss McGlory," Montanari commented, increasingly delighted with his spirited model as she began to pace the studio excitedly.

"I've an idea," she announced, "a *wonderful* idea! Tell me quickly, can you do your dolls life size?"

"What you want is a mannequin," Montanari said with a bemused smile. "There are plenty of them."

"Yes, but the bodies are wrong and the faces, if there are faces, are stiff, and the hair is yarn or wool, and I want—"

"*Do* slow down"—Montanari laughed—"and tell me exactly what you have in mind."

"We're putting a plate glass window into the front of our salon that I'm to model in, but if we also had a life-size doll—one that looked like me—she could be there when I wasn't. It would cause a sensation on Broadway!"

"I'd think so." Montanari nodded happily. "There are mannequins, but none is good enough to do you justice. Their faces are usually made in mask factories, the hair is badly attached, the teeth false, but worst of all, the bodies aren't . . . natural. Twenty years ago when mother showed her first baby doll at the Crystal Palace Exhibition, there was a mannequin introduced made of seven thousand pieces of wire that could be bent to surprisingly lifelike positions, but still . . ." Montanari gently lifted one of his dolls and removed her cream-white wool dress, handling the tiny buttons with ease. "This twenty-inch lady, who would certainly blush at being so unceremoniously undressed, is the Princess Alexandra of Wales, wife of Edward, Prince of Wales, England's future king. Without her Worth gown, you see, her contours leave something to be desired."

"But if it were possible to achieve the loveliness of classical statuary . . ." Caitlin paused. "Could you? In wax?"

"Yes," Montanari said very slowly, "I think it could be done. Wax and rubber. There's a new process with rubber that could be adapted. That's one of the reasons I came to America, to talk to Mr. Goodyear. But I hesitate to—"

"Oh, don't be coy with me," Caitlin bubbled with excitement. "Say what you mean!"

"If *you* will agree to be my figure model, I'll

create a mannequin so lifelike one would have to touch her to know whether or not she's warm flesh and blood."

"If Heather can pose for you—sky-clad, as they say—I don't see why I can't," Caitlin pronounced.

Montanari was pacing now, rubbing his fine hands together gleefully, his eyes gleaming. "We would do the face in wax, solid wax. Our lids are set in separately, the eyes, too. We're particularly good with eyes—we buy hundreds of pounds of them from a glass factory in Germany—but yours I will have custom made, the color matched to perfection." He laughed with delight. "We set each real hair into the wax, and then it's sealed with the merest touch of a hot iron. Our women are unequaled in lashes and . . ."

"Yes? What's wrong, Richard?" Caitlin asked.

"Your hair," Montanari answered with a look of despair. "The color is so very extraordinary. How will I ever be able to match it?"

"What do you usually do? Where do you find your curls?"

"We buy them. From nunneries, from peasant women whose heads are coifed most of their lives and feel no loss, from those in difficulty who need money. I must have a lock of yours to try to find a near match."

"Agreed," Caitlin said, catching up a scissor

and severing a curl without concern. "When shall we begin?"

"Now, if you're not too tired," Montanari answered, beginning to set up an easel.

"Not at all, but I'm supposed to meet my friends to go dancing, and I've had nothing to eat."

"Don't worry. I'll send a boy with a message to your friends. We'll meet them later, if you like. I'll have dinner brought in—wine, pheasant, champagne, *anything* your whim desires."

"All of it. But I've a question," Caitlin said, stepping behind the screen to undress. "Who will the mannequin belong to?"

"To you; my gift. I'll create only one. The dolls, though, will be mine to do with as I choose. They will be so beautiful, I expect to sell a great many of them."

"At a very high price?" Caitlin asked.

"Certainly. But that will vary with the dress and boots and so on," he answered a bit absently, absorbed now with the tools of his trade and the light.

"I've one demand," Caitlin called from behind the screen.

"Oh? What's that?"

"The doll costumes are to be made by my friend. There is a superb stitcher at the salon, poor little Kathleen, who can do anything any Parisian modiste can, I promise," Caitlin said, emerging into the well-lit room, moving with her usual unself-conscious grace to the model's platform as Montanari watched appreciatively in awed silence. His hands, as before when he drew her profile, moved quickly to capture Caitlin's perfection, to recreate and possess it, as his warm brown eyes touched her. He never looked away, never spoke as he worked, circling her, tearing sheet after sheet from his large pad, pausing only to tack the finished sketches about the walls of the studio, until, without any warning, the door swung open unexpectedly.

"Why don't you knock, damn you?" Montanari exploded. Not looking up to see who'd entered, he pulled off his velvet jacket to drape Caitlin's nakedness and only turned around when she spoke, the sudden softness in her eyes as they fixed on the intruder rousing his interest.

"Don't bother," she said, shrugging off the jacket. "*He's* seen it all before."

Montanari saw the possessive, dark exultation in Quinn's eyes as they met Caitlin's unflinching, beautiful blue stare that was at once taunting and inviting. Beautiful as she'd been, there was about her now, the artist realized, a different warmth, a glow that hadn't been there a moment before. He knew that her anger, when she spoke again, was false.

"You, Mr. Jones, are trying my patience," Caitlin pronounced. "If you don't stop following me about, I'll . . . I'll—"

"You'll what, Caitlin?" Quinn prompted, scowling. "Come now, don't be tongue-tied."

"I'll turn you in to the police, that's what," she snapped, unable to maintain her poise.

"And I'll turn you over my knee if you don't stop teasing like a naughty little girl." He laughed, starting toward her as she grasped Montanari's jacket, draped it about her, and danced away to hide behind the screen, her silvery laugh filling the room.

"Quinn, my friend"—Montanari winked—"you are, to my everlasting regret, already acquainted with my new model. Will you join us for the evening? A light supper and dancing?"

"Dancing? With that imp?" he teased, as Caitlin in riding pants and boots stepped lightly to the center of the room.

"But she's a splendid romp of a girl, Quinn," Montanari defended, "even got up as a lad. However, I'd planned to take her home first to dress."

"But we're only going to Harry Hill's," Caitlin protested. "Then maybe down to Kitt Burns's Rat Pit. He saves his best terriers for Saturday nights. The East River supplies all the rats one could need and the fights are rather entertaining," Caitlin goaded Quinn.

"You can't bloody well frequent such places!" Montanari exclaimed, shocked. "Not a lady like you!"

"She was going to introduce you to the wickedness of vulgar New York, was she, Richard?" Quinn asked with a raised brow. "She knows rather less about all that than she pretends."

"You, of course, are *the* expert in such matters," she quipped. "Was it one of your hoydens arrested for shooting the Ninth Avenue El?"

"Shooting what?" Montanari demanded, horrified.

"Some rather gay New York girls took a little after dinner pistol practice. It seems the elevated trains passed their hotel window at just the right height. I had to leave before it all started." Quinn winked at Caitlin.

"Pity," she smiled back before turning to Montanari. "It's him or me, Richard. You choose," she said. "I've seen all I care to of Mr. Jones today, or ever for that matter," she added a little less emphatically, admiring Quinn's dark grace as he crossed to the window and glanced into the street.

It was the first time she'd seen him in evening clothes, his sleek elegance heightened by the velvet-trimmed broadcloth cloak across his wide shoulders. He emanated a quiet confidence and such certainty of his own mastery that Caitlin had to remind herself who he really was—a gallows bird turned bird of prey. She had often seen the type at The White Elephant. He was one of the legion of anonymous rogues who regularly took New York by storm. No one knew who they were or where they came from, but money and style took them everywhere. Caitlin couldn't help but admire him in some deep, secret place in her heart. They were, after all, so alike. She would soon be playing the same game in London that he was in New York, and if she was half as good an adventuress as he was a rogue, she would snare herself a duke in a snap.

"My carriage is waiting, Miss McGlory," he said. "I'll take you home to change. I'm giving a late supper at my hotel suite, and there's a particular reason I'd like you to be there."

"Oh, I can just imagine your 'particular reason,'" she responded, returning his intimate smile.

"Say you will come?"

"Only if Richard agrees. I don't trust you. Besides, I've nothing to wear," she sighed dramatically. "I've no evening clothes at all, or wraps, or slippers."

"Borrow the lace dress I ordered. It must be ready, or nearly." His hands rested on her shoulders as he placed her riding cloak about them.

"The lady for whom it's intended . . . she

won't be pleased that her magnificent gown's been worn before she's even seen it," Caitlin objected mildly, leaning back against Quinn for a moment.

"I promise you she won't mind at all," he answered.

Chapter Twenty

Caitlin's entrance at The White Elephant that night, her first appearance there in nearly six months, was nothing short of spectacular. When the double doors of the hall were thrown open by her two handsome escorts and she stepped across the raised entry to the balustrade above the polished dance floor, the musicians, as if on cue, stopped playing. The interrupted dancers stared, and men leaning at the bar glanced quickly over their shoulders then slowly turned and stared, too, at the satin-draped, bejeweled beauty looking about with what appeared to be curiosity, though Caitlin was actually doing a quick count of the Saturday night crowd, an old habit with her.

The sudden hush brought Billy McGlory hurrying from a back room brandishing a broken bottle he intended to use to stop a knife fight, the only event that ever plunged his rowdy establishment into near silence. The gesture of a bar girl's shoulder directed his eyes to Caitlin, and, with a roar of wild laughter, Billy took the entry steps in double leaps to catch her in his arms and whirl her about, sentimental tears standing in his eyes.

"I shouldn't be lovin' you up so, should I, now you've become such a grand young lady? I can't help myself," he said, flourishing a large, white pocket handkerchief.

"Oh, Billy!" Caitlin sighed. "You must do whatever you like. I'm not any different than I was before. I'm your little girl still, and I'll always be, even if I'm dressed up like a princess."

"You're a woman too, Caty, so soft and lovely. I couldn't admit to it before, because I didn't want to lose you. It wasn't right of me to try to hold on so; it wasn't fair."

"You'll never lose me, Billy McGlory, no matter what!" Caitlin said, near tears herself until Billy began to laugh with uproarious delight.

"Drinks for everyone—on the house!" he shouted to the murmuring crowd below. "Caty McGlory's come back home where she belongs!"

There was a rumble of approval from the dancers as the band took up a waltz, Caitlin's favorite the musicians remembered, and she followed Billy toward his table near the bandstand. Before she quite reached it, Quinn pulled the evening cape from his shoulders, relieved Caitlin of her satin wrap, and passed both to the accommodating Montanari. Quinn pulled her onto the floor and into his arms, moving to the music with the lithe grace she found so irresistibly attractive. They were again the center of attention when the others gave them the floor, their swirls and turns becoming wider and faster. The black velvet skirt of Caitlin's gown flared, the sweeping, pale yellow lace bodice—jewel embroidered with dripping pearl drops and fire opals, garnets and aquamarine beads—caught the light as Quinn led her around the floor. Exuberant with high spirits, she threw her head back and laughed, the low, rich sound so mysteriously lovely, Quinn drew her closer to him and stopped at the center of the floor to kiss her lips. As his arm circled her slender waist and her hand rested on his neck, another hush fell over the crowd. With just one fiddle playing the faint strains of the waltz, the pair seemed lost together, alone in some beautiful dream.

There was a burst of raucous, good-humored applause when they reluctantly parted to look into each other's eyes, oblivious to everything around them until someone tapped Quinn's shoulder and spoke.

"If you don't mind, *I'll* take the lady for a turn about the hall, now."

Quinn shrugged off the fellow with a fast, frowning glance.

"I mind. The lady's with me," he said.

"I said I'll take her for a turn about the floor, for old times' sake," the man repeated so insistently that Caitlin peered at him around Quinn's shoulder.

"Why, Layton Weetch!" She smiled. "Meet Mr. Jones. Quinn, this is the Mr. Weetch I once told you of."

"The cause of your banishment to Silver Hill?" Quinn asked coldly.

"The very same." Caitlin nodded, wondering how she could ever have thought Weetch in the least interesting. He now seemed to her course featured and foppish in his fancy-man's garish clothes.

"Thanks, Weetch, for the service you did me," Quinn said casually, his calculating wolf's eyes cold and pitiless as he sized up the man.

"I did you no service. Out of my way!" Weetch sneered, offering his hand to Caitlin again as a crowd began to form a circle about them.

"Be careful. It's liquid courage you're showing, Layton," Caitlin said icily. "I will not dance with an inebriate, and if—"

Quinn pushed Caitlin roughly aside as a

pistol Weetch pulled from his boot discharged once, shattering the long mirror behind the bar, then went off again as Quinn crashed into Weetch, toppling him and sending him sliding across the smooth surface of the floor amidst the shrieks of the dance hall girls and the angry shouts of Weetch's numerous cohorts. Deserting the bar *en masse*, they all came at Quinn, who kept them at bay with his fists, dropping one after the other with precisely placed blows while still keeping an eye on Caitlin. Tripping one man with a strategically extended foot, she snatched up the broken bottle from beneath Billy's table and was pursuing another with the cold, purposeful wrath of an avenging Fury as her uncle and the hall bouncer moved into the roughhouse crowd, fists swinging.

When it was all over ten minutes later, the dance floor was littered with half-conscious, moaning forms, and the whole place was in a shambles: tables upturned, chairs broken, shattered glass everywhere. The large canvas of a fleshy nude hanging over the bar had fallen, and standing beside it, getting her breath, Caitlin noticed the model had been Montanari's Heather. Worried, she looked about for the doll maker and discovered him seated exactly where she'd seen him last—at their table, a sketch pad open before him. He was drawing furiously, the finished sheets piling up beside an unopened bottle of champagne.

Caitlin's silvery laugh caught Quinn's attention, and he came toward her, his most winning boyish smile lighting fine gray eyes.

"You did right well, ma'am," he said with a Western drawl as he filled a glass for each of them, half and half with golden champagne and foamy dark stout.

"Mm, what's this?" Caitlin asked, licking her lips with pleasure after her first taste.

"Black velvet, an interesting combination of refinement and earthy strength. Where'd you learn to fight like that, imp?" he asked, raising his glass to her.

"Runs in the family. Ask Billy," she said as the big man joined them.

"Quite a welcome home they give you, hey, Caty?" Billy beamed. "But then this lad causes a rowdydow every time he comes in here. Have you ever thought of takin' up the boxing profession, Mr. Jones? You could make a go of it."

"And ruin his looks? His face is his fortune for a confidence artist like Quinn. How's Mrs. Faithful's fortune coming along?" Caitlin asked sweetly.

"She's in my pocket." Quinn winked. "But you shouldn't mention such things in front of your uncle. He might not think me suitable." Quinn raked back his hair and waited for Caitlin's question, which came at once.

"Suitable for what?" she asked, eying him warily.

"As a husband for his niece. You're going to marry me, Caitlin," he said with such certainty, she was nonplussed for three seconds at least.

"Marry you? Not in a millennium, Quinn Jones. Not if hell freezes over; not by a ghost of a chance, or a dog's chance, or a snowball's chance in hell. Not," she said pertly, angered by his supreme self-confidence, "if you were to beg *forever*, you blackleg land pirate, you ass in lion's skin, you . . . you wolf in sheep's clothing!"

"You're turning me down then?" Quinn asked.

"How perceptive you are." Caitlin twinkled back at him, while Billy McGlory looked from one to the other as if watching a badminton match.

"Care to take a flyer on it?" Quinn offered.

"Why not? Sure as fate, I'll win," she replied. "What's the trade-off?"

"Not being able to resist a wager runs in the family, like brawling," Billy explained to Quinn pridefully. "But Caty," he added, turning to his niece, "you'd best be cautious. You may win your bet with me—you've only got a few weeks to hold out—but Quinn here . . . I think he's a man like myself, who only wagers on a pretty sure thing. Besides girl, you haven't considered his proposal."

"Billy McGlory!" Caitlin exclaimed, appalled and furious at her uncle's inexplicable turnabout just when she needed his support.

"*You* are the one who wants a McGlory in the Social Register!"

"Right as rain you are, Caty love, and I have been informed that the connections and background of Quinn are—"

"Caitlin knows enough about my background already, sir, without you prejudicing her further, one way *or* the other," Quinn interrupted. "I wouldn't want your niece to marry me for anything but myself—or for love, or money. Any pretext will suit."

"Love's got nothing to do with this, Jones. Now, stop stalling and state your terms," Caitlin said impatiently. The scoundrel was crooked as a ram's horn, she knew, and there had to be some underhanded twist in the game, but for the life of her, she couldn't imagine what it might be.

"If you, McGlory, are not my wife, loving or otherwise, before six months have passed, I'll gift you with anything in the world your heart desires—jewels, furs, magnificent gowns, a Swiss chalet, a Venetian palace—wealth enough to make you independent for the rest of your life."

"Will you climb mountains and plumb ocean depths and sail the world around to bring me whatever treasure I ask you for?"

"You know I'm a gypsy at heart, Caitlin," Quinn said with indulgent good humor. "I'll be at your command." He bowed.

"I'll settle for a fistful of diamonds, I think," she mused.

"Hey, you two got it all wrong," Billy grumbled. "In the fairy tales I read to you, Caty, the prince would have to prove himself by great feats of courage so's he could *win* the princess. Why would he go to the bother if he'd already lost her?"

"But what if *I* lose?" Caitlin asked, not very seriously. She'd almost dismissed that possibility out of hand.

"The way I see it, Caitlin McGlory," Quinn said softly, "if you lose, we'll both have won the world."

A soft exclamation escaped her, and her eyes were filled with a questioning, hopeful wonder when they met Quinn's. Then she forced herself to turn away.

"Billy," she asked, "will you be our witness and arbiter?"

"I will," he replied, ponderously serious. "But I think you both should know, I'm biased."

"Well . . . that's only natural. You can still be fair, can't you? I'm sure Quinn will understand and—"

"*You* don't understand, Caty. I'm biased, but not in your favor. I'll be rootin' for the lad every inch of the way," Billy bellowed with a deep laugh. "I got business to do. I'll leave it to you two to work out the finer points."

"You, of all people, Billy, wanting respectable connections and worrying about bad blood and . . . well, I'll take on the pair of you and still win," Caitlin said with a condescending blink at first one and then the other before Billy hurried off, still chuckling. She faced Quinn then with aloof aplomb.

"Are there any rules?" she asked. "What if I were just to disappear for six months and surface again to claim my prize?"

"All's fair in love and war, but a lady of your dauntless fortitude wouldn't take the coward's way," Quinn shrugged. "There's no challenge in that, and if there's no challenge, where's the fun? Besides, I'd find you, no matter where on earth you tried to hide. You can't run away, not this time, not from me ever again. In fact, I think I won't ever let you out of my sight. If you spend every waking hour of every day with me, Caitlin, for the next six months and then turn me down, then if you can turn your back and walk away, I'll have to let you go. But you won't be able to. I'm *betting* on it." Quinn laughed devilishly.

"Waking hours only?" Caitlin asked with a touch of mock disappointment in her wide, innocent eyes.

"Night and day, if you prefer. I wouldn't put you out of my bed if I happened to find you there." Realizing that Caitlin was up to something that would, no doubt, be irksome, Quinn watched her now with cold, flat eyes.

"What a very gracious invitation. I'll accept on one condition." She smiled gleefully, ignoring his wolfish look.

"And that is?"

"Agree to my condition first, or I won't play at all," she pressed him, leaning back against the bar casually.

"Let me be sure I understand what you're up to, imp. You will promise to be available to me at my pleasure day and night for the duration of our wager," he probed, "if I agree to just one blind condition to be imposed by you after we've struck our bargain, and the bet is on?" He was leaning on the bar beside her, one boot heel hooked over the brass rail, watching her from the corner of his eye. She was making it too easy for him, he decided, and she was no fool; far from it. There had to be a catch, but once he had her in his arms, he reasoned, once that beautiful, responsive body was in his hands again, nothing else would matter. All her clever little wiles and devious tricks would count for nothing.

"It's a deal." He smiled. "Now, what's the condition?"

When she turned to him, her blue eyes were

shining triumphantly. "The condition, Quinn, is that you never ever touch me, not even once, no matter what the situation or circumstance in which we may find ourselves."

"Will I be permitted to hand you in and out of your carriage and hold your cloak?" Quinn asked with barely controlled anger.

"But that's not the sort of touching I mean, and you know it. Of course you may do those things. I'll expect you to be the perfect gentleman. I know you can be when you choose to." Caitlin's teasing was sweet and playful. Quinn glared at her in stony silence, his eyes hard as steel, his jaw clenched tight, until, unexpectedly, he began to laugh. The sound came from deep in his throat and then, to Caitlin's perplexed unease, he threw his head back and positively roared.

"Stop that and tell me what's so funny!" she demanded in a pout.

"First, I've a question. What if I should lose patience and just take you by force? You're setting up a dangerous situation, you know."

"If you do any such thing, the game's forfeit for you. You lose," she answered, laughing herself now.

"And what if you should ask me to assuage your magnificent passions, my pleasure-loving lady. Am I to deny you?"

Put at her ease by Quinn's now easy, casual manner and thoroughly enjoying the cat-and-mouse game, Caitlin answered without stopping to think. "That won't happen but . . . just supposing it did, for argument's sake only you understand, you mustn't decline to please me, not ever!"

"Well, for argument's sake only, Caitlin, tell me, would it mean you'd lost if such an unlikely occurrence were to take place?" Quinn finished the last of his drink and took a deep swallow from Caitlin's glass that was still half full.

"Of course not." She laughed. "The only way I can lose, no matter what I do or where I go, is by actually finding myself married to you within six months' time. That's the deal."

"You think the deck's stacked in your favor, don't you, my overly clever little imp? It's heads I lose, tails you win, isn't it?" Quinn asked with a startling surge of the whiplash anger Caitlin had seen in him before. "You're wrong. You've backed yourself into a corner, Caitlin, though your ingenious little plan did give me a moment's pause, did give me visions of the torment I'd suffer, having you within my reach but having sworn on my honor not ever to stretch out a hand to caress all that provocative loveliness you'd be flaunting. I remember, Caitlin, exactly how you look when you're flushed and glowing with roused passion." Quinn had moved close to her and his voice purred in her ear, hot and intense and dangerous. "You remember the touch of my hand on your beautiful breast, how those sweet, hard, berry tips tingle when my teeth work at them even a little? You *must* remember how it feels to come awake and smile up into my eyes with your fine legs already parting and your tight depths smooth and warm and ready for me. Do you remember, Caitlin?" he asked in a rough whisper, standing close behind her now, an arm to either side, imprisoning her against the mahogany bar, his breath warm at the curve of her neck. "Come now, tell me what you'd like me to do to you; tell me the way you told me every night at sea aboard the *Aglaia*, when you were naked and wild in the light of a sweet new moon, offering up every secret, soft inlet and taking me—"

"Stop it!" she whispered, her head fallen back against his shoulder.

Steadying her trembling form with a protective arm about her waist, Quinn found Caitlin's reflection in a triangle of unbroken mirror behind the bar. He was assaulted by her acute, flamboyant beauty, and she seemed to him as fragile and soft as a sigh.

"Caitlin, you *are* going to be my wife; you won't hold out even half the time. If ever you're really in my arms again, you won't want to leave me; you won't be able to, 'til death do us part."

She broke away from him, summoning all

her adamant, stubborn strength that he'd nearly forgotten in the tenderness of the moment.

"You, Quinn Jones, are an arrogant, self-concerned, deceitful libertine. I could spend every day and night with you, six months . . . six years . . . six *hundred* years and not be fooled again!"

"What is it you're talking about now?" Quinn asked gently, wanting to calm her, knowing that anger made her wild and reckless.

"You were off to England, asking me to tag along for your amusement, planning all the while to marry your heiress once you got there. Now you're proposing marriage to me, but unless you're planning to add bigamy to your list of crimes, someone's going to be a bit miffed to say nothing of disgraced and dishonored." Caitlin drank the last of her black velvet in one long swallow and brought the glass down on the bar so hard it shattered.

"Don't worry about a few more shards. In this mess, no one will notice," Quinn said slowly.

"You, sir, are avoiding the subject I've just raised. What about this betrothal of yours?"

"You mustn't believe everything you hear, my little innocent, particularly if the source is a drink-befuddled character like Gordon Finley. He tends to get facts confused when he's under the influence."

"Are you saying that what he told me was lies?" Caitlin asked.

"Not exactly. There was a kernel of truth there, but nothing was settled, no banns read, no plans made. Now I understand why Gordon's working so hard. He's trying to atone for the damage he's done. He never did admit to it. Bartender," Quinn signaled, "two more velvets."

"Only a kernel of truth?" Caitlin asked doubtfully. "And what's Gordon working at with such diligence?"

"He's doing some investigating for me, of the sort he did for Dunn years ago. Gordon's a natural sleuth, likes prying into other people's business, but he makes brilliant connections. Incidentally," Quinn said almost as an afterthought, "Gordon wrote that he found what is probably a notation of your birth, Caitlin, in a parish ledger at Cardiff."

"You . . . you three-story liar! I don't believe a word you say. But . . . if it's true," Caitlin went on, trying to stay calm, "if there's even so little as another of your kernels of truth in this, then he knows, and you, too, what my mother's family name was, and I could find them and . . ." Caitlin held her breath. "Tell me?" she asked.

"I can't tell you, Caitlin. The ink ran—spilled wine or something. Her name was illegible, but Gordon's going to try to find the marriage record of one Patrick Michael McGlory and Damaris something."

"It *is* true; it *is*!" Caitlin clasped Quinn's hand and began pulling him after her. "That *is* her name. We must tell Billy at once! He'll want to know." She came to a sudden stop and spun about to glare at Quinn suspiciously. "Why is Gordon doing this?"

"I told you, he was looking for information I need and came upon the McGlory name—Jean McGlory, your godmother, and Patrick, and you. I've got to get back to the hotel. I'm expecting guests. You tell Billy the news and then have Montanari bring you along in about an hour. And, Caitlin? Try to stay out of trouble until then, will you? I won't be here to come to your rescue again." He winked and strode off before she could say another word.

When Caitlin burst in upon him, Billy was ensconced at the commodious roll-top desk in his office, giving directions to the cleanup crew about to put The White Elephant back in order.

"I broke a glass myself," Caitlin announced excitedly, greeting the men, who were old friends, and interrupting Billy in mid-sentence.

"And that's what you came running in here to tell me all in such a bluster and blather? I ain't seen you like this since you found that litter of kittens in the alley when you were eight years old." He laughed affectionately.

"No, no that's not what I want to say, and I can't wait—"

"I'm done with this lot anyway. They are going to put things to rights after your little homecoming party," he said, ushering the men from the office and closing the door after them. "Now then, tell me your news."

"Billy! Darling Billy," she said, taking both his large hands in hers. "I will, but first you must tell me about Jean McGlory."

Billy's eyes opened wide, and all the color drained from his craggy face as he dropped into the nearest chair, tearing at his top collar stay. Caitlin sank to her knees at his side, terrified until he patted her hand indicating that he was all right. "Pour me a glass of water, will you, Caty?" he asked in a strangled voice, and when she did, he gulped it down, begged another, then hid his face in his hands for a moment while she waited and worried over him. As she started toward the door, deciding to get help, Billy called her back and placed a chair for her facing his. His manner was formal, controlled, more serious than Caitlin had ever seen him. He waited until she was settled, cleared his throat, clasped his knees with big knuckled hands, and finally spoke.

"Jean McGlory, Caitlin, was my sister," Billy announced with a doleful, haunted smile.

"But you never told me about her, not one word, and she was . . . is my aunt, my father's sister, too," she said.

"Your father's twin, Caitlin. I never thought to hear her name spoken again as long as I live, but I always knew she would haunt me in hell for all eternity."

"But why? *Tell* me what you mean. Just say it out, Billy," Caitlin said softly.

"It was the year of the famine that I did . . . what I did. Those were the worst of times in Ireland. I found myself orphaned and all of twelve years old with those two little ones to look out for. They wasn't much younger than me, only a year, but I was their big brother see, and I . . . we took to the roads with all the other vagrants. There were thousands lookin' for a crust of food and a bit of work, but there was nothin' to be had, Cate, 'specially not for three starvin' tykes. We went into England . . . and—I know I never told you, Caty; I *know* I always said your father tried his luck in Wales and I sailed straight from home, from Ireland. Well, I lied." Billy was standing with his back to Caitlin now, looking up at the ceiling and rocking on his heels. She sat unmoving in a frozen calm, waiting for him to go on.

"We three went together, part of an army of wide-eyed, lost youngsters and frightened, displaced wives thrown out on their own, deserters, card-sharpers, vagrants—the worst rabble. There were gangs of poachers in the hills and a lot of barn burning going on in the countryside, fire bein' the true weapon of the oppressed. There'd been a rising of the Welsh miners not long before we got to the Rhonda Fawr Valley. They hadn't much to give when we begged at the little houses terraced above the river. Respectable people turned away and pretended not even to see us, thousands as we were. It was natural we should drift into Merthyr, natural that we should stay with other Irish who crossed over Jackson's Bridge into the . . . the most depraved part of a sinful city. They called it *China,* Caitlin; that's how little control the authorities had in that part of the city when we got there. A few years later the evangelicals came in and the reformers and journalists. Little Sodom, they said it was."

"Billy, please, tell me about Jean?" Caitlin asked.

He turned to face her. "But you must know how it was so you won't judge me too hard when you've heard what I done," he said in a pleading voice. "Those was hellish times; you have to know that."

"I'll try not to judge at all," she answered simply.

"We went to the hiring fairs, which were no better than slave markets," Billy continued, "but there were so many willing to do anything for a pittance, I couldn't get a job of work at all. Almost got apprenticed to a rat catcher once, but he refused to have the little ones."

"You're stalling, Billy. Say what you mean to," Caitlin insisted.

"I had to get the fare somehow to go to America. It was the only way to any future at all, so . . . I gave Pat the last copper we had and sent him off to buy a bit of bread. When he was gone, I sold Jean away like chattel."

"You . . . sold her?" Caitlin questioned, seemingly calm though her knuckles went white as she clutched the chair arms. "To *whom* did you sell her?"

"To a woman who ran a very *fine* house in London, she said, catering to *real* gentlemen only, she said. Mrs. Drabble frequented the hiring fairs regular, filling special orders from her rich clientele. One of her gents had an appetite for fiery, green-eyed virgins with skin like milk and . . . a smile to rival the sun for brightness. That was Jeannie," Billy said with a catch in his voice before striking the wall with a heavy fist. "That was Jean all right, and Drabble wanted her, kept after me and after me, promising to feed the child well and pay me what seemed a fortune. I still can hear that woman's wicked voice tellin' me it was only a matter of time before winter came and we'd freeze or we'd starve or both. Then, Drabble said, I'd *have* to go her way."

"And she was right," Caitlin whispered as she slowly stood, not knowing what to do or say, wanting to comfort Billy in his distress. But she was sickened and pained by the terrible tale he'd told, and held back. "What did my father do after . . . ?"

"I told him she'd been . . . stolen away. He was near mad with pain, looking for her everywhere and asking after her until, one day, Patrick discovered I had money, too much of it, enough for passage to America for us both. He wouldn't take so little as a half penny from me, wouldn't speak a single word, just turned and walked away, tears pouring down his ruddy cheeks like rain.

"You . . . let him go?" Caitlin was incredulous.

"Oh, Caty, I followed him a long way up the London Road, and then . . . then, yes, I let him go, and I shipped for America and never saw neither one ever again. So when you come to me sick and lost and all alone, Caty," he went on quickly, "it was like I was given a chance to make up for the wrong I'd done. I wanted you to have the *world*, to be safe and warm always. When you ran off, it was like losin' them all over again. Help me, Caty! Tell me you forgive me!" Billy implored. He dropped into his chair and, elbows on his knees, buried his face in his hands.

"Oh, Billy, my heart is breaking for you and for them," Caitlin said sadly, kneeling beside him, resting a hand on his shoulder, "but to ask me to forgive you . . . it's not up to me. Billy," she went on, "why did you never, in all this time, try to find her?"

"The years go rolling by so fast, Caty. At first I was too poor to do anything about . . . what I'd done, and then . . . then I didn't want to—I was afraid to rake up old coals."

"I'm not," Caitlin announced, getting to her feet. "I'm going to book on the first steamer out of New York for England, and Billy?" He looked up at her with pained eyes. "You are going to win our bet, because I'm asking you to fund this voyage."

"I will if you want." He smiled wistfully. "But I already bought you your pistols. I was that sure you'd win, so you might as well have 'em. They're in the leather case on the shelf." He gestured. "But Caty, why do you want to borrow trouble? It may be best to leave things as they are. What do you hope to find, girl?"

"The truth, poor Billy"—she smiled kindly—"about Jean and my mother and me. Now I must go. Quinn's expecting us."

"Caty!" Billy called after her, bringing her a few steps back into the room. He was slumped in his chair, looking very tired but relieved. "Thank you for hearing me out," he muttered. "And . . . for not judging me too hard."

"I'm *glad* you told me. It's better you did."

"And, Caty?" he added, almost smiling. "I hope you lose your other bet, too."

"What? And marry that desperate character, Jones? Then there'd be wickedness and bad blood on *both* sides," she said, not quite jesting, as she hurried off.

Chapter Twenty-One

Caitlin arrived a bit breathless at Quinn's suite at the Fifth Avenue Hotel with Richard Montanari in tow. She'd poured out Billy's sad story to the doll maker as they'd come on foot from The White Elephant. The intensity of her emotions and the brisk walk in the chill winter night had heightened Caitlin's high complexion and set her eyes gleaming. The extraordinary jeweled dress, revealed when Richard took her cloak, caught the subtle glance of every woman in the room. The men just stared openly, and Warren Abingdon materialized at her side at once.

"It *is* the Mystery Princess of the park! I *knew* I'd find you, but I didn't dare hope it would be so soon!" Warren exuded.

"Mr. Abingdon." Caitlin smiled, offering her hand.

"Mystery Princess, *will* you tell me your name *now*, or must I get Jones to introduce us?" the boy asked, glancing about for Quinn. Caitlin had spotted him at once. His deep-set gray eyes met hers even as he listened attentively to that silly Miss Gouvenour to whom Caitlin had taken such an instant dislike at the salon.

"Don't disturb Mr. Jones," Caitlin said, gazing into Warren Abingdon's adoring eyes. "We'll do nicely without him." Taking the boy's arm, she moved toward a linen-covered table, noticing Quinn begin to move in her direction, stopping to talk with his guests on the way. His dark, powerful good looks, the confident dynamism he radiated, made it difficult for her—and the other women in the room—to look away. Caitlin knew how the long muscles stirred in his arms and rippled across his back with each stride, envisioned—when he retrieved a lady's dropped glove—his rangy body knifing the water as he dove from the deck of the *Aglaia*. Flushed, she looked about furtively, wondering how many other women in the room had the same thoughts of Quinn to dwell on. Mrs. Faithful, perhaps, talking to the older gentlemen in the cutaway? The tall young woman in blue silk in the window alcove? Possibly even that dreadful Miss Gouvenour. Caitlin glowered.

"Something wrong?" Abingdon asked solicitously as Richard Montanari joined them.

"Nothing is ever wrong with this lovely lady. Her little moods come and go, like April breezes." The artist smiled in his gentle, quiet way.

"How well you've come to know me, Richard. I'm starving," Caitlin declared, taking the doll maker's hand as casually as if he were an old friend and turning her attention to the table where ranks of silver trays and iced Dresden bowls proffered lovely delicacies. There was caviar—red and black—oysters, smoked pheasant and tongue, lamb kidneys in aspic, quail liver mousse, varieties of patés, and all sorts of sweets, tortes, petal cakes, and crystallized fruit in a very tempting array.

"May I be of service, Princess?" Warren asked with a courtly bow. "Just whisper in my ear and anything your heart desires—"

"Warren, I warn you for your own good; Miss McGlory has an insatiable appetite and I know exactly what she likes," Quinn interrupted. "I'll see to her needs from now on." He gave the crestfallen boy a confidential wink and slipped a possessive arm about Caitlin's waist.

"Quinn, introduce us properly," Warren implored. "I was about to propose to her for a second time today, and I still don't know her name."

"What a coincidence, Warren," Quinn replied with a wry laugh. "Caitlin McGlory, *do* allow me to present Warren Abingdon and his cousin, Ivy Gouvenour," he added as the girl who had trailed him across the room joined them.

"We've met, after a fashion," Miss Gouvenour said with a disdainful glance. "You *are* the clothes model at Overton's, are you not? Quinn is so original to invite you. One doesn't often meet tradespeople at such functions as this."

"Oh, doesn't one?" Caitlin asked with a lethal smile. "But isn't it awfully dull for you, always listening to the asininities of the upper tens?"

"What quaint American phrase is that, Caitlin?" Richard Montanari asked, trying to ease the tension.

"The upper tens are our aristocracy, Richard, my love, the ten thousand best families in the country, like the Four Hundred, only not quite so exclusive. Meet one of them, Miss Gouvenour here, though two tradespeople in one evening may be more than she can comfortably deal with."

"Caitlin!" Quinn said in a low, warning tone.

"Delighted to make your acquaintance, Mr. Montanari," Ivy Gouvenour said stiffly. "What sort of work do you do?"

"He's a doll maker and an artist. I model for

him, too. Richard," Caitlin said with a wicked gleam in her eyes, "wouldn't Miss Gouvenour make an ideal subject for a baby doll, with her gap-toothed smile and little upturned nose? Of course, she might not agree to pose for you in the nude, as I do. Would that matter?"

"Oh my! I would never!" the girl spluttered. "You might be interested to know, Miss McGlory, that I, too, have been asked to do modeling, but of a more respectable sort, of course. Guiseppi Fagani is painting the nine reigning belles of New York Society as the Muses of Classical Antiquity. The portraits will hang in the entranceway of the new Metropolitan Museum. I will sit for Thalia."

"The comic Muse? That is appropriate. Do you like art, Miss Gouvenour?" Caitlin asked pleasantly. "Quinn, as you no doubt are aware, is a collector. I'm sure you and he have talked quite a lot about art." Caitlin had taken a place on a circular velvet *causeuse* at the center of the room beneath a tiered crystal chandelier. Ivy Gouvenour settled beside her and the three men hovered about them, not knowing what sort of fireworks to expect.

"My father *adores* the landscapes of Fred Church. And I, too, like them, particularly *Heart of the Andes*," Ivy prattled. "People have lined up by the thousands and *paid* just to look at it, even quite common people," she marveled.

"Do tell?" Caitlin said, exchanging meaningful glances with Richard. "I'd wager Ivy—may I call you Ivy? I'd wager that your favorite painter is Bougeureau."

"How *did* you know?" Ivy asked.

"We tradespeople are very shrewd; we have to be to make money. Am I right, Richard?"

Montanari's inherent politeness prevented him from commenting one way or the other, and Caitlin, not wanting to make him any more uncomfortable, turned to Quinn instead.

"Does Miss Gouvenour know *your* opinion of Bouguereau's work? All those fat, naked nymphs and excited satyrs?"

"*Caitlin*!" Quinn said again with ominous undertones. "You'd best—"

"It's bad art, Ivy. I'm sorry to be the one to have to tell you so." Caitlin shook her head sadly.

"How can it be bad? He's immensely popular and his list of prizes goes on and on," Ivy said defensively. "He's decorated churches, mansions—"

"Mansions of the parvenu, Ivy, of the *nouveau riche*, of *tradesmen*. His paintings are like porcelain plates—very shiny. Now I think I will have some of that lovely food, if you'll excuse me?" Caitlin smiled, leaving her companions speechless.

"Still want to marry her, Warren?" Quinn laughed, starting after Caitlin.

"More than ever!" the young man said fervently. "She is clever and so . . . so passionate. I adore women of strong opinion and intense feeling!"

"She's vulgar, Warren. Proper girls don't talk about naked nymphs. They don't heap their plates either, as she's doing!" Ivy sniffed.

"She eats divinely," Warren said with breathless adoration, causing his cousin to roll her eyes at the ceiling and move off to mingle with the other elegant guests who were arriving from parties and theatres and concert halls all over the city.

"You are an ill-behaved brat," Quinn whispered, relieving Caitlin of her full plate and guiding her across the room with a firm hand at her waist.

"What are you doing? I still haven't had a single bite to eat," she complained.

"You'll need more than food if you don't behave and do as you're told. Now smile like a gracious lady and get yourself through that door opposite or I won't be responsible." There was no mistaking the meaning of the low growl in his voice, and Caitlin stopped, looking up at him with a provocative, wide-eyed glare.

"Quinn!" she said with exaggerated shock. "You *can't* be serious. All these people are here and—"

"Don't push me or all these people will

know just how serious I am," he gritted. Grasping her hand, he now began to lead her, treading a tortuous path through knots of guests, doing well until they came upon Leila Faithful.

"Caitlin, darling!" the woman exclaimed. "How perfectly lovely you look!"

"I adore *your* dress, Mrs. Faithful." Caitlin smiled.

"Oh, I'm so glad. It was made by the most fashionable designer in New York. That's what I shall tell all my friends. I'm leaving for home in a few hours, so you must say goodbye to me now and promise to call if ever you should be in London. There are a dozen or so families that simply own England. I'll gather the eligible sons for your perusal. Perhaps at a dinner, or a country weekend. I . . . dear, what *is* the matter with *him*?" Mrs. Faithful wondered as Quinn, glowering, tried to lead Caitlin away. "Isn't he ill tempered this evening? I don't suppose he's introduced you to anyone here?"

Quinn's grip tightened on Caitlin's hand as she shook her head "no," afraid if she attempted to speak she would laugh instead.

"*I'll* have to see to it, then," Mrs. Faithful pronounced and she did, with a vengeance. Before she was satisfied that she had done her duty, the society portraitist, Fagani, was insisting that Caitlin pose for him as Erato, the

Muse of the Poetry of Love; the landscaper, Church, was considering changing his specialty so that he, too, could paint her, a half-dozen men had asked permission to call on her and leave their cards, and as many women couldn't help asking who had created her gown. By the time Quinn got her behind the locked bedroom doors, she could feel the radiant heat of his anger and something more—a dark Dionysian passion she understood in her own wild heart.

Devouring her with his eyes, Quinn became the untamed, dangerous creature of her dreams, stepping out of primeval, shadowy woods to claim her again. She stood silent, motionless, aching with longing that had grown unbearably in the weeks they had been apart.

"You're so lovely, it hurts to look at you. I love you, Caitlin; I *want* you now. Will you give over?" he said, not moving either, leaning back against the locked door, hands at his sides.

"I . . . will, you *know* that," she answered, "but . . . we mustn't call it . . . don't call it love because . . . I'm leaving; I'm going away."

"Are you, now?" he said in a velvet-soft purr, undoing his shirt as he crossed the room. His eyes were brilliant with dark fire as he was irresistibly drawn to Caitlin's bedewed perfection, her helpless innocent freshness. She whirled away with a little sob as he neared her.

"Do you know," he went on, "how tortuous it's been being close to you these past days, always wanting you and never touching you?" It was the low wooing tone, insistent and seductive, that shattered her reserve and sent her in tears into his waiting arms.

"I *do* know, but why did you have to come back?" she cried, hiding her face against his shoulder.

"I wasn't through loving you yet, that's why, and Caitlin, now I know I will never be." His hands were at the fastenings at the back of her dress.

"Quinn," she whispered with a trembling smile, "what of all the others, all those *other* women?" She helped him slide the dress from her shoulders and stepped out of it with a high-kneed prance to undo three layers of petticoats one at a time. Leaving a lace and silk trail behind her, she moved toward the bed wearing pantalettes and a flimsy Grecian bend corset that accentuated her full curves above and below.

"Some of my women *were* friends. Most were just lovers," he said, watching her with pleasure. "Where'd you get those slippers?" he asked. "The heels must be three . . . four inches."

"They're part of the costume," she began, leaning forward, both hands on the bed, to kick them off.

"Don't," Quinn said in a tight voice. "Don't *move.*" And then he was behind her, undoing her coiled hair, his breath hot at the nape of her neck as he pressed to her. She felt the quick, cold touch of steel on her skin as he cut the silk ribbon of the pantalettes. She felt his heat as he surged against her, forcing her legs wider. His hands cupped her breasts that were cradled and thrust forward by the corset before his touch slid to her hips, holding her, directing her eager undulations as he entered the dewy, silken warmth she offered, wanting all of him at once, telling him so, demanding that he keep nothing from her. One serpentine, muscled arm circled her waist, and his hand caressed her flat belly then slid to and manipulated the tiny, rigid risen shaft below. She uttered one stifled cry as he lifted her to kneel on the bed, kneeling with her, never letting up in his violent battering surges, not letting her go until they slowly sank forward together, breathless and sighing. Even then he still held her, rolling to his side, keeping her body locked to his, the two still joined, the shuddering passion still touching them after their love was, for the moment, spent.

Caitlin didn't protest when he cut away her corset with the silver knife. She sighed sleepily as he covered her with a down quilt and awoke with a smile an hour later when he returned with a tray of food, the finest delicacies the hotel could provide at three in the morning.

Quinn watched Caitlin stretch awake, her perfect body in the sleep-tossed bed shimmering to life, wide blue eyes trusting and innocent as the day he had found her.

"Once"—he smiled—"kettle drums and trumpets were played only for kings and queens. They should be sounded now, for us."

"Why?" she asked, her eyes flitting from him to the tray, not knowing which she wanted most.

"Because we, miss, are violently, profoundly in love." He placed the tray on a bedside table and pulled up a chair, resting his heels on the edge of the bed. He poured wine and raised his glass.

"How can you be sure?" she asked, selecting a turkey leg from a full platter.

"I've had experience. And dreamers don't lie."

"Oh? Did I say something, you rogue, when you had me . . . defenseless?" She took a swallow of wine and, balancing a plate on a raised knee, laid back against the pillows. Before she had quite finished, he rose to remove the food and was atop her, upsetting her glass, tasting food on her lips, tonguing droplets of wine from shoulder and breasts as his body covered hers. Their fingers laced, he pulled her arms above her head, his weight holding her down as she struggled laughing.

"Now you *are* helpless. Now tell me you love me. *Tell* me!" he demanded.

She bit her full lower lip and shook her head no.

"Tell me!" His voice rasped in her ear, the undertone of anger softened by desire. Still she resisted, writhing beneath him, her silvery laugher rising.

"Never!" she giggled as he rolled her above him and spanked her twice, eliciting an indignant complaint before he forced her lips down to his, a controlling hand behind her head holding her until she began to soften and respond then moved into her when he had pulled her knees up beside his hips. She arched back as she moved above him, so that his hands were freed to do as she asked in a lush, low, sighing voice.

"I love you. I love you. I *do*," she said over and over, looking into his eyes with her direct, depthless blue gaze, seeming to Quinn so unbearably lovely, so innocent and trusting he wanted to hold her in this one perfect moment balanced at the brink of time forever.

"I love you," she repeated later. "I love you and I'm *terrified*. You won't ever leave me again? I couldn't bear it!"

Her ingenuousness, the absolute certainty

with which she'd declared her love, finally, and promised herself to him forever made Quinn laugh with delight as he caught her to him and kissed her. "If you're planning to spend the rest of your life with with me, lady, you'd better get dressed. Our ship sails before dawn."

"What are you talking about?" she asked in surprise, sitting up as he rose and pulled on a tweed dressing gown. "You *were* going to leave me!"

"No, actually I was going to abduct you if you must know," he said seriously. Gathering her scattered lingerie, he held up the slashed corset. "This is beyond repair. You'll have another made in London. I've never seen anything quite like *you* in *it*." His eyes softened as he glanced at her.

"Quinn, be serious. This is no time for . . . jesting, or anything," Caitlin insisted adamantly, sitting cross-legged on the bed. "Explain what you're talking about."

"We're sailing aboard the *Napoleon* for Le Havre, and you, my love, had better have something on before the transfer men come for my cases."

"You *are* serious. But what about my things and my job and sitting for Richard Montanari and deserting Billy again without a word and . . . I need breakfast . . . and coffee. I have to think about this," she said with a pout, pulling a sheet about her and beginning to pace as Quinn calmly dressed.

"You've given Ann some good ideas she can put to use without you, Montanari can work from a photograph until he meets us in London, and we'll send a message to Billy. Oh, and we'll breakfast aboard ship. That solves all your problems. Now if you don't get dressed, I'll just have to take you as you are, which might be just as well. I don't plan to let you out of the stateroom for at least the first week at sea." Dressed and sleekly handsome, a blue sheen of beard darkening the planes of his lean face, Quinn held the jeweled gown ready for Caitlin. Still she held back.

"Now is the time to be daring. In one wasted moment, my beautiful wild gypsy princess, a door may close forever," he said softly.

When Caitlin came toward Quinn with a lilting, silvery laugh, incandescent, alight with love, she was the loveliest thing he'd ever seen.

"Why Le Havre?" was all she could say. Her doubts dispelled, her decision made, she was euphoric with a surging sense of freedom. The future was an open golden road before them.

"Le Havre because the French steamers are by far the most elegant and the food much superior to what the English and Americans provide. Besides all that, we'll be traveling with friends. Ready?" he asked, placing Caitlin's satin cloak over her shoulders and glancing quickly about the room. "Why are you looking at me that way?" he asked when their eyes met.

"I'm wondering what you're doing to me, Quinn Jones," Caitlin said in the husky little girl's voice that always made him smile.

"Loving you," he answered, extending his hand.

Chapter Twenty-Two

Steam from the tall stacks of waiting tugs drifted through pools of gas light swirling with the fog of the threatening winter dawn. Caitlin and Quinn stopped briefly on the deck after boarding the *Napoleon* to look at the waking city beneath a sleeting sky.

"Next time you see this sight you'll be Mrs. Jones," Quinn said, pulling off his lamb suede coat and wrapping Caitlin in it. Dressed in just a little lace and satin, she was shivering violently, and he ushered her below as the first snowflakes began to fall.

"Are you planning to keep me in England for six months?" she questioned as they followed a steward through a maze of narrow passageways.

"You aren't holding me to that wager now that it's all settled between us," Quinn said with the flash of a grin. "I'll get the captain to marry us before we make a landfall."

"I don't know about this," Caitlin answered, suddenly quite serious. "I mean, I already lost one bet today . . . yesterday, whenever," she added, trying to make light of the subject. "And I don't like losing."

Quinn brought her to a stop with a hand on her shoulder and swung her about to face him, pressing her against the wall as another passenger, nodding politely, hurried by.

"There's no way you *can* lose, Caitlin McGlory," he whispered fiercely. "I told you that. Besides, you can have your fistful of diamonds anyway as a wedding gift," he added, lifting her through the doorway of their stateroom. Inside, a full tub steamed, a cheery fire burned, a bottle of French champagne waited chilled in a bucket, and there were flowers everywhere—on the marble-topped chest, on the mantle, the bed tables.

"No dandelions; I'm sorry," Quinn smiled, relieving Caitlin of his coat and her satin evening cloak and starting on the fastenings of her dress.

"I'll have to make do, won't I, with glasshouse lilies and rosebuds?" she answered, still shaking with cold.

"Into the tub," Quinn ordered, "or I'll be nursing an invalid from here to Le Havre." With undisguised pleasure, he watched her step out of her dress and stretch naked before the mirrors, the lilting curve of her breasts lifting, taut muscles moving beneath creamy skin.

"Do you know what happened to Narcissus? Move!" Quinn growled.

"There *are* other ways of getting warm." She laughed, scampering to the tub as he started toward her. She sank into bubbly water that closed about her like a soft, warm blanket. Suffused with a lovely weariness, she let her head rest back, her eyes drifting closed. "Now," she said, "tell me who you really are, Quinn Jones. I've promised to spend my life with a man I scarcely know."

"You may never," he answered coolly.

"Quinn, *please.* This is no time to jest. Tell me something, anything." Caitlin sat forward to sip from the delicate flute he'd placed in her hand. "Tell me why you built the North Mountain mansion. Start there."

His angular face was all at once severe and his gray eyes unreadable until she smiled. To her surprise, he turned away with a low oath just as the ship began to move. There was a deafening blast of the whistle and hoots from the tugs alongside that made any talk at all impossible for a time. When the noise subsided, Quinn removed his jacket, rolled up his sleeves and pulled a chair close to the fire, resting his boot heels on the marble edge of the hearth.

"I built the mansion and furnished it and began to fill it with the most beautiful things I could find—silver and china and jewels and clothes—all for a girl destined never to set a foot there or lay eyes on all those treasures." Quinn spoke slowly, intently watching the flames with narrowed, pained eyes.

"Was she someone you loved very much?" Caitlin asked hesitantly, hurting for him, wanting to comfort him though jealousy twisted in her heart. "Who is she?"

"She was my sister, Caitlin, and, yes, I loved her. Glenda was a sprite, a delicate flower, fragile from the day she was born. She was bedridden most of her short life, and there was a game we played by the hour as children, building our special castle in the air. Our mother provided us the details down to the least lintel and cornice of her 'family' manor in Wales. She described it to us over and over just as her mother had to her with such longing that I swore I'd take them both there one day, when I was grown." Quinn refilled his glass and Caitlin's.

"Did you?" she asked.

Quinn shook his head. "When I discovered we were just a colonial offshoot of an aristocratic family, and sprung from illegitimate roots at that, I decided to build my own mansion. Nova Scotia was the nearest thing in the world to the Gower Peninsula with its wild landscape and towering tides. I hoped that wanting to see what I'd created for her would *make* Glenda walk, and then, when I got there, the clear air would have been *good* for her, would have made her strong." Quinn lapsed into silence, staring into the flames.

"But Glenda and your mother never came to Nova Scotia?" Caitlin prodded softly as she stepped from the tub and swathed herself in deep folds of warmed Turkish toweling.

"They died of the cholera while I was . . . away," Quinn said. "If I'd been there, it could have been different, but I lost them both."

"I'll *never* leave you; I swear it," Caitlin said in a trembling voice, and when Quinn glanced up at her he was bemused to see her beautiful eyes brimming with tears that began to slide down her flushed cheeks as she came into his arms. Her innocent candor, the undisguised tenderness of her emotions, made Caitlin seem terribly vulnerable and Quinn held her close in protective arms for a long moment.

"You're damn right you'll never leave me," he growled with mock ferocity, catching her up and swirling her about, then setting her before a mirror. Slowly and thoroughly, he dried every glowing inch of her slender body. Hands lingering, tongue tasting, he traced her long lines and swells, and when he'd done they were ready for each other again and she turned back the satin bed covers.

Quinn was still asleep when Caitlin awoke and quietly went to peer out of the porthole. She was amazed to see the dusky rose glow of evening behind them and black darkness ahead. They'd slept the day away, it seemed, the rhythmic throb of the great engines a kind of mechanical lullaby, the roll of the ship a cradle rocking. A stab of hunger reminded Caitlin that she hadn't eaten in a long time. Trying not to disturb Quinn, she tiptoed to the dressing room to find her one gown, imagining the stir she'd cause appearing in all her jeweled magnificence for dinner in the ship's galley.

"Someone's been at work," she mused, noting that all but one of Quinn's trunks had been unpacked and removed. She opened the mirrored doors of a recessed closet and was delighted to find hanging there, neatly pressed, every outfit she'd modeled for Quinn during his numerous and infuriating visits to the salon. Even the magnificent wedding gown was there among the day dresses and riding suits. Flinging open the doors of a cabinet above, she found bonnets and scarfs. In the papered, scented drawers of the steamer trunk there were bed gowns, lingerie, gloves of leather and of lace. Fat, bulging jewel cases were tucked in with satin sachets and garters, fans—her favorite among them, nested in silk.

Caitlin went back to bed and lay quite still, studying Quinn's profile as he slept, his face cradled on his arm, a down quilt pulled up to his shoulders. Wanting him to waken and losing patience, she rolled back the covers and ran a caressing hand through his black, satin hair. He only moaned a little. She traced a finger down the long channel of his spine, then stretched to her full length, she slid over him, her hands on his broad shoulders, her breath hot at the nape of his neck. He stirred in his sleep and mumbled, trying to buck her off, but she clung to him, sitting up finally like a jockey on a horse, leaning low and forward to whisper in his ear. "You were so damn sure of me, bringing all those clothes . . . sure of me from the first instant, you deceiving, manipulating, arrogant, two-faced—" She was pounding his back with her fists when he rolled her off and had her pinned before she could say another word. Glaring down he suggested she shut up and behave if she knew what was good for her. Happily, she agreed, and, soon after, they dressed and went to dinner.

"But it *can't* be the Burleighs," Caitlin cried, instantly recognizing the doctor's bulky form and Cedre's solid figure beside him. They both turned, smiling at the sound of her voice, and she virtually flew across the lounge and into the doctor's welcoming open arms before placing a kiss on his wife's ruddy cheek.

"He didn't tell me you two were going to be here," Caitlin complained with a glare at Quinn, who stood back, enjoying her excitement as she led Cedre to one of the built-in benches near a small fireplace while Wade pulled up a pair of wicker chairs.

"We *three*," the doctor corrected. "Little Nealon is asleep below in the care of one of the attendants. You'd hardly know him, he's grown so much since you were our guest. Well, isn't this a fine surprise for you, Caitlin?" He laughed.

"Oh, it's delightful!" she answered, settling beside Cedre while Quinn went off to see about their table.

"I *told* you love would save that lad, didn't I, Cate?" Cedre asked with a smug smile. "I've never seen him so easy and so pleased."

"It's all come right, has it?" Wade chortled. "You look beautiful, my dear, radiant and beautiful."

"You were both right . . . about him and about me. I can't believe how right it is. It . . . frightens me a little," Caitlin said, a shadow touching her smile. "Well, now confess, you two. What are you doing here?"

"*We* are Quinn's guests. He invited us to

make this trip and see his unfortunate friend, Mr. Hawker, that he told us about. I think Quinn has more confidence in Cedre's skill as a bone setter than in my medical expertise, but we'll both do our best for the man. Do you remember what Quinn told us about Hawker, Caitlin?" the doctor asked. "He's the poor fellow with the crippled back."

"The man shot in a hunting accident? Yes, I do remember." Caitlin nodded. "I was never convinced that it was an accident, given Quinn's questionable past," she said.

"Your suspicions are partly correct, my dear." Wade nodded. "It seems the man was actually wounded trying to escape the authori ties. He's a professional poacher, Quinn tells me. Started doing it out of need back in the bad old days; keeps at it now out of political conviction. Green growing things and wild creatures of the earth belong to us all, no matter whose land they're on—that sort of thing."

"Quinn went to jail in Hawker's place," Cedre continued. "The old man was caught red handed and Quinn, who was at the scene with some writer or journalist, took Hawker's bounty at the last minute. They had to let the poor man go and got Quinn instead. Of course, we had to pry that bit of information out of your Mr. Jones, Cate. He's not one to brag on himself, is he?"

"No," Caitlin answered. "No, he isn't . . ." She was on her feet the instant Quinn beckoned, moving to his side to slip her arm through his. "The Burleighs are a lovely surprise. Got any more for me?" she asked, rising on tiptoe to kiss him.

"Wait and see," Quinn answered with his best boyish smile, ushering her ahead to their table where Mrs. Faithful was seated beside a distinguished gentleman with a neat gray mustache and gray hair combed straight back. He was introduced as Mr. Bask of Liverpool and described by Leila Faithful as somewhat hard of hearing, though pleasant.

"Lovely dining room, but small!" Caitlin said loudly, turning about in her well-padded swivel chair. It was bolted to the floor like all the furniture in the dining salon that was built about an open circular stairwell. There were Roman Ionic columns, potted palms, and the finest linen, crystal, and china on the tables.

"Should be lovely," Mr. Bask answered just as loudly. "First class salon should be lovely and small. Only one hundred and sixty-six first class passengers on this ship. There's a thousand third class, but you won't see them."

"Mr. Bask is a great traveler. He knows all about boats." Mrs. Faithful smiled. "But I want to know all about *you,* Caitlin. Why didn't you say you'd be sailing with us?"

"I couldn't tell you what I didn't know

myself, could I?"

"You just up and left on impulse? How . . . American!" Leila laughed. "But what about your obligations, your family, poor Richard Montanari, so taken with you and not finished with his work?"

"He's already done a lot of sketches and also, I asked that a photograph be sent to his studio. Fortunately, I'd had one taken only a few weeks ago," Caitlin explained. "The background is full of foggy extras, but I show quite clearly."

"Did you actually go to a spirit photographer? There was one arrested for fraud only a few days ago, along with his seer. Two old ladies complained they'd been had," Mr. Bask announced in a loud voice.

"Alfred, that *is* interesting," Leila commented, "but you needn't shout. You are the only one hard of hearing, remember. I read in the papers about this Mummler and Madame DeLisle and I—" Leila began.

"That's where *we* went!" Caitlin interrupted excitedly as a white-gloved waiter placed bowls of leek and potato soup about. "The Wily sisters must have put the snitch on. There was another man there, too, Mr. DeLisle. He didn't say much."

"He slipped away, Caitlin," the doctor said, "but you might be interested to know his name wasn't DeLisle. It was our old friend, Robin

Edwards. He has a real flair, it seems, for the tricks of the spiritualist trade."

"*That's* how they knew about . . ." Caitlin rested her spoon for a moment. "If ever I see that man again, I will probably do him in. They certainly put on a show for us—music and bumping and spirit writing and vapors and . . . they knew something only Quinn and I could have . . ." She glanced at him and flushed a bit. "Well, the charlatans!" she huffed.

"I went to Charleston," Mr. Bask announced. "Had a fine time. Good for one, travel, especially for me. Men of my head size should get about. The phrenologists told me. They said I had great enduring powers that suited me for roughing it in the colonies."

"I don't think they meant America, dear; at least not New York and Charleston. Chicago perhaps; Africa certainly," Mrs. Faithful mused. "Mmm, what have we here," she asked as the cold hors d'oeuvres were served and wine glasses were filled with a burgundy Quinn had selected and tasted.

"*Cerneaux,*" the waiter said. "Green walnuts marinated in salt and pepper and wine vinegar. There's an eel paté also. The warm appetizer will be *la gougere,* a cheese pastry."

"It *is* fine, traveling with the French," Wade pronounced, taking a swallow of wine. "Now," he said, turning to Caitlin, "what's this about running off, young lady? It's not the first time, and every time you do it, someone's sick with worry over you."

"My fault, doc," Quinn defended her. "I kidnapped the lady again, more or less. This time we made certain our messages got to the concerned parties."

"You've done this before? How romantic," Leila sighed. "How wicked! But you seem to have been all packed," she added, noting Caitlin's dress, a deep-sleeved ivory silk with tiers of tucking and bands of lace.

"My abduction was a premeditated one and perpetrated by a villain with excellent taste"—she laughed—"in clothes, wine, food—"

"And women," Bask barked with an approving twinkle, followed by general laughter.

The sprightly conversation continued as the courses came and went one after the other until late into the evening. By the time the party was enjoying demi tasse and dessert of caramelized fruits cooked in red wine, the rolling of the ship had increased and occasional violent lurches set dishes sliding.

"We seem to have run into a storm," Leila Faithful complained, standing. "You shan't see me 'til it's over, which may be days from now. I don't do well in heavy weather, but if one travels in late January, one must put up with what one gets, mustn't one? Good night all." She smiled wanly as Bask, too, stood to help her to her cabin.

"Brandy, Jones?" the doctor bellowed, patting his ample girth beneath a taut vest hung with a gold watch chain. "No rumble of weather can lay me low, not with such meals as these and wines and brandies to be enjoyed for the next two weeks!"

"I'll join you of course, Doctor," Quinn answered, "and the ladies will no doubt enjoy a visit," he said, placing an affectionate hand on Caitlin's shoulders as he stood behind her chair.

"I'm looking forward to it." Cedre smiled. "Caitlin, come to the cabin with me now to see Nealon. I don't know how the rolling will affect him, and he's never been left with a stranger before."

Quinn and the doctor watched the ladies cross the now nearly empty dining salon, grasping the backs of chairs and edges of tables as the ship lurched through the storm. The crystal drops of a great gas-lit chandelier danced above the table, and the two men moved into a comfortable, dimly lit lounge where the doctor ordered a creme de cassis and Quinn a Chartreuse on ice.

"Well," the doctor demanded after settling into his chair, "when's it to be? When are you going to marry the girl? If she were my daughter, sir . . . or niece, I'd have you horsewhipped for ruining her reputation and not doing right by her." Agitated, the doctor raked his wild gray beard, then brought his hand down hard on the arm of his chair for emphasis.

"*Le gouter, messieurs*—after dinner snack?" a steward interjected, setting down a tray of sweets. "*Nonnettes, biscuit de savoie,* caramels," the man intoned before staggering off as the ship rolled violently.

"Doctor, I'd have the captain down here to marry us this instant, if the girl would have me," Quinn explained with his best smile. "She won't—not yet—and I don't know why. I've decided it's best to humor her, for a while anyway."

"And what about the Montressor woman you'd planned to wed?" the doctor asked, relaxing a bit and tasting a caramel.

"It was never definite. I'll explain things to her when I meet her in London."

"And your inheritance, my boy?" The doctor smiled, pleased with Quinn's answers. "What's happened to the missing Montressor heir?"

"My friend Gordon Finley, whom you'll meet, Doctor, has been doing a bit of investigating for me, very quietly. Someone's been tampering with relevant documents, but Gordon will get to the source, if anyone will. By the way, in the course of his sleuthing, he's come upon a notation of Caitlin's birth in Cardiff. That's part of the reason she agreed to this voyage. By the time we dock, Gordon may know all about her past and the missing Montressor. I've never really told Caitlin about . . . my past, so if you'd keep my secret just a little longer, Doctor? Another drink?"

"Absolutely, my boy!" Wade said, raising his glass. "To both, keeping your secret *and* another drink. So she won't marry you, hey? Cedre will find out why; I'll *bet* on it."

"I'm *afraid,*" Caitlin said. "I'm afraid to marry him." She and Cedre were in the Burleigh's cabin ensconced amidst plush upholstery and pink and white satin drapings. They talked as the baby slept peacefully in his railed crib despite the storm's batterings.

"Afraid of what, for pity sake," Cedre asked with a touch of impatience. "It's quite apparent you've already gifted the man with your innocence—that's the only frightening part for most girls."

"He's wild and violent and . . . and criminal; that's why I'm afraid."

"He wouldn't hurt *you,* Caitlin McGlory. Be sensible. Besides, at least some of what you heard about him was lies, rumors, half truths. A lot of men sow a few wild oats before they want to be settled and take up the strictures of respectability. And you were saying such nice things about him at dinner." Cedre shook her head sadly. "It would take the wisdom of the Seven Sages to fathom your heart, my dear."

"I don't want to be settled; I don't want to be respectable, damn and blast it all!" Caitlin exploded.

"I see." Cedre nodded. "Why not?"

"Because . . . I'm afraid I *can't* be settled and respectable, and I'm afraid to marry and have children with a wild man like Quinn. Because . . . because my father was a vagrant and my mother a murderess and my uncle a coward and blood always tells—like produces like. *Your* children all have fine characters, I'm sure, but what if they didn't?"

"Caitlin, where am I to begin?" Cedre asked, throwing up her hands. "Everything you've said is . . . nonsense, pure nonsense, and only hypocrites and fools would tell you differently. It's circumstance that drives some men to do dreadful things, and it's love and warmth and cherishing that make a child strong. If you won't listen to me, talk about it to Wade, please!"

The baby awoke just then and, gurgling prettily, sat up in his cradle, looked about, and a bright smile lit his flushed face as he raised his arms to his mother. Cedre lifted him and settled him at once in Caitlin's arms. "There's nothing so sweet as that in all the world, Caitlin, but if you don't want them, you needn't have them. There's a device in the chemists' shops now that prevents it."

"One of the girls at Billy's told me about that," Caitlin said, lifting the laughing baby above her head and cooing at him as the door opened. Quinn, who had come to claim her, stepped into the cabin and was charmed by the picture they made.

"You can have one of your own if you marry me," he grinned, an offer that caused Caitlin to burst into tears. She stood, deposited the startled baby in his mother's arms, and hurried off to their own cabin.

"It's all the excitement," Cedre said in response to Quinn's questioning, concerned expression. "She'll be fine if you give her a moment."

The winter storm raged on for days unabated, keeping most of the *Napoleon*'s passengers cabin bound. Unaffected by the weather, Quinn and Caitlin had the ship very much to themselves until Dr. Burleigh made his late afternoon appearance each day for a game of cards and a good talk, but mostly for dinner, which was unfailingly excellent although the chef did have some difficulty keeping his sauce pans upright.

Through those fog-bound days, Caitlin felt she was living in some perfect, magical season out of time as she and Quinn—cared for attentively by a crew with little else to occupy it—wandered through the opulent luxury of the steamer's lounges, drifted through deserted passageways from game room to reading room to dining salon then back to their stateroom. They spent most of their time there, though for different reasons than other passengers kept to their cabins.

"You must be Triton's daughter, just as I suspected," Quinn told Caitlin after three stormy days had passed. "You're a natural sailor or else a mermaid to be able to cope with the elements as you do."

"I've always loved storms." She shrugged casually, nibbling a delicacy—a *filet de hareng* —from one of the small trays regularly delivered to their cabin.

"This storm must be your fault," Quinn accused with a raffish smile. "You displayed yourself like a shameless sea witch last time we sailed together. I think Aeolus wants a look at you again, but you're mine; don't forget it," he said with a wicked laugh. He pulled her closer as they curled in bed sipping sherry.

"Let's taunt him." Caitlin laughed back. "Let's drive old Aeolus completely mad. Take me for a walk."

Swathed in a long, dark, Tartar sable cloak Quinn had had made for her, the hood pulled close to frame a laughing face, Caitlin lured him on deck where they did several turns arm in arm despite the pelting sleet and cold wind. Coming round a corner to face directly into the teeth of the storm, she loosened her cloak to let the wind toss her auburn curls and touch her glowing ivory skin. Naked beneath the fur but for high-laced boots, she posed like a figurehead in the prow of the ship, her back to the wheel house, calling on the King of the Winds to do his worst, until Quinn, in a barely controlled rage, tucked the cape close about her glistening body and quickly carried her below.

"You bloody little fool! You'll catch your death, and that's no figure of speech where you're concerned," he hissed furiously, kicking a chair close to the fire and dropping her into it. After calling a steward to prepare a bath, he handed Caitlin a snifter of warmed brandy and sat opposite her, glaring in angry silence, his face severe, his expression cruel.

"What *is* the matter with you?" she asked with a little sigh of exasperation. "I was only *playing*."

"Bad little girls play. Sensible people don't tempt the gods. They know they'll be punished if they do."

"Well, I've been doing such things all my life and nothing's happened yet," she said airily, falling into a pout as the steward moved about the cabin with hot water and towels. She was distinctly annoyed by Quinn's patronizing, bossy manner and decided to tell him so without mincing words as soon as they were alone again.

"You do sulk masterfully," he glowered, going to latch the door behind the departed steward, "but it won't do you any good with me."

"Who the devil do you think you are, Quinn Jones, telling me what to do and what not?" she demanded angrily, beginning to undo her boot laces as the fur slipped open to reveal a round, ruby-tipped breast. "Nobody tells me what—No!" she exploded in furious surprise as he placed one foot on a chair and unceremoniously hauled her over his leg, face down.

"You were right the other day," he gritted. "There is more than one way to get warm when you're chilled. See how this method suits you." Her smooth skin was pale against the dark sable when he slid the fur above her waist and, to her flabbergasted, speechless disbelief, proceeded to spank her soundly. It lasted only a minute or two, but that was all it took to have her begging him to stop and when, to her discomfort, he planted her firmly back in her chair, the flush on her beautiful face matched the one he'd brought to her bottom.

Startled eyes wide, biting her quavering lower lip, Caitlin watched Quinn go down on one knee to finish undoing her boot lace before he met her awed stare.

"I think I'm going to be your husband one of

these days—that's who I think I am, and I damn well will tell you when you're acting like a frivolous little fool. Do you understand me, Caitlin?" he demanded, his tone one of confident but tender mastery.

She just nodded and pouted, blinking back tears.

"I spent a lifetime looking for you, and I don't intend to lose you—*ever*," Quinn went on quickly, his voice now rough edged and low. "I want to wake every day of my life from now on feeling your lovely fingers on my skin." He took her hand to his lips. "And seeing the morning light in your eyes." He kissed first one fluttering lid and then the other, gently. "I intend to see you, Caty, my own love, in the golden air of every spring, running to my arms through fields embroidered with wildflowers. I want to love you in the forests of evening with nightingales singing and the scent of pines all about us . . . take you through mountains of dreams into all the silver mists of dawn. If anything were to happen to you"—Quinn paused—"if I were to lose you now, all my nights would last forever," he whispered, wooing her with his eyes, caressing her with hands that slid beneath the fur. Her parted lips met his and he lifted her, holding her against him.

"I love you," she whispered. "I *do*, and you must remember that if ever sad days come."

"There won't be sad days," he growled, "not as long as we're together. I'm your destiny, Caty; our story's all written and you couldn't change the ending if you wanted to."

"I don't want to change one thing," she sighed softly, clinging to him for a moment before she looked into his warm, gray eyes.

"Do you know—you never called me Caty before," she said with a dazzling jubilant smile.

Chapter Twenty-Three

"I think you should buy the best push chair they have. It is a gift to your son from Quinn and money is not an object," Caitlin told Cedre in a not-to-be argued-with tone. The two were being directed by Leila Faithful along Oxford Street, the center of the London baby carriage trade.

"That nanny person you found for us, Leila, prefers a three-wheeled perambulator for babies of Nealon's size. There!" Cedre pointed. "That looks handsome and solid."

"Solid is the correct word, ma'am," a salesman agreed, materializing at Cedre's elbow. "Birchwood body with five coats of paint, real leather splashboard, steel springs, iron handles, and an opal glass pusher. The Queen's babies had no better than this."

"Is it Morocco leather?" Caitlin asked, caressing the well-padded carriage lining with an appreciative hand.

"Yes, ma'am, real Morocco, as well padded as the finest coach. When will your daughter be confined, may I ask?" He smiled at Caitlin.

"No, you may not ask," she responded with an impish smile. "I'm not even married—yet."

"Beg pardon, miss," the man mumbled, his cheeks scarlet. "I—"

"We will take this one," Cedre said impulsively, her desire to relieve the poor man's embarrassment overcoming her disinclination to spend so extravagantly.

"Caitlin, how could you," she admonished when the fellow went off to get his order book. "Leila did tell us that in England some things are just not done—or said. Making such risqué personal remarks is one of them."

"He was so endearingly stuffy, I couldn't resist." Caitlin laughed. "It wasn't kind of me. I'll apologize."

"No, no, that would only make it worse," Leila insisted. "You Americans can get away with what we English can't. Your foreign accents make it hard for clerks and others to know your class. Rather than insult an aristocrat, even an eccentric one, they'll overlook a lot. If you'd been English, he probably would have refused to sell that fine pram to you after such a . . . well, such an indelicate remark. Incidentally, when *do* you and Quinn plan to be married?" Leila asked casually.

"I don't know; soon, I suppose. We're trying to decide that, and don't you start badgering me, too, Leila Faithful, like everyone else." Caitlin frowned slightly.

"I simply can't fathom you Americans and that is all there is to it," Leila answered, shaking her head. "Well, we must hurry now," she added, giving instructions that the pram was to be sent round at once to her house in Kensington and ushering her two companions off to Regent Street. There, some of Richard Montanari's finest dolls were on display at Cremer's.

"Soon, we shall be seeing little Caitlins among the other beauties." Leila smiled. "Come, come, don't dawdle," she admonished, leaving the shop to move briskly along Regent Street. "I . . . what *is* the child doing now?" she demanded of Cedre as Caitlin, fallen into a thoughtful mood, lingered behind her companions to study a blue-eyed baby doll in a satin gown and cap.

"I think our Caty hasn't quite made up her mind about really growing up, independent as she is. Once she's agreed to become a wife to Quinn and the mother of his children, she won't be able to use her little girl wiles and tempers whenever the mood strikes her. That's my view of it," Cedre speculated. "Do you agree?"

"I'm not so sure," Leila mused. "She can be so perfectly in control, so elegantly sophisticated one minute, and then the next—just look at her *now*!"

Caitlin was rocking the doll in a scallop-edged cradle suspended from ornately carved, double-footed posts. At the head, a gilded angel holding gossamer draperies smiled serenely down on the sleeping "infant" below.

"Caitlin!" Leila called. "Come *along*. We're to meet Quinn for tea, and I've lots more to show you before. Perhaps," she added in a lowered voice to Cedre, "we could help her make up her mind. I know she adores your baby son. We'll show her other little ones, too. They can be so wonderfully seductive, even irresistible, to a woman in love as Caitlin is."

"Has she ever told you about her past? Her worries about it, I mean?" Cedre asked, slipping her arm through Leila's as they walked. "It seems there's a bug under the chip somewhere. She's afraid there's a strain of wickedness in her that will show up in her children, particularly if Quinn is the father."

"I noticed right off she suffers from the delusion that he's a notorious evildoer. What's that about?"

"It's an idea she got into her head the day they met, and he refuses to dissuade her of it. He wants her to take him as he is, so to speak, no matter what he might be. They are an uncommonly stubborn pair." Cedre sighed.

"But so perfect together and striking, to say nothing of romantic. He adores her and he will have her. Men like Quinn are not easily thwarted."

"I agree." Cedre nodded. "Men like Quinn can be tenacious, calculating, pitilessly acquisitive in their pursuit of what they want. There's no deflecting them. They must possess completely the painting . . . the sculpture . . . even the woman they've fallen in love with, I'm afraid."

"But *I'm* afraid Caitlin might be one of those women who simply will not be possessed, not in the way Quinn intends. She is a free spirit with her own stubborn streak," Leila said thoughtfully.

"But," Cedre went on to conjecture, "I think Quinn loves her enough to understand her, to help make it happen."

"And I think she loves him enough to trust him more and more each day and help him to help it happen. They will be one of those rare and fortunate couples, as passionately in love all their lives as they are now. Their every meeting will be a tryst, their every touch will always bring a charming blush to her cheek and that simmering heat to his incredible eyes." It was Leila's turn to sigh.

The women had reached Hamley Brothers and waited for Caitlin, who was coming along quickly now, looking very bright and pretty in a narrow red wool reefer coat with white fur cuffs.

"That baby doll *was* one of Richard's. Now what?" she asked, glancing at the sign above Hamley's door. "'The Court Toymen,'" she read. "Really?"

"The Hamleys supplied Her Majesty's children, all nine of them," Leila confirmed, ushering her guests inside where a delightful racket of clockwork toys, music boxes, and children's voices greeted them.

Deciding to bring a gift to Nealon, Caitlin inspected a roundabout, a horse and buggy, alphabet blocks, dancing bears, and a quacking duck that laid eggs. Finally, she chose a green felt lettuce from which, at the turn of a key, a rabbit poked its head. Starting toward the door, she paused to watch a small boy in an Eton suit—short, dark worsted jacket and light trousers—crank the handle of a music box.

"I must have that." She laughed to her companions. "Which way are you walking? I'll follow you in a few moments."

"Along Piccadilly to St. James." Leila smiled indulgently. "Quinn's taken the doctor to Lock's for a bowler. The carriage is to meet us there, so don't be too long."

"I could never recall very much of what

happened before I was . . . sent to my uncle Billy in America," Caitlin bubbled over, coming upon her friends in front of Lobb's bootery, near Lock's. "But today something very sweet and odd is happening. Amidst the toys and dolls . . . little wisps of memory keep teasing. What's this melody, do you know?" she asked, undoing the wrappings of the music box and turning its crank.

"But that's *Green Gravel,* Caitlin," Leila smiled, "—a nursery song every English child knows.

Green gravel, green gravel, your grass is so
green
The fairest young damsel that ever was
seen . . .

"'I'll bathe you in milk'"—Caitlin took up the words—"'and dress you in silk, and write down your name with gold pen and ink.' I know it! I must tell Quinn. Someone did sing it to me once long ago. I can hear the sweetest voice—"

"Not like *my* froggy croak, do you mean?" Leila asked with mock affront. "There's your amorist now, looking elegant as always. That's because he dresses like an Englishman. He has his things made here in London."

"But he and Wade are coming out of a wine merchant's now." Caitlin laughed, already in motion, irresistibly drawn toward Quinn. Caught on a sudden brief blaze of white winter sunlight before the London sky went gray again, she was dazzling with love as she came into his arms.

"If ever you hope to be regarded as respectable by the English," he said against her brow, "you *will* have to learn some restraint."

"I don't care about the English; just kiss me." She laughed, turning up her lovely face, velvety lips pursed, eyes closed. He did, as the others reached them.

"It's not *done* here you know." Cedre smiled at Caitlin. "We've purchased the most extravagant baby coach I've ever seen," she told her husband and slipped her arm through Wade's.

"Like my new hat?" he asked, clearing his throat self-consciously. Backing off to study him with his wild gray beard and long, steely gray hair beneath an elegant, shiny black bowler, Cedre couldn't help laugh before she planted a kiss on his cheek.

"I don't care either if it's not done. You look so spiffy and handsome, doc, I couldn't control myself." She smiled. "It's been such a lovely day, I can't imagine anything else that could possibly happen to improve it."

"Caitlin McGlory . . . Caitlin *Montressor* McGlory, I should say, you are heiress to most of your grandfather's sizable fortune and mistress of Montressor Manor, his estate in Wales," Gordon Finley announced, as proudly as though he himself had engineered the whole thing. Though still very thin, his narrow face lined and weathered beyond its years, Gordon was looking well in properly tailored, good clothes, and his lanky frame had filled out a bit since she had last seen him. "Of course," he went on self-importantly, "there are two cousins, very removed cousins, who are both limited beneficiaries now. They would have shared everything if you hadn't been found in time."

"But she *has* been found and we must celebrate," Leila Faithful insisted. "I know it's tea time but champagne is in order nonetheless."

The tea room Leila had chosen was an elegant one, with velvet banquettes and low, marble-topped tables dripping lace doilies. There was hot milk for coffee, thick cream for the tea, buttered bread, ratafias, and chocolate glace biscuits, among many other dainties.

Subdued and thoughtful, Caitlin sat holding Quinn's hand, not able to sort out all the feelings that were coursing through her. The image of herself she had had all her life—the canny waif who would have to make her fortune through cleverness and hard work, the rootless outsider who would have to maneuver her way to social respectability—had just been shattered. She had been transformed, made, as if by magic, an aristocrat, had even been provided with generations of solid ancestors whose portraits were hung in some decaying castle in the Welsh countryside.

"It's like . . . like Cinderella," Caitlin breathed, "except that I already *had* a prince . . . of sorts. Do you know the ballad of the lady and the gypsy?" she asked, looking around the table. Her companions seemed to her oddly sober in light of the wonderful news.

"Of course we know it," Leila answered. "It's the story about a fine lady who ran away from her new wedded lord; she who put off her silk-finished gown and gave up her goose-feather bed with the sheet turned down, all to ride off with her gypsy lover. *You* shan't have to do any of that, you lucky girl. What you and Quinn have is love, pure and simple and—"

"'If pure love exists,'" Gordon intoned, "'free from the dross of our other passions, it lies hidden in the depths of our hearts and unknown even to ourselves.'"

"That's one of La Rouchefaucault's maxims, nearly two hundred years old," the doctor said with a self-congratulatory smile as Gordon glared at him suspiciously.

"'Lovers' vows do not reach the ears of the gods.' Who said *that*?" Gordon challenged, pulling a flat blue bottle from his breast pocket and sipping.

"Ovid, of course. The gods know more about lovers' lies, that sort of thing, than we ever shall, thank heaven. A lot that passes for love is . . . well, not. What are you imbibing, sir?"

"A patent medicine recommended by a practitioner in Hyde Park as a brain tonic, a cure for headache, neuralgia, and melancholy, among other things. Having given up alcohol after I talked too much, I'm finding this most effective," Gordon said, looking at Caitlin. "I haven't had so much stamina since I was a boy."

"It's a good anaesthetic, man, but to use cocoa extract as you are"—the doctor sat forward, breathing heavily, his big shoulders shifting from side to side"—you'll end up in Betlehem Royal Hospital without even knowing your name!"

"Bedlam, do you mean, sir?" Gordon asked, stubbing out a mere ash of a cigarette and lighting another. "Perhaps, perhaps, but they would surely have put me there before now, if it weren't for my new tonic. Speaking of Bedlam," he went on, turning back to Caitlin, "I've learned from Dancy that her mother, Mrs. Pallett, has spent some considerable time within its forbidding walls, put there apparently by the abusive Mr. Pallett. David and Dancy fled England, she finally told me, because they caused the wretched man's demise. He was the worst sort of devil catcher, a pious nonentity, one of those hypocrites who practiced the opposite of what he preached. He was—pardon ladies—forcing himself on poor Dancy," Gordon said in a chilled voice, "when somehow he slipped over the edge of a precipice into the sea, never to be heard from again."

"How terrible!" Caitlin said, tears standing in her lovely, sympathetic eyes. "But where is Dancy now, and what's being done about it?"

"Everything's being done for her; Quinn's seen to that. Dancy and David are staying in a secure gamekeeper's cottage on your property, not far from the Montressor Mansion. James Hawker is their gracious host. After you visit your 'silk' in the city first thing in the morning, we'll be off to Wales. Hawker needs doctoring and Dancy needs you!"

"Why a lawyer?" Caitlin asked.

"Once you sign a paper or two, the Montressor wealth is yours to do with as you wish."

"At once?" she asked with disbelief. "Right then?"

"Caitlin, yes, right then." Quinn smiled, taking her hand. "You can walk away with more thousands of pounds than you could carry, but my advice is to draw what you need. The rest will be safe in Mr. Barlow's competent hands. Where are you going now?" he demanded possessively.

"To comb and fuss a bit. After all this, I'm too restless to sit! Do you know that Barlow is competent?" she asked.

"He handles Quinn's affairs in The City and does very nicely," Gordon stated, reaching again for his medicine bottle. "Do you all know about the ghost of Threadneedle Street?" Caitlin heard him ask the others as she left the table. "It's an old woman who haunts the inner courts of the Bank of England. Seen by many, . . . When will you tell her?" Gordon demanded of Quinn, glancing over his shoulder to be sure Caitlin was out of hearing. "You are making us all accomplices in a perilous game."

"The fond gazes of lovers, Quinn," the doctor added, "make boundaries about them, make it easy to forget the rest of the world, but it's there; it will intrude, and you must tell Caitlin the truth before she hears it some other way."

"Love takes skill, Quinn, and work. It's not so easy as falling off a log," Leila chimed in. "If you give her reason to distrust you now, lord knows what may happen."

"If you ruin it now, if it's lost now, in the springtime of your lives, you'll regret it later when sad memories come rushing down the years. It will be too late, then," Cedre exhorted.

"Tell her who you are, my boy—a perfectly respectable son of a banker; tell her that you and she are distant cousins, that you've known about this for—"

"Doctor, I learned she was a Montressor only yesterday when we reached London, not before," Quinn protested, "though it may appear otherwise. Gordon wrote, but we'd left before the news reached New York."

"All the better. Tell her *now*."

"As soon as I've spoken to Melusina. She's to be in London tomorrow," Quinn explained. "I'll follow you to Wales in the next day or two. Does that satisfy you all?" he asked, standing. Caitlin was making her way toward him across the tea room, lovely in a gray and white brocaded satin day dress trimmed in Alice-blue taffeta, black velvet ribbon, and black and white silk lace. Just before she reached the table, she hesitated.

"*You*!" Quinn heard her say angrily. As the man she was staring at got to his feet, he grabbed his hat and broke from the room, sending a tea tray shattering in his rush to the door. At the threshold, Robin Edwards turned to the silent, crowded, shocked room, gave Caitlin a knowing smile, blew a fiendish kiss in her direction, then disappeared into the London dusk. Barely able to contain her anger, Caitlin resumed her place beside Quinn and said nothing until a fresh pot of very hot, very dark tea had been brought.

"I told him I'd kill him if ever I saw him

again," she said finally.

"Caitlin, my dear, his sort will simply sink into the slums of Whitechapel; St. Giles will devour him. Now let's have no more talk of killing," Leila Faithful said with a worried glance at Quinn.

"You're right," Caitlin agreed too quickly for Quinn's comfort. "Gordon!" she said brightly. "What have you to tell me about my mother and father? I am almost afraid to ask after what I've heard before."

"You needn't be afraid. I'll tell you only that much. There are others who will say more, and you will like everything you hear." Gordon smiled.

"People who knew them?" she asked, toying with Quinn's hand. "Who, Gordon?"

"James Hawker for one. Lady Fleur Outerbridge for another. She rode to hounds with your mother. They were girlhood friends. Their country places were only a few miles apart. Also the former Miss Chantal Outerbridge—Mrs. Wells now—the daughter of Lady Outerbridge. She thinks she remembers you, too, Caitlin."

"Fleur is delightful, Caitlin," Leila said enthusiastically. "Her daughter, Chantal, is also, though she is very different from her mother. More tea?" Leila poured beautifully and enjoyed being center stage as she did.

"Yes, thanks. How are they different?" Caitlin passed her cup.

"Fleur spends her life in rather a relentless pursuit of pleasure . . . perfectly innocent pleasure, one hears. She lives a very lavish life full of flowers and jewels and expensive carriages, spends money with magnificent abandon, entertains graciously, dresses expensively. There is always a retinue of admirers, usually young, seeing to her comfort. Lord Outerbridge has always encouraged her flings, probably because she allowed him to indulge in his own pursuits. He's a notorious philanderer. He keeps several mistresses in Mayfair—Daisy and Luffy and Betty, that sort—and he is a regular at all the . . . well, the most interesting houses. He and his wife simply *adore* each other, no question. It's a good match."

"Could I have a retinue of admirers?" Caitlin whispered to Quinn.

"No," he said flatly with lethal coldness.

"I didn't think so," she teased.

"Lady Outerbridge seemed proud of the fact she had been betrayed—my word, not hers—before her honeymoon was over." Gordon sputtered.

"Quite so." Leila nodded. "But Chantal is Fleur's antithesis. She's been married three years to Quentin Wells. She adores him and has already given him three daughters. Domesticity suits Chantal. She simply glows among the baby frocks, always reeks deliciously of rose powder, and, though not by any means a beauty at a ball, she is charming with an infant's little mouth at her breast; no wet nurse for *her*. You must meet Chantal, Caitlin, right off."

"Of course." Caitlin nodded. "But Gordon, you mentioned my cousins and a Mr. Hawker. Do you mean Quinn's Hawker?"

Gordon nodded but kept silent for once, much to Caitlin's irritation.

"We have to go back to the hotel." Quinn got to his feet abruptly and, still holding Caitlin's hand, pulled her after him. "You'll all excuse us now and expect to see us at Leila's in Kensington for dinner at nine."

"Just one more question, please Quinn," Caitlin insisted. "Gordon—Jean McGlory, what about *her*?"

"I found only that one notation, nothing else." Gordon shrugged.

"I'll try to find her myself," Caitlin said, her eyes pained for a moment. "Now that I have the means to help her, perhaps I can make up just a little for the harm Billy did all those years ago."

"Miracles do happen, Caty, if you help them," Cedre said. "*You* should know that as well as anyone."

"Yes." Caitlin nodded, meeting Cedre's eyes. Then she responded to the pressure of Quinn's hand on hers. "We'll see you later." She smiled over her shoulder.

"Why are you rushing me so?" she asked testily as Quinn helped her with her coat, even adjusted the matching fur-trimmed bonnet. "I wanted to ask Gordon about Mr. Hawker. It is an odd coincidence about your friend."

"Hawker will tell you himself anything you want to know. Now I want you all to myself. I've been civilized long enough. I haven't touched you for hours, which is bad enough, but now you're going to be away from me for days. I intend to store up enough of you to get me through." His boyish smile shattered Caitlin's resistance. She curled lovingly into the possessive curve of his arm that rested about her shoulder, and they stepped out of the tea room into a cutting wind that swept round the corner.

"They're plucking geese in Yorkshire," Caitlin said softly, wistfully, catching a snow drop on her pointy tongue. "I remember someone saying that, a woman in a window seat, mending, while we watched the flakes fall. Quinn?" She looked up anxiously. "It won't be . . . different with us now . . . now that I have all this money?"

"Of course it'll be different, imp—better. You can keep some of your precious independence if you don't have to come to me for every silly thing once we've married. In fact, I might just let you support *me*," he teased.

"That's too much independence, thanks. The Wiley sisters warned me about rakes like you." She sniffed. "The ladies were very adamant about avoiding fortune hunters."

"Who in blazes are the Wiley sisters, and what was their view of lecherous ravishers?" he asked with his best wolfish leer as their carriage pulled up.

"They are the dear old things who blew the gaff on Robin Edwards and his partners," Caitlin explained as he handed her in.

"I don't want you worrying about that lowlife. I'll see he's taken care of so he never troubles you again, understand me, Caitlin?" Quinn demanded, climbing up after her. Without answering, she drew him into her arms and urgently kissed him even before the carriage door had closed. Enthralled with each other, neither noticed Edwards huddled against the tea shop wall. Hat low, collar up, he watched them with hate-filled eyes until their carriage turned a corner and was out of his sight.

"Did I ever tell you about Ingrés?" Quinn whispered into Caitlin's ear, his arms about her.

"He's the Parisian painter who adored the female body. You told me that much," she sighed between kisses.

"Monsieur Ingrés would take Madame Ingrés to the ballet," Quinn said, his hands sliding beneath Caitlin's coat to caress a soft breast, "but the sight of the ballerinas in their tights," he went on, his hand now moving up along her leg beneath her skirt, "so . . . pleased him, he would hurry Madame from the theatre at intermission . . ." Quinn's demanding mouth was on Caitlin's, her silken, pointed tongue darting against his.

"Yes, at intermission?" she prompted breathlessly.

"They would leave at intermission, and he'd have to have her in their carriage on their way home."

Caitlin was half reclining in a corner, looking up at Quinn with laughing eyes.

"They must have had a greater distance to go than we do," she said naughtily.

"We've far enough," Quinn growled, his hard body covering hers.

Chapter Twenty-Four

"He is twisted as a stick and aged before his time, but Jim Hawker's spirit has never been broken," Dancy told Caitlin. She had come some miles down a steep, narrow woodland path for a first glimpse of her friend, and now the two climbed, agile and pretty as a pair of yearling fawns, toward a small stone house set into the side of the wooded hill. "He's very pleased you're coming to see him. He's gotten rather worked up about it . . . brushed his hair and insisted we help him into his Sunday jacket. Caty," Dancy said with a shy smile, "we were told you've come into the Montressor fortune, that this is actually your land we are walking over now."

"I can't really believe it myself." Caitlin laughed. She moved with fine grace, climbing steadily and never seeming to tire. She stopped though when the skirt of her walking suit snagged on a low branch.

"It's so beautiful here, so rough and pure, just as David said. On this mountainside, with these trees straining for light, twisting their branches toward the sky, the stream with the misty vapor rising—I feel I've been here somehow."

"See the brick chimneys there?" Dancy pointed. "Just poking through the trees? It's *your* manor. Want to go see it?"

"I'm not . . . ready yet," Caitlin said. "When Quinn is here . . . Tell me, how is David?" she asked.

"Oh, now he's home and he's wonderful. He rides often with the poachers, which makes me . . . anxious. He goes out at dawn to fish with coracle men in their leather boats. He's even been up north to the farm to see Mother. I can't . . . not yet."

"Is she very bad?"

"She's never very good," Dancy answered, placing a hand on Caitlin's shoulder. They stopped again, this time in a wild glade warmed by a splash of late sunlight. "Mother's always been a trembling, frail creature, beset by her own demons, and I'm very like her sometimes. That frightens me, you see. I don't often go to see her."

"Gordon told us about your stepfather," Caitlin said simply.

"He'd been . . . it went on all my life, his trying to force himself on me—from the time I was seven or eight, anyway, when he married Mother and adopted us. We were always running away, David and I. The last time, he almost had his way with me before I . . . I pushed him. I never meant to," Dancy said, closing her eyes. "After it happened, we ran away again, to America. David and I thought I'd be hanged for a murderess if I were caught, but now Quinn says it isn't so, and Gordon agrees it was . . . self defense. Gordon!" Dancy smiled affectionately. "With all his silly talk and quoting, he's really a very wise man, and kind."

"I think he loves you, Dancy," Caitlin said softly.

"I don't want . . . that kind of love, not his or any man's, not after what I've done," Dancy said wildly. "I still feel that man's hands on my skin, feel him forcing me . . ." Dancy shuddered and hid her face from Caitlin. "Gordon says he'll be content to stay by my side forever and never want . . . *that*. He does want to marry me, though, Caitlin." Dancy smiled tearily. "Even after—"

"Of course he wants to marry you. What happened was never your fault; don't you understand?" Caitlin said intensely.

"I understand, yes, but I can't *feel* that way." Dancy shrugged, wiping her eyes with a pocket handkerchief. She stood. "Come along or poor Jim will be overly excited by the time we get to the cabin."

"Dancy . . . I thought Gordon had a wife," Caitlin stated.

"She died of the cholera years ago. There's a child in America that Gordon insists isn't his. We make a singular couple, don't we? Gordon and me, we're a fragile pair, but we do share what few strengths we have between us. It helps." Dancy laughed, starting off again up the mountain path. "Wait 'til you meet Hawker," she called. "He's a wonderful man, and Caitlin?" Dancy waited. "The two people in all the world he loves most are your father and Quinn Jones."

"So, you are one of *cymry cymraeg*, the Welsh speakin' Welsh!" Hawker said to Caitlin when she greeted him in his own lovely, flowing language.

"David taught me a little," she answered, looking up at the very tall figure who'd stood to greet her. A soft-spoken man with gentle, dark eyes and thinning pepper and salt hair, he was, as Dancy had described him, pained and bent, leaning heavily on a pair of thick wooden walking sticks.

"Please sit down, Mr. Hawker," Caitlin said, her sympathies, as always, clear in her eyes.

"He's hard as nails, always has been," one of the young men in the room bantered, setting chairs for Hawker and his guest. He was bolder than the others in the room who had been struck silent at Caitlin's entrance. "It's not every day a beautiful Welsh princess comes in out of the glades to visit," the young man said with a smile.

"That's Owen," Hawker told Caitlin. "Those other fierce fellows are Tom, Llewelyn, and Gareth, and your friend, David, of course, who's going to bring us each a cup of mead, aren't you, David, to make us easy in our talk? When will the doctor be comin'?" the old man asked.

"Any moment. He and his wife climb more slowly than Dancy and I."

"No wonder," Hawker laughed. "Who could keep pace with a pair of agile mountain deer like you two? And Quinn, when will he come?"

"In a day or two," Caitlin said with a look that told Hawker everything.

"I see." He nodded. "I'm pleased for him that he's got you to love him so. You've saved him, I can tell."

"That's what I told her would happen. I told her it was a dangerous gamble," Cedre Burleigh said, stepping into the cabin, short of breath and a bit bedraggled after her climb, "but Caty's a born gambler, I think."

"It's a merciless drizzle out there, man, turning now to ice," Wade huffed, dropping his mackintosh and striding to shake Hawker's hand. "But we are damn glad to be here. We'll take a cup of whatever it is you're taking a cup of, and then we'll see to the patient."

"Tomorrow will be soon enough," Hawker insisted. "Tonight we'll visit and talk. There's much to be said, and we don't often have such a houseful of guests way off in these wild mountains and never such special ones. I wouldn't keep Caitlin waiting to hear the story I have to tell. Ah, here's Mrs. Holyoake." He greeted a rosy, round woman who peered in from the kitchen. "She's the best cook in Wales, and we'll be eating tonight, courtesy of Miss McGlory," Hawker announced with a twinkle.

"Me?" Caitlin asked. "I don't understand."

"Every bite you take was runnin' over your land not long ago," he explained, much to the delight of the men gathered in the cabin who roared with laughter.

"Perhaps the lady would go out with us tonight," Owen invited, "to see how it's done. It'll be safe enough. Her gamekeeper, Griffiths, don't bother us in the sleet and chill."

"*My* . . . gamekeeper?" Caitlin stood and looked questioningly at the men who had gone quiet again all at once.

"The trustees and executors put Griffiths on

us. Your grandfather and me, Cate, had an agreement going back years, to when we were both not much more than boys. 'Mr. Hawker, do you shoot?' he asks me one day, seeing me in my long, covert coat with all the secret pockets and me limping along with my sawed-off rifle down my pants leg. 'Yes, sir,' I replied, not wanting to lie to him. 'Then I give you permission to go on my land,' he says. Now, giving a poacher permission is like taking the sugar out of the ginger bread, but I respected the man for his generosity. He was not like others who'd deny the earth's bounty to starvin' children so there's plenty of game when they bring their fine friends from London to shoot for the sport of it. I have poached on *their* land more for revenge than gain, and they never caught me until—"

"Until Griffiths shot him in the back," Owen spat, "and he couldn't run, and that's when the American, Quinn, saved his life. Jail would have killed him, bent and pained as he is."

The room went absolutely still. The men, now seated with the others about a large, rough-hewn table, looked grim until Hawker, in his gentle, commanding way, changed the tone of the gathering.

"Boys! We outdo them every time we match wits with 'em; we run circles about 'em and we feed ourselves and our friends right well. We own the woods and copses on moonlit nights. We are honest rogues and we take care of our own. Lookin' back, memory for me is good. I wouldn't have had it any other way."

"'For he lives twice who can at once employ the present well, and ev'n the past enjoy,'" Dancy recited. "Gordon taught me that."

"Your Gordon is a fine man, no matter what he may think of himself." Hawker laughed. "Want to know about the time we fooled the bailiff over to—"

"I want to know about my father, please," Caitlin said very seriously. She stood, taking heavy platters from Mrs. Holyoake as the woman came and went and setting them about the table.

"I found Patrick McGlory when he was working as a crow starver for a shilling a week," Hawker began at once, "throwing rocks at crows to keep them off the corn. They had him feedin' the pheasants, too, on raisins soaked in gin, and, him starvin' himself, he snitched those raisins and staggered like a drunkard. All of twelve he was, mind, and wild with a pain and sadness it would take years for him to speak about. He did finally, after he and your mother married and he brought her home here to me. She was the most beautiful little thing . . . like you." Hawker went on speaking in a low voice to the enthralled company, his eyes on Caitlin, the food growing cold. "There was a portrait of her done that same year before she run off. She was seventeen. It could as well be you. You'll see for yourself when you go up to the mansion."

"And was he—Patrick—very handsome?" Caitlin asked dreamily as Cedre began passing the platters.

"He had hair the color of oak leaves in autumn, eyes blue as yours, and a smile like summer sunlight. Those two were like somethin' out of a fairytale, so in love, destined for each other always, but destined to lose each other, too, and they seemed to know it. They could never have enough of each other, would never be parted for more than hours. They were like . . . like shootin' stars. Their flame was blinding and quickly spent."

"How did it happen?" Caitlin whispered.

"The fever. She tried to bring him through it, and when she couldn't, she knew she'd not last long either without him. That's when she took you to Lady Outerbridge."

"Not my grandfather?"

"That lonely, stubborn old fool, rattling about in his empty castle. He never forgave her for runnin' off with her famine Irish lad. He wanted you, though. She'd taken you to him to show you off, and he adored you. But he was old, and she was afraid of what would happen to a mere babe after he died. There were relations wanting the old man's wealth. On her own death bed, Damaris made Lady Outerbridge swear to send you to America where you'd be safe, and never to speak of you again."

"They couldn't have hated my uncle Billy so, if she asked that?"

"I think your father did forgive him, but I don't know about Jean."

"They found her, I know."

"Yes, Caitlin, they prowled the slums of London for months and found her just walking along one day, humming to herself and clutching a doll like she was a little child. She saw Patrick, slipped her arm through his, and began to prattle as though she'd never been gone, though five years had passed since he'd lost her."

"Too great a shock can affect the mind that way," Wade Burleigh said somberly. "Did she ever remember her London life?"

"Never, but she kept trying to get back there, kept wandering off, and one day she wandered off for good. That was just after you were born, Caitlin. They searched again but never found her. Your mother had some ideas about what haunted Jean. Maybe she told Lady Outerbridge. She never told me."

"Take me to her," Caitlin said.

"At this hour? Through the dark?" Cedre Burleigh protested. "Caitlin, what has waited all these years can surely wait until morning.

You haven't eaten one—"

"It *can't* wait," Caitlin insisted, "and these gentlemen are expert at getting about in the dark. Will you take me?" she asked Owen.

"My pleasure," he said, already on his feet.

"Thank you." She smiled then whirled about to face James Hawker again. "How could my uncle say they were wild?"

"They were—wild and beautiful, always in motion like wild birds in flight. Your father wasn't a man for a pie and a pint and a dog at his feet by the fire, nor was your mother one for the spinning wheel or the drawing room. There was a restlessness about them I—"

"And she didn't abandon me or . . . murder him?" Caitlin demanded.

"She insisted they go together into a part of Merthyr where the fever was raging, to help, so you could say she took him to death's door. But he'd have gone without her if he could have made her stay behind," Hawker insisted. "Now, as for abandoning you,"—the lines etched on Hawker's long, somber face deepened—"the last word on her lips was your name."

"Oh! Mr. Hawker, thank you," Caitlin said, kissing his cheek as her eyes flooded with tears. "Dancy," she sniffed, "will you go with me to Lady Outerbridge?"

Dancy nodded and went to get her cloak

at once.

"If Quinn should come," Caitlin said at the door, "you'll tell him where I've gone?"

"Of course, you silly." Cedre laughed. "Now, if you're going, get on your way. You're letting in a draft."

Chapter Twenty-Five

"I'm so glad I was here visiting Mother or I might not have gotten to see you," Chantal Wells told Caitlin warmly, passing three formal drawing rooms to usher her into a cozy family parlor, a room done in an Arabic motif with stenciled walls and Persian rugs and needlepoint portraits of birds. "I *do* remember you." Chantal smiled. "I remember being terribly angry that you'd invaded my nursery, but when you left I cried. I remember that, too."

"We couldn't have been more than four or five," Caitlin mused. "I wish *I* could recall." She found Chantal's open, unaffected friendliness delightful. She was a plain girl with light hair and unremarkable features, but she radiated a warmth that was endearing. She'd come tripping down the stairs pushing back her hair, wearing a dark dress, cuffs rolled to the elbows, and a spotted apron, explaining that she'd been bathing her newest baby and that her mother would soon be down.

"It can be a very great burden for some women, being extraordinarily beautiful, as Mother is," Chantal said. "She can't appear as less than perfect to anyone, ever. Still, I wish that I looked as much like her as you resemble your mother. You are the image of her, Caitlin."

"But you can't remember *her*!" Caitlin protested. "She died before—"

"It's her portrait at Montressor Manor I'm thinking of. It could be you. In fact, there are generations of Montressor ladies hanging, and you've a resemblance to several. Ah, here's Mother."

Fleur Outerbridge rustled into the room in a great sweep of pink satin dressing gown, her sugary blond hair piled high, her arms outspread as she approached Caitlin. "You could *be* Damaris, darling Caitlin, standing there at that hearth as she used to do so often. Turn round. I want to see how you've grown. Damaris would be so pleased with you. Have you ordered up tea, Chantal?" Fleur asked.

Her daughter nodded and withdrew a little, as was her habit, to a side chair as Fleur led Caitlin to a settee. The woman's fingers glittered with rings and her blue eyes sparkled.

"Dancy tells me you are about to marry," Fleur smiled, her heart-shaped face beneath its crown of blond hair very beautiful, belying the fact of a grown daughter and three grandchildren in the nursery upstairs. "To an American, Dancy says. Is that wise?" Fleur's concern seemed genuine.

"Mother thinks North Americans are barbarians or something very like." Chantal laughed.

"Well, they are all in trade, aren't they?" Fleur's light laugh filled the room. "What does *your* American do?"

"Well . . . he does investments," Caitlin pronounced, realizing with a start she couldn't say exactly what Quinn did. "And he collects art," she added.

"That is nice—a little culture. I hope you're madly in love?" Fleur asked. "I shall give you a ball. Now, I must finish dressing. There's a dinner at Lord Layton's."

"Mother is all romance, Caitlin. She thinks life is unbearable unless one is blindly in love or giving a ball," Chantal explained affectionately. "Do let her give you one."

"Yes, of course, but before you go, Lady Outerbridge, will you tell me about my aunt?" Caitlin asked urgently.

"But my dear, your mother was an only child and that of your grandfather's old age. Her mother didn't survive the birth. I don't understand." Fleur looked charmingly confused.

"Tell me about Jean McGlory, my father's twin sister," Caitlin pressed. "Mr. Hawker thinks my mother might have talked about Jean to you."

"Oh, my dear, that was all so sad, I've nearly erased her memory altogether. It was as if she'd never grown up. She was a charming, lovely, perpetual child. I don't *know* what ever happened to her or to her children," Fleur added insistently.

"I'd no idea Jean *had* any," Caitlin said, going to stand by the mantel again.

"That was your mother's explanation of it all. The girl talked to her dolls quite rationally, you see; they had names and all. Your mother thought the babies were in London, that that was why Jean kept trying to go back there though Jean herself didn't really know that. Ah, here's my darling Dancy. Another of my precious strays. I must dress, but in the morning we'll have a good talk." Fleur sighed, drifting from the room in a pink satin rustle.

"Have you been to the Montressor house? In daylight, you can see the chimneys from here," Chantal said, pouring three cups of tea. "This place is a castle with battlements and all. Yours is a fortified manor, really, with the sea crashing below. It's beautiful."

"I'm not ready to go there yet." Caitlin smiled distractedly.

"Would you like to see the nursery? Perhaps you'll be comfortable there," Chantal said, aware of Caitlin's restlessness.

"You're very kind." Caitlin smiled. "How did you know I was—"

"Restless?" Chantal laughed. "If one is the very unbeautiful daughter of a very beautiful woman and a man who is quite blind to women who lack that attribute, one develops certain sensitivities to compensate for the disappointment one has caused. I can read my father's moods in a way that startles and even interests him and captures his attention. Because I'm not beautiful, my mother trusts me, and I am her best friend. Now, you must see my daughters who are beautiful *and* clever."

After climbing three flights of oak stairs, the last quite narrow, Caitlin, Chantal, and Dancy came into the nursery at the top of the house. The room was warmed by an open coal fire burning bright behind a wire mesh safety fender with a brass rail. A pot of hot milk rested on a trivet, and the air was fragrant with rose powder. There was a glazed blue chintz cover on the bassinet with curtains to match and colored beads threaded on the rod of a baby chair where a little girl of about two, in a muslin gown, sat with a large bowl of broth. Another child, her golden hair shining, was curled in a window seat, and a nursemaid in a full white apron with white collar, cuffs, and cap sat in a rocking chair cooing lovingly to the very small girl she held in her arms.

"Someone is plucking geese in Yorkshire." Caitlin laughed. "Oh, I remember! I do really, every detail—the cork floor and the counterpanes and the smell of hot milk—it's like coming home."

"It's my favorite room in this vast castle." Chantal smiled. "And it always has been. What else do you remember?"

"Mother, sitting in that window seat, sewing. She was the most beautiful—Dancy!" Caitlin said suddenly. "We must go back to London at once!"

"No!" Dancy laughed, looking up from the little girl in the push chair who was her special favorite. "Emmeline won't allow it, will you, Emmeline?" she asked. Dancy stood and took Caitlin's hand. "Why do you want to go? It's so lovely here and Quinn won't be long and—"

"I must find Jean McGlory. I can't bear being happy and thinking she may be alone and lost still, after all this time. Come with me?"

"Of course I will. Did you ever doubt it?" Dancy shrugged dramatically and kissed Emmeline goodbye.

Chapter Twenty-Six

Melusina Montressor learned only accidentally from her country hostess that Quinn Jones was in London and squiring a party of Americans about the city. Melusina returned to town at once, sooner than she had planned, even though it was inconvenient for her to do so and costly as well. Her townhouse had to be opened, the servants recalled, and supplies laid in.

Living as Melusina did in genteel poverty, always at the brink of financial disaster, she had very nearly become a perpetual house guest among that idle segment of the aristocracy always in need of distraction and amusement. If nothing else, Melusina Montressor was distracting, carrying from noble house to noble house the juiciest bits of the most scandalous gossip. She was skilled at playing on the vanities of her hostesses, and each woman she titillated with nasty news of others in their circle felt she alone was Melusina's true friend. Melusina actually had no friends. She regarded all her rich and privileged acquaintances with hidden contempt heightened by an acid jealousy that had eaten away at her since childhood. Urged by an ambitious mother to reach for upper rungs of the social ladder, Melusina had made excellent use of the Montressor name. She'd had little else of value. Her father was a remote cousin, a poor relation of the rich and landed Montressors, and her mother was near-gentry with no money or position to trade on, something of an embarrassment to her daughter who had adopted all of the worst snobbish attitudes of the class to which she aspired and none of their aristocratic virtues. Melusina was personally offended by the very existence of the lower classes and tried to avoid them whenever possible. On those occasions when she had no choice but to pass through Victoria Station on her way to some grand country estate, or to make one of her frequent trips to Petticoat Lane for the inexpensive clothes she was forced to wear, Melusina's disgust was boundless, and she thought of the poor as an inferior species of human, a view bolstered by some of the most highly respected scientific theorists of the day.

Melusina Montressor was not an unattractive woman. She had heavy dark hair and fine hazel eyes, but, although a prominent chin and pointed nose precluded her being designated a beauty, there was nothing so very wrong that she should not have been able to catch a respectable husband before reaching the advanced age of twenty-seven. She had come close once. A timid, aging viscount had almost asked, but he had been, at the last hour, frightened off by Melusina's viperish meanness that did exude on occasion from beneath her controlled and false angelic shell. She had almost given up hope when the executor of the Montressor estate contacted her, and then Quinn Jones had appeared, reviving abandoned hopes of marriage.

Melusina's vindictive fantasies sent her into transports of vicious delight. Once in control of the Montressor fortune, she would dress beautifullly, spend profligately, and dangle her magnificent catch—Quinn—before her envious, lascivious lady friends. He was *perfect*—irresistibly handsome, both cultivated and tigerish, quite untamed beneath his elegant exterior, rich in his own right, and a Montressor besides. Even Melusina, who had always been repelled by even the thought of a man touching her *that* way, decided she might not mind it with Quinn, might actually enjoy it as some of her female acquaintances admitted to doing. She really never had believed them before, but now, she mused, there might be something to it.

So Melusina returned in a rush to London, to her house on Wimpole Street. She invested in her wine cellar, got the larder filled, ordered a load of coal, brought in the butler, the cook, and one parlor maid, and then, when all was ready, sent a message to Quinn's hotel to say that she was back in town and eager to see him. It took two days for him to respond.

Quinn Jones had appeared on Melusina's doorstep in jodhpurs and boots, one of those rugged North American mountain coats over his shoulders, collar up against his dark hair, the expression on his hard, handsome face intense. He'd explained to her quickly, kindly, about the other heir and his impending marriage. He'd smiled and taken her hand to his lips. If he could ever do anything for her she was to let him know, he'd said, and he hoped she'd come to the wedding. Then he was gone, off to Wales and his American heiress, who had to be the cleverest, meanest schemer on earth to have won out and walked off with everything Melusina had wanted, had already counted on.

In pale, drawn, icy fury, she had had the fires extinguished in the upstairs rooms, dismissed the servants quickly, and changed into an old, faded day dress, carefully wrapping away the almost new one she'd worn for Quinn. Making a mental note to return the expensive brandy to the vintners, Berry and Rudd, she took a moderately priced bottle of crusted port to the drawing room and sat alone behind closed shutters, sick with disappointment and rage, trying to decide where to turn and what to do next. By the time she'd reached the sediment at the bottom of the bottle, she was almost ready to emigrate to Australia. It was then she remembered the note that had been waiting for her the day she'd opened the house. The paper was cheap and the handwriting rough. Repelled, she'd torn it in half and . . . done what with it? she wondered now in panic. If only she hadn't burned it, if only it was still on the desk . . . Melusina tore up the steps and with a shaking hand unlocked the library door. The note was there, torn and crumpled as she'd left it. Carefully smoothing it flat and placing the pieces together, Melusina could read the name and address at the bottom.

In less than an hour, Robin Edwards was, much to her disgust, ensconced in her parlor, sipping her expensive brandy. He was nothing more than a lout with a pretty smile, but he was telling her all sorts of fascinating things about Quinn Jones and Caitlin McGlory. Melusina filled Robin's glass again.

"He's left, miss, gone just this morning," the desk clerk at the Durants Hotel told Caitlin.

"Mr. Jones was riding north, not training, taking some horses up, he said. He's kept the rooms, if you wish to—"

"Yes, thank you, we will later," Caitlin answered, disappointment written all over her lovely face as she turned to Dancy. "We'll do this alone," she said despite Dancy's worried look.

"Cremorne Garden is bad enough in summer when there're lights and music and hundreds of dancers. Now, Lord knows what low, desperate characters may be prowling," Dancy protested.

"Think of the positive side. One of the prowlers might be your Mr. Gladstone, the prime minister. Quinn told me he often wanders about, rescuing prostitutes, taking them home to tea and a good life. He might know about Mrs. Drabble's place," Caitlin lectured, leading Dancy along.

"How do you know about this Drabble person?" Dancy asked suspiciously.

"When Billy told me about Jean, he mentioned the name of the woman who'd paid him."

"But that was more than twenty years ago," Dancy protested, still hanging back.

"It's all I have to work with," Caitlin said adamantly. "If you don't want to come . . ."

"You don't think I'd let you go alone?" Dancy snapped, quickening her pace.

They took a hansom to Queen's Gate and walked through the thick mist of a cold February night toward the Cremorne Gardens in Chelsea. They traversed the deserted gravel paths there, arm in arm, talking in lowered voices as they glanced nervously about.

"It's very pretty in the summer," Dancy explained, "with the music and dancing. You can have lemonade or sherry under the elms, the flower boxes are all filled with geraniums, and if one didn't know why the men and women were here, one couldn't guess by looking. It's all very discreet. Oh! Look there."

Between two widely spaced, mist-clouded gas lights, a man and a woman leaned close against a wall.

"You can't ask them anything," Dancy whispered in panic.

"Why can't I?" Caitlin demanded. "Perhaps they'll know about—"

"You're such an innocent." Dancy laughed. "Don't you know what they're doing there?"

"No!" Caitlin said, her blue eyes very wide as she peered over her shoulder. "We had better go. I didn't realize it would be this way. Oh, if only Quinn were here!"

Arms linked again, eyes on the ground, Caitlin and Dancy walked very briskly back toward Kensington. They had decided that Leila Faithful might be able to help when, with little gasps of fright, they collided with a large, blue-coated figure who stepped out of the shadows to block their way.

"Where are you two going?" a gruff voice demanded.

"To Mrs. Faithful in Kensington," Caitlin answered at once in a breathless whisper, and the disapproving eyes of the tall policeman softened a little.

"What are you two young girls doing in the park at such an hour?" he asked, taking in their good clothes and modest manners.

"Actually, we're trying to find Mrs. Drabble's," Caitlin announced boldly, never one to let a good opportunity slip by her.

The man went red in the face and then laughed, slapping his knee once or twice before regaining his somber, authoritative manner. "You had me fooled there for a flash, looking like two respectable girls. Mrs. Drabble's establishment is in Mayfair, a convenient location for her tony clientele. Want an escort?"

"It isn't what you think," Caitlin said indignantly. "We're trying to find someone. Perhaps you could help, officer." She smiled her prettiest.

Half an hour later, Caitlin and Dancy were climbing the steps of Mrs. Drabble's townhouse while police officer Arnold, a considerate man who, not wanting to discourage trade, waited for them out of sight across the road. The proprietress led the way upstairs toward her private apartment, stopping to let her guests peer through tinted glass into one of the rooms they passed. There, a young man, slender as a jockey, with long blond hair nearly to his shoulders, stood rigid and silent, gripping the posts of a bed as a half-dressed girl gleefully laid a row of stripes across his back with a fine switch.

"He'll reciprocate in kind, though he requires that she be tied and rather more vocal and animated than he is," Mrs. Drabble explained after providing her guests with sherry and biscuits and settling into a deep red velvet sofa. "If you want to work for me, you should know in advance that we provide varied services here. Our specialty is young virgins, so if either of you are properly qualified, we could do well at an auction."

Dancy paled and set down her glass. "No, no," she said quickly. "You don't understand. We've come looking for someone."

"I'm sorry," Mrs. Drabble said, her puffy face going serious. "I should have known by the look of you, but respectable girls don't often find their way here. In fact, this may be the first time I've ever been paid such a call by the likes of you. Well?" she demanded.

"Jean McGlory," Caitlin said, and Mrs. Drabble's eyes narrowed.

"That was more than twenty years ago," the woman answered. "Why do you care?"

"She was my father's sister," Caitlin said, leaning forward anxiously, "and if I could find her—"

"She's a respectable married woman now with her own children to think of, her own twins, a grown boy and girl. She may not want to be found by you."

"But you can't decide that for her." Caitlin's anger was rising. "I've learned that her mind was undone by . . . by what happened to her here, and she may need help; no one seems to know."

"*I* know," Mrs. Drabble said. "She's been helped and I'll tell you how, but then I don't ever want to see you again, do you understand?" When Dancy and Caitlin nodded, she began to speak.

"Jean *was* undone, as you say. One brief half-hour here seemed to have destroyed her forever. She was an extraordinarily beautiful girl, heavy red hair like . . ." Mrs. Drabble shook her head, staring at Dancy. "Red hair and green eyes like yours, and the sweetest smile. Lord Outerbridge paid a small fortune for her maidenhead. I don't mention his name casually. I think you should know it." Mrs. Drabble looked directly at Dancy this time, who closed her eyes and rested her head against the chair back. "He's enjoyed more than one such innocent here, but only Jean ever reacted so strong . . . and he was distraught at what happened, paid me to keep her for him only, visited her regularly but never touched her again after that first time. When the twins were born he arranged for them to be placed at a very good baby farm in the North. And then, when she ran away, Lord Outerbridge searched . . . and found her. He went on paying for the twins' care for some years until Jean seemed better, and then he arranged a marriage for her with a man from up near Devil's Bridge in Wales. He even bought them a farm, I've heard, and brought the children to her. Later, Lord Outerbridge put the boy into the Navy when he was of age. He sometimes took the little girl home when Jean went bad in her mind, on and off. I often wondered if Lady Outerbridge ever realized . . ." Mrs. Drabble's voice trailed off and Dancy slowly opened her eyes.

"She did," Dancy said. "I know that now, and she never minded at all. She was always kind to me. To Lady Outerbridge I was more than a governess; I was a part of the family. . . . Cate, can we go?" she asked with a tearful smile, and Caitlin could only nod assent and offer her hand.

"This *is* the night for discovering long lost kissing cousins." Caitlin laughed. Exuberant over their discovery once the shock of it began to subside, she and Dancy had walked back to Durants, stopping at Leila's to announce their news and look in on Nealon Burleigh, asleep in an upstairs bedroom. Accompanied on their way by Officer Arnold, who was nearly as pleased as they, Caitlin and Dancy chattered about all the things they would have done together if only they had found each other before, and they planned the things they would do from now on—have all their babies at exactly the same times, if Dancy ever had any, and bring them up all in the same nursery so they would never feel lost and lonely as their mothers sometimes had. More seriously, they had talked of bringing Billy McGlory and his sister, Jean, together, but that they knew would take time and care.

"We must leave first thing in the morning. If I don't see Quinn soon, I won't be able to bear it," Caitlin was saying as she took the keys and a message from the Durants' desk clerk. "I want to marry him right now, this instant, but if Billy and Ann will come over, we'll wait. We'll have a grand wedding, and you'll be my bridesmaid, Dancy, and I'll be yours when . . ." It was then she read Melusina's note and handed it to Dancy.

"She's not *my* cousin," Dancy said with a joking little sniff, "but if you decide you like her, I will, too, as long as you don't like her better than you do me. Let's go round right now. I want to see her!"

"At two in the morning?" Caitlin hesitated, but not for long. "Let's! I'm too wildly excited to sleep anyway, and if she seriously thinks she is going to be our cousin, she'd better get used to our quirks at once."

Melusina's house on Wimpole Street was all lit up as Caitlin and Dancy arrived and, relieved of their wraps, they were shown into a comfortable drawing room. They had barely had time to investigate in their usual inquisitive way, when their hostess appeared, silently materializing at the door with outstretched hands. "Cousin Cate," she gushed, striding toward Dancy who gestured with an upturned hand, setting Melusina off in the proper direction. Caitlin tolerated a stiff hug. "I had hoped you would come round this very evening. I waited for you. It is too bad that our third relation, Mr. Jones, couldn't be with us tonight for this historic meeting that should have taken place—" Melusina stopped to gaze at Caitlin with concern. "But what's wrong? Did I say something to upset you?"

"*What* Mr. Jones?" Caitlin demanded. "He never mentioned you."

"Mr. Quinn Jones, your countryman, a Montressor several generations removed on his mother's side. It's an illegitimate branch, but on his death bed your grandfather recognized their call on the family fortune. Did Quinn never tell you? That sly rascal, and now I've ruined his surprise."

"What surprise?" Dancy said, moving to Caitlin's side.

"Why, that he and I will also share in the inheritance, in a limited way, of course. If you hadn't been found, Caitlin, Quinn and I would have had it all. We'd planned to marry and solidify the family, but now that you are the heiress . . . well, now I learn that you, not I, will become his wife. No matter, the money and estate stay in the family either way. We must toast your happy future." Melusina nodded, ringing for her hastily recalled butler.

"He . . . he didn't know until a few days ago that I was . . . who I was. Gordon just informed *me*," Caitlin said coldly.

"But my dear, Quinn went to America to find you, if he could. After he did, he sent that Gordon Finley here to formalize matters by unearthing the relevant documents. I'm sorry . . . I didn't mean to disturb you, but I thought surely you already knew everything I'm telling you. But then Quinn *is* such a notorious confidence man, such a clever manipulator, perhaps he was afraid you'd think he was marrying you for your money, which can't be the case, can it? And even if it were, what matter? I mean, you are so obviously in love, just as he told me earlier today, that—"

"He didn't know about the estate, I tell you,"

Caitlin said in a shaking voice.

"Poor darling. I *am* sorry, but it's best these things come up before one has taken an irrevocable step, sworn fidelity for a lifetime and so on. Even if Quinn hadn't received a letter from his Mr. Finley relating the facts—"

"But he *did*," Caitlin interrupted with a terrible look. "He *knew* about my aunt, Jean, and where I was born. Go on, please, Melusina."

"My dear cousin, with no documentation at all, he would have known at very first sight exactly who you were, because he'd seen the portrait of your mother at Montressor Hall. But surely, none of this matters," she repeated.

But it did matter. Ignoring Dancy's tearful pleas to hear an explanation from Quinn, Caitlin absolutely refused to see him again—ever, she insisted. She left at once for Wales with Melusina in a sumptuous, lacquered black coach emblazoned with the family crest of Melusina's good friend, Lord Ruthven Glendenning, called Ven, who was a member of the peerage and heir to several titles. He escorted both ladies north, gallantly assuming the task of educating Caitlin in the lifestyle of the class to which she now belonged. Liberating her from commonness was the way Ven described what he was about, a phrase that earned him a slow, coldly amused stare from his "student," whose icy blue eyes made Glendenning uncomfortable and more than a little angry. He would be called handsome by some, Caitlin told herself, openly studying him. He had small, even, almost girlishly pretty features—restless light eyes shaded by long blond lashes and a thin, dissatisfied mouth that lent him the appearance of a spoiled child. He was pale and wan, his transparent skin the color of watered milk, and his bony hand gripping the blue velvet arm rest of the carriage would be, Caitlin was sure, very cold to the touch. Ven was slim as a jockey, though tall, with long blond hair reaching nearly to his shoulders.

"Are you uncomfortable, Lord Glendenning?" Caitlin asked innocently as he sat rigidly straight, moving rarely and then with stiff, set shoulders.

"I seem to have caught a bit of a chill. It's stiffened my neck," he answered, the expression in Caitlin's bold eyes making him feel she knew more about him than she possibly could or should. His eyes glazed for a moment as he imagined Caitlin in the place of the girl he had had last night at Drabble's.

Ven was the first to look away. He glanced into the dusk of a London street as the carriage rounded a corner where a bedraggled girl stood shivering in a light cape.

"Rather pretty, some of these costermonger's daughters." He smiled.

"She'll freeze, pretty or not, if she doesn't get

out of the cold," Caitlin worried.

"They are different than you and I, my naïve little cousin." Melusina laughed. "Don't waste your sympathies; *they* don't feel the cold as we do."

"No matter what you Americans may think, there is a difference between us and them," Ven said with a supercilious laugh. "They are born with a capacity for criminality. They should all be transported for the first infraction or made to do the floorless jig as they call hanging."

"I quite agree." Melusina nodded. "I've heard from Mr. Griffiths, our gamekeeper, that there's quite a lot of poaching on our land. Perhaps Ven could be helpful in putting a stop to it while he's your house guest at Montressor Manor."

"No, he won't put a stop to anything, and it's *my* gamekeeper," Caitlin corrected in a clipped tone. "I'll handle the poachers on *my* land in my *own* way. Grandfather gave them permission to take what they needed. I plan to do the same."

Ven and Melusina exchanged quick glances. "Of course it is your property, and you do exactly as you wish," Melusina said, patting Caitlin's hand. "You Americans are all so tender-hearted. Quinn expressed the same sentiment to me once, when he thought he was about to become lord of the manor."

At the mention of Quinn, Caitlin turned her face to the window, seeing little through a blur of tears, remaining motionless and silent for a long while. As the carriage moved steadily along the darkening, lonely road, Caitlin, haunted by regrets, tried to call up all her stubborn strength and passionate pride to quell the pain that thoughts of Quinn brought with them. But it didn't work. The loss was too great, the wound too deep, and she let herself sink into her sadness, not fighting it at all, knowing that only time would ease it, though fifty or a hundred years, she conjectured, probably wouldn't be quite long enough.

The arrival at Montressor Manor, something Caitlin had anticipated with delight when she thought Quinn would be at her side, was a grievous experience for her without him. She passed silently beneath the towering stone arch and climbed the old stone steps, knowing what she'd find even before the house, her mansion, came into view. Tucked against a mountain and touching the sky, it looked out over nearly hidden cottage rooftops to the sparkling sea beyond. Its classic Palladian façade was identical to that of Quinn's mansion in the North Mountains above Fundy Bay, but instead of Gordon Finley in all his rumpled, disreputable charm, a battalion of liveried servants was ranged across the marble steps to greet their new mistress who rose to the occasion despite everything. Smiling, she offered her hand to the butler, the housekeeper, and to the cook, to the upstairs maids, parlor maids, and scullery maids, to footmen, coachmen, stable boys, and lackies, hesitating only when she reached the gamekeeper with his net bag and six or eight barking corgis tumbling about his ankles.

"I've heard about you, Mr. Griffiths," she said icily, and the massive man shifted from foot to foot, his small, hooded eyes like a ferret's as he wrinkled his knob of a nose and doffed his cap. "I hope you been hearin' good, miss," he said, but she'd already moved on to greet the master of hounds, a shepherd, and the poultry girl shivering in a skimpy shawl. Caitlin pulled off her own cloak, wrapped it about the child's shoulders, and strode inside, butler and housekeeper at either elbow. In the grand entrance hall where the portraits were hung, generations of Montressors smiled down at her, the last of a line going back to the wild Welsh princesses who rode the ancient mountains with their men long ago in some distant, shadowy past, their brave beauty preserved in these paintings. For the last hundred years the Montressor women had been painted by the great portraitists of England—Reynolds and Gainsborough, Romney and Hoppner. From heavy gilt frames they stared down, some wistful, some bold and coquettish, others romantic in soft, filmy, form-following gowns. The young mothers painted with their rosy, laughing babies were charming, but most affecting for Caitlin was the portrait of her own mother, Damaris. As she stood transfixed before it, at last remembering the beautiful face and the melodic voice of the mother who had been lost to her so long, the old housekeeper, unable to maintain her unruffled calm, burst into tears, nearly causing Caitlin to do the same.

"I'm so sorry, miss, but seeing you beside her . . . it does bring back such sad memories and lovely ones, too. I do hope you'll be happy here with us."

"Thank you." Caitlin smiled, caught up in memories of her own. "I hope the same," she added, turning to a portrait, more than a hundred years old, of a tall, dark man with gray eyes soft as velvet.

"The resemblance to Quinn is slight but unmistakable. Will you see him, Caitlin? You owe him that much."

Shocked, she turned to find Dr. Burleigh standing beside her, his kindly eyes full of concern.

"Oh, I'm so *glad* to see you," she said, tears starting as he caught her in his arms. "How did you get here, and how did you know . . . what's happened?"

"Dancy told us. She came directly up to Hawker's place. Quinn's there, too. You must see him," the doctor said.

"No, I won't, and I don't owe him anything," Caitlin said softly. "He *lied* to me."

"He loves you, Caty. He knew nothing of your inheritance when he lost his heart to you. You two were so loving and close. Caitlin, how can you do this?"

"Time will make strangers of Quinn and me, Doctor," she said wistfully.

"Perhaps, but memory will rush down all the long years, and you'll have sore regrets always about what you're doing today. Quinn's an honorable man, Cate. You do him an injustice."

"Doctor, turn around, please," Caitlin asked and heard his breath catch when his eyes fell on the portrait of her mother, Damaris Montressor. Dressed in a green velvet riding habit, her titian hair loose and flowing, wide blue eyes sparkling, the beautiful, glowing girl in the picture could almost have been Caitlin herself. "Tell me *now* that he didn't know," she said sadly, leading the speechless doctor into the library for tea with her house guests, cousin Melusina and Ven Glendenning.

Dr. Burleigh was only the first of Quinn's

advocates, who, without Quinn knowing it, kept coming to Montressor Manor, one after the other, again and again, through the slow weeks of February and March. Cedre came with Nealon and Dancy, Gordon, too, and the doctor almost daily. Even James Hawker on his way to a London hospital stopped, looking sad and frail.

"You are wrong headed, miss. I have to say it. I love Quinn," Hawker said, "like my own son, like I loved your father. Quinn would share his last loaf with the hungry; he's that giving. He wants you for *love*, not money, my girl!

Caitlin was gracious and genuinely pleased to see Hawker, to see them all, but she was adamant about Quinn, and they all left feeling they had failed but vowing to try again.

In the spring, Owen came to the larder door, hat in hand, to plead Quinn's case.

"He's runnin' wild with the pain of it," the poacher said softly. "He's drinkin' and wenchin' and gamblin' like a madman, fierce as a wolf, always ready for a fight."

"I'm sorry," Caitlin said, her heart twisting with pain. "I can't help him."

"He's talkin' about abductin' an heiress, so don't be surprised if—"

"You'll remind him that I'm a superb shot. I had the best teacher." She barely managed to smile as she turned away.

"Miss, you are lookin' kinda peaked," Owen called after her. "Would you be wantin' to ride out with us of an evenin' now the weather's warming?"

She ran back toward him really smiling for the first time in ages. "Yes! Yes, I would!" She laughed. "If I don't get free of my . . . constant companions, I'll soon be good for nothing at all but presiding at the heads of dinner tables and pouring tea for the neighborhood peerage. Midnight at the stone bridge?"

"Midnight at the stone bridge." Owen laughed back, smitten by her dazzling loveliness.

It was two months later, in May, that the announcement was made. Caitlin Montressor and Ven, Ruthven Glendenning, Fifth Earl Altamont, Eighth Duke of Devon, were to be married on the first of June, at Montressor Hall. Half of England was invited. In size and splendor the wedding would rival the Queen's, who, it was hoped, now that she had come out of seclusion, would attend. Melusina Montressor, who had taken up residence with her cousin, would be bridesmaid. Another cousin, Dancy Pallett Finley, would be matron of honor. The bride's uncle, Billy McGlory, formerly of Dublin, late of New York, would give his niece in marriage. Lady Fleur Outerbridge, a family friend, would hold the wedding ball.

"You can't marry him, Caitlin. The man's dangerous. He's got a mean reputation," Owen said. He and the others sat with her, at three in the morning, around a very low, sheltered fire, roasting part of their night's catch and drinking some home-brewed spirits.

"I can handle Ven Glendenning," she snapped.

"Some of the girls tell terrible things," Owen said. "They won't have nothin' to do with him round here. He's got to go up to London for what he wants. You *can't* marry him, not with a man like Quinn wildly in love with you."

"It doesn't matter to me now who I marry. There'll never be another man like Quinn. But I *won't* have him. Ven is . . . convenient, he needs an heir, and he'll give my son a title. It will work. Best of all, my uncle will have what he wants. I couldn't have done better unless I were to marry the Prince of Wales." There was a cold sadness in Caitlin, a lost-little-girl fragility touching her vibrant beauty that made every man there want to fight her dragons and keep her from harm. "It's just self-indulgent to marry for love; Melusina told me that," she reported with a short laugh. "It's social position and wealth that matter; money and glitter and luxury last, Melusina says. Love doesn't."

"It gives me a chill, like a ghost walked over my grave, hearin' you talk like that," Llewelyn said.

In the weeks she'd been riding with the poachers, slipping out every night dressed like a boy in cap and jodhpurs, the men had grown easy with Caitlin and open in their talk.

"We were going to keep dark about this, but we must tell you now—Quinn's leavin' for France day after next. Says he's never comin' here again," Tom said.

"Wish him a good journey for me," Caitlin responded. "I must go." She stood and, with a lift from Owen, was quickly in the saddle. "Tomorrow, then?" She smiled. "It'll be my last ride for a while. The ball's next night and the wedding the day after."

"Tomorrow," they all murmured, sad and subdued as she rode off.

A mile down the path, with the chimneys of the mansion looming against a dawning dark blue sky, she nearly rode down the gamekeeper, Griffiths, leading a young boy with a rope around his neck and describing the swift justice to be expected from Lord Glendenning before another sun rose.

"Let loose of him or I'll let some daylight into *you,*" Caitlin commanded, trying to force her voice into the lower registers, keeping back in the shadows of shaggy, overhanging trees.

The boy, who stopped before Griffiths did, was jerked to his knees by the large man who peered into the darkness, scowling. "I ain't afraid of no pair of boys," the keeper laughed meanly. "I'll have your friend's face in the dirt if you are not on your knees beside him in a trice."

The first shot Caitlin fired sent a bullet whining close to Griffiths' cheek. The second shot went into the dirt at his feet. When he dropped the rope, the boy stood and came toward his rescuer.

"Run, you fool," Caitlin urged as he stared at her face, dumbfounded, before disappearing into the woods. Digging her heels into the sides of a fast chestnut gelding, bent low over the withers, she passed Griffiths at a full gallop, disappeared down the path, and tore into the stable yard just as the sun was just beginning to glow over the hills. By the time she'd put up the gelding and was hurrying toward the larder door of the mansion, there was light enough for Ven, peering from his window, to see her wild tumble of titian hair as she pulled off her cap and danced up stone stairs to disappear inside.

Three hours later, rested and dressed, Caitlin passed Griffiths leaving the house as she was on her way to the breakfast room where she found Ven and Melusina in intense conversation. They went silent as she entered.

"You look fresh and pretty as usual." Melusina nodded to Caitlin. "Sleep well? You're looking particularly bright this morning, and your dress is most flattering."

Caitlin wore a dotted black on white, long-sleeved over-jacket, pulled in and belted at her tiny waist. Her skirt was white, trimmed with lace and black velvet along the hem. Onyx rings, earrings, and beads complimented the dress, and she had tucked a dandelion, one of the season's first, at her throat. Caitlin smiled and crossed the room to pull open heavy brocaded draperies before going to the sideboard, heaping her plate and filling her coffee cup.

"What was that snitch Griffiths doing here?" she asked. "I want him dismissed at once."

"Why such urgency?" Ven questioned irritably. His expression, as usual, was ill tempered and egotistical. He was pale with boredom, his dissatisfied mouth curling in a mild grimace.

"I think the man's done a superior job," he continued. "He came to tell me of an illicit distillery he's discovered. That sort of thing has been a problem since the Wine and Beerhouse Act closed down so many pubs. I don't want you worrying about Griffiths, Caitlin. You know my view that excessive exercise of the mind impairs general efficiency. When the vital powers are concentrated in one place, they are diminished in another. It's not healthy."

"You have the most amusing ideas, Ven," Caitlin said dryly, adjusting the silver *epergne* at the center of the table. "What else did Griffiths say?"

"He reports a new member of the criminal classes roaming your woods—a boy who is a very good shot and a superb horseman. I told Griffiths to keep a special watch for him. I need a new rider before the next Epsom race. By the way, Caitlin, I've something to discuss with you. When I was last in town, I passed Cremer's in Regent Street. There's a doll there with your name and the resemblance is clear."

"Ven, why didn't you bring me one?" Caitlin asked. "I modeled for the man who made it, Richard Montanari. That's *my* doll."

"This sort of thing won't go on after we're married, Caitlin. It's . . . common and repulsive. You must ask the fellow to destroy the things at once. I'l buy them all if necessary."

"You will not," she answered, her reckless eyes blazing with anger. "If you think the dolls are common, you must see the life-sized mannequin in Ann Overton's salon window in New York. Ann's written to say it is a perfect likeness of me. She'll tell you herself when she and Billy arrive for the wedding." Furious, Caitlin stood and left the table abruptly, starting for the door.

"Where are you going?" Ven demanded. "By

God, I'll teach you some manners when—" He went silent at a cautioning look from Melusina.

"Let her go. You will have the authority to do whatever you wish to that . . . that Corinthian bagatelle after you're married. Let her be for now. Don't upset things so carefully arranged. I need her money and so do you."

"Corinthian bagatelle? What a quaint phrase for a whore." Ven laughed. "You are quite right, as usual. When I have all the sweet charms of the creature exposed and she's at my mercy, she'll quickly learn her place. I sense a restlessness in her, though. I think we'd best have some means of controlling the baggage should she think of bolting at the last minute. Telegraph your very useful American friend in London, Mr. Edwards."

"He may be useful, but one would not want to call such a low and sorry lot as Robin Edwards a friend." Melusina sniffed. "He will, however, do anything you ask if you promise to let him have your future wife to himself for an hour or two. That, I think, is *all* Robin Edwards lives for."

The new May moon, low in the western sky in the small hours of the morning, touched Caitlin's ivory body with fingers of caressing light. She lay, after her night ride, in a restless, troubled sleep amidst tumbled bed clothes, her hair dark against pink satin sheets. She sighed and called out once and tears slid from the corners of her eyes that flicked open slowly. "Thief! Prowler and thief," she whispered, looking up into Quinn's gray eyes before her willowy arms enfolded his neck and she drew him to her. His hard, ravenous mouth took hers and then he was gathering her slender form in his arms as she was shaken by long, silent sobs. All the sadness, all the hard-held tears of the past lonely months were loosed at his first touch, and Caitlin could do nothing but cling to him, trembling violently.

"I was halfway to Paris," he managed to say, brushing her brow with his lips.

"Don't ever leave me again," she answered, almost unable to speak for the ache in her throat.

He held her in mute anguish and rage, thinking what a near thing it had been, knowing he'd almost let her go, almost lost her forever.

"I'll love you until my dying day," he said, his voice a growl of thunder.

"I don't care what you've been or done or why you want me—none of that matters. All that does is that you never leave me." She looked up at him then, love dancing in her lovely eyes, and saw that their time apart had taken its toll. He was leaner and darker, the strong lines etched a little deeper in his handsome face.

"It was such a near thing," she said, holding to him. "We almost lost each other forever. Can you ever forgive me my stupid, stubborn pride? I wanted you so, but I was . . . hurt and angry and—"

"In an evil hour," he interrupted, "I was persuaded by demons not to tell you the truth about who I was, not until you'd proven your love by marrying me no matter what I might have been. It was a stupid and dangerous game and—"

Caitlin kissed him to stop his words then looked up. "It's a game you've won." She smiled. "I do, I will, forever and always. Now tell me, how did you get here?"

"Like Romeo, Caty, I scaled your balcony." He shrugged.

"You *didn't*!" she said, horrified. "You told me you didn't take such chances. It's hundreds of feet."

"I said I wouldn't risk my life for nothing. This . . . you . . . you're everything I'll ever want. Let me love you now," he said, his voice smoky and hot as he carried her back to the pink satin bed, lowering her gently. She was alabaster and ivory in the glacial moonlight flooding the room, her lawless beauty a desperate dream come true. She was soft and warm and wanting, and desire overcame him as he pulled off his clothes and went to her, the menacing look of a wolf, of a Tartar prince on his face and in his hungry eyes. The ruby tips of her breasts stood against his muscled chest as he lowered himself over her. Her slender legs parted and, kneeling between them, he came into her fast, her body arching, rising to his, meeting each repeated, strengthening thrust with increasing urgency. From a single point in her soft depths, drops of liquid fire spread and flared until she was wrapped all around in golden ribbons of silken flame. With possessive, unrestrained power, Quinn's lean body reclaimed Caitlin, made her his as she had never been before. As soon as the long ripples began to pass down her flexed and glistening body, they touched his, too, and they were caught together in a roll of exploding thunder and light that seemed never to end. But it did, and they began all over again, and again, taking each other with a love-starved greed, not satiated, not able to stop, until the night was almost gone. Then in the darkest, stillest time between moonset and sunrise, they lay very close, touching each other, coiled together as if, after so long and terrible a time apart, they couldn't let go. They couldn't lose sight of each other either and resisted sleep until every word that had been left unsaid was spoken, all secrets shared, and promises made.

"What about . . . Gordon's wife?" Caitlin asked hesitantly after a quiet time. "If you don't want to talk about it, don't. I'll never ask you again."

"I want you to know everything, Caitlin; all there is. There'll be no more secrets, understand?" She nodded and he pulled her closer to him. "I was seventeen and working in my father's bank. That's how Flora and I first met. I didn't even know Gordon then; I just saw that she was very pretty and charming, one of those helpless women who bring out the protective instincts in certain men. Well, to make a long tale brief, we met on the street one day and she asked me home—to fix a broken window, I think it was. Her husband, she explained, was away a lot. His detective work for Dunn took him all over the midwest and there were little things at home he hadn't time to tend to. One of those things turned out to be *her*. On a night that I was taking care of Flora, my father's bank was . . . not broken into, but robbed. The theft had to have been done by someone who had a key and who knew how to get in and out without touching off the night alarm. Everyone associated with the bank had an alibi. Except me."

"But you had one. You were with Flora—Quinn!" Caitlin said wide eyed. "You wouldn't compromise her and she wouldn't come forward when they accused you. Oh, how sad!"

"I said I was innocent, and I expected my father to believe me. He didn't, so I joined

Grant's unit next day and went off to war. I never went home again. Some years later, when Flora was dying, she sent for my father and told him the truth."

"And then you went to see him and made it up?" Caitlin asked.

Quinn shook his head. "There was too much anger in me then and stubborn pride."

"I know a lot about that." Caitlin took his hand to her lips. "We'll go together."

"There's something else you should know, Caty. Flora had a child that she claimed was mine. Gordon just told me about her."

"Do you believe it?" Caitlin asked quietly.

"I don't know, but my father did. He's raised the little girl since Flora died. He adores her, I've heard; has given her everything, a lot more than he ever gave us."

"Don't be angry. He'd lost all of you, remember? You and your mother and your sister. Whether she was your child or not doesn't matter. A lonely old man and a lost little girl have probably enriched each other's lives immeasurably."

"I do love you, Caitlin." Quinn smiled.

"Good! That's settled then." She nodded, kissing him. "So, I'm not getting a wild gypsy prince or a dangerous desperado after all. I'm getting a perfectly respectable, or almost respectable, Midwestern banker," Caitlin laughed, jubilant with love.

"Don't be complacent. You'll learn how

dangerous I can be if you ever try to get away from me again," he glared, pinning her beneath him. "How much do you love me?" he demanded. "You'd better have the right answer, or you'll find out now how dangerous I can be."

"All these months, since I've had money and land and connections, when I could have demanded anything in the world I wanted, all I dreamed of was you. Now, think of all the lovers that ever were or ever will be in the world. Just think about that. Are you thinking? Are you?" she asked with whimsical charm.

Quinn nodded.

"Good. Now think how much love that is. Quite a lot, would you agree?"

Quinn nodded again.

"I love you more than all of it combined," she pronounced. "Is that a good answer?"

Quinn nodded once more, but then, charmed by Caitlin's kittenish, uninhibited happiness, he couldn't suppress a warm, low laugh as he caught her to him.

"Where's all the slowness you were always touting?" she asked with a giggle before he kissed her to silence and made love to her again, not slowly at all.

"What shall we do . . . about everything?" Caitlin asked. The new morning glistened on the hills outside their window bright and warm when they woke, refreshed by a few hours' sleep, to breakfast in bed on a tray of food Caitlin had brought from the kitchen. Supposedly preparing for the evening's ball, she'd left instructions that she was not, under any circumstances, to be disturbed. She planned to spend the entire day, except for visits to the kitchen, lost in Quinn's arms.

"Run off with me now," he said as he finished his coffee.

"I can't do that to Billy again. He and Ann will be here late today. I'll tell them and Ven after the ball. I do owe him that much and then"—she smiled with delight—"I'll follow you to the ends of the earth, if you'd like."

"That won't be necessary. You decide where you want to live. Where's home to be Caty, love?"

"Nowhere, not yet. I want to see the Seven Wonders and sail the seven seas first, and then we'll decide. The Welsh coast is beautiful and Nova Scotia is, too, but somehow not *home*. Perhaps one day they will be, but not now. Wherever you are—that will be home until we decide."

"That's fine for a gypsy princess, but what about building a nest for your chicks? I want a lot of them."

"They'll be like us, like you and me, free flying, at home anywhere . . . everywhere in the world like we'll be . . . like a band of gypsies. How does that sound?"

"Perfect," he pronounced. "Let's start now, making our gypsy tribe," he leered.

Even by late afternoon, it was hard for them to part, though the separation would be brief. Finally, Quinn dressed and leaned above Caitlin, who was still nestled in bed, and bestowed a goodbye kiss on her tempting lips.

"I'll see you at the ball," she purred languidly. "I'll meet you at the stone bridge after it's all over. I'll be ready to go."

Chapter Twenty-Seven

"You didn't have to dance every dance with him, did you?" Ven greeted Caitlin sharply as she stepped into the library, still wearing her magnificent jeweled gown. It had caused a sensation at the ball, particularly among Ven's aristocratic set. They were told that the dress was created by the American designer, Ann Overton, who was herself looking elegant in wine satin and long ropes of pearls.

It had been an extraordinary evening. Earlier in the day, Dancy and David had brought their mother, Jean, from her farm to Montressor Manor, to meet the brother she hadn't seen in twenty years. True to form, Billy McGlory was overwhelmed with emotion until Jean, in a rare, happy, and lucid moment, threw herself into her brother's arms and told him that nothing had been his fault. They'd all been children cast out into a cruel world, pawns of fate and fortune. That was that, she said. Nothing could be done about it now, and he must stop his whimpering at once, or she'd refuse to dance with him at the ball. Billy had bellowed with laughter, pounded a startled Ven on the back, kissed Caitlin, and gone off to find himself a drink.

During the ball, Gordon stayed sober, Dancy got slightly tipsy, and Richard Montanari arrived, all smiles, with Kathleen Toole, the sewing girl he'd hired away from Ann to design clothes in his London factory. They were in love, Caitlin was sure, and Kathleen, like any woman in love, glowed with a new and touching subdued beauty. Cedre and Wade Burleigh, who had come back from London that morning, reported that James Hawker was recovering well from his surgery. Baby Nealon, they told Caitlin, who had been left in the charge of his nanny, was beginning to say a few words in a decidedly English accent.

Leila Faithful, with Mr. Bask at her side, spent three minutes talking to Ven and hurried to Caitlin. "Darling, you can't really be marrying that grinding bore," she whispered and was quite shocked to learn that, no, Caitlin actually was not, but she was to please keep her mouth shut, as the grinding bore hadn't yet been informed. Lord Outerbridge, a tall, gray, distinguished-looking man, danced with Jean and took Dancy once about the floor, while his wife, Fleur, and his daughter, Chantal, saw to their hundreds of guests. Fleur agitated Ann by saying in a very positive way to one of the young guests, "My dear, a woman's weakness is her only strength." Ann swooped in and carried the girl off to set her straight at once.

It was Ann who knew, without being told, that Caitlin would never marry Ruthven Glendenning. Ann knew that the instant Quinn made his entrance, sleek and handsome in dark formal clothes, black onyx studs, and cuff links flashing. He never took his superb eyes off Caitlin, who glowed with a most extraordinary beauty that had nothing whatsoever to do with Ven, Ann noted.

"Why don't you tell me exactly what little trick you're up to now, you clever girl," Ann whispered in Caitlin's ear as they stood at the punch bowl. When she had been fully enlightened by Caitlin, Ann shook her head, looked in exasperation at the ceiling, and offered to break the news to Billy later when they were alone. And at just about the time she was doing exactly that—telling Billy that Caitlin was running off with Quinn . . . again—Caitlin was informing Ven that there would be no wedding. He said nothing, just walked to the library door and closed it, then turned to Caitlin and burst into a high-pitched, nasal laugh that caught her off guard.

"I'm glad you're taking it so well." She smiled. "I am sorry, Ven, but—"

"You don't know how sorry you're going to be," he snapped, coming toward her, a grimace on his thin lips. "Sit down. I've a few things to say to you."

With a sigh, Caitlin did as he asked, thinking she'd been overly optimistic to expect he wouldn't make some sort of scene. Deciding to be patient, she was completely unprepared for what followed.

"You *are* going to marry me—no, no, do not interrupt. Hear me out. Then, if you've anything to say, I'll listen, briefly. I had anticipated that you might try to pull a little caper like this, so I've had your old chum, Robin Edwards—ah, I see you *do* remember Robin Edwards." Ven smiled evilly as Caitlin stood and went to glare out the window. "Robin Edwards has stolen the Burleigh baby, who will not be returned until several days after you and I wed. You've no choice. No wedding, no baby—ever."

"I don't believe you," Caitlin gasped, starting toward him with clenched fists.

"If I ask Melusina to bring in the nanny who is just next door, you will believe me."

"Why, you smarmy, disgusting—I know *all* about you, Ruthven Glendenning. There already is talk here, in the town, about your . . . odd habits, and it just so happens, I myself saw you at Mrs. Drabble's. If you try to go through with this, the whole world will know what you are."

"Mrs. Drabble's?" he sneered. "Whatever you may have seen or heard there is nothing compared to the games I intend to play with you. I have an isolated lodge north of here, well equipped for my purposes. When I tire of you, my dear, I'll return that child to his parents; not before. If you don't cooperate, they'll never see him again."

"You can't . . . do this! Quinn won't let you," Caitlin said, apprehension building.

"Perhaps you'd be happier about it all if I tell you that Edwards will be joining us. We'll be taking a nice, fresh, virginal servant girl along, too, for my particular pleasure. Now, you will meet Jones as you planned and tell him you will never see him again. Griffiths and I will be listening, be sure of that."

The most terrible moment of her life, Caitlin decided later, was when she told Quinn that she wasn't going with him. Standing there on the stone bridge in her ball gown and shivering though wrapped in fur, she told him in a flat, cold voice that she'd decided to marry Ven after all and it would be best if they never saw each other again. He'd looked at her for a time, in silence.

"These are for you," he said finally, extending his hand to offer her a fist full of diamonds.

"No!" she gasped. "I . . . I don't want them."

Without another word he hurled the diamonds away to let them fall like raindrops into the river below. Then he turned to leave and Caitlin, for the first time in her life, collapsed in a faint. Griffiths carried her home.

Caitlin McGlory was an exquisite bride. The beautiful, fitted dress of ivory satin and antique lace, the dress that Ann Overton had made and Quinn Jones had bought for her, elicited sighs of admiration from the women who watched her move very slowly down the long aisle between the rows of chairs set up in Montressor Hall. Flower girls, ring bearers, and bridesmaids had come before and waited as the bride, who seemed a bit pale beneath her feathery veil, appeared to lean for support on her uncle's arm as she made her way toward the groom. Ven Glendenning waited, smiling.

They made a fine couple, most of the five hundred guests agreed. The slender, blond aristocrat and the delicate, beautiful American were an unusual match. Though there had been some unpleasant talk about the groom, he was considered one of the most eligible bachelors in the British Isles. It was no small accomplishment for an American, no matter how rich, to make such a catch. Today, though, she was looking poorly, some of the guests noted. Her magnificent high coloring and her glimmering, vibrant beauty seemed subdued. Nerves perhaps? some wondered, as she stumbled and actually dropped her bouquet. Something was definitely wrong.

"Caty," Billy had whispered, "you don't have to do this. I'll take you out of here now, peerage or no peerage."

"I'm all right, Billy," she'd whispered, glancing away to hide the tears beginning to well in her eyes. It was then she noticed an odd thing. Sitting very upright and conspicuous in an aisle seat, dressed in his rough tweed, Sunday best jacket, was Owen Colver, the poacher, with, of all things, a dandelion stuck in his lapel. Curious, Caitlin began looking about and saw his cohorts everywhere, weathered countrymen in dress-up jackets, sporting her favorite yellow flower. Looking down, she discovered a dandelion among the flowers in her bouquet, saw them mixed with the pink roses that decorated the hall. It was Quinn's doing—she knew it was—but where *was* he, and what on earth was he up to? She stopped still and looked about, and the guests murmured at the bride's strange behavior as she met Owen's eye. He winked and she began to laugh, knowing then it was all going to be fine. Still stalling, she stumbled and dropped her bouquet again, and as she did, the hall doors burst open. Quinn, like a marauding Tartar prince, mounted on a fierce, snorting, black stallion, rode at considerable speed down the center aisle of the hall and gathered up the now glowing, laughing bride, to hold her on the saddle before him protected in the curve of his arm. Eyes dark with fury, his severe, angular face a mask of cold rage, Quinn flayed Glendenning's pale face with two strokes of a riding crop when the man tried to reclaim Caitlin, grabbing at her with long, pale hands.

She tossed away her bouquet, lifted her veil, and folded her arms about Quinn's neck as he kissed her deeply then pulled the pawing stallion about and surged back up the aisle leaving pandemonium behind them as the poachers took charge of Ven, Griffiths, and their retinue. Quinn guided the stallion down the marble steps of the mansion, and then he and Caitlin disappeared through the great stone arch, the train of her gown flying like a victorious banner.

"Since you're already dressed for it, Caitlin McGlory, will you marry me?" Quinn smiled, as they slowed, entering the forest.

"Oh yes, of *course* I will, Quinn Jones." She sighed. "But when did you know something was wrong?"

"Ten minutes after I left you. You're a

terrible liar. You always were. I came back for you—to the stone bridge—and saw Glendenning with a torch trying to gather up the diamonds from the water."

"But the baby?" she asked, tensing. "What about Nealon?"

"We'd have come for you sooner if not for him, but we just got a telegraph saying he's safe with Mrs. Drabble. She called the police as soon as Edwards brought Nealon to her to keep hidden. The whole lot of them are under arrest by now," Quinn said as they reached the stone bridge, where some members of the wedding party—the poachers and a few close friends—had gathered, bringing the minister with them.

Quinn and Caitlin were married at midday on the first of June in the year of 1872, beneath the towering trees of the wild Welsh hills, the rich scent of pines swirling about them as they came into each other's arms as man and wife.

"I've won the bet," Caitlin whispered. "I held you off for six months and a day. It wasn't easy."

"If we were in New York now, where we made the blasted bet, *I'd* have won. It's still yesterday there." Quinn laughed. "But you know, love, we've both won everything. Ready to go, Mrs. Jones?" he asked.

"Ready, Mr. Jones." She smiled, taking his outstretched hand.

Epilogue

On a lovely fall day in mid-October of 1874, when the leaves in Central Park were showing color and the paths were busy with prams and tricycles, Ann Overton McGlory pushed a sleeping baby in a very fine English perambulator along the Mall toward the fountain. Walking beside her was a little girl wearing a white smock dress with dark stockings and high boots. Chestnut ringlets protruded from beneath the child's tiny white cap. Her pale blue eyes showed a quiet intelligence and mild curiosity as she looked about, keeping pace with her mother without complaint. "Where is my father's niece to meet us?" the child asked in a tone that was nearly a perfect echo of her mother's usually cool and disinterested voice.

Today, Ann was anything but cool and disinterested. Caitlin and Quinn, whom she hadn't seen in two years, had returned to New York the evening before and were guests at the Fifth Avenue mansion of old friends. Ann had promised to meet them at the fountain at noon and she was already five minutes late. Lifting the little girl to sit at the front of the pram, cautioning her not to disturb the sleeping infant it held, Ann went along more quickly than before until she heard someone call her name, and then Caitlin was coming toward her, beautiful and elegant, holding the hands of little boys in each of hers and smiling her dazzling smile. Quinn, striding beside them, was strikingly handsome as always, his slightly sinister expression somewhat softened, Ann thought.

The women were close to tears as they fell into each other's arms. Quinn stood back, enjoying as he always had the lovely, musical sound of feminine voices. He watched Ann introduce a beautiful little girl, who stood rolling the baby carriage back and forth until Caitlin stopped her to peer inside.

"He's three months," Ann said. "Patrick William McGlory. His sister, Jean, is—" Ann looked around to find her daughter engaged in serious conversation with Caitlin's twin boys, who were dark haired and gray eyed and as graceful as their father. Like their mother, they were never still, always in motion, bright and glimmering as light on water, Ann thought, blessed with all Caitlin's wildfire exuberance and energy.

"They are beautiful." Ann smiled, admiring their sailor suits. "I know British boys aren't breeched until they're six, but ours can't be kept in gowns and curls that long. Can you tell them apart?"

"Nicholas is just a touch heavier than Tony, but it's not easy." Caitlin laughed, reaching for Quinn's hand. He quickly gave it, coming close and encircling her waist.

They haven't changed at all, Ann thought. They're as wildly in love as the day they met.

"I should have been married in scarlet, you know," Ann told their hostess, Brigida Hawkes, and Caitlin. The three sat in the Hawkeses' Fifth Avenue library that overlooked a large garden where their children, now including Brigida's four, romped in the fading afternoon.

"I was already carrying Jean when I caught your bridal bouquet, Mrs. Jones," Ann explained, taking up her knitting.

"I hear it was tossed with a special élan unknown in the history of bouquet tossing." Brigida laughed. "It was quite a wedding, I gather. Whatever happened to your sinister nobleman, Glendenning, and the others?"

"No one actually went to jail for kidnapping Nealon Burleigh. A very remote colonial appointment was arranged for Ven in Khartoum or somewhere by his influential family. *Your* friend, Robin Edwards, eluded the authorities, but his fate may be worse than a life sentence in Her Majesty's jails." Caitlin smiled smugly. "He actually married Melusina Montressor, and they fled to the Australian outback to raise sheep. It must be a fate worse than death for Melusina, with her genteel affectations. She must be making Edwards's life horrific, I'm sure."

"Yes." Ann nodded. "Edwards deserves her. Now, Caitlin, you'd better hurry and tell us all your other gossip before the gentlemen arrive for dinner."

"Delighted." She laughed, settling comfortably into a deep arm chair. "Dancy and Gordon are living happily at our North Mountain estate on Nova Sctia. They like the isolation and the settled, quiet life."

"Any sign of progeny?" Ann asked.

"Not yet, but I haven't given up hope. Now, David Pallett is another matter. I don't expect he'll ever marry, though he'd be a great catch for some girl. He's caring for the Montressor Mansion, hunting with the backwoods lads, riding to hounds with the gentry and is content to make infrequent trips to London for a new pair of boots now and again. Speaking of London," Caitlin went on, "we saw Richard Montanari on our way through. He's married to Kathleen, and they have a little boy of their own. The doll business is booming, and Richard's going to name a new doll after my next baby, if this one's a girl, as Quinn hopes it will be."

"I could see Quinn was quite taken with my little Jean." Ann smiled. "Well, where do you think *your* daughter might be born, Cate? It'll be your turn next to use Nealon Burleigh's English baby buggy. But I'll have to know where it's to be sent. You vagabonds just amaze me." Ann shrugged.

"I think . . ." Caitlin hesitated, "that our next baby will be born in California, but I'll have to let you know for sure. We're training west. We'll be leaving next week and making a stop in Illinois, at Galena. Quinn hasn't been home in a dozen years."

Caitlin and Quinn stood hand in hand talking on the platform at Galena station and watching their twin boys who climbed admist trunks and boxes, undaunted by the disapproving stares of the station master.

"If he's not here in five minutes, I'll hire a rig to take us out to the house," Quinn said, beginning to pace the platform with long strides. Caitlin followed at his side with short, quick steps.

"Be patient. Give him a chance. It isn't any easier for him than you, you know," she said, and Quinn quickly drew her to him and kissed her.

"I love you." He smiled. "I don't know how I lived . . . before. There he is," Quinn added almost indifferently, turning her to face the tall, gaunt man who was striding toward them. The young girl walking at his side easily matched his fast pace.

"She's absolutely *beautiful*!" Caitlin whispered to Quinn. "She's like a purebred, long-legged colt. How old is she?"

"About fourteen," Quinn said, his unsmiling face severe and cold, his gray eyes fixed not on the girl but on the man who stopped a foot from them and stuck out his hand. His coloring was different from Quinn's—fairer. It was his build and facial structure Quinn had inherited; those extraordinary, hard, angular lines were there in the still-handsome older face.

"Quinn." The man nodded once. "Welcome home."

There was a brief, tense moment until Caitlin took charge, calling the little boys to meet their grandfather who became enthralled with them at once. Then she turned her attention to the girl, Evangeline—Eve for short, the beautiful child insisted—and she smiled Quinn's magnificent, winning smile. She was tall, like her father and grandfather, but finer boned, the angularities of her face softer and more delicately sculpted.

"I brought you a doll from London." Caitlin smiled. "But I think, now that I see you, you might be too grown-up for it."

"My father sent mail order to London for one of your dolls last year, after you wrote to us about visiting." The girl smiled. "It's very lovely, like you. I'm pleased to have another."

"Your . . . father?" Caitlin repeated, glancing at Quinn, who had accepted the old man's hand, finally, and now turned to the lovely girl at Caitlin's side.

"It's odd," Eve said, her smile mirroring Quinn's, "to meet a brother you've never seen before in fourteen years."

A week later, the farewell scene at the railroad station was very different from the arrival. There was a lot of easy talk and warm laughter, hugs, and kisses. Invitations were made, promises given, even a few tears shed as the train pulled out and Caitlin leaned from the window to watch Mr. Jones and Evangeline standing hand in hand, waving goodbye.

"Some things are better left untampered with." Caitlin smiled tearily up at Quinn. "He *does* cherish her so—you can see that—and they did promise to come west."

"As usual, you're right." Quinn smiled back, taking Caitlin's hand. "I wanted her with us, but he needs her and she loves him. If you give me a beautiful little girl or two," he said, glancing down at the twins he held in his lap, "I'll be content."

They sat close as the train gathered speed, and they shared the joyous, soaring sense of freedom that heralded the beginning of every new adventure.

MORE RAPTUROUS READING

WINDSWEPT PASSION (1484, $3.75)
By Sonya T. Pelton
The wild, wordly pirate swept young, innocent Cathelen into an endless wave of ecstasy, then left with the morning tide. Though bound to another, the lovely blonde would turn one night of love into a lifetime of raging WINDSWEPT PASSION.

BITTERSWEET BONDAGE (1368, $3.75)
by Sonya T. Pelton
In sultry, tropical Morocco, Rosette would forget the man who had broken her heart. And forget she did in the tantalizing embrace of mysterious, magnetic Mark – who knew he'd always keep her in BITTERSWEET BONDAGE.

AWAKE SAVAGE HEART (1279, $3.75)
by Sonya T. Pelton
Though Daniel craved tantalizing Tammi, marriage was the farthest thing from his mind. But only Tammi could match the flames of his desire when she seductively whispered, AWAKE SAVAGE HEART.

THE CAPTAIN'S VIXEN (1257, $3.50)
by Wanda Owen
No one had ever resisted Captain Lance Edward's masculine magnetism – no one but the luscious, jet-haired Elise. He vowed to possess her, for she had bewitched him, forever destining him to be entranced by THE CAPTAIN'S VIXEN!

TEXAS WILDFIRE (1337, $3.75)
by Wanda Owen
When Amanda's innocent blue eyes began haunting Tony's days, and her full, sensuous lips taunting his nights, he knew he had to take her and satisfy his desire. He would show her what happened when she teased a Texas man – never dreaming he'd be caught in the flames of her love!

Available wherever paperbacks are sold, or order direct from the Publisher. Send cover price plus 50¢ per copy for mailing and handling to Zebra Books, 475 Park Avenue South, New York, N.Y. 10016. DO NOT SEND CASH.